"If *The Proposal* and *While You Were Sleeping* had a baby, it would absolutely be *The Catch*! Such a wonderful mix of enemies to lovers and small-town tropes. [Lea] once again knocks it out of the park with her sharp banter and steamy tension!"

—Sarah Adams, *New York Times* bestselling author of
Beg, Borrow, or Steal

"Amy Lea knows how to write heart-clutching romance. *The Catch* is a real catch, and I can't wait for readers to devour it."

—B.K. Borison, *New York Times* bestselling author of
First-Time Caller

"Amy Lea's brand of rom-com feels like 2000s nostalgia with modern, intelligent heroines and unputdownable writing. Evan and Mel's slow-burn romance comes with everything: smart humor, chest-aching emotion, stakes that had me invested from the first page, and happy tears for their well-earned happily ever after. I loved every page."

—Tarah DeWitt, *USA Today* bestselling author of *Left of Forever*

"An adorable small-town romance. . . . Mel and Evan's love story will *reel* you in, and it's the perfect way to end Amy Lea's Influencer series."
—BuzzFeed

"Lea's talent for writing complicated but ultimately likable characters is on full display as things between Melanie and Evan become more and more comically disastrous before they start to get better, and her expert knack for comedy makes this story a standout."

—*Kirkus Reviews* (starred review)

Tara's quest to find herself a second-chance romance of her own is swoony, hilarious, and ends in the perfect HEA."

—Emily Wibberley and Austin Siegemund-Broka, authors of
Book Boyfriend

"A gorgeous friends-to-lovers slow burn, *Exes and O's* is filled with fun, charm, and an appealing hero who sees and loves the protagonist for exactly who she is. A perfect mix of relatable characters, hilarious banter, and steam, *Exes and O's* is for everyone who has wondered about past relationships and future loves."

—Lily Chu, author of *Drop Dead*

"I flew through this book—Amy Lea packed every sentence with so much hilarity and heart. Get ready for some trope-y goodness in *Exes and O's*, including a meta awareness of those same tropes that's a blast to read. If you love the roommate vibes of *New Girl*, a heroine who's unabashedly 'extra,' and a hero who accepts her for who she is, you won't want to miss this one!"

—Alicia Thompson, *USA Today* bestselling author of
Never Been Shipped

"The resulting romance is as sensitive and swoony as it is self-aware, playfully engaging popular romance tropes. This is a winner."

—*Publishers Weekly* (starred review)

"*Exes and O's* is equal parts tender and laugh-out-loud funny, with an earnest appreciation for the romance genre singing loudly from every page. With her sophomore novel, Lea proves she's here to stay."   —*BookPage* (starred review)

"Fresh, fun, and extremely sexy. *Set on You* is a romance of unexpected depth."

—Helen Hoang, *New York Times* bestselling author of
The Heart Principle

"*Set on You* is energetic, steamy, bubbly, and so, so fun. But more than that, it's also a hugely important book that celebrates body positivity in the most joyous way possible."

—Jesse Q. Sutanto, *USA Today* bestselling author of
Next Time It Will Be Our Turn

"*Set on You* is the best kind of workout: one that ups your heart rate with its swoony hero, makes you sweat with its slow-burn tension, and leaves you satisfied with its themes of empowerment and self-acceptance. With a fresh, hilarious voice and a deeply relatable protagonist, this romantic comedy is enemies-to-lovers gold."

—Rachel Lynn Solomon, *New York Times* bestselling author of
What Happens in Amsterdam

TITLES BY AMY LEA

• • •

THE INFLUENCER SERIES

Set on You
Exes and O's
The Catch

The Bodyguard Affair

The

BODYGUARD AFFAIR

AMY LEA

············•◆•············

Berkley Romance
NEW YORK

BERKLEY ROMANCE
Published by Berkley
An imprint of Penguin Random House LLC
1745 Broadway, New York, NY 10019
penguinrandomhouse.com

Book design by Daniel Brount

Library of Congress Cataloging-in-Publication Data

Names: Lea, Amy, author.
Title: The bodyguard affair / Amy Lea.
Description: First edition. | New York: Berkley Romance, 2025.
Identifiers: LCCN 2025004214 (print) | LCCN 2025004215 (ebook) |
ISBN 9780593641781 (trade paperback) | ISBN 9780593641798 (ebook)
Subjects: LCGFT: Romance fiction. | Novels.
Classification: LCC PR9199.4.L425 B63 2025 (print) | LCC PR9199.4.L425 (ebook) |
DDC 813/.6—dc23/eng/20250204
LC record available at https://lccn.loc.gov/2025004214
LC ebook record available at https://lccn.loc.gov/2025004215

First Edition: December 2025

Printed in the United States of America
1st Printing

The authorized representative in the EU for product safety and compliance is
Penguin Random House Ireland, Morrison Chambers, 32 Nassau Street,
Dublin D02 YH68, Ireland, https://eu-contact.penguin.ie.

AUTHOR'S NOTE

Thank you a million for choosing *The Bodyguard Affair* as your next read. While this story is generally light, I would be remiss if I did not include the following content warnings: detailed accounts of childhood abandonment, homelessness, and a parent with early-onset Alzheimer's disease. Notably, the depiction and severity of Alzheimer's in this book is informed by research and medical consultation, and reflects one fictional character's experience. It is not intended to represent all experiences of those living with Alzheimer's, nor those of their families and caregivers. Alzheimer's disease affects each person uniquely, with symptoms and progression varying widely based on individual circumstances and medical factors. Please take care while reading.

The Bodyguard Affair also portrays a *fictional* Canadian prime minister and his family, as well as fictional heads of state, government officials, and political parties. In particular, the book features a fictional private security detail responsible for the protection of the prime minister. Incidents, dialogue, and characters are products of my imagination and are not intended to depict actual events or people. I also want to acknowledge that, in reality, Canadian prime ministers and other high-ranking government officials are guarded by the RCMP's Protective Operations Close Protection Units.

Please note that any inaccuracies regarding political protocol, policies, or terminology are my responsibility alone and likely have been changed for creative reasons. They are not to be taken as factual and accurate accounts or views expressed by the government of Canada.

The
BODYGUARD
AFFAIR

CHAPTER 1

Andi

There's something liberating about sitting in a crowded bar, elbow to elbow with drunken strangers, casually writing a piping hot love scene.

Until tonight, I've avoided writing in public, mainly because I'm an easily distracted individual, an unintentional eavesdropper. When the women next to you are having a "serious sitdown" with a third friend who is "almost certainly" being catfished by a bald man in a trailer park in Manitoba, one can't just tune it out. Then there's Taylor Swift's newest single about her big breakup with Joe blaring over the speakers, her poetic, lyrical genius filling me with life and withering imposter syndrome simultaneously. Or the man in a toque joking that I'm "hard at work on the next bestseller," a well-meaning quip that's both depressing and as likely as a short, mild Ottawa winter (hint: highly improbable, practically statistically negligible). Even the piece of lint on the sleeve of my sweater can induce a brain fart.

Then there's the ever-present risk of someone glancing at my tablet, seeing my latest penis euphemism, and being so scandalized, they choke to death on a mouthful of bar nuts. A touch dramatic? Maybe. But one has to consider these things. Ottawa is a reserved, buttoned-up city.

To be fair, the patrons at this bar are too busy drinking and socializing to care about the stone-faced woman sitting in the corner, wrapped in her emotional support cardigan, lost in her quest to make fictional people fall in love. That, or they can't decipher my tiny size 8 font.

Distractions aside, being in public offers a wealth of inspiration, like the women secretly playing footsie under the table next to mine while on dates with unsuspecting men. The petite lady who can barely keep her hands off her man as he twirls her around on the strobe-lit dance floor.

I'm not sure why I haven't done this sooner. With the intensity of my new day job, getting words down in the privacy of my apartment is becoming a rarity. That's why I'm taking advantage of the time until my best friend, Laine, shows up.

The crowd melts around me as my fingers dance across the keyboard, barely keeping pace with my brain. With each keystroke, I slip deeper into my starry daydream of a fictional world. It's an enchanting place where men aren't trash and there are gentle, sugary forehead kisses aplenty. Where every touch is laced with a tenderness that makes you feel weightless. In my little world, love doesn't fizzle, it endures. It scoops you up and holds you tight in its warm embrace, making good on its promise to never let go. It makes you feel like everything will be okay, even if it won't. I'm so lost in my own head, I barely register when someone tugs my hand.

"I should have known I'd find you hiding in the corner," Laine shouts over the pulse of the music, eyeing my tablet screen with her heavily lined hawk eyes before I can slam it shut. "What are you doing?"

"My to-do list for work," I say quickly, cheeks aflame with the heat of my blatant lie as she hands me a gin and tonic. Here's the straight-up truth: I haven't told anyone about my writing since I started a couple months ago. Not even my best friend, who knows everything about me, down to my monthly cycle. Maybe it's superstitious and silly, but if I tell people, it's no longer mine. It's no longer a magical, sacred project I can escape into, tend to in my quiet moments. It feels too new, too raw. Sharing it with people, particularly Laine, who will demand to read it, opens it up to scrutiny and critique that I don't have the mental fortitude for—yet. In fact, I'd rather hurl myself into the rapids of the Ottawa River than live with the knowledge that, somewhere out there, a human being has read my words and may have *thoughts* (good or bad).

While I love Laine, I already know she would judge me. Hard. Anytime I pick up a romance novel around her, she rolls her eyes and suggests something with a gold Pulitzer Prize stamp on the cover. If you looked on her bookshelves, you'd only find classics, war and terror academia books, and poetry.

So, for now, I write for me.

"Come dance!" Laine barely waits for me to shove my tablet in my bag before dragging me onto the congested dance floor. "Love the one-piece. Very Audrey Hepburn meets Catwoman," she decides, twirling me around. It's a far cry from skintight, high-gloss pleather, but Laine has a tendency to give aggressively ego-boosting compliments. The jumpsuit in question is black chiffon with a flirty keyhole back, not that it's visible under my cardigan. But for a woman working in politics, nothing feels better than abandoning the tyranny of tummy-control pantyhose.

I close my eyes, drink, and let the lights blur around me in a red haze. For the first time since my breakup three months ago, I'm feeling playful, rebellious, and, dare I say, a smidge sexy—until I have to use the bathroom. In a one-piece.

Comfort aside, I hadn't considered the logistics of peeing in a one-piece. So here I am, vulnerable, outfit around my ankles, boobs out, praying whoever just walked in can't see me in all my nude glory through the alarmingly wide crack in the stall door.

And then the worst happens. Because of course it does.

While I'm mid-pee, the door flings open to a pair of startlingly blue eyes. I've never seen eyes this striking—like the artificially colored blue raspberry Kool-Aid my little sister and I used to chug straight from the plastic jug on those swelteringly humid summer days in our top-floor apartment with no AC. The kind that stains your tongue and teeth for a week.

The eyes in question belong to a very startled man.

At least, I'm pretty sure it's a dude. The bathrooms in this bar are unisex, individual stalls.

We let out simultaneous screams, though mine is more like a piercing wail. I flail about on the toilet like an injured flamingo, endeavoring to cover my ugliest bra—thick straps, "nottonight" beige, probably three years too old to deserve any place in my drawer. It's so bad, I forget to hide my lower half, which is covered by sweet nothing. This exact moment is why I don't often leave my house.

"Shit!" He slaps a palm over both eyes and stumbles backward into the sinks in a blind frazzle. "I am so sorry. The door wasn't locked, I—" I can't hear the rest, because he quite literally dashes out of the bathroom, leaving the stall door swinging wide open.

With a groan, I hobble off the toilet to close the door. The lock was broken all along. Go figure.

Before someone else walks in on me, I wash up and beeline it back to the dance floor in search of Laine. No sign of her freshly permed curls anywhere. A quick scan tells me she's migrated to a booth along the back wall. She's cross-legged, in what appears to be deep conversation with my ex-boyfriend, Hunter, who's come straight from the office, based on his sweater-vest—a staple in his office wardrobe. Tonight's vest is mustard yellow.

I'd nearly forgotten that Hunter was coming tonight. Then again, why wouldn't he? He's Laine's friend, too, and when we split, we made an agreement that we wouldn't let it affect our group dynamic.

The three of us met over a year ago as sun-starved baby interns working for Eric Nichols, the leader of the Democratic People's Party (DPP)—the third party that no one ever expected to win. I used to consider it the best day of my life. The day I started my dream job and met my best friend and my boyfriend.

The three of us got closer when our contracts were extended for the election, and again when the DPP won and transitioned into power. We did everything together. Morning coffee runs, lunches at the office, eyes bloodshot, poring over spreadsheets, take-out containers sprinkled over our desks. Weekends exploring museums, doing Parliament tours, dominating at trivia pub nights, consuming ill-advised late-night poutines with too many toppings. The usual things poli-sci geeks do for fun in the nation's capital. Laine used to joke about being the third wheel, but these days, it feels like *I'm* the third wheel.

But I don't let myself think about that. Not right now. Tonight is a happy night. We're celebrating Laine's official promotion to permanent staffer with health and dental benefits. She signed the offer letter today after dreaming of being one of the few East Asian women on the Hill since being elected class president in grade five. Give her thirty years and she'll be the next prime minister of Canada. I'm calling it now.

Whatever Laine said must have been funny, because Hunter is dangerously close to falling face-first into her ample cleavage. I catch the subtle way he squeezes her shoulder affectionately, his thumb tracing a smooth circle down her arm—a move he used to do with me. Our eyes meet as I approach, and he flashes her one last frat-boy-president smile before slinking out of the booth to give me my spot back.

"Andi Lenora Zeigler!" He shouts my full name heartily, brows raised, as though my existence on earth delights him. Ever since we broke up, he tries a little too hard to be congenial in public. Excessive arm pats, laughing way too loudly at my jokes. "I never got to congratulate you on the new gig."

"Oh. Thanks. And congrats to you, too. I know communications was your dream," I say, barely hiding my cringe. We sound like coworkers by the watercooler, not exes who dated for nearly a year and shared a dingy apartment above a dim sum place in Chinatown.

The crease between his brows deepens in a dramatic show of sympathy. "Don't worry, you'll join us soon. Once you do your time as household staff." He says it so quickly, I'm too caught off guard to respond. Household staff, aka my new role as the prime minister's wife's assistant, isn't exactly considered prestigious or desirable.

I wait for him to fully disappear toward the bar before squeezing in next to Laine, who uncharacteristically averts her gaze to her lap the moment I make eye contact. I contemplate telling her what Hunter just said, but then I remember the one rule: Never put Laine in the middle. She'd never take sides anyway. Instead, she'd come up with endless explanations:

You know Hunter, he doesn't have a filter!

He didn't mean it like that, Andi. He has a good heart. The best. Did you know he volunteers with Big Brothers Big Sisters?

"Some guy just walked into my stall while I was peeing," I announce instead, keeping my head low.

Laine's brows shoot up to her hairline. "You didn't lock the door?"

"I thought I did, but it was broken. And that's not even the worst part. The guy saw *everything* because I had to take this whole thing off." I motion to my onesie.

"Full bush?" she asks, because apparently that's an important detail.

"Not full. But overdue for a wax." Not that I'm planning on getting one. No one's venturing downtown anytime soon. No point in subjecting myself to socially sanctioned torture just to impress a man.

Laine erupts in booming, witchy laughter, following it up with a smack on my thigh. She does that when something particularly amuses her (which is most things). Her tendency to feel every morsel of emotion with her whole body is one of the things I love most about her. Her intensity is what makes her excellent at her job. When she's finally collected herself, she turns and pops her head over the back of the booth like a gopher peeking out of its burrow, scanning for predators. "Who was it?"

"I don't know. I was too mortified to get a good look at him." Aside from his eyes.

She slaps the back of the booth like she's at a high-energy sporting event. "Andi, is that him?"

I duck my head even lower, chin to chest, making a triple chin. Highly attractive. "Not looking."

"Code red. Code red. He's coming over. And he's kind of . . . hot. Not really your type, but—"

I shrink inward, averting my hard stare to the ring of condensation pooled on the sticky table. I will not make accidental eye contact with whoever just saw me nude, hunched over on the toilet. I refuse.

"Uh, hey." It's definitely him. It's the same deep, rough-around-the-edges voice that yelled *Shit!* in the bathroom. There's a weight to it, a grit that stops you in your tracks.

I don't look up. If I can't see him, he can't see me.

After three of the longest seconds of my life, my theory proves false.

"Andi? He's still here," Laine informs with a sharp poke in the ribs.

Death, please take me.

I begrudgingly lift my eyes, raking them over a pair of dark-wash jeans, a gray Henley T-shirt covering arms more muscular than I've ever seen up close, a prominent Adam's apple poking through a dark, neatly trimmed beard. His face is boyishly cute, with a slightly bulbous nose and ears that stick out a little from beneath overgrown waves the color of dark roast coffee. And then there's those blue eyes, crinkling at the corners, twinkling even in the dim bar lighting.

Laine is 100 percent right. He is not my type. And by "not my type," I mean aesthetically superior to me in every way, face and body.

Before I can slither under the table and disappear forevermore, those eyes latch on to mine. He raises his hand, fingers hesitating in midair, like he hasn't decided if he's committing to a wave or a handshake. Apparently, he decides on neither, shoving both hands into the pockets of his jeans.

"Uh, hi?" I say.

"Hi." He stops, the apples of his cheeks turning a touch pink above his beard. "Sorry. I already said 'hi.' Um, I think we, uh, just met in the bathroom?" He jerks his thumb back in the direction of the bathrooms, squinting adorably at me with one eye.

"Yup. We sure did," I yelp.

"I wanted to apologize and make sure you were okay."

"Oh, uh, thanks? I'm okay." As *okay* as one can be mere minutes after a stranger inadvertently saw their naked body.

I expect him to do us both a solid and leave, but he lingers. "It won't happen again," he assures me with a dip of his chin.

"You won't walk in on an unsuspecting stranger in the bathroom again?" I clarify, my gaze stuck somewhere around his full, soft-looking lips. I can barely look at him without my cheeks heating, wondering if he's secretly judging me about my lazy grooming.

"Never. I'm gonna peek under the stall first to make sure it's unoccupied." He stops and winces. "Actually, never mind. Peeking under the stall . . . that's equally creepy, isn't it?"

"Yup. Sex predators tend to do that kind of thing."

"I swear I'm not a sexual predator. Or a predator of any sort. God, I can't believe I just said that. I feel horrible about the whole thing." I can tell he's genuine, based on the furrow of his thick brows, the downturn of his shoulders.

"Don't. It wasn't your fault. The lock was broken. It's all good," I say, sitting up a little straighter.

I'm not convincing enough, because he's still rooted in place, hands twisted in front of his torso. "Are you sure?"

"Yes, I'm sure. I fully accept your apology." I meet his eyes reluctantly.

"Okay. Well . . . have a good night?" He cheerfully pats the top of our booth before backing away, one side of his mouth quirking into a lopsided smile that sends a single spark pingponging down my spine.

"Have a good—bye." I slow-wave, watching him turn away into the crowd. He rakes his hand through his waves and strides back to the bar, plunking down beside another guy in a backward ball cap who's also scarily fit, tattoos decorating both arms.

Laine gives me another slap on the thigh, though this one is with purpose. "Um, are you ill?"

"What?"

She shoots me a hard stare from under her thick lashes. "Bathroom guy. He's . . . hot. Weirdly hot. Like, does-not-belong-in-Ottawa hot. I wonder if he's a Sens player or something. He kinda has that hockey guy swagger. And the shaggy hair. Minus the wet dog smell."

I don't recognize him, not that I'm familiar with the Sens

roster. As someone with weak ankles and zero bodily coordination, I don't exactly follow sports. "So?"

"So! He was flirting and you let him walk away. You don't let guys like that walk away," she says, apparently under the delusion that I've sent the love of my life away into the mist, never to be seen again.

"He just came over to apologize," I assure her. He smiled at me a fair bit, but I assumed those were sorry-I-accidentally-saw-your-pubes smiles. Like the way I smile weakly at panhandlers outside my apartment.

Laine emits a disgruntled sigh and levels me with a look that screams, *Come the fuck on*. "He was interested. He's still looking at you. Right now!"

I brave a look, confident she's lying to boost my morale.

Shit.

She is not.

Our eyes meet again and he grins, revealing dimples. *Dimples*. The kind I write about. Sweet Christ. I swiftly look away, back to the relative safety of Laine.

"A few days ago, you were lecturing me about staying single and focusing on my career," I remind her. Laine isn't normally one to push romantic relationships. She swears by being a singleton and doesn't plan on marrying, ever—hence her condemnation of romance novels.

"And I stand by that," she says, pausing to finish her gin and tonic. "But there's no harm in a one-night stand with some random you'll never see again, especially if it helps get you out of your funk. I mean, look at him. He just looks like he knows his way around down there."

"I'm not in a *funk*. I just got a new job," I point out.

For some reason, Laine is concerned that I'm not over the breakup. Maybe she's right. Hunter and I were only dating a year, but it felt like longer, especially after we moved in together so soon.

On our first day of work, he'd sent me a DM on our internal messaging system that read, *Coffee?* He was as consistent with the messages as he was with his sweater-vest collection. We'd trade jokes about our boss and her tendency to send frantic emails without subject lines or punctuation, or worse, entire emails *within* the subject line.

He was passionate, realistic, and analytical about everything, never saying things he didn't mean. Whenever he wanted to make a purchase, like a new pair of dress shoes, he'd spend hours and hours researching. He came from a prominent family in the city with a long history in politics. Something about him just oozed reliability—something I'd never had before. And so I let myself trust him. I let myself fall. Fast.

Everything was perfect, until the lead-up to the election. Hunter was tasked with coming up with social media slogans and captions for the campaign. He was overwhelmed with other work, so I stepped in to help, coming up with three. One of them was actually used in the PM's victory speech the night of the election: "There's no us versus them. Only us."

I never expected him to credit me after the fact, but he never acknowledged my role in helping him, even privately. It was like he actually convinced himself he wrote it. He started talking over me in meetings or, worse, correcting me in front of our boss. Things like this happened more and more toward the end of our internship when it became clear there would be only one job opening on the media and communications team, a role both of us wanted.

One night in bed, he'd rolled over and said, "You do realize only one of us can get the job, right?"

"Yeah. I know. And I'll be happy for you if you get it," I'd said genuinely.

"Same," he'd replied, though he couldn't look me in the eyes when he said it. Instead, he went around and around, explaining how this job was his *dream*. How he'd always regret it if he put our relationship first over his career (not that I ever asked him to).

"I could . . . not apply," I'd offered weakly.

The moment that came out of my mouth, I knew I'd lost myself entirely. I'd actually offered to sacrifice my dream job for him, after working my ass off to get scholarships for university and grad school.

He didn't take the suggestion well, because me stepping aside would mean he "didn't earn it."

After that, things were awkward for a solid month. When he started sleeping on the couch and stopped sending me DMs and niche political memes throughout the day, I knew it was over as fast as it began.

We ended things mutually, amicably, high-fiving to "staying friends." Both he and Laine helped me move out a week later, the day he got the job over me.

I never told Laine the gritty details, because airing all my grievances about him would have put her in the middle. Besides, it was easier to keep things civil.

"Laine, I'm very over him," I assure. Even though seeing him still makes my stomach pinch. Not in an *I miss him* way. More of a *he hurt me and never took accountability* way.

Laine works down a swallow. "Actually, I'm glad you said that. Because I've been meaning to talk to you about something—"

"Look, I'm not bringing anyone back to my place tonight except a falafel shawarma platter with extra garlic sauce," I cut in before she can lecture me.

"Okay, but will a falafel bring you to orgasm?" she asks.

I snort. "Close to it. I think you have too much faith in men. Hunter never got me there, and he had a year to figure it out."

Her entire face creases, pained. "Hunter and I like each other." It comes out so fast, I almost miss it.

In fact, I'm about to pull my phone out to preorder my shawarma for tonight when she snatches it and turns it face down on the table, like I'm a toddler with no impulse control.

"Did you hear me, Andi?"

I blink. "You and Hunter . . . like each other?" I repeat that approximately seven times before the meaning begins to sink in. "As in . . . more than friends? How—why didn't you tell—"

Laine launches into a long-winded confession while I drift in and out of consciousness, only coming to when she casually mentions how Hunter's original DM was actually meant to be for *her*. He mistakenly got our names mixed up (ha ha, so funny, right?) and was surprised when *I* poked my head over the cubicle wall and took him up on coffee. Here is where she stops to pledge that he "genuinely" fell for me, but that there was always something unspoken between them. Of course, they only came to that realization "way after" we broke up.

I think my body is slipping into shock, because I can't move, or swallow my drink. I think I'm passing out, because in a blink,

I'm lying in the booth, legs up in birth position (minus the stirrups). Laine and Hunter (who swoops in out of nowhere) are above me, fanning me with napkins, asking if I'm okay and if I require medical assistance.

I manage to sit up with a violent cough, taking in the sight of them—my ex and my best friend—sitting side by side next to me, touching. *Touching.*

Realistically, the signs have been there for weeks, ever since we broke up. Laine has been "busy" nearly every night and weekend, which I chalked up to us starting our new jobs and me getting lost in my writing. But then last weekend happened. Laine told me she was too busy with work to hang out, only to post a shot of her fancy cocktail on social media hours later. Five minutes later, Hunter posted a photo of the same drink, from the opposite angle. Again, I chalked it up to the fact that the two of them now work at the Privy Council Office (PCO)—the department that supports the PM and Cabinet—together, while I was all the way at 24 Sussex—the PM's official residence. Naturally they were going to become closer after seeing each other at work daily.

I have to stop myself from going forehead into table. "So you two are . . . together? As in dating?"

They look at each other, barely containing their bliss, and nod simultaneously, as one. Hunter even takes her hand and squeezes it for emphasis.

Laine offers a weak smile. "I told Hunter I couldn't make it official until I had your blessing. I figured, since you two broke things off so mutually and you no longer have feelings, that you'd be okay—"

"Yes, I'm okay with it. Of course I'm okay with it," I say a little too quickly, mouth bone-dry. Because of course I am. I have to be. It's been three months, technically almost four, since things went awry. It's not like I've been brokenhearted over him. So why does the sinking sensation in my gut feel like betrayal? Isn't dating exes against girl code?

"We never expected it to happen," Hunter continues, as though I've asked for a repeat of their origin story. To my horror, he starts listing all the reasons they're perfect for each other, as though I'm the hard-to-please De Niro–esque father-in-law with some sort of authority or say in the matter. I sit there, red-faced, nodding aggressively, pretending to be completely and totally on board with this. I have no choice in the matter. Laine is my best friend. I have to support her, right? It would be selfish otherwise.

At one point I must zone out, because Laine pokes me in the rib. "Andi? You good?"

"Fantastic," I say with more enthusiasm than I feel. I don't know if I'm happy, mad, or sad; all I know is I need to get the hell out of here. Stat. "You know, maybe you're right. Maybe I should celebrate tonight. Love is in the air, after all," I say, butt-scooting out of the booth as fast as humanly possible (not very fast).

Laine punches the air, victorious. "That's the spirit! Go get that celebratory peen. You deserve it."

In my shock and delirium, I amble my way to the crowded bar, where I spot him. Bathroom guy. He's still in conversation with his tattooed friend. I don't know what comes over me. Maybe jealousy, a desperation to prove myself after Hunter and Laine. But I approach. Rapidly. Aggressively.

He sees me coming in hot before I can talk myself out of it, his lips parting in surprise.

In my limited experience, guys who look like him are usually the grunting, brooding-in-dark-corners types. But there's a lightness, a warmth to him that's strangely comforting. Kind of like holding your frozen, winter-kissed hands over a toasty outdoor bonfire. It takes me off guard. So much so, I let out an *ahh* sound before saying *hi*, which comes out like, "Ahoy hoy."

Jesus.

My greeting hangs in the air for a brutally long moment.

"Ahoy hoy?" he replies, unsure whether to laugh or not.

I decide to push through, not acknowledging it, even though I'll never forget this moment as long as I live. "I, uh—I realized I forgot to introduce myself. I'm Andi Zeigler." There's a pause, like he's waiting for me to continue. Only, I don't know what else to say about myself. "And I'm, um, well—I don't know what I'm doing or saying anymore, so I'm just going to leave now. Bye!" I spin on my heel to make a run for the exit. This was a terrible idea. Falafel platter, here I come!

A few strides away, a hand on my shoulder gently turns me back around. Bathroom guy is smiling at me and I don't sense pity. He extends his other hand and says, "Nice to meet you, Andi. I'm Nolan Crosby," without a beat, totally casual, as though I wasn't fleeing him.

Nolan Crosby. It suits him.

"I don't do this often," I decide to inform, as if it weren't blatantly obvious.

"Approach guys at bars?"

I shrug. "Ask guys to go home with me."

His right brow flicks up. "Oh? I'm coming home with you?"

"No!" I scream. I'm much worse at this than I ever realized. With Hunter, it was easy, because he did most of the talking and charming. I barely had to say two words. "I mean, unless you want to?"

He watches me for a beat, and I'm certain he's about to back away slowly, like that GIF of Homer Simpson vanishing into the bushes.

"I have food!" I add, for no good reason.

This must pique his curiosity, because his eyes brighten on the spot. "Food, huh? What kind of food?"

"Well, actually I'll have to stop at the twenty-four-hour grocery on the way home. I only have cherry tomatoes in my fridge," I say, racking my brain to take inventory. I might have some old olives from a solo charcuterie night weeks ago. Do olives expire? "But I'll make you something good. Like . . . pierogies."

He tilts his head like he's trying to assess whether I'm serious. Apparently he decides I am, because he says, "Sure, I could go for pierogies."

CHAPTER 2

Nolan

Y ou really don't have to make me food," I assure Andi as we zigzag through the produce aisles in Peevey's, her neighborhood twenty-four-hour grocery. Bad call on the name, in my opinion.

She peers at me warily over her shopping cart, which is humongous compared to her. "This is the third time you've said that. Do you think I'm a bad cook or something?"

"No, not at all." I mask my hesitation, eyeing the cart, which contains a single bunch of green onions and three loose pears (no bag). And we've been here for at least fifteen minutes.

"Then do you not want to hook up?" she asks, pouting those glossy, plump lips. It's disorienting, the twinge I feel whenever I look at them.

Truthfully, my hesitation is more about my own guilt over being here instead of home, where I should be on my last night before going on a six-month military deployment. "Do *you*?" I ask pointedly.

"Yeah. I do." She doesn't sound hesitant in the slightest, leveling me with a wide, earnest expression. My stomach free-falls. Under bright grocery store lighting, her eyes are hazel, not brown.

"Okay, then I do, too," I say, more turned on than appropriate in the middle of the produce aisle.

I hadn't noticed her in the bar before walking into her stall, but I recognized her when she emerged minutes later. She stood out in the crowd. Her posture was stiff and tense as she fidgeted with the sleeves of the oversized sweater covering her jumpsuit.

She wore her dark hair in a tight bun, which kind of went with her whole vibe of hiding in the back with her friend. Her eyes darted nervously to the door every five seconds, as though searching for an escape. When I went to apologize, she avoided all eye contact and angled herself in the opposite direction, arms folded tightly over her chest.

So when she approached me so brazenly minutes later, I was stunned. Even more so when she asked me to go home with her. I'd misread her, and I don't misread people, ever.

"In case you couldn't tell, I don't normally do random hookups," she declares. I don't know if it's a vulnerable admission or a warning.

"What changed?"

"Certain events have happened in my life recently. But I won't bore you with the details." Her eyes bulge at the cost of lettuce before she mumbles, "Who am I kidding? I'm not getting any vegetables."

I try not to laugh as I follow her dutifully down the cracker aisle like a puppy. "You wouldn't bore me, but I understand if you'd rather not share with someone you don't know."

"Meh. I mean, you've already seen . . ." She waves a hand vaguely to her lower half.

I stumble back and grab at the shelf for balance, nearly taking down a neatly lined row of Cheez-It boxes. "No. I really didn't see anything. I think I actually blacked out."

"Are you just saying that because you feel bad for me and my ugly grandma bra?"

"Nope. And it wasn't ugly, by the way."

She furrows her brow and points at me. "Wait, you said you blacked out and didn't see anything!"

"I said I blacked out and didn't see your . . ." I vaguely gesture back at her, and she fills in the blanks. "I didn't say I didn't see above the waist."

She hides her face behind a Triscuit box before chucking it into the cart as if it wronged her.

"It really wasn't that bad. And who cares what your bra looks like? Good tits are good tits regardless of the bra." For a second, I'm scared that was too vulgar a statement. That's what happens when you're exclusively around guys 99 percent of the time—you lose your filter.

But it makes Andi smile. "That might be the most romantic line I've ever heard."

I pretend to bow, relieved. "I'll be here all night. Or as long as you want me."

For the next half hour, we zip down every single aisle. She fills the cart with more random items, like a bag of fresh-baked crescents rolls from the bakery section, sliced turkey, a jar of hot mix pickles, and frozen pierogies. Then we do a second loop "to make sure we didn't forget anything," as though there was a method to the madness. It's a good thing, because she adds marble cheese, sour cream, and bacon (for the pierogies).

"You seem to know your way around," I note.

She shrugs. "Grocery shopping is overwhelming. That's why I like this place. It's never busy, at least not late at night when I come after work."

I'm about to ask her what she does for a living, but she spots a cheesecake display in the bakery and doubles back.

"Don't judge. This cheesecake needs me," she says, cradling the plastic container like a baby.

I assure her I'm not judging, and we finally head to check out.

Her place is a couple blocks away, which would normally be fine if we weren't carrying heavy groceries, and if it weren't minus-20 degrees Celsius. I insist on taking all but one bag, leaving her with the lightest one. She protests, but ultimately concedes once she realizes she's not getting them from my grip.

"Wow, you really live where all the action is," I say as we turn a corner down a dark side street. There's at least thirty people sitting in clusters around the sidewalk. I immediately slip into work mode, posture erect, senses heightened, scanning every person, shadow, alleyway, and doorway for any sign of danger.

"Yup. I had two criteria: no roaches and close to Roger's Diner so I can have easy access to their mozzarella sticks. They're my writing fuel," she says far too casually, seemingly unfazed by the people. She probably does this walk all the time, which actually makes me feel worse. This area is sketchy for anyone, including me, let alone a young woman by herself at night.

"Writing fuel? Are you a writer?" I finally ask, trying to mask the worry in my voice as we pass by the biggest clusters of people, most of whom seem too strung out to do more than watch us with vacant stares. There are still some stragglers toward the end of the block, but not as many.

She doesn't respond for a few moments, and I'm worried I've hit a nerve until finally she says, "Yeah. I am. Well, kind of. It feels weird to call myself a writer. I only just started."

"A beginner is still a writer," I say, intrigued as we round a pile of snow shoveled inconveniently onto the sidewalk.

Before I can ask a follow-up question, an older homeless man in an oversized coat and boots with a hole in one toe approaches, eyes focused directly on Andi. Instinctively, I step in front of her, shielding her.

"Hi, Ted! How are you today?" She waves over my shoulder before going around me.

He bows his head, covered by a nice warm knit hat with a pompom. I'd peg him at around fifty, but he could be younger. His skin is weathered, patchy with some sores. Both hands are visible and relaxed, not clenched. "Well, I'm still kickin'. Got treatment for my frostbite today."

There's no edge in his tone, just softness, so I relax my stance marginally. Over the years, I've gotten better at trusting my gut. Good instincts are important in my job. You either have them or you don't. They have to be instant, because sometimes, you need to make life-or-death decisions on the fly. And there is zero room for error.

"That's great news," Andi says, her shoulders dipping in relief.

"And how's my baby boy doing? He still limping?" Ted asks.

"Lars is doing really well. His paw seems healed. He went for a nice run with me this morning. I'll bring him by tomorrow morning."

Ted dips his head politely again. "I'd like that. Thank you."

Andi studies him for a moment. "You sure you're doing okay?"

He looks down, twisting his hands. "I didn't make it to the Mission in time for supper."

She immediately makes a grab for the grocery bags in my grip, gets on hands and knees, and riffles through them on the sidewalk. "I almost forgot, I picked up some of your favorites." She pulls out the pack of crescents rolls, sliced turkey, three pears, and a box of Wheaties (low sugar).

I thought those items were really random, but I never would have guessed they were for someone else.

Ted's eyes widen, welling with appreciation as she piles them in one bag and hands it over. He takes it gratefully, clinging to it like a lifeline. "You're really trying to fatten me up with all this fancy food, aren't ya?"

"Sure am. It's going to be a cold winter."

"Not with you around. You always brighten my day." He flashes her a broad smile, which she happily returns.

"Have a good night, Ted. See you in the morning."

Ted dips his head in a nod before eyeing me suspiciously, like he's just realized I'm here. "This your friend?"

"Yeah. This is Nolan," she informs him.

He watches me for a beat. I suppose he decides I'm safe, because he gives me an approving nod before waving us off. "Take care of my Andi, now. She's my guardian angel."

I have many questions, but my first is, "Who was that?"

"Ted. He lives at the Mission down the street. He's harmless, by the way. Most of them are," she adds as we turn into her apartment complex. It's a redbrick six-story walk-up with an old, rusty fire escape barely hanging on to the side of the building.

"Seems like a nice old guy."

She swipes her key fob, and we trudge up the creaky stairs. "Oh yeah. He's hilarious. Reminds me of my grandpa on my dad's side. I'm temporarily watching Lars since it's too cold for him to be on the street."

"He has a dog?"

"Yup. And he takes better care of that dog than housed owners. Gives him most of his food, the comfiest blankets," she informs me. "That's actually how we met. Lars started following me home looking for scraps, and then Ted and I got to talking. He was worried about the cold weather at night and said he might have to surrender Lars to the shelter. If he had, he'd never have gotten him back because of Lars's breed and temperament. They'd have put him down, and that would have broken Ted's heart. So I offered to keep Lars at my place."

"That's really nice of you to do that for someone you don't know," I tell her. And I mean that. Not many people would go out of their way for a stranger and their dog.

She lifts a shoulder in an easy shrug. "Everyone falls on bad times sooner or later. The only difference between me and someone like Ted is that I'm lucky enough to have a safety net."

That statement strikes me as she leads me up all five flights of stairs. I'd never really thought about that before. It's easy to say it would never be you. But it could be, if you'd been born into certain circumstances. If you'd made a few wrong turns.

Lars is wary of me immediately when we walk in and attempts to hide under the coffee table in the living area, though he barely fits. He's huge, at least eighty or ninety pounds of solid muscle by the looks of it, with a short, sandy coat. "Sorry, he's sketched out by people he doesn't know after living on the street. Especially men. Are you okay with dogs?"

"I love them. I miss having one around," I say genuinely.

"You don't have one of your own, I take it?" she asks.

The closest I ever got to having a dog was whenever my sister and I were sent to live with Aunt Shelly. She had a ten-pound bichon frise, Matilda, who ferociously growled at me and nipped my ankles whenever I got too close. And by the time I'd built enough trust with her, either Mom would come back or we'd get sent to live with another family member. I never stayed in one place long enough to have a dog of my own, though I always dreamed about it.

"Nah, I wish. I'm gone too much with my job. Wouldn't be fair to the dog." I bend down to peek at Lars under the table. He lets out a low growl, so I back up to give him some space. I got used to dealing with street dogs while on tour overseas. Most are wary and generally distrusting of humans, unless you give them food regularly.

She watches me, and for a second, I think she's about to ask what my job is. Then she seems to decide against it, settling for, "Understandable."

"How about you? I take it you're a dog person?"

"In a way. I never had one of my own, either. My sister and I begged my parents for a dog every year at Christmas. But they always said it was too expensive. Then, when we could afford one, it was 'too much work.' 'Too much responsibility.' We got betta fish instead. Those colorful ones," she says, her tone tinged with latent disappointment.

I laugh. "Ah, the good ol' starter pet."

She shrugs. "My sister always forgot to feed hers and clean its tank, so I ended up taking care of both of them. Not that they lived long. Poor M. Sea Hammer and Swim Shady."

I dip my chin. "Rest in peace. Great names, though."

While she unpacks the groceries in the kitchen, I sit a distance away on the floor and try to coax Lars out. Andi hands me a slice of marble cheese, which works like a charm. Lars inches out from under the table just far enough to gobble the cheese from my palm. I expect him to take it roughly, maybe even bite me. But he takes it gingerly, just barely brushing my palm with his lips before backing away to safety underneath the table, hitting his head in the process. After he devours the cheese, he inches out a little farther, nudging my hand with his big wet nose for more.

Andi hands me another cheese slice, which brings him out from underneath the table entirely.

"He likes you," she says, watching as Lars tentatively sniffs my lap, in search of more cheese. "Make yourself comfortable. I'm going to, um, freshen up," she informs me, her voice going higher.

"No rush," I call over my shoulder, while dodging a sloppy kiss from Lars.

"Sorry for the mess, by the way." Her voice is slightly muffled by the wall between us. "I moved in last month and haven't had the time to unpack."

I pan around for the mess she's referring to. There are a couple boxes stacked in the hallway, a half-drunk glass of water, a notebook, a laptop, and some crumpled paper on the coffee table. Nothing out of the ordinary for a writer. "You're one of those people who apologizes for mess when there's zero mess, aren't you?"

"You don't think this is messy?" she calls from the bedroom.

It looks clean to me, nondescript even. Off-white walls, plush cream carpet. All the furniture is also of the neutral variety, no fluff, no patterns or designs. She hasn't put up any artwork, personal photos, or vases or candles on her shelves or tables like you'd usually find in a woman's place, not to stereotype. At the very least, she does appear to have a hefty dead bolt on the front door. The same can't be said for the sliding glass door. The lock latch looks broken. There's only a wooden stick wedging the door closed, which looks like the snapped end of a broom handle. The locks on the windows also leave a lot to be desired. I could probably bust them open with one hand. At least she's on the top floor.

"I've seen worse," I tell her through the wall. "Your place is very clean. I mean, aside from the half-put-together desk," I say, eyeing it in the corner near the sliding glass door, which leads to a small, snowy balcony. It looks like an IKEA desk, with only one side assembled.

"Ah, yeah. I ordered it because it said easy assembly. It is not, for the record. And I'm pretty good with instructions usually. Shit. I totally forgot to boil water for the pierogies."

"Oh, no worries, I'll put them on. Just—uh . . ." I attempt to get up, but fail. I don't know what I do, but at some point, Lars decides I'm an okay human and plops his massive body into my lap like a baby. He's asleep, heavy, his warm head resting on my chest. I feel bad moving an inch. He seems comfortable.

Andi comes out in a tank-top-and-shorts pajama combo, which accentuates her curves. Shit. Her long hair, which was previously in a bun, now cascades down her back in thick waves. It's lighter when it's down, with some blond highlights framing her face. She's really fucking stunning in an understated kind of way.

And then there's her body. Small waist. Slender, soft legs. As she walks toward me, it becomes clear she's not wearing a bra. A zing fizzes through my chest, traveling lower, landing somewhere highly inconvenient. I immediately avert my gaze as she laughs at the sight of me and Lars. "You found yourself a new best friend."

"Looks like it. Is he always such a suck up?"

"He's a gentle giant. Wouldn't hurt a fly, though you wouldn't know it to look at him." She calls him over and he nearly knocks me over with his wiggling butt as he licks her bare legs, trying to get as close as possible for an ear rub. He seems to really like Andi.

She approaches, shifting her weight back and forth on either foot. "So . . . should we . . . get to it?"

When she inches closer, peering up at me with those big eyes, awareness rushes through me from head to toe. She smells citrusy, like a mixture of grapefruit and oranges. "It's okay, we don't have to rush."

"I figured most people would just . . . go home and bam. Penetrate."

A laugh rockets out of me. "I guess that's how it usually happens."

She covers her eyes, the flush of embarrassment tinting the apples of her cheeks pink. "As you can see, I'm terrible at this."

"You're doing just fine," I assure her, smoothing my fingertips down the inside of her arm, over her elbow, and fuck, her skin is soft. Encouraged, she relaxes into me, the peaks of her full tits pressing against my chest.

My breath hitches at the contact, and the air shifts. My fingers twitch to lift her off the floor, to feel those thighs lock around my waist as I carry her to the bedroom and touch her every-fucking-where. But there's something about this woman that makes me want to slow down and savor every second. My thumb traces the soft line of her jaw, finding its way to her pouty bottom lip, breathing her into me until she tilts her mouth up to meet mine.

She pushes up on her toes and comes in faster, harder than I expected. Our lips crash together. And by lips, I mean teeth. The collision is so hard, I have to take a step back to get my bearings.

She slaps her hand over her mouth, eyes wide, mortified. "I am so sorry," she whispers, gingerly reaching to touch my lip with the pad of her thumb. "Shit. I think your lip is bleeding."

I run my tongue over my lip, tasting that coppery note of blood. It stings a bit, but not enough to shift my focus from her. Honestly, if anything, I find it kind of funny.

I lace my hands in hers and give a reassuring squeeze. "Don't even worry about it." I tilt her chin back to me and gently catch her lips with mine to show her it's okay. And holy shit. She tastes like she smells: tart, fresh, electrifying. Every swipe of her tongue against mine leaves a tingle in its wake. And when she arches her hips into me, dragging her nails down my back, I lose the power of speech entirely. Every thought, every word, all logic and reasoning go up in smoke. With a swift movement, I pick her up and do exactly what I wanted to do. Carry her across the threshold and into the bedroom.

It's not as smooth as I'd hoped in the darkness in an unfamiliar apartment. But the silver moonlight filtering through the blinds offers enough light to find a wide cedar dresser with an attached mirror. I set her on top of it, her thighs clinging to either side of my torso like a lifeline.

"Is it okay if I take this off?" I ask between kisses, tugging at the back of her tank top.

She nods and helps me pull it over her head.

"Fuck," I barely manage as her breasts fall out. I've always considered myself more of an ass guy, but I've officially changed my mind. I'm so fixated, I barely notice she's made quick work of getting my shirt off.

Her gaze blazes from my chest and down my stomach, followed by the soft pads of her fingers. "Whoa. Sorry, I just . . . haven't touched real abs. Ever."

"You've touched fake ones?" I clarify, trying to maintain an iota of control as her hand drifts to my waistband, where things are growing more and more uncomfortable by the second.

"I once dated a guy in high school who had so little body fat, he had a bit of a six-pack. But yours look hard-earned. Do you even eat carbs?"

I slide her a cheeky grin. "More than you'd think."

"Liar," she whispers, her thumb dipping lower and lower beneath the hem where my skin burns, wanting her.

"Do you have a condom?" I whisper, trying to suppress the urgency. "I don't have any on me." Hooking up with a woman was certainly not on my agenda for this trip home.

"I might." She hoists herself upward a little too hard, smacking her head on the mirror behind us.

"Jesus. Are you okay?" I ask, cradling the back of her head as she hops down from the dresser. That sounded like a hard hit.

She plops on the edge of the bed, defeated, head in hands. "I'm sorry, I'm absolutely shit at this," she informs me, her tone sour as she flicks on the lamp by her bedside table. Her room is smaller than it looked in the dark, though still fairly nondescript. The furniture is nice and new, but there are still no photos or personal items, aside from a small bookcase overflowing with paperbacks, a bottle of pink nail polish, and some hair ties on the side table.

"We don't have to do anything," I say genuinely, lowering myself onto the mattress next to her. "And not because I don't want to." I really fucking do. But in the yellow glow of the lamp, she looks . . . sad. If she's not in a good state of mind, maybe hooking up with her isn't the best idea. The last thing I want is for her to wake up tomorrow morning filled with regret.

She nods, biting her bottom lip before leaning back against the wooden headboard. "I just feel bad. I got you here under the pretext of food and sex and you got neither."

"Even without food or sex, this is the best night I've had in a long time."

"You're not just saying that to make me feel better?" she asks skeptically.

"I don't lie to make people feel better, Andi." I look her in the eye when I say it, because I mean it and I want her to know it.

She nods, seemingly accepting it, however reluctantly.

I debate whether I should take this as a cue to leave. The last thing I want to do is linger and overstay my welcome. But she still looks sad, and honestly, I like her company. I want to know more about her, so I settle myself on the side of the bed.

"So you mentioned you're a writer?" I ask, hoping it'll lighten her mood or at least take her mind off what just happened.

"A wannabe writer, I guess. I'm not published or anything. No one has ever read a word of anything I've written."

"Doesn't mean you're not a writer. If you put pen to paper, you're a writer."

She shrugs and bites her bottom lip again, unsure.

"What do you write?"

Red flushes her face. "I'm scared to tell you. You'll make fun of me." My gut twists at the idea that she feels like her passion isn't something to be proud of.

"Why would I make fun of you? Do you write knock-knock jokes or something? Instruction manuals for bizarre household items?"

"Pet obituaries, actually." She holds the lie for all of two seconds before folding, erupting into a laugh along with me. Seeing her smile again feels like pure sunshine breaking through the dark.

"For the record, it's a noble profession. Pets are purer than most humans, and they should be honored," I argue.

"Sorry. I know. I'm avoiding. But since you asked . . ." She watches me for a second, the mattress creaking as she shifts closer, like she's telling me a secret. "I write romance novels. God, it feels weird to say that out loud." A deep breath escapes her lips, and the tension in her body melts away. She actually looks relieved.

"You write full-length novels?"

"Well, I've written one and a half so far. I just started. My first is about strangers, Bryce and Layla, who meet on a train, connect, and agree to meet up on the same day of each year for five years. One year, he doesn't show up, and then a year later, they become coworkers. I'm starting on my second, about a prime minister's personal assistant. I'm going to call it *The Prime Minister & Me*."

Holy shit.

"Andi, do you realize how cool that is?" I lean forward, astonished by how casually those words came out of her mouth. Why is she not an ounce proud of herself?

Another shrug.

"You've literally written an entire book and a half. Who else can say that? Not many people." At least not people who I come across day to day. When she still refuses to admit how kick-ass she is, I continue on. "Actually, my sister, Emma, loves romance novels. She used to steal my grandma's old paperbacks and hide in the closet reading them, way past her bedtime. I think she has one of those e-readers now. Anytime she can get a break from the kids, she's glued to it."

She glances up at me, encouraged. "Your sister sounds like my kind of girl."

"She's sweet, but she has a dark side. If I ever interrupted her while she was reading, she'd literally hiss at me."

"Never get between a woman and her happily ever after," she warns, a smile flirting at the edge of her mouth.

"I'm guessing you're a hopeless romantic like Em?"

She turns her soft gaze back to her lap. "Not really. I'd consider myself more of a realistic romantic."

"What does that mean?"

She lifts a shoulder and pulls her legs tight to her chest. "I think true love exists to some degree. But that happily-ever-after, everlasting romance we're told to hold out for? I'm not so sure. In my experience, those initial butterflies, the lust and sexual chemistry in the first few months or years of your relationship, fade with time until you're left clinging to *what was*."

Wow. I didn't expect her answer to be so bleak, even if it isn't far from the truth. "Damn. Who hurt you?"

"No one in particular. Life, I guess. Don't get me wrong, I think those lightning-in-a-bottle moments exist. The ones that sweep you off your feet and leave you winded. The moments that inspire all the great love stories and make you believe in magic. That's what I love about writing romance. You get to capture that snapshot in time when real life is better than any dream. The moments that make life worth living. Will the characters experience hardship later on? Fight? Fall out of love? Maybe. But we as the reader or writer get to experience the pinnacle of their love. It's joy in the purest sense. It may not always be realistic, but it makes me giddy and hopeful in a way I haven't felt since I was a little kid who believed in Santa and the Easter Bunny. It makes me feel like anything is possible. At least, for a moment," she finishes, voice wistful, almost hopeful.

I've never been a romantic myself, but I could listen to this woman talk about her writing all night. There's something beautiful about the way she describes it. The way her eyes glint, starlit with possibility. The subtle curve in the warmth of her smile. It stirs a deep ache in me. A longing, a homesickness for a feeling I've never actually felt, if that's even possible. How can I miss something I've never had?

I've also never heard anyone talk this openly about love. When you're in my line of work, conversations about love go about as far as a crude joke in the mess hall.

"And no one has read anything you've written?" I ask, bewildered by this woman.

"Nope. I don't know if anyone ever will. I thought about

trying to get published. I did all the research on the best agents and publishing houses, but I'm also considering self-publishing online. I don't know. My new job is proving to be pretty demanding, so finding pockets of time to write is hard."

"If that's your dream, writing, I mean, I think you should pursue it. With everything you have," I tell her.

She eyes me for a moment. "How can you say that when you haven't read my work? What if it's complete crap?"

"If your writing is a sliver of the magic of what you just said about love, I can tell you with absolute certainty it isn't complete crap. Listen, what you said about real life being hard and wanting to give people that hope and escape was fucking amazing. Imagine what your stories could do for someone else going through a hard time."

She fidgets, running her fingers through her hair. "The issue is, my day job is kind of . . . serious. I wouldn't be able to tell anyone. The books can get a little . . . uh, steamy."

"First, who cares what other people think? But if you really want to stay anonymous, you could use a different name. Don't writers do that all the time? Then no one would know it's you."

"True. That's a good idea, actually." She keeps twisting the ends of her hair, seemingly mulling it over.

"Are you open to any suggestions?" I ask after a couple moments of easy silence.

"Sure."

"Don't name your main character Bryce." I'm only half joking.

She clasps her chest in mock offense. "Why not? What's wrong with Bryce?"

"Let me put it this way, I've never met a Bryce I liked," I tell her, leaning against her headboard.

She cocks her head like a dog, and it's so adorable, I force myself to look down at the floral pattern on her duvet cover. "How many Bryces have you met?"

I count on my fingers. "Two. And a half. One was a toddler mid-tantrum, so it's hard to judge. But in my limited experience, they are one of two things: arrogant pricks or foot doctors. Unless that's the characterization you're going for."

She clutches her stomach as though she's holding in a laugh. "Bryce is actually in medical school, so you're close. If I change it, will you buy a copy if it ever gets published?"

"I may not be your target audience, but I'll be first in line," I promise.

She narrows her gaze at me. "Why aren't you my target audience? Because you're a dude? Men can read romance, too, you know."

"No, I just mean, I don't really read. Haven't read a book since high school," I confess. It's not that I don't like books writ large. But after years in the military, my attention span is too shot to sit idle and stare at words for long periods of time. "I'm also not really much of a romantic, either."

"No?"

"I think love probably exists . . . if you're lucky enough to find someone to put up with your bullshit for fifty years. But I don't think it's for me. Never wanted to settle down and do the whole white-picket-fence-and-two-kids thing." Unlike my sister, who was desperate to have a family of her own, the family we never had growing up, I've always maintained the opposite philosophy. How could I ever be a good husband or parent when I've never seen a functional example of either up close? Not to mention my work schedule and the fact that I'm never home.

"What was her name? The woman who hurt you?" she asks knowingly.

That's a loaded question. So I start with the easy answer. A cop-out. A fraction of the truth. "Angelica. She said she'd go to the prom with me, so I got her a corsage, borrowed a shitty suit from my friend's dad. Turns out, she had a whole other date," I say, only realizing now how long it's been since I thought about that.

"That's seriously savage."

"Right? Guess it was my fault, in the end, trusting someone named Angelica."

She cackles, mirroring my position, turning to face me. It's an intimate position, especially for two people who've only known each other a couple hours, tried to hook up, and failed. But I don't feel the urge to turn away and face the ceiling after revealing something personal. This feels comfortable, like I've known her for years.

"I went to university with a girl named Angelica," she tells me. "She could reduce anyone to tears with just her words."

"That tracks."

"Can you pass stern judgment on the name Hunter?" I have no idea why she cares about my opinion so much, but it's intriguing nonetheless.

"Who's Hunter? Your ex?" I prod.

"You're very perceptive. How'd you know?"

"Oh, just the complete and total angst in your voice when you said his name." I bump her shoulder lightly.

"A lot of regret, actually," she adds.

"I went to elementary school with a Hunter. He used to put his entire mouth on the nozzle at the water fountain, if that tells you anything."

A laugh rockets out of her. "My Hunter—" She stops herself, grimacing. "Sorry. He's not *my* Hunter. Anymore. He's . . . Laine's Hunter now. I guess."

"Who's Laine?"

"My best friend. The one who was with me at the bar tonight. Long story." She waves her words away like the subject isn't worth talking about. I don't want to upset her, so I leave it alone.

We sit in a comfortable silence for a few moments before she bolts upright. "I almost forgot. We have cheesecake!" Before I can respond, she scurries off the bed and races into the kitchen, only to return with the cheesecake and two forks.

Three-quarters of the fluffy, cloudlike cake is devoured within fifteen minutes. "God, this is good. Better than sex, I think," she says through an indecent moan that makes my stomach free-fall.

"You think so?" I ask, shifting my leg to hide her effect on me.

"Definitely."

"You're not having very good sex, clearly," I point out, leaning back against the headboard, my stomach fully satisfied.

"You're right about that," she says with a shrug. "That's why I brought you back. I kind of figured you'd be good at it."

"Ah. And you don't think so anymore?" I tease.

"Oh, no. I think you'd be amazing at it. Me, on the other hand—"

She furrows her brow, stressed all over again. So I place my hand on her forearm and give her a reassuring squeeze. "It's okay, Andi. Let's just enjoy the moment."

"Thanks for being so . . . nice tonight," she says, laying her head back, eyes to the ceiling, hands folded over her stomach.

"Well, I did walk in on you in the bathroom. I had some making up to do," I remind her. "Like I said, probably a top-ten worst thing I've ever done."

"Now I need to know what other nine things are on this list," she demands, a wry smile creeping over her face.

"What I'm about to admit might shock you."

She leans closer. "I'm ready to be shocked."

I pause for dramatic emphasis. "When I was seven, I cut a girl's braid off in class because she kept whipping me with it."

She barks out a laugh. "That's . . . terrible."

"Told you. Okay, your turn. Worst thing you've ever done."

She doesn't hesitate. "When I was eighteen, I scraped the side of my stepdad's fancy car in a drive-thru and lied, saying it was my sister, Amanda, who did it. She'd just gotten her learner's permit, so it was believable. It was, like, a thousand dollars' worth of repairs."

"Shit. Do they know it was you now?"

She laughs guiltily. "No, actually. I never told them."

We go back and forth, trading confessions into the darkness. They get progressively more serious and also hilarious. She tells me about how she accidentally dated a guy in high school when she was in university. "When I was in fourth-year university, I met this guy at Bulk Barn. We went for the same sour gummies. He looked my age, or at least I assumed. We exchanged numbers and he asked to pick me up for a date that night. And he did. On his bicycle. He asked me to get on the handlebars. I don't know why, but I did. It was just too awkward to say no and I thought maybe he was just environmentally conscious. That should have been my first clue. I finally figured out he was a senior in high school when he used his high school student card to get us a discount at the restaurant. Needless to say, there was no second date."

We both laugh until we're doubled over in bed, clutching our stomachs. After I get the chance to recover from that one, I decide to confess something serious.

"All right, last one. I just found out my mom, who I barely have a relationship with, was diagnosed with early-onset Alzheimer's disease—a disease that affects her brain, causing memory loss, personality changes, and overall cognitive decline. And I'm about to leave on tour. Tomorrow. For at least six months."

I hold my breath, but I'm met with silence. Nothingness. Shit. I've taken this too far. Andi thinks I'm a complete and total asshole. And she would be 100 percent correct. Who the hell leaves their sick mother for six months, even if she wasn't exactly mother of the year?

I sit up and brave a glance, only to realize Andi is not harshly judging me. At least, it doesn't look like it. She's on her back, head tilted slightly to the side, clutching her cheesecake fork to her chest. Her breathing is slow, heavy, and consistent. She's . . . asleep.

Thank fuck.

It might have felt comfortable confessing that in the moment, but in hindsight, it's probably for the best she didn't hear it.

I stay for a couple more moments, waiting to see if she'll wake up. But she doesn't. I consider my options. I could stay, but it feels wrong to sleep here without explicit permission. Besides, after seeing how uncomfortable she was about hooking up, I don't want to embarrass her even more, or make things awkward tomorrow morning once the alcohol wears off.

Maybe it's best I just go on my merry way. Before leaving, I make sure to refrigerate the rest of her cheesecake and give Lars another piece of cheese. I also finish assembling her desk, which takes all of five minutes.

The last thing I do is write a quick message on a sticky note and leave it on the desk.

I put your cheesecake in the fridge!

—N

PS. You should ask your landlord about fixing the lock on your sliding door.

CHAPTER 3

Andi

PRESENT DAY

Not everyone can say they've touched the prime minister of Canada's boxer briefs. On multiple occasions.

That statement sounds far more scandalous than it actually is. Like most things in this life, the truth isn't all that titillating. Folding and packing the PM's unmentionables is just a typical day in the life of me—the personal assistant to Gretchen Nichols, wife of the Right Honorable Eric Nichols.

I sigh, staring at the ominously high pile of tighty-whities, wondering how many I can stack before they topple over. You'd think after Underweargate (when a pair of Eric's tighty-whities ended up on eBay for $750), he'd diversify his underwear collection. Maybe add a splash of color, a playful pattern. But he has not, which is a *choice*. I respect it.

Technically, the housekeepers are responsible for laundry,

but after Underweargate, the Nichols family is understandably less trusting about who handles their unmentionables. And after three years as Gretchen's PA, I've been deemed trustworthy of the privilege. Lucky me.

I won't lie—there are times I wonder how I got here. When I landed that coveted summer internship with the Democratic People's Party fresh out of university, I was bright-eyed, idealistic, hell-bent on sticking it to the man and making the world a better place for those who need it most—one policy memo at a time. As it turns out, jobs on the Hill are Hunger Games–level competitive. So when the manager of the household staff called me out of the blue and informed that the PM's wife urgently needed a PA with a "get-up-and-go" spirit and "sparkly" personality, I took the position, no questions asked.

I left out the part that I possessed neither of those qualities, because I wasn't in a position to be picky. I was freshly single, in my own apartment, and I needed the money, badly. Besides, I know firsthand how quickly life can go downhill if you find yourself unemployed for too long. I also mistakenly assumed the job would offer enough flexibility to pursue my side passion: writing romance. And it did for a few months, until Gretchen realized I'm allergic to the word "no" and took over my life.

Now, my days are packed from dawn to dusk: fielding phone calls from Gretchen's pesky mother, steaming her capsule wardrobe of neutral linens, or hand-burying the Nichols children's deceased pet hamster in the backyard (and arranging its themed "gone but not FUR-gotten" funeral). Instead of writing sweeping love stories in my spare time, I'm in a constant state of catch-up. I'm lucky if I can get a few sentences down a day.

To be fair, being Gretchen's PA isn't as bad as it sounds, even if her intensity terrifies me. Over the years, I've come to believe that changing the world isn't always about grand, lofty ideals and fancy policy documents. Maybe making a difference is in those small, honorable everyday tasks, like playing Jenga with Eric's undies. The deeds that require you to roll up your sleeves and get your hands dirty, literally.

I'm about to start unpacking Eric's socks when the bedroom door bursts open. Gretchen charges in like an impeccably dressed beige storm cloud and stands over me. "I know I texted you about packing that champagne satin dress for dinner, but I was looking at pictures from the fitting and I think the cowl neck makes me look boxy, don't you? I can't even wear a bra with it. I know nipples are *in*, but mine are way too aggressive. This is what happens when you exclusively pump-feed two children," she cautions, peeking at them disapprovingly under her blouse.

As a childless woman with my original nipples, all I can do is nod and pretend to understand the struggle. Most of the time, all Gretchen wants is to be heard.

"The beige one doesn't scream romantic anniversary dinner, either," she continues, lips pursed. The word "anniversary" catches my attention.

Shit.

She doesn't know. This is the third time I've had to be the bearer of bad news in the past few months.

Thankfully, she's gotten good at reading me. It takes her all of two seconds to figure it out.

"Eric canceled again, didn't he?" she demands before I'm forced to say it aloud. As a former attorney, the woman is scarily perceptive.

I dip my chin, softening my gaze. "I know you were looking

forward to it." She and Eric had plans to spend the weekend in
Mont Tremblant for their sixth anniversary, hence the packing.
It was going to be a weekend of fine dining and relaxing couple's
spa treatments. I booked the entire thing months ago, and just
like that, I'll be spending the afternoon combing through can-
celation policies and negotiating refunds.

She's more upset than she's letting on, by the way she's furiously digging at her cuticles, shoulders squared in an effort to
look casual and unaffected. Tension aside, she's still absolutely
stunning. Her bone structure is otherworldly and her poreless,
tanned skin makes me want to cry. Then there's her long, thick
hair that always looks windswept, like she walks around with a
fan blowing on her at all times. If she doesn't receive at least one
compliment on her lush locks, it's a bad day for her. If I didn't
know she was an attorney, I'd assume she was a cover model.
Canadian designers are constantly sending sample pieces in
hopes she'll wear them.

She huffs. "What's going on this time?"

"It's Kirkwood," I tell her, because really, that's all she needs
to know. Kevin Kirkwood is the minister of finance—well, former minister as of 6:00 a.m. He stepped down publicly, and now
they're scrambling to find a replacement.

"Sex scandal?" she confirms knowingly.

I nod.

She lets out a throaty, marginally evil laugh, her eyes narrowed to slits. "I knew I didn't trust him the first time we met.
He was trying to guess the bra size of every woman at the table.
Then, at the end of the night when I was going to leave, he
claimed I owed him a hug."

She's not lying. I've lost track of how many times I dodged advances by men like Kirkwood as an intern.

"Who did he stick it in this time?" Gretchen asks before I can say anything.

"The nanny." It's not the first time Kirkwood has been embroiled in a sex scandal. In the two times previous (both interns), it was just whispers on the Hill with no actual proof, like most scandals of this nature. But this time, the nanny herself came forward with receipts (i.e., screenshots of laughably bad sexts where he had the audacity to type the word "bosom," as well as a terribly angled dick pic for good measure), which hit the media, finally exposing his trash bag ways once and for all.

"The nanny." Gretchen lets out a derisive snort. "So uninspired. If you're going to have an affair, at least do it with some pizzazz. Some flair. We never hear of them sleeping with the gardener, or the Amazon delivery person."

A feeble laugh bubbles up from my throat. "All right, so I'm going to cancel all the weekend bookings."

Gretchen grumbles, mentally incinerating the suitcase with her amber eyes. "It would have been nice to actually spend our anniversary together. I thought with the House rising for the summer, we'd actually have more time together," she says, referring to the months when members of Parliament return to their home constituencies for the summer. "But he's busier than ever, if not more with the G20 summit. And with the election coming up in the fall, I won't see him for months." She's not wrong. The election is in October, and while Eric is predicted to win again, the months leading up are jam-packed with travel, events, and general campaigning.

"I'm sure he'll make it up to you . . . after the election," I say hopefully as she disappears into the mahogany-paneled walk-in closet.

"I doubt it," she says over the *clank* of metal hangers and the *woosh* of fabric. "It's always something." Her words strike me in the heart, and I can't help but remember the starry-eyed look she used to give him four years ago.

During the election campaign, Gretchen would stop by his office. He'd stop whatever he was doing to wrap her in his arms and plant tiny kisses all over her face and neck when he thought no one was looking. They were even advised to cool it in public to appease the conservative-leaning voters. Fast-forward to now, and she and Eric don't even sleep in the same bed.

It doesn't help that Eric travels constantly, domestically and internationally. And when he is home, he's usually in his office until the late hours, reading a stack of briefings that comes up to my boobs until he falls asleep on the couch.

I tilt my chin, unsure what to say, aside from, "I'm sorry, Gretchen."

She rights her posture immediately, as though refusing to admit the disappointment to herself. "It's fine. It's what I signed up for, isn't it? Honestly, I'm more pissed about missing out on that hot stone massage than anything else." She flicks through her phone mindlessly. "Think you can book one for me today?"

"Absolutely."

"Now that my weekend is free, I should probably go for lunch with Mireille, the owner of that restaurant with those brushed gold caramel dome desserts. We need some more big-ticket items for the gala's silent auction. Oh, maybe you can help me with the kids' variety show costumes," she continues, her mind always racing with things to do, just like mine.

"Oh. Right. Um, actually, I was going to ask if I could have Saturday off." She purses her lips and I can already tell the thought of it stresses her out. So I add, "But never mind. I'll be here if you need me." I don't bother explaining that I had plans with my sister, Amanda, while Gretchen was supposed to be away. It's been weeks since we last saw each other, which feels like an eternity, given we were two peas in a pod as kids, running up and down the halls of the run-down social housing complexes we lived in for years.

My sister and I were going to do lunch and then peruse a flea market, where she would inevitably buy more novelty junk she doesn't need. Thankfully, Amanda won't mind if I cancel. She only recently moved here from Toronto, and already she has a million friends or acquaintances she can call, unlike me, who has exactly one friend, who is now blissfully engaged to my ex.

Besides, when you have a job like mine, a social life is basically impossible. "I'm going to meet the event coordinator at the Chateau to confirm the dimensions for the stage this afternoon," I note. Gretchen is a bit of a micromanager and likes to know what I'm up to, which is fine by me.

"Go home after that," she instructs me. "We have the Squamish trip next week. You'll need all the rest you can get." Squamish is a mountainy town north of Vancouver, BC, and happens to be Eric's riding, aka his hometown, where he was originally elected as a member of Parliament before being named the party leader. They're going for two days to meet with local constituents. "Seriously. I'll be checking your location to make sure you're home by a decent hour."

I catch myself mid-yawn and nod, though we both know leaving early is merely fantasy in this line of work. By the time I complete everything on my to-do list, it'll be well after dinner. But that's typical. There are no set hours, especially with the twenty-four-hour news cycle, which is why my ringer is always set to max volume, even in the middle of the night. You never know when the next scandal will break.

"I'll have to see how it goes with the—" I'd continue, but her attention is pulled to the doorway. Eric is standing there, tie askew, bags under his eyes. He looks visibly stressed, presumably by the whole Kirkwood thing. "Sorry, am I interrupting?"

Gretchen folds her arms over her chest. "What do you need?"

"I just wanted to . . ." He pauses for a beat while I hold my breath, praying an apology is to follow, or it's about to be a nightmare weekend for all of us. But instead, he looks at me and says, "Introduce Andi to my new CPO."

By CPO, he means close protection officer, aka the James Bond–esque folks with earpieces who follow the Nichols family around 24/7. Gretchen hates it, but given Eric's popularity, it's necessary.

It was a little unnerving when I first started working for Gretchen, having someone dressed in all black lurking around in the shadows, watching your every move. But I've gotten to know most of them pretty well, particularly Ben, Kyle, and Jo-anna, her main CPOs, considering how much time they spend around us. They're pretty down-to-earth if you can learn not to be personally offended by their disapproving expressions.

The new CPO's head is turned, looking in the opposite direction. From my vantage point, his hair has an I-just-got-out-of-bed look to it and the collar of his white dress shirt is a little loose.

He's not wide and beefy like some of the CPOs. He's leaner, with a figure reminiscent of a soccer player—muscular and agile, but not overwhelmingly hulking. Though based on the way I have to crane my neck to look at him, he's tall.

When he finally turns his head, our eyes meet in a devastating flash of blue.

A hot surge of recognition shoots through me. I know him.

CHAPTER 4

Nolan

"Any traction on another posting?" I ask into the speakerphone, cutting straight to the chase. I lean against the brick wall where all the household employees apparently loiter on break.

My boss, Jones, emits a long groan that tells me I'm pushing it. He's sick of these weekly calls from me, begging for news. Any news. "Fuck's sake, Crosby. I told you last week, I'm working on it, but it might take longer than we hoped. Maybe six months."

"I can't do six months," I tell him straight up. The thought of enduring a gray, miserably frigid Ottawa winter makes me want to walk into oncoming traffic. If I have to freeze my nuts off, I at least want it to be somewhere interesting, like . . . Siberia. At least the vodka is strong there.

"You really are an impatient bastard, you know that?"

"So I've been told."

He pauses. "I don't want to pry, but shouldn't another posting be the least of your concerns right now? Don't you want to stick around for a bit?"

"My mom has a spot in a specialized facility come September. Way better care than I can give her," I remind him, tamping down the frustration. "Once she's settled, I've got no reason to stay here."

He doesn't miss a beat. "Don't your sister and her young kids live in Ottawa, man?"

"Well, yeah. But—"

"Crosby, you should really consider some family time. A slower pace of life might be nice for you."

I roll my eyes. It's been great seeing Emma and the kids, but I'm not cut out for suburban uncle life. The mere thought of accepting her constant invitations to various apple orchards and petting zoo farms gives me hives. "A slower pace of life? What am I, ninety?"

Jones chuckles. "Nothing wrong with a little sedate, geriatric activity. Knitting improves hand-eye coordination."

"Yeah. I'll see if I can find the time in between fucking bingo and shuffleboard. If I don't die of a boredom-induced heart attack before then," I add darkly. I'm fully aware I'm acting like a self-indulgent child right now. And I feel like shit about it. I like Jones. I respect the hell out of him. He's a retired special forces guy who started his own private security firm, where he contracts out internationally. In the two and a half years I've worked for him, he's been great at keeping the postings flowing. Until now.

"See, that sunshiny personality is exactly why I hired you."

I promptly ignore his sarcasm. "And like I said, I'll go anywhere you want to send me. Antarctica, Nebraska, even Gary, Indiana—"

"Gary, Indiana? Jesus. You really are a desperate man." He sighs, like he's dealing with a young, highly stubborn child. "Look, I'll see what I can do, but no promises. You won't believe how hard it is to find someone who actually wants to go to Ottawa and replace you." It's a running joke that no one in their right mind would want a close protection posting in Ottawa, mostly because it's known to be a snoozefest. It's also viewed like a punishment. Somewhere you're sent when you really fucked up on assignment. Jones literally did the running man when I told him I needed to take the Ottawa posting, however temporary.

"Oh, trust me, I believe it." I snort, covering my mouth when Eric, of all people, peeks his head around the corner. I did not expect Eric—the PM of Canada—to be lurking around the employees' break area. But I'm learning quickly that Eric is not your average PM. I hang up the phone immediately.

"There you are! I have someone I want you to meet," Eric says, ushering me to follow him to his office.

He makes random conversation about the next hockey game as we head down the long, narrow corridors of his residence. The route to the main bedroom is complicated. I know, because I spent days studying the floor plan of this place.

I hover outside the doorway for a moment, assuming he's officially introducing me to his kids or something.

Only, it's not his kids. He steps aside, revealing a woman.

It hits me instantly. The slight upturn of her nose. The fullness of her lips.

It's Andi. The woman I ghosted three years ago on the tail end of one of the worst weeks of my life.

I've thought about her a fair bit (a fucking lot) since that night. Lying in her bed eating cheesecake, talking about her writing, and harshly judging names. It was the most fun I'd had in a long time, and a welcome distraction from reality.

She eventually fell asleep mid-conversation, so I left. Part of me has always regretted not leaving my number at the bottom of the note I left her. But I wasn't looking to be tied down. That still hasn't changed.

When she spots me, she makes a *gah* sound reminiscent of an ailing walrus, and her eyes go from curious to horrified. Her mouth is curled into an accusatory frown as she clutches her chest, conducting a slow inspection, starting at my feet. When she reaches my face, her eyes widen in recognition. At least, I think so.

"Um . . ." For a second, I think she's going to acknowledge that we know each other. But she doesn't.

"Hi," I finally manage, my voice cracking like I'm twelve years old again as I take her in. She looks the same as she did that night. Hair in a bun, tweed skirt, black tights, and an oversized sweater. The hot librarian look has never really done it for me. Until now.

She slow-blinks, her expression uncomfortably vacant, lips pressed into a thin line. Her posture goes rigid and guarded, fingers interlaced in front of her, tense as fuck. Just like it was that night in the bar.

The silence stretches and my stomach plummets. Either she doesn't remember me at all, or she does and absolutely hates my guts. I wouldn't blame her. It was a classic dick move to leave without notice, even if I did build her desk.

"I'm Nolan Crosby," I add in a rather pathetic attempt to extract a morsel of recognition out of her. A bead of sweat drips down my temple, and I have half a mind to turn around and run. What is wrong with me? Why can't I read her? In all my years of service, I've never been this fucking nervous. I'm officially malfunctioning.

"Nolan," she repeats, slow and assessing, gaze still focused on some point in the middle distance. "I'm Andi."

Thankfully, Eric cuts in. "Andi Zeigler is Gretchen's personal assistant. She's the best," he explains. "And Nolan is from Hexcorp. Former special forces."

Andi slow-nods, seemingly unimpressed. Not that I blame her. "Welcome to the team."

I scratch the back of my head, trying to suppress the urge to ask if she remembers me. I'm not sure I can handle the embarrassment if she doesn't. Or worse, the possibility that she actually did hear my confession that night and has decided I'm an awful person, which, fair.

"Andi, can we talk?" Eric asks, snapping me out of spiraling completely. Putting the job first comes naturally to me. It's what I've always done, because distractions can be deadly.

I dip my chin and say "Thank you" before stepping out to give them some privacy.

I don't run into her again until the next day in the staff kitchen. She's bent over the sink, scrubbing her forehead. I spend far too much time debating whether to keep walking or say something, finally landing on a weak "Hi, again" over the running water.

I think my surprise appearance startles her, because she pops up from the sink, her eyes wide in a mild state of panic. When she turns to me, I see it instantly. There's half a *Deadpool* tattoo directly in the middle of her forehead. "Hi."

I bite back a laugh, failing to keep a straight face. "I didn't peg you for a tattoo kind of girl."

"Josie and Jason decided I should have one. For the sake of my street cred," she informs, referring to the Nichols children.

"Ah, right, your street cred."

"Any chance you know how to remove a semipermanent tattoo?" she asks.

"Dish soap and a lot of scrubbing would probably do it." I step forward and grab a square of paper towel from the counter, pouring some soap and warm water over it. "May I?"

She nods, and I gently lift her chin, careful not to make weird, prolonged eye contact as I move the paper towel in small circles over the tattoo, removing it little by little. She tenses a bit where my skin brushes against hers. It's not my imagination that her breathing quickens as I work.

When her gaze flickers to mine and darts away, everything goes quiet. Her skin is as smooth as I remember beneath my fingertips. Thankfully, most of the tattoo comes off quickly, aside from some stubborn red and blue residue . . . which I suspect will stick around for longer than she wants it to.

"How do I look now?" she asks hopefully when I step back to assess the damage.

"Less prison pod boss. Now you look like someone who would politely ask for my commissary," I tease.

She emits a sigh of relief, running her index finger over the red area where the tattoo was. "Exactly the vibe I was going for. Thanks for helping, Nolan."

"Ah, you remember my name?" I ask, shamefully fishing.

"You told me yesterday. Besides, Nolan's not a very common name. But Nolans strike me as kind," she says, finally meeting my eyes for longer than a millisecond.

"Kind?"

"Kind enough to carry a woman's groceries for many blocks in the dead of winter and eat cheesecake with her until she falls asleep." She flashes me a brief, crooked smile and my entire body instantly relaxes. Well, shit. She does remember me. And she doesn't hate me.

"So you do remember me."

"I'm surprised *you* remember *me*," she counters, eyeing me as I lean my weight against the counter.

"You're hard to forget, Andi." And I mean that.

She runs a hand over her smooth bun contemplatively. "So you're the new bodyguard?"

"I prefer close protection officer," I inform, tamping the corners of my lips down in an effort not to grin like a maniac.

"Same difference, no?"

"Absolutely not." I clutch my chest, feigning offense. "Bodyguards are massive, beefy dudes in dark sunglasses whose job is to look lethal and intimidating. A CPO's job is to blend into the background and prevent issues before they arise," I explain, repositioning my lean as her curious gaze trails back over me. I don't think it's my imagination that it lingers a little.

"Fair. But for the record, you don't look discreet. I think you could kill someone with your bare hands."

So I've been told. "Noted. I'll work on looking less murderous going forward."

She cracks a slight smile, and I take it as a victory. "You know, I always thought you were a hockey player, or some sort of pro athlete."

"Really? Sorry to disappoint."

She shakes her head. "No—I just never would have guessed . . . even though you did tell me to get a new lock on my patio door. I always regretted not asking you more about yourself that night. But I was trying to keep things—"

"Casual," I finish. "And to be fair, I wasn't a CPO back then."

"No?" She eyes me curiously.

"I was in the military at the time. Left a couple months after and went private. Trying something different," I say, which is the line I've been telling all my colleagues. I refuse to be that guy unloading all my personal baggage. "Are you still writing?"

Her brows draw together, but before she can respond, a sharp ding interrupts us. She pulls her phone out of her pocket and practically darts for the door in a panic. "Sorry, I need to pick up the flower order ASAP."

"No worries," I say quickly before she disappears around the corner. "But we should talk sometime."

She pauses in the doorway. "About what?"

"The fact that we know each other." I lower my voice when I say it, just in case anyone is in earshot.

"We do know each other," she agrees. "And now we work . . . in the same place. Do you think that's a problem? A conflict of interest?"

I shrug. "No. I mean, nothing happened between us. Aside from my lip injury and your head injury."

"You can say it," she says, mouth curling into a smirk. "It was a horrible hookup. I know."

I don't have an opportunity to deny that statement, because her phone dings again and she vanishes down the hall.

CHAPTER 5

Andi

I t's just a rule that if there's a semi-attractive man around, I'll make a fool out of myself," I say to Amanda over the phone. I'm speed-walking, trying to finish my errands for Gretchen before tonight.

"You mean you don't think face tats are sexy?" Amanda asks. This isn't the first she's heard about Nolan. I told her about our brief encounter after it first happened. So of course, I had to update her. And cancel on her, yet again, for the second time this week.

"No, Amanda. They are not."

"I beg to differ. The last guy I went out with had one. It was his first name in italics down his cheekbone. Hendrix," she says dreamily.

"I'll never understand why people get their first name tattooed on their bodies. Are they afraid to forget it?"

"It suited him. You'd have to see it up close to appreciate it," she argues, though I highly doubt that. "Anyway, you really need to learn to reject hustle culture. There's no glory in the grind, trust me. Just irreversible wrinkles, eye bags, and a dusty nether region."

We have this conversation pretty much every time we talk. Amanda finds any capitalist 9–5 schedule to be "deeply disturbing spiritually," let alone my 24/7-on-call schedule (with theoretical vacation time). I see her point. This lifestyle isn't for everyone. When I first started, I didn't think I'd last more than a year. But over time, I got better and better at anticipating Gretchen's needs, understanding exactly what she wants, when she wants it, to the point where I've become indispensable. A necessity in her life. Needed. And it feels good to be needed for once.

Still, sometimes when I'm utterly spent at the end of a long day with no more energy left for my writing, I wish I could be more like Amanda, who lives life unencumbered by routine or rules in general. She's an artist, always has been. Ever since we were kids, she could be found collecting funky-shaped twigs, rocks, or shells in the sand at the beach to be fashioned into unique pieces. She calls herself an environmentally conscious artist, who exclusively makes her art out of recycled trash and/or well-loved objects to highlight the impact of waste and "mindless consumption" on the environment.

She walks the walk, too, refusing to drive or live in one particular place, to my parents' utter horror. Live in a van for a year on Vancouver Island? Check. Join a nudist commune? Check.

"Ew, please don't say 'nether region' ever again," I beg.

Of course, she screams it into the phone, cackling.

"Are you in public?" I ask, hearing a flurry of chatter in the background.

"Sure am. I'm at the liquor store, actually. I was grabbing some pinot for our night. Though since you're no longer joining, I'm going trashy before I go out. Malibu and Wild Vines," she adds.

"Have I ever told you how jealous I am of your ability not to care about what people think? Even our mother."

"Oh my god. Speaking of Mom. She called me the other day, solely to complain about the drama with ladies at the country club over the food drive charity. Apparently, one of them knew about her past and asked her to give an account from personal experience in a speech at the banquet. Kind of an inspirational, *Look where I am now, this can be you, too* sort of schtick," she explains.

I snort at the mere thought. "Mom must have been absolutely horrified that anyone knew she used to be poor."

"Oh, she's livid. She asked Dave if they could sue for defamation, as if it's a big lie or something."

"Amazing how quick you can forget you were ever on welfare, huh?"

"Truly. Anyway, enough negativity. I gotta go. The cashier just asked for my ID," she informs proudly. "I have one last request."

"Nope," I say preemptively. I think I know where this is going.

"Talk to the bodyguard again. I mean, what are the chances that you'd run into him again after all these years? Let alone work with him? It's gotta be a sign or something."

"Bye. Love you," I say as I pull up to Gretchen's dry cleaner.

Admittedly, seeing Nolan again threw me for a loop. All I could think about was waking up alone the next morning, my entire chest coated in cheesecake crust crumbs. I think I may have had some dried bits on the corner of my mouth. No wonder he got the hell out of Dodge. Besides, it was for the best. It's not like I wanted anything more, except for a chance to redeem myself in bed.

"That's how one-night stands work. They aren't supposed to stay," Laine kindly reminded me when she called the next morning (to make sure I was *okay*) after she and Hunter sprang their big news on me.

After a couple months, I started to think I'd imagined Nolan. Over the years, he became a faceless, very muscular blur. Surely any memory I did have of him was my overactive imagination filling in the blanks. There's no way I'd met a wildly attractive man who encouraged me to keep writing, to publish my books, to pursue my passion. Maybe I dreamed him up entirely, like I tend to do. Because lightning-in-a-bottle moments like that don't happen to me. The kinds you could write an entire romance novel about.

The only lasting proof that he was real was my assembled writing desk, as well as the sticky note he left on top, which I kept in my underwear drawer of all places. But the moment I saw him standing in Eric's doorway, I knew for certain he'd been real.

Since that night, I'd self-published three books in the span of two years under the pen name A. A. Zed before Gretchen took over my life. None of the books sold more than a couple thousand copies each. In fact, I probably invested more money into editing, cover design, and marketing ads than I got back (the joys of self-publishing). But it was nice, sprinkling a little bit of happiness into the world. To this day, I still get messages from readers asking when my next book is coming. I never respond, because honestly, I don't know the answer. Maybe it's my complete and total lack of free time, but I've had zero inspiration.

Until now. It's the first time in forever that my fingers itch to fly across my keyboard again. I spent the whole night curled under a blanket at my desk, letting my brain roam freely, the familiar, satisfying soft click of keys under my fingertips. When all was said and done, I'd written over four thousand words. Admittedly, they were rusty words. Probably not meant for consumption by anyone but me. Still, finding my rhythm again filled me with a satisfaction that I haven't felt since I wrote my last book.

As usual, I don't have a lot of time to nurture the spark. Yesterday Eric practically begged on bended knee for my help. He's desperate to "make it up" to Gretchen for ditching their anniversary weekend. I may not have recent real-life experience with romance, but I know Gretchen.

So I booked them a private room at her favorite vegan restaurant, La Maison. I even ordered hundreds of dollars' worth of orchids for aesthetic purposes. And because Eric really needed the brownie points, I hired the same harpist who played at their wedding as Gretchen walked down the aisle.

Two minutes before Eric showed up at the restaurant with Nolan, Gretchen called to inform me that she wasn't coming.

"Why not?" I asked, unable to mask the disappointment. I didn't spend all night making a slideshow montage of their life together for nothing.

"Let's not act like you didn't plan this entire night for him,

Andi. He didn't lift a finger, aside from plunking his ass into the chair. And I'm the one who should make the effort to put on a bra and go all the way there? For what? So he can give me the same old excuses he always does?" She proceeded to hang up on me and sent my next two calls to voicemail.

So now it's just me, the harpist, and Nolan crammed into a tiny, candlelit room, watching Eric quietly sob into his fancy vegan polenta dish. And yes, it's as awkward as it sounds.

I've never seen Eric cry before. Not even out of happiness when he won the election. He's generally a sunny, upbeat guy—the kind of person you'll rarely catch without a smile. Without his usual team of assistants around, I'm not sure what to say, if anything.

Nolan slants me a brief glance laced with mild panic from his post by the door, as if to say, *What do we do?*

I turn my palms to the ceiling and shake my head, deliberately ignoring how well he fills out that suit. Must focus on the task at hand. "Um, would you like me to get the food to go?" I ask Eric, as gently as possible. I'm used to dealing with Gretchen, but Eric? Not so much.

His dark eyes flick up, meeting mine desperately. "Andi, what can I do to fix this? I feel like I've tried everything." His tone is one of complete dejection.

"Um, I'm not sure I'm the best person to ask—"

"You are," he pleads, panic edging his voice. "You spend more time with her than anyone." Technically, he's right. Gretchen lost most of her close friends at the beginning of his term, mostly due to her lack of freedom. She can't make plans on a whim without security approvals. With the kids in school all day, I'm the person she has the most face time with. And after thousands of hours spent with her, I'm fully aware that this rift between them is anything but simple.

I hesitantly pull Gretchen's would-be adjacent chair out and sit. "I guess the first step would be understanding all the factors that have led to this."

"She's upset because I had to cancel Tremblant, right?" he asks simply, his shoulders slumped. Oh, Eric. "Upset" is a generous descriptor. She also used some colorful language, calling him "willfully obtuse." Despite running a whole-ass country, he remains as clueless as most men.

"Well . . . that's part of it." I drum my fingers in the space between us, debating whether it's my place to get into it. It's really not. I'm just a low-level assistant. Then again, Gretchen is too angry to explain it in a way he'll receive it. Maybe a go-between is exactly what they need. Maybe I missed my calling as a couples therapist. "It goes back further than that. She's been feeling like you haven't prioritized her or the kids ever since you took office."

His face crumples. "But what choice do I have? She knew how demanding the job would be and she agreed to it, encouraged it. I try my best to eat dinner with them when I can. Just last month, I bought her that necklace she wanted." He accidentally knocks over the stone saltshaker as he talks. He's always had a tendency to talk with his hands.

I catch it before it falls over completely. "Look, the grand gestures are sweet. But in the end, what she values most are the small things. Little ways to show you really care."

"Like what?"

"Compliments, putting on her favorite song, small reminders

of good memories, a touch here and there. Being present instead of always checking your phone, going through your emails. It will all add up. She just needs to know she and the kids are number one." Am I, a very single woman with zero romantic prospects, really giving marriage advice to the prime minister of Canada right now? What is my life?

He rubs the back of his neck, like he's not so sure, before leaning in close. "Can I tell you a secret? I'm worried it's over between us. We haven't had a real conversation in months. She doesn't even let me near her anymore."

"She loves you," I insist, looking him in the eye so he knows I'm telling the truth. "I can tell by the way she still looks at you, the way she still talks about you."

"You think?" he asks tearfully, doubling over in the chair, finger-massaging his temples. He looks like a dejected puppy who's been kicked out of the house into the rain by his beloved owner.

"Of course. If there's any couple who can make it, it's you two," I assure, mostly to give this poor, broken man some much-needed hope.

I think it works (thankfully, because I'm grossly unqualified to give in-depth marriage advice). He considers that for a couple seconds, a promise of a smile flitting across his sharp features before he reaches out to give my hand a quick squeeze. "Honestly, I don't know what I'd do without you, Andi."

"Well, you'd have to fold your own underwear, for starters," I point out, pushing my chair back when he stands, giving Nolan the signal that he's ready to leave.

He gives me his trademark sunny smirk as he smooths down his suit. "Let's not get ahead of ourselves."

CHAPTER 6

Nolan

We've done so much good work in the past few years, but there's so much more to do together. I've had the privilege of speaking to Canadians across our country at length about the greatest challenges we face today, like the rising cost of living and childcare.

"It brings me back to my own childhood. As early as nine years old, I was shoveling driveways, delivering newspapers, doing anything I could to make extra money to help my mom put food on the table, pay for the necessities, and sometimes, we fell short. We'd go hungry, or play cards over candlelight because our electricity would be shut off. And that's not acceptable. That's not something I can continue to accept for you."

The lines are delivered with such eloquence and down-to-earth charm, it smacks you upside the head and leaves you a little winded. You'd never know this affordable childcare press conference was thrown together in a day as a distraction from the Kirkwood scandal. And you definitely wouldn't know Eric spent all last night crying in a dimly lit restaurant like a groom jilted at the altar.

Based on the volume of cheers and hollers, you'd think it's a boy band onstage, not the PM giving a speech about subsidized childcare. Then again, Eric Nichols isn't your average politician.

The crowd is eating it up, as always. Honestly, I don't know what kind of magic this is, but I want whatever he's having. I have a theory that Eric could stand behind a podium, recite a nursery rhyme, and still receive a roaring standing ovation. The man has a special knack for maximizing every moment, every gesture, and knowing when to slow down and pause for impact at exactly the right times.

"Onward together, toward a better future for us and our children."

"Eric, I love you!" an unassuming middle-aged woman screeches. She proceeds to shove her way to the front of the crowd with more force than you'd expect for someone wearing a T-shirt that reads BLESS THIS MESS.

"FP Martina White is on the move, fast approaching Tousled Wave," I warn Ivan through my earpiece. I recognize her face from the photos shown during the team briefing earlier this morning.

The Close Protection Unit has deemed Martina a "fixated person (FP)," aka a stalker. Brent, the team lead, describes her as a forty-two-year-old who's under the delusion that she and the PM are star-crossed lovers.

Since Eric became PM, she's shown up at every single one of his local events. She's also sent an astonishing number of emails and tweets professing her love, which, when printed, take up two three-ring binders. Her dedication is both frightening and a little admirable. And while it's been determined that Martina is generally harmless as far as a risk of violence, we keep close tabs to ensure that doesn't change.

"For fuck's sake. I'm on her," Ivan grunts in response. "Welcome to your first week on the job, Crosby."

Ivan and I are perfectly positioned by the time Martina gets to Eric, reaching for his forearm. When she holds on a couple seconds longer than comfortable, I discreetly loosen her iron grip from behind, giving Eric a chance to escape naturally without making a scene. Then, Ivan swoops in, subtly blocking Martina from following.

It seems simple. So much so, I guarantee no one in the crowd, nor those watching on the news, notices anything peculiar about the entire exchange, which is exactly the point. That entire "simple" maneuver was one of countless scenarios we close protection officers practice in advance of situations like this. These basic, easy protocols keep the principal—aka the PM—safe.

Still, I keep a couple paces behind Eric as he makes his way through the crowd, shaking hands and generally hypnotizing citizens with his strikingly white smile. Usually, no one gives a shit about Canadian politicians, but Eric is different than any former PM, or most world leaders, for that matter. The team calls it the Eric Effect.

I assumed taking this job would be similar to all the other times in the military when I did protection for a political leader or dignitary. But unlike anyone else, Eric has a 74 percent approval rating, which is twice the approval rating of his political party at large. And he does it all simply by being himself. He was voted *People* Magazine's "Sexiest World Leader" twice in a row; women have a tendency to throw themselves (and their bras) at him. One passing glance at his singular right dimple and it's clear why. See, most Western world leaders have a look: white, male, and aged sixty-plus. But not Eric.

Picture a walking Disney prince, dazzling charisma and all. In all his time in office, his only scandal was getting caught on camera sneaking a cookie from his pocket during a royal event at Buckingham Palace. Because of all this extra attention, Eric is the only PM in history to require private, specialized security for himself and his family above and beyond the security provided by the federal police, which is where my team comes in.

Since the press has a complete field day whenever he leaves his residence, Eric conducts much of his daily business from his home office—the only exceptions being scheduled events and Wednesdays, when he attends House of Commons Question Periods.

Eric briefly makes eye contact with me, steeples his fingers, and moves them apart. It's our silent code we agreed upon yesterday. When he wants me to come closer, he draws his fingers together. And when he wants me to back the fuck off like right now, he draws them apart.

As a true "man of the people," he spends an extraordinary amount of time at each event among the crowd, just socializing. At least that's what my boss tells me. This is my first event with him. Case in point, he's just moved on from shaking a frail old man's hand to playing peekaboo with a cherub-faced baby.

"Did we ever follow up with the RCMP about mental health services for Martina?" Eric asks the moment we finally shuffle him into the Suburban. It occurs to me that it'd be easy to be a dick and make fun of her in private, but the bastard seems to genuinely care about her mental health.

"We can follow up on that," I assure, making a mental note.

"Please do." Eric shoots me a teasing glance. "Hope that bra didn't leave a mark on your face." On the way out, someone flung their bra at him, and of course, the clasp hit me in the side of the face instead.

I shrug. "Better that than a fist, I guess."

"We've had our fair share of those," Ivan notes from the front seat. "Eric routinely shows up on most punchable politician lists." The downside of being popular with the majority is that he's vehemently hated by an asshole fringe minority who don't want to see a half-Indian guy from the projects as their nation's leader. And that fringe minority is loud.

"It's true," Eric faux-brags. "But you don't need to worry about me. I can handle myself."

"He's not lying," Ivan informs. "The man has a black belt and a law degree. He could fuck you up and turn around and sue your ass." That's part of his wide appeal. He isn't some rich kid who grew up steeped in privilege, or closely connected to politics. In fact, his mother raised him and his brothers on her own, while working full-time as a personal support worker for people with physical disabilities. He put himself through university, and then law school, where he worked for legal aid for ten years, which was where he met his wife. After getting frustrated with the legal system, he tried his hand at politics with the goal of making real change. And he has.

Ivan tilts his head to me. "Crosby, I sent you the floor plans and videos for the Squamish trip, which you're joining, by the way," he informs, referring to Eric's two-day trip back to his home riding. This is news to me. As the new guy, I didn't think I'd be traveling so soon.

A couple guys from the team have been there for a week already, casing everything out down to the floor plans for the venue, hotel, restaurants, and coffee shops the PM will visit, as well as each and every route for the motorcade. It seems like overkill to the average person, but it's standard in this line of work. Everything must be preplanned to minimize risk. This job is all about prevention. If an incident does happen, we've already failed.

Before I can respond in the affirmative, Eric turns to me. "Is that okay? I know you're taking care of your mom and—"

In all honesty, it gives me some anxiety. The whole reason I took this contract was so I could be here for the summer—until a spot opens up for Mom in the assisted living center. At the same time, I'm too new to decline work.

"It's all good. She'll be fine. Appreciate it, though." I wave him off casually, casting my hard stare out the window as we pull through the gates of 24 Sussex, which is swarmed with media, presumably here about the Kirkwood scandal.

The moment we exit the vehicle, one of them steps forward, his microphone pointed at Eric. "Any comment regarding the rumors about you and your wife's personal assistant?"

CHAPTER 7

Andi

I wake up to two alarming texts. The first is from Laine.

LAINE: Hey! The friendliest reminder that the deadline to RSVP to the wedding is next week. We'd love to have you there. XO -L

Ugh. That feeling. The dread that always gathers in my gut on the rare occasion her name pops up on my screen. These days, my friendship with Laine consists of a few texts back and forth with some variation of *We must hang out soon!!* with many exclamation points and emojis, but ultimately no follow-up. In fact, I found out about her and Hunter's engagement last year via social media. And two months ago, it came in the mail in the form of thick cardstock with a loopy script font, which read:

The presence of your company is requested for the wedding of

Laine Hall and Hunter Williams

Frankly, I was shocked to be invited. I still haven't RSVP'd, despite the wedding being in less than two months. In Mexico.

I'd rather have uncontrollable, explosive diarrhea at a fancy foreign dignitary event than travel to a Mexican resort to celebrate their nuptials among an intimate group of family and close friends. But if I say no, I look bitter. Declining would also solidify the end of our friendship, and I don't know if I have the heart to make it official, despite the writing on the wall.

So I do the mature thing: avoid it entirely and move on to Gretchen's text.

> GRETCHEN: See me in my office this morning when you arrive. It's URGENT.

The aggressive use of caps lock gives me pause.

That's odd. These days, Gretchen isn't normally awake until around ten, which gives me plenty of time to get her clothes steamed and coffee and breakfast ready. When she texts, she's intensely specific about what she wants. This vague and ominous text gives me nothing.

Heart hammering in double time, I throw on a wrinkled pencil skirt and cardigan from the pile on my floor, toss my hair into a quick bun, and hightail it to work on foot with no makeup. This will have to do.

I burst through the employee entrance twenty minutes later, rain-soaked hair sticking to my forehead. The door leads into the staff kitchen, where the household workers congregate for breaks.

The voice of Noella, one of the nannies, roots me in place by the door. "It's always the quiet ones you have to look out for."

"I always thought she had a crush on Eric. Guess it wasn't so innocent," says a softer voice I recognize as that of Ann, the head chef.

"Do you think she'll get fired for this?" Noella asks.

Whoa. Something big must have gone down. Normally, I keep close tabs on the news cycle. It's my job to stay informed. To know exactly what Eric and Gretchen are talking about at any given time. But after the whirlwind of last night's impromptu restaurant gesture, I went to bed early and didn't have a chance to scroll through the headlines this morning.

I poke my head around the corner like a gopher, curious. "Hi," I squeak, removing my coat before I start sweating profusely from the humidity. The temperature in this old house only knows two extremes, arctic chill or Satan's asshole, and right now, it's the latter.

Noella and Ann simultaneously jump at my presence. They let my greeting hang, gaping at me in silence, like I'm a sinister ghost of prime ministers past or something. Normally, they're friendly with me—more so Noella, who provides daily updates on her foster cats. She jumps at the chance to talk to adults whenever she can, since she spends most of her time with the

Nichols kids. Ann, on the other hand, hates me and my entire essence since the time I mistook her lactose-free string cheese in the communal fridge for my own. Ever since, she's labeled all her food items in bold blood-red Sharpie.

"Who are we talking about?" I ask, trying again.

Ann just eyes me up and down from behind her wire-framed glasses, lips pressed together as though she's trying to hold in a laugh. I place my hand over my mouth, auto-assuming there's something on my face, or food in my teeth.

Clearly, I was too abrupt and accidentally interrupted a private conversation. I've never been great at reading people, especially when they're in groups. Inevitably I always feel like the odd one out. The one who gets the least amount of eye contact. The one who awkwardly stands there, nodding, like a bystander to the conversation. I've always preferred one-on-one friendships because of that.

"Glad you're both having a good day." Before I can embarrass myself more, I scurry to the bathroom to do a mirror check before going to Gretchen's office, only to find nothing on my face or in my teeth.

I'm trembling by the time I arrive at her office. Gretchen glares at me in the hallway before my direct view to her is disrupted by Eric, who's just leaving. He inches past me in the doorway without so much as a passing glance. Odd, especially after our heart-to-heart last night. He's a busy man, but he usually at least says *hi* to me. Maybe he's embarrassed about crying in front of me?

When I enter, Gretchen gives me an icy look that could freeze a large nation. She's not an overly warm and fuzzy person, but she's never been this cold to me. Not even after I accidentally spilled coffee on one of her favorite cashmere sweaters in my first month.

As I round her oak desk, it's clear we're not alone. In the chair on the far right is Bethany, director of media relations, with the box-dyed red hair that always looks a shade of purple.

"We have a serious situation." Gretchen's abrupt, clipped tone isn't lost on me. What the hell is going on?

"A situation?"

"A PR nightmare," Bethany says, enunciating with precision. She shifts her whole body toward me, the toes of her blue matte heels dragging against the carpet.

"What can I do?" I ask instinctually. As a PA, remedying the situation is always my first priority, even before understanding what the situation actually is.

"Maybe you can tell us," Bethany says cryptically.

I rack my brain, trying to figure out what the hell I did wrong, but come up with nothing. Maybe Nolan told someone we knew each other? Not that it should be a big deal, since nothing happened between us. Besides, everyone on the Hill knows one another (and sleeps together, occasionally). "What's going on?"

Gretchen turns her desktop monitor to me. The screen is opened to multiple internet tabs, all of which appear to be media articles.

I suck in a shaky breath, mentally prepping myself to read headlines about Eric and Gretchen splitting up, or maybe even divorcing. Did things go that south since last night's failed anniversary dinner? Maybe that's why Eric was in such a mood.

But the articles aren't about Gretchen and Eric. They're about Eric and . . . *me*.

CHAPTER 8

Andi

SCANDAL AT THE TABLE: PM AND ASSISTANT GETTING COZY AT INTIMATE DINNER

RESTAURANT PHOTOS FUEL SPECULATION ABOUT ERIC NICHOLS AND WIFE'S ASSISTANT

ERIC NICHOLS' RUMORED STEAMY AFFAIR WITH WIFE'S PERSONAL ASSISTANT

WHISPERS OF INFIDELITY: PM'S DINNER DATE RAISES EYEBROWS

And then there are the photos.

They're of last night. And admittedly, they look bad.

It's a direct shot of Eric and me at the table—the harpist and Nolan cropped out. Beside the candles and flowers, Eric is leaning in close. It looks like we're staring dreamily into each other's eyes.

If that's not bad enough, there's a couple shots where it looks like he's touching my elbow, when really, it's when he accidentally knocked over the saltshaker. And then there's the last few photos, where it appears we're holding hands, even though it was merely a one-second squeeze. Nothing remotely intimate or romantic. In fact, I've always considered Eric a remarkably cooler, older brother figure.

With each new headline and accompanying photo, I lose a year of my life. I think I'm having an out-of-body experience. It's like I'm watching myself, pale like Casper the Friendly Ghost, death-clutching Gretchen's chair with my sweaty hands so hard, I'm shocked the leather doesn't puncture. My heart thrashes, desperate to burst free and run out of this house. Out of this city. I'm certain both Gretchen and Bethany can hear it. And probably everyone in the whole house, for that matter.

My eyes latch on to Gretchen's, bypassing her hard stare. "Gretchen, I swear to you, there's absolutely nothing like that going on. We were just talking. I was giving him advice about how to fix things with you," I assure her, clumsily explaining the saltshaker incident and the quick hand squeeze. "I don't—I don't think that way about Eric. Ever. You guys are like family to me." Those words sound ludicrous coming out of my mouth. But how does one eloquently convince their boss they're *not* sleeping with their husband?

"Actually, there's more. It's not just the photos," Bethany warns.

My brows shoot up. "More?" What more could there possibly be?

Gretchen opens yet another tab and my gut curdles.

A partial image of a dapper man in a suit with a shadowed

outline of Parliament in the background takes up the entire screen. It's my second book, to be exact. *The Prime Minister & Me*, about an affair between a prime minister and his assistant. It's my steamiest book—as in 11/10 eggplants on the heat scale, a departure from the low-heat, angstier vibe of my first book. It was probably the most fun I've ever had writing.

At the time, work was starting to take over my life. Escaping into a made-up world about a fictional silver fox of a PM and his assistant having hot sex on various surfaces around Parliament proved an excellent escape. A far cry from the gritty, bureaucratic world of real-life politics. It was also easy to write, because inspiration was all around me.

I open my mouth to speak, but my shock mutes me.

Before I can cobble together a sentence, Gretchen cuts in. "After the photos leaked this morning, the media naturally did some digging on you and found this . . . *erotic novel*." The way she says "*erotic novel*," as though it were written by the devil himself, is exactly why I used a pen name to begin with.

"It's speculated to have been penned by you. A memoir of sorts. Look familiar?" Bethany asks. "The media have called, requesting comment for their follow-up story."

"Memoir? Follow-up story?" I cringe, heat emanating from my cheeks, throat, and entire body.

"Linking you to the book," Bethany explains. "They see it as added proof of the affair. They'll be publishing the story tomorrow."

I want to throw up. Even under all my layers of polyester and wool, I feel naked. Entirely exposed. That's why Noella and Ann were looking at me sideways. Everyone thinks I'm some sex-crazed freak who's having an affair with Eric, or at the very least, fantasizing about it. And worst of all, my boss thinks I've written a self-insert erotica about her husband.

Her. Husband.

The prime minister of Canada.

Fuck my life.

Death may be a welcome alternative.

"You know the opposition is already popping bottles in their offices, hoping this and the Kirkwood scandal will be the catalyst that shifts public opinion. So please, please make my day easier and tell me this isn't you. That the photos mean nothing," Gretchen says. The anger hardening her face has softened slightly, replaced by what looks like a plea.

I mentally assess my options. The photos are completely innocuous. But the book isn't. I did write it.

I could admit it, explain that the story has nothing to do with Eric or me. That it merely served as a setting for two completely fictional characters who bear no resemblance to me or Eric. Nothing more, which is the cold, hard truth.

But would Gretchen and everyone else actually buy it? Would they really believe it was simply a work of fiction? Regardless, I could never be Gretchen's PA as well as a romance writer whose books include some seriously scorching face-sitting scenes by chapter 3. Not to mention, my mom would burst into flames and disintegrate into ash if she ever read a single word.

My second option is to deny it all. Aside from the initials, the pen name isn't linked to my real identity in any tangible way. I've gone through painstaking efforts to keep the two identities separate.

"Andi, was it you who wrote this book?" Gretchen asks again, growing increasingly uncomfortable with my silence. "I don't want to accuse you of anything, but there are things in here that only an insider would know."

"You read it?" I ask, my jaw ticking.

"Well, I skimmed it, of course, but had to stop at *erect peach nipples*. God knows I'll never get that half hour of my life back," she continues, not bothering to hide her distaste.

"No. Of course I didn't write it." I twitch when the words come out, just waiting for her to call me out like she always does.

She watches me for what feels like an entire year.

My body feels like it's ready to burst into flame under the pressure. But what other choice do I have? If I admit to being A. A. Zed, I might as well kiss my job goodbye. My entire reputation would be tainted as a mistress / smut memoir writer.

Even if I could prove I'm not involved with Eric, everyone would think I'm creepily obsessed with him. That every sexy scene in that book is based on my real thoughts, even though it's not. No one would take me seriously, ever again. And worse, it could cause even more tension between Gretchen and Eric. The last thing I want to do is make her feel like she can't trust me around her husband.

Bethany continues through my silence. "Given the security situation around Eric, it would be a conflict of interest. If you did write it, now is the time to fess up so we can fix this."

Conflict of interest. No shit.

And so it's decided: Nothing positive can come from admitting it. Denial is my only option.

"I did not write it, and nothing is going on between me and Eric," I repeat, careful not to let my voice waver under Gretchen's searing gaze. I feel like Bill Clinton saying he *did not have sexual relations*. God, I hate lying.

Gretchen shifts her elbow onto the armrest, staring at me, waiting for me to crack. A millennium passes until she finally says, "Okay. I believe you."

I have to stop myself from flopping out of my chair entirely.

With Gretchen's support, Bethany switches her tune. "The media has no tangible proof that you wrote it, aside from speculation regarding the initials and the fact that the author also lives in Ottawa, according to their biography."

"How do we make the headlines go away?" Gretchen asks Bethany, as though she's a genie in a bottle who can make all of this disappear in a puff of smoke.

"We cannot, under any circumstances, allow the public to believe the story has any validity, especially months before the election. So as of now, our stance is to do nothing aside from feed the news positive stories about Eric and Gretchen. Other than that, we ride it out and hope it goes away. Luckily, these headlines haven't made it to mainstream news outlets. We think Eric responding to the rumors will only bring more attention to them."

"Right," I say. That's one thing I'll never understand about world leaders. You have to portray this outdated, picture-perfect family image in order to have any clout with voters. A solid family unit exudes the image of stability and relatability.

"We need everyone to believe Eric and Gretchen's marriage is strong," Bethany continues, biting her tongue when she realizes how that sounded. She glances at Gretchen sympathetically. "Not that it isn't strong. I just mean—"

Gretchen puts her palm up. "It's fine."

"So that means, ideally, Andi and Eric should not be spotted publicly together, even with you present," Bethany says to Gretchen.

"But wait, what about Squamish? That's tomorrow," I point out.

"I don't think it would be wise of you to join any upcoming travel. But—" she continues, pausing to look at Gretchen.

"I insisted. I said I'm not going anywhere unless I can bring you. You not coming would look more suspicious, in my opinion. If nothing is going on, why wouldn't I bring you?" Gretchen says firmly, her gaze meeting mine hopefully. "You'll still come, right?"

"Of course," I say dutifully. In a weird way, it feels kind of nice to be needed, even though it would be better if I didn't go. "Listen, I'm sorry about all of this."

Gretchen gives me wide eyes. "Why? It's not your fault some weirdo snapped pictures of you guys. I bet the opposition did it on purpose. I bet they even wrote the book themselves to stir shit up. They knew where we were weak and thought they'd exploit it," she says cynically. Based on the shifty look on her face, she's already strategizing.

After a couple minutes of Gretchen and Bethany trading conspiracy theories while I nearly expire in my chair, Gretchen dismisses us.

Bethany springs up from her seat, grateful to leave, but not before telling me, "The Close Protection Unit is going to give the book a read to make sure there's nothing of concern. They might ask you some questions, but I wouldn't worry too much about it."

Normally I'd stick around to make sure Gretchen doesn't need anything. But today, I bolt out of her office and down a quiet corridor. I steady myself against the wall, hands on knees, practically gasping for breath.

And then it hits me. Nolan.

He was the only other person at the restaurant last night. He's also the only person who knows about my writing. Did he leak the photos and the book to the media?

He doesn't strike me as the kind of person who would do that. In fact, if I were a betting woman, I'd have guessed he'd be the last person to expose me. What would he have to gain?

At the same time, how odd is it that days after he's hired, I get doxed? It's too big a coincidence to ignore.

CHAPTER 9

──────◆◆◆──────

Nolan

Y ou've all probably heard the rumors about this book by now."
Ivan brandishes a brand-new paperback with *The Prime
Minister & Me* scrawled across it in fancy lettering. The exact
same title Andi told me her next book would be called.

She actually published her book. She fucking did it; at least
it appears so. Technically, it could be a coincidence. But if it was
her, pride swells inside me, even though I barely know her.

"Um, what are these rumors?" I ask, leaning in to get a better
view of the book. Truthfully, there was a lot of whispering going
on today. But I purposefully try not to eavesdrop. People's personal business is not my concern, and I have enough of my own
shit to deal with.

"Gretchen Nichols's PA, Andi Zeigler, is the author," Mike
says through a snort, propping his forearms on the table.

"*Rumored* author," Ivan corrects.

Rowland lets out a hearty laugh. "The PA?"

"The book was published two years ago, along with two other books. And the initials and location of the author match," Ivan clarifies.

"Okay, but there are one million people who live in Ottawa. Probably a good number with those same initials. Doesn't mean it's her," Ben points out from the end of the long table.

"Andi has denied it," Ivan notes, which makes me sad. "Eric and Gretchen aren't putting much stock into the rumors. But given the accusations of sensitive insider information in the book, we need to do our due diligence and investigate." Ivan slides the book toward me on the table. "The honor goes to you. As the newest member of the team. Some nice plane reading for Squamish tomorrow."

I pick up the book, running my finger over the glossy cover in awe.

All the guys around the table crack up. It pisses me off, the way they're eyeing maybe-Andi's-book derisively like it's trash or something. Now I understand why she was so against people knowing about her books to begin with. I'm tempted to tell them off and ask if they've written any whole-ass novels lately, but I hold my tongue. If she's claiming she didn't write it, the last thing she needs is me drawing attention to it.

Mike tips his chin to me as I stand. "Happy reading, Crosby."

Never thought part of my job would entail reading a romance novel, but here I am.

The moment I step into the hallway, a figure pushes me to the right. It's Andi, using her entire body weight to shove me toward a random, nondescript hallway door. Realistically, she can't move me an inch unless I let her. So I do.

We're in a dusty storage closet. It's dark, though my eyes adjust fairly quickly. The shelves are neatly filled with maintenance tools, linens, fine china, and crystal glassware I assume is reserved for official dinners. There's a stack of miscellaneous paintings and historic-looking household items piled in the corner, alongside boxes hand-labeled as state gifts. There's an antique side table to the left, its ornate legs jutting out at an odd angle, leaving little space for us to squeeze in comfortably.

We're practically chest to chest, close enough that I can feel the warmth of her breath skating across my throat. It's a little exciting, if I'm honest, until I see the look on her face. Her eyes are narrowed into a furious look that could wither the entire vase of Gretchen's fresh flowers on the table in the hall.

"We need to talk," she announces, poking me hard in the chest while eyeing the copy of *The Prime Minister & Me* tucked under my arm.

I swallow. "Uh, in a storage closet?"

She ignores that, piercing me with an accusatory stare. "Was it you who leaked the story? Don't lie."

Ah. That's what this is about. "Of course not." Frankly, I'm really fucking offended she would think that.

She conducts a scrutinizing once-over. "Because you're the only person who was at the restaurant last night. And you're the only one who knows I write romance."

I level her with a *come on* look. "If you don't count the harpist, the waiter, the chef, and all the other customers in the main dining room. And I never even told anyone we knew each other, let alone that you were a writer."

She lowers her shoulders slightly, her fingers flexing and twisting at her sides. "I'm sorry for accusing you. I'm just really . . . stressed."

"Stressed because you're the real author?" I wager.

Her brows furrow. "No, of course I'm not."

I study her face for the truth. It's a source-handling technique that I've always been good at. Liars tend to either avoid eye contact or overcompensate by staring a little too long. Andi has never been one to make prolonged eye contact, so it's difficult to tell.

Liars also tend to fidget, touch their face, or make rapid movements with their hands when under a microscope, which she's doing.

"I didn't write it," she repeats, her lips pursed.

It takes all of five seconds for her to buckle under my stare.

"Fine. I wrote it. It's my book," she admits, leaning her whole body weight on the shelf behind her, as if the admission extracted all her remaining energy.

I don't know what comes over me, but I pull her in for a hug. "You actually did it! Do you even realize how freakin' amazing that is?" I say as I pull back. It's a complete understatement, of course.

Even three years and published books later, she still can't handle the compliment. Instead, she buries her face in her hands, peeking at me through the crack. "But you should know, the book has nothing to do with Eric. Or me. I've never thought of him like that, ever. I was just . . . writing what I knew, I guess."

"You don't need to convince me. And I'm really proud of you," I say genuinely.

She tips her head, evidently not in the mood to celebrate her achievements right now, which is fair. Her job is on the line. "You won't tell anyone, right?"

Technically, this is a huge conflict of interest. I'm supposed to be investigating this. At the same time, it's none of my business, or anyone else's, what she does with her own time. So I look her in the eye. "Andi, it's fine. I would never tell anyone. It's no one's business but yours," I assure her. And I mean it.

She steadies herself against the shelf of linens, hands on hips. "God, this is a nightmare."

"It is."

"I mean, you were there last night. Nothing about that exchange seemed inappropriate, right?"

"Not that I could tell," I agree. Nothing struck me as odd, which is why I was so shocked by the rumors. "All of this is going to blow over. You know the truth and so does Eric. That's all that matters."

She looks relieved to hear that as she fumbles for the closet doorknob. "Thanks, Nolan."

CHAPTER 10

Andi

Someone is in the hallway when Nolan and I emerge from the dark depths of the storage closet. It's Gretchen, because of course it is. Life really has it out for me today.

She's gliding past, mid-stride, as Nolan and I burst into the light. I'll admit, it looks bad. We're both a little disheveled and sweaty from the lack of air circulation, swatting the cobwebs from our clothes and hair.

Her head snaps in my direction, and her amber eyes lock with mine with scary, hawklike precision. "Oh, there you are! I was looking for you."

"I was just—"

Before I have the chance to shove Nolan back into the closet, her eyes dart over my shoulder to him, towering behind me. Her mouth lifts in a coy smile as the pieces slide into place in her head. "Mr. Crosby."

Oh no.

"Hi," he says, giving her a weak wave. "Sorry, I—um, I'm going now." He gives me one last look and darts off down the hallway, my book tucked under his arm.

And then it's just me and Gretchen. I expect her to ask what the hell we were doing in there. I've even summoned a half-baked excuse about asking him to fetch an obscure item from the top shelf since he's vertically gifted and I am not. Instead, she just nods her head, motioning for me to follow her.

We end up back in her office, which doesn't exactly give me the warm and fuzzies since our meeting fifteen minutes ago.

"It wasn't what it looked like," I declare the moment she closes the door.

"I owe you an apology," she says, ignoring my statement as she leans her hip on the desk, arms folded over her chest.

"For what?" I ask, tepidly sitting the edge of my butt in the chair.

"Our meeting earlier. I know it probably felt like an ambush, with Bethany and the whole book thing. I was so shocked by the rumor and I could tell you were hiding *something*."

I slow-nod, unsure where she's going with this.

"I had a feeling there was something up when you asked for Saturday off. You never ask for days off," she points out, like she's trying to convince herself. "But now it all makes sense. There's something going on between you and Nolan."

My first reaction is to cough, violently. I'm basically a mangy alley cat hacking up a lung. It's so bad, Gretchen offers me a sip of her own latte, which I take gratefully. "Thanks," I rasp.

"When did it start?" she asks with uncharacteristic interest, her expression smug.

"When did what start?" I counter, flustered by Gretchen's

sudden interest in my love life. She's never shown much interest in me in general for three years.

"You and Nolan," she declares, like it's obvious.

I half cough, half laugh. Me and Nolan? "Oh, I think you misund—"

"Normally I would tell you to keep it on the down-low so you don't have to get HR involved. But I was thinking, *not* hiding might be a good thing." She drums her nails against her coffee cup, a smile creeping across her lips.

I've barely even digested the fact that I'm not getting fired, at least not today. And now, she thinks Nolan and I are dating?

Here's the thing, relationships on the Hill happen all the time, and for good reason. Political nerds who work inhumane hours are simply happier with other political nerds who also work inhumane hours. But when it does happen, you're obligated to report it to HR, and generally, it's frowned upon to work on the same team, or in each other's general vicinity. Even more frowned upon is PDA at work.

I'm about to say, *No, you have it all wrong*, when the smile practically splits her face. "Actually, this could be a really good thing, you being with Nolan. You know how powerful insider gossip is on the Hill," she says, working through it in her mind.

"Are you saying that if people see Nolan and me together, they're less likely to think I'm having an affair with Eric?" As nuts as it sounds, she has a point. If I were dating someone, people would be less inclined to see me as some sex-crazed weirdo/ mistress.

"Exactly."

Here's the point where I should take my space and set her straight. But because I'm a perpetual people pleaser, I just sit there, nodding like a lunatic as she goes on about upcoming events we should attend together, like the breast cancer gala at the end of the summer. "Oh, and the Redblacks game next weekend. Eric can't go. Shocker. You two can take our seats in the box," she adds, referring to our local football team.

Cue the sweat again. "Oh, um, that's too kind. But things are really . . . new with us and I'm so busy with work—"

She waves my words away like mere houseflies. "When I was in my twenties, I was busy with law school, apprenticing, and a part-time job. I barely had time to eat. But I didn't let that stop me from dating. At one point, I was seeing four men at once, including Eric."

"What made you choose him?" I ask, grateful for the opportunity to pivot the conversation to her.

"Well, one of the men showed up at my apartment in a fedora. So he was automatically out." She pauses to chuckle. "But Eric. He wouldn't take no for an answer. Not in a creepy way. The others were just . . . passive. If I was busy and didn't call them back once, they'd give up. But not Eric. He was persistent. He left messages, purposely tried running into me at the library. He joined my study group for a class he wasn't even in." She stares wistfully out the window, tormented by memories of better times. For a moment, I think she's about to cry, until she switches gears. "Anyway, sorry to call you in under these circumstances. Go home for the day. See you at the airport tomorrow for Squamish! And I'm assuming you already know, but Nolan is coming. I'll make sure you two get to spend some romantic time together," she adds with a wink.

My cheeks heat with the fiery flames of hell when she says "romantic time."

Turns out, I'm going to need one more (massive) favor.

CHAPTER 11

Nolan

What are you reading?" a soft voice asks. It takes a half second to register the fact that my mom is standing behind me, peeping over my shoulder.

A jolt of mortification rips through me, and I slam the book shut, face down.

Would it be too obvious to fling it under the bed? Dive over it with my whole body like it's an improvised explosive device? Incinerate it with my eyeballs? Sadly, I do nothing but sit there, clammy, my jaw and fists clenched. I feel like I'm a prepubescent kid again, getting caught peeping at those convenience store nudie magazines under the covers at my grandma's.

"Can you please knock?" I ask, unable to mask my irritation.

Mom rolls her eyes. "I didn't know you were in here. I thought you went to work already."

"I'm leaving later today. Going away for two days on a work trip, remember?" I remind her.

"Right," she says, though I don't think she actually remembers.

"Theresa will be here soon," I say, referring to one of her nurses. "And I'll finally be out of your hair for a few days."

Surprisingly, a frown overtakes her face instead of the relief I expected. I've been home for a few weeks now, and so far we've been butting heads the entire time. She hasn't taken well to me moving in and taking steps to establish order and routine, despite trying to keep the same schedule and rules as my sister did. Aside from accusing me of hiding her belongings (like the TV remote), she gets upset when I ask her to take her medication or to eat meals at certain times. Irritation and anger are apparently a common and normal symptom of Alzheimer's.

In the rare moments she isn't arguing with me, she goes in the opposite direction, trying too hard to be the mom she never was. Like the other night when she decided to have a "serious conversation about the past" before I left for work.

The moment she started bringing up how proud she was of me and Em and how she thinks I inherited her "adventurous streak," I shut down and left. No way in hell was I sitting here, listening to her take an ounce of credit for what we've become. Honestly, I'd take her anger over that any day. At least I know it's authentic.

Apparently, she's in a rare good mood, because she circles back to my book. "Hey, that's my book club pick!" she exclaims, plucking it out of my grip with a knowing smirk.

"Huh?" I blink up at her, only now aware that I'm a little clammy. Okay, a lot clammy. This book is steamy.

"I started reading it on my Kindle yesterday for book club. All the ladies were talking about it. It's in the papers," Mom informs nonchalantly, sitting on the edge of my bed, her legs dangling casually, as though buddy-reading a romance novel is a totally normal mother-and-son bonding activity. Out of pure instinct, I shift away, putting an inch of space between us as she runs her fingers over the annotated tabs I've made to mark any mention of potentially sensitive or procedural passages.

For the first time in a couple days, Mom seems to be having a good day, based on her playful demeanor. Her movements are relaxed and steady, expression clear, eyes bright. She's also wearing her signature deep red lipstick, which she tends to forget most days.

"I didn't know you were in a book club," is all I can think to say.

"Yup. With some other ladies in my support group. Dr. Yang recommended it. To keep sharp." She taps her head three times.

Who is this woman and what has she done with my actual mother? The one who spent most nights (and days) barhopping until she was refused service. The one who opted for months-long adventures with random men instead of being at home with her kids. The one who dressed like she was nineteen instead of thirty, and acted like it, too.

Ever since I moved back a few weeks ago, I feel like I've been living in an alternate dimension. Due to her Alzheimer's, her days consist mostly of the same routine. Drinking tea in the morning, leisurely strolling around the neighborhood with her nurse, gardening and bird-watching in the backyard, followed by watching television at night. The weathered skin and yellowed teeth from years of abusing her body are the only lingering remnants of her old life—along with her obsession with all things leopard print.

When I don't respond, she continues on. "The book is fast-paced. And sexy. Some of those office scenes . . . the one where they get caught in the bathroom?" She fans herself. If I wasn't approaching a mortification-induced death before, I'm teetering pretty fucking close right now.

I sink into the mattress, wishing to disappear entirely. "Actually, I'm kind of busy. I'm heading to the airport soon so I need to start packing."

"Do you want breakfast to go?"

"It's fine. I don't really eat breakfast."

Yet another reason to believe she's been body-snatched. Despite her angry mood swings, she's invited me to join her for breakfast nearly every day since I've moved in. It's part of her daily routine, which Theresa is keen on cementing, so long as it's safe for her to make, like toast, or yogurt and berries, or premade hard-boiled eggs. Predictability is important. As is allowing her the independence she needs for her mental health.

Still, daily breakfast is ironic, because she never bothered to make sure Emma and I ate breakfast when we were kids. If we were lucky, she'd slap a box of sugary cereal and a carton of expired, curdled milk on the counter before slinking to the couch to sleep off her hangover. We got by using the breakfast club at school—until I realized it wasn't a magical place with bottomless eggs and toast. It was for poor kids, as my asshole peers pointed out. So I stopped going, preferring the ache of hunger to shame. Haven't been a fan of breakfast since, unless you count black coffee.

Mom parks herself on the edge of the bed, the mattress creaking under her weight. "I had no idea you read."

There are a lot of things you don't know about me is what I really want to say, but don't. In times like this, I think about what Emma would tell me. *Give her a chance.* I wish I could forgive as easily. Though it's easier to forgive when you don't know the full story.

In all fairness, Mom apparently turned things around before her diagnosis. A year or two after I first enlisted in the military, Em had her first baby at nineteen. She gave Mom an ultimatum: She couldn't see the baby unsupervised unless she got sober. After that, Mom got herself into a treatment program and stopped drinking. She picked up a job at an antique shop in Westboro and, according to Em, was a completely changed woman, though I was never around to witness it.

Work became the perfect excuse not to visit for holidays or special occasions. Maybe part of me didn't believe it, and the other half didn't want to get my hopes up for fear she'd slip back into her old ways, like she always did.

"It's for work. And I do read," I lie. Maybe I'll start, because this book is *good*. It's also suspenseful, with the whole assassination attempt subplot. I started it last night with the intention of skimming it just enough to write my report. Instead, I ended up staying awake until two in the morning. I'm over halfway through and I don't want it to end. Reading Andi's words wraps me in the same warmth and comfort I felt the night we met.

Mom clasps her hands together. "Oh, I got Theresa to pick up cornflakes. You like them with just a little bit of milk, don't you?"

It was Emma who didn't like her cereal the slightest bit soggy, but I don't bother correcting her. Mom does this with a lot of things. Talks to me about food I apparently loved as a child, or shows I'd watch "on repeat." Emma chalks it up to her Alzheimer's disease, but truthfully, she did this long before that. I think it's her way of trying to make herself feel better about missing out on so much, though it's hard to give her that win. Especially when her version of my childhood is entirely inaccurate.

"Sure." It's easier to *just go with it* (as Emma would say), even if it isn't true. Otherwise, it might confuse her.

I'm desperate to change the topic to literally anything else. "By the way, I got all your groceries and meals prepped for the week. They're in the fridge, labeled by time and day of the week. Anything else you think you'll need before I leave?" I'm due at the airport in about an hour for the Squamish visit. Ivan and I have to do a security sweep of the jet before departure.

She shakes her head, knee bouncing, avoiding my gaze. "I'm fine on my own. Besides, I have Em. And Theresa," she adds.

The timeline differs for everyone, but according to her doctors, Mom is on the cusp of entering what they refer to as "the middle stage"—a worsening of symptoms. She now requires more professional care and a stringent routine, because otherwise, she'd potentially forget things like dressing, bathing, and cooking. She also gets winded easily and struggles to carry on conversations without forgetting words or losing her train of thought. It's the stage before the last—when she'll become potentially nonverbal and lose the ability to eat, walk, and use the bathroom without assistance. I try not to think about it too much.

Until recently, Mom got by with the help of Em. For years, Emma stayed home with her kids, so her schedule was flexible. But when the opportunity came up to start her own salon, which involves grueling hours, Em hired Theresa, a nurse. Theresa takes Mom on errands, ensures she's eaten, assists with bathing and general hygiene, and doles out her meds. Up until recently, Theresa only came part-time, because Mom was okay to be left alone for a couple hours here and there. But it's started to become dangerous. Just last week, she left the stove on for hours after making a pot of tea. I immediately went out and bought a teakettle that automatically turns off once the water is boiled. Now that she requires all-day care from Theresa, the bills are becoming wildly expensive. We couldn't afford someone both day and night, which is why I took a short-term contract here in Ottawa and moved in with Mom until a spot opens in a home. I couldn't let Em sacrifice her salon after all those years of taking on the brunt of Mom's care.

Still, in-home care is unaffordable long-term. Luckily, we found an affordable memory care facility Mom liked. It has a space starting in September, which means I get to leave sooner than expected. The only problem is that Mom frequently forgets she's moving there.

"And remember, I'll be back in two days," I remind her.

"Oh, that's nothing, I'll barely have time to miss you," she says with a wide grin. She doesn't like to acknowledge her illness, and I don't want to be too overbearing, because it upsets her.

"If anything, you should be gone more," Mom says, continuing through my silence. "All you do is work, sleep, work out, repeat. It's hardly a way to live, sweetheart."

"Well, I have a job. Adult responsibilities," I say, though it comes out more pointed than I intended. "And I really don't have time for much else."

Either she doesn't notice my tone or chooses to ignore it. "You haven't dated since . . . what was that woman's name? Charlene?"

"Charlene was my high school girlfriend, Mom. You're thinking of Penny."

"Right! Penny."

I grunt, mostly because I hate talking about Penny. I met her last year in the States through one of the guys at work. She happened to be mutual friends with a guy I worked with. She was smart, worked in IT, and was able to work remotely.

I wasn't looking for a relationship, but she seemed different than anyone I'd dated in the past. We were together for over a year, not that we saw each other much. She was the first girlfriend I had who didn't seem to be overly concerned with my work schedule. In fact, she said she thought it was "sexy" for a man to put work first.

Penny seemed to be perfect for me and my lifestyle, so much so, I even brought her home to meet Em. A month later, she told me she'd actually met someone else while I was away. I was pretty fucking crushed. But to be fair, I understood. I'd been gone six months, so what the hell was she supposed to do for half a year? Sit at home and write me love letters?

We broke up and I moved back home. Not that I've ever considered Ottawa to be home. All I have here are shitty memories of being moved all around the city like a shelter dog no one wants. I'm just biding my time until Jones calls with a new posting so I can have my old life back.

"What happened with her?"

"Long-distance didn't work." Barely anyone in my line of work has relationships—successful relationships, at least. Being away from home seven or eight months of the year and leaving without notice, not being able to tell your spouse where you are, isn't exactly a recipe for a successful relationship. In fact, I'm pretty sure the divorce rate is hovering around 90 percent, no exaggeration.

"Well, I don't want to keep you from your big trip. But I'll miss having you here, even if you do boss me around," Mom teases.

I roll my eyes. "Reminding you to eat and take your medication isn't bossing you around, Mom."

The thought of leaving her fills me with dread. We may not be close, but she's my mom, after all. If she needed someone, technically there'd be no one else to call aside from Emma, and the last thing I want is for Em to think I don't have things under control. In the years she took care of Mom without me, she never once requested my help.

I wrap Mom in a goodbye hug that feels awkward and forced and grab my bags.

One summer. I can do this.

CHAPTER 12

Nolan

The media is impossible to miss when I arrive on the tarmac. They're jammed like cattle into the designated media zone outside the *Challenger*—the PM's refurbished Airbus A-330-200—chattering among themselves while busily setting up their equipment.

The media attention has been wild, and has gotten even worse since yesterday when news of the book broke.

Ivan and I are the first to arrive. There's a lot that has to happen before the PM boards the plane, including ensuring the jet is free of explosives, weapons, nefarious surveillance equipment, all that fun stuff. I'm also helping Ivan verify the identities of all the passengers, including the captain and the flight attendant, and securing all the exits. And then there's the media to keep at bay.

"Are they usually out here like this?" I ask him as I approach, jabbing my thumb in their general direction.

Ivan is standing outside the plane, surveying them. "For Eric, yes. Not usually in this volume, though, unless he's leaving or returning from a high-profile visit."

It's a good thing there's two of us, because over the next hour, more and more media personnel arrive. In my short time in the role, I recognize some familiar faces. They're alert, ready, pens poised, hungry for a juicy headline. Some have tried to talk to me, casually asking me questions about Eric's alleged affair, none of which I respond to.

When a black SUV rolls up, the energy shifts from anticipation to frenzy.

I hadn't gotten word that the motorcade was arriving yet, so I head over to the car. Must be one of the press secretaries or advisers. The vehicle door swings open and the reporters on that side go wild. Based on the sheer rush of microphones and flashing cameras, I assume it's the minister of environment. She's joining for Eric's announcement about a new electric car plant near Squamish.

Turns out, it's Andi commanding the attention. Pathetically, her being on the trip is the thing I've been looking forward to most. A zing of hyperawareness shoots down my spine as I speed-walk to her.

By the time I approach the car door, she's halfway out of the vehicle, balancing a tray of coffees, donuts, and a garment bag. And when the coffee teeters in her palm, the camera flashes quadruple, paparazzi desperate to capture anything remotely interesting.

"Andi, care to comment on the authenticity of your memoir?" one of the reporters shouts, jostling her way to the front.

"How long have you been having an affair with Eric Nichols?" another one asks.

She turns around and stares at them like a deer in headlights, shielding her face from the ridiculously bright camera flash. Her discomfort is palpable, almost painful. She looks fragile, small in her knit cardigan, frozen in place.

I position myself between her and the reporters like a shield, guiding her on board.

"Thank you," she says gratefully, letting out an audible sigh of relief once we're inside.

"No worries. That was intense." I watch her closely, a pang of sympathy stirring as I set the coffee tray on a side ledge. "Do you usually get here so early?"

"No. Normally I come with Gretchen, but she's riding with Eric and I'm not supposed to be seen or photographed anywhere near him, given the whole . . . scandal," she explains, placing the donuts next to the coffee.

"Makes sense." I'm surprised she's even coming on the trip at all. Then again, I suppose it would be equally suspicious if she didn't.

"Find any bombs?" she asks teasingly, righting her face only when Ivan arrows a stern look from where he's verifying the emergency equipment.

"There were a few bombs stashed under the emergency peanuts, actually. Taken care of, though," I assure, smiling reflexively.

"Damn. We probably shouldn't joke about that. Isn't it illegal to say 'bomb' on a plane?"

"It's not illegal," I note. "But probably frowned upon around the PM. Best to get it out of your system now."

"Well, thank you for your service." She pretends to salute me, plopping into the aisle seat in the first row. She immediately whips out a tablet from the leather bag over her shoulder and plugs it into a charger. "Hey, actually, I'm glad you're here early. I wanted to talk to you about something."

I stiffen. This sounds serious. "Sure, what about?"

She scratches at her throat, leaving a red welt before leaning in to whisper, "I kind of got us into a . . . situation."

"A situation?" I repeat, glancing at Ivan, who's otherwise occupied.

Before she can elaborate, the crowd outside erupts with excitement, which can only mean one thing: the arrival of the PM.

CHAPTER 13

Andi

I don't get a chance to drop the proverbial bomb on Nolan—i.e., tell him about the whole Gretchen-thinks-we're-a-couple thing and beg him to go along with it. Because when Eric and Gretchen arrive, things get chaotic and he's urgently required outside.

It's a bloodbath out there, at least from what I can hear in the comfort of the jet. The reporters shout a myriad of scandal-related questions at Eric, like, *How is your marriage? What about your children? How long before you announce your divorce?*

The last day has been absolutely wild. Ever since the book was linked to me in the media, my phone has been flooded with DMs from random people. I've had to temporarily disable all my accounts. For the first time in months, my mom called me yesterday, in a tizzy over me dishonoring the family name and whatnot.

"All the women at the golf club are asking me about it. It's so embarrassing," she complained. I choked back a laugh. Last time I saw Amanda, she was joking about how many times in one conversation Mom references her fancy golf club frenemies, who she's obsessed with impressing. The count often reaches the high teens.

"None of it's true," I reiterated for the fourth time in five minutes.

"I really hope not, Andrea. Especially this . . . racy memoir. Your father and I—well, not your father. *I* raised you better than that. Your grandmother would roll over in her grave if she knew about this. It would be so embarrassing for the entire family." By the disappointment in her tone, you'd think I'd committed some unspeakable, violent crime. She then launched into a tirade about how she *knew* this role as PA was "bad news." That it was nothing more than a "glorified maid" position.

"You know, we could sue them for this. Dave has a lawyer friend who specializes in defamation. I bet he'll—" she started, referring to my stepdad. I like Dave enough, mostly because he rarely says a word, unless you bring up outer space (his obsession). But his family is similar to my mother's. They're judgmental, the types who make you feel like you're under a microscope. The first time Amanda and I went to his place for Christmas as teens, we overheard his mother laughing in the kitchen about how we used the wrong forks at dinner. Ever since, Amanda has purposely used the wrong utensils on the rare occasions we visit, including a salad fork to eat her soup (while maintaining a straight face).

"Mom, it's fine. Eric's and Gretchen's legal teams are handling this," I assured. It's a partial truth. Their teams are handling it, but only for Eric and Gretchen's benefit. Not mine.

I couldn't get her off the phone fast enough. I had bigger things to worry about, like the wild fact that *The Prime Minister*

& Me rocketed to #45 in "Erotic Fiction" and #90 overall on the Amazon charts.

When I first saw it, I thought for sure it was a glitch. I spent all morning refreshing the rankings, waiting for it to descend back to its rightful place, buried under millions of other books. Until now, my work has never cracked the top 100 of anything, not even the top 500,000.

A fresh wave of guilt washes over me as Eric and Gretchen board. Gretchen's forced smile disappears the moment she enters, as does her grip on Eric's hand as she beelines it for her usual seat. She promptly slaps on her satin sleep mask and reclines, conveniently ignoring the flight attendant's soft warning that she'll need to be in an upright position for takeoff.

Eric carries on like everything is sunshine and rainbows. He's his usual friendly self, greeting the staff, making sprightly small talk before turning to me. "Andi, listen, I'm so sorry for all of this. It's all my fault," he whispers.

"How is it your fault?" I counter.

"I'm the one who made you set up the whole dinner. Made you stay late and talk."

I shake my head, repeating what Nolan told me. "It's no one's fault, except whoever snapped those photos. We both know the truth."

He blows the air from his cheeks, seemingly grateful for my understanding. "It's true. It'll all blow over soon enough, I'm sure."

There's strain behind his smile. No doubt this rumor is taking a toll. This added stress was the absolute last thing they needed in their relationship. And then there's the kids. I'm sure they're getting asked about it at school.

"Andi, did you bring the templates for the table numbers and place cards?" Gretchen snaps out of nowhere, shooting upright. Her tone cuts the air, and everyone stops. I hold back a laugh, because her sleep mask is still on and she's not even remotely facing my direction.

"Yes, they're on your tablet," I say, standing to fetch it from her bag. I make quick work of pulling them up before she removes her mask.

She takes one look at them and nearly incinerates me with her grimace. "These are the wrong ones."

They aren't. Last week, Gretchen was going back and forth between the floral templates or the plain ones. I know this for a fact because she ranted for a solid ten minutes about how the plain ones were too "pedestrian." "You said last week you wanted the floral ones," I point out politely.

"Yes, but I wanted them to be pink. For breast cancer. The entire theme of the gala. Obviously," she hisses.

Gretchen is notorious for thinking things and not verbalizing them, then mistaking it for a real conversation. I don't bother to correct her, especially not when she's in a mood. So I just lower my head and nod. "I'll get the pink ones."

I'm furiously scouring the depths of the internet for similar pink templates when the rest of the staff arrive, including Stephanie, Eric's chief of staff. She's understandably overwhelmed by the reporters and spills coffee all over herself two seconds after boarding. I rush to help clean it up before the air staff have time to react, mostly out of guilt. After all, I'm the reason for all the disorder outside.

There are whispers from the front of the plane. I try to strain to listen to their conversation, only picking up bits and pieces from where I'm sitting at the back of the jet.

It's really a problem.

Have to deal with it sooner rather than later.

Whether Gretchen likes it or not.

Oh god. This doesn't sound good.

My stomach twists. What if they're right? What if Gretchen decides it's not worth the media spectacle so close to the election? What if she fires me, or is forced to? This kind of rumor is the worst-case scenario for an election campaign. The last thing they need is me being photographed anywhere near Eric. Every photo, every look, scrutinized by the public for any sign of a torrid romance between us, which, frankly, is laughable. Compared to Gretchen, who's basically a supermodel, I look like a Smurf in a dowdy cardigan.

I glance at her. She's still reclined, mask back on, hands folded over her chest like an Egyptian mummy. I thought she might stick up for me, remind everyone that she's the one who insisted I come on the trip despite the controversy. But she remains in tomb position.

"Don't worry about them," Nolan whispers, slipping into the aisle seat across from me.

The moment our eyes meet, I consider ripping the Band-Aid off and asking him to be my pretend boyfriend right here, right now. But how does one casually ask for that kind of favor?

Oh, hello, Nolan. You barely know me, but will you do me the honor of being my fake boyfriend so people don't think I'm sleeping with the prime minister?

Would you be willing to risk your new job to lie on my behalf? I'll name a character in my next book after you.

Your mission, should you choose to accept it, is to kiss me in public. I'll try not to cut your lip with my teeth this time.

God. The possibilities just keep getting worse.

He could have a girlfriend, a fiancée, a wife, multiple children for all I know. So naturally, I sit there in agonizing silence, pretending to be engrossed with the ultraserious task of choosing a template while internally spiraling about what my life has come to.

About an hour into the flight, Gretchen comes to the back. She no longer looks like she wants to kill me. In fact, when she crouches down in the aisle between Nolan's and my seats, her face breaks into a grin. I guess her nap did wonders.

"You know, I was thinking, you two should take the night off when we get there. Maybe go on a date or something. Remember that restaurant you booked for us for my birthday last year? The one that served rattlesnake and kangaroo?" Gretchen asks, glancing eagerly between me and Nolan.

Between snake and kangaroo in a food context, it takes me a moment to register what she's just said. *A date.* When Nolan flashes me a look that screams, *What in the world is this woman talking about?*, my stomach descends into my asshole.

Oh no.

No. No. No.

A nasty smoker's cough rockets out of my throat, and it turns the heads of all the passengers up front. Even the stewardess springs into action to bring me a glass of water. I've never wanted to disintegrate into the fabric of the chair more than I do right now. Now would be a good time for the oxygen masks to drop from the ceiling. Even a brown paper bag would do.

"Oh, um, thanks for the suggestion," I manage through a wheeze, praying she'll leave without another word.

She does not. "It's superromantic. Tell them you work for me and see if they'll give you guys a mountain view. Oh, and make sure you two amend the room booking," she says, winking at a very confused Nolan.

He sits forward, brows creased. "Room booking?"

"You two have separate rooms. You only need one since you're together. Best to cut costs for trips like this, especially before the election. It'll be audited and scrutinized each way to Sunday," she says with a knowing brow raise before slinking off back to her seat.

Nolan turns in my direction, gifting me with a bewildered expression. "What was that all about? Is it normal for employees to . . . share rooms?"

"Um—no." Shit. How do I even begin to explain? "For the record, I'm really, really sorry." Sorry seems like a good place to start.

"Sorry? For what?"

I peer around, ensuring everyone is occupied or out of earshot. "Gretchen thinks we're dating," I whisper, lightning fast.

He blinks in rapid succession, seemingly too stunned to speak. I can't tell if he didn't understand my mumble, or if he's as appalled as I am with myself. "Wait, what? Why would she think that?"

"She saw us coming out of the storage closet and assumed we were canoodling in there."

His entire face lights up with a grin. "Did you just say 'canoodling'?"

"What's wrong with canoodling?"

"Do you mean fucking?" he asks bluntly.

Pin prickles erupt everywhere. Why is my body reacting like this? I will never be able to unhear Nolan saying the word "fucking" in that deep, baritone voice. I will also never get the barrage of images out of my mind. Clearly, I need to write a closet sex scene.

"No!" I squeak. "I meant canoodling. It's an all-encompassing word. It could mean anything from kissing to touching to, yes, technically having sex."

He raises a brow. "If you say so. You are the writer."

We've seriously gone off track, so I turn my legs in his direction and lean in. "Look, I didn't get the chance to come up with an explanation on the spot with everything else going on. And now it's too far gone. She thinks we're a legit couple. Boyfriend and girlfriend."

He lets out a low whistle, taking it all in. "Jeez. She seems . . . very invested in you."

I don't have time to explain that she's desperate to fix this affair situation in any way possible. If us being a couple helps to quell the rumors on the Hill, she's going to do whatever she can to make it happen. Instead, I settle on, "Gretchen is very passionate."

"Well, I'm, uh . . . flattered, I guess, to be your pretend boyfriend?" he says, though I'm not so sure. He tugs at his collar, watching me expectantly.

"Just so you know, you don't have to do this. Say the word and I'll fix it," I tell him genuinely. I'd rather jump out of this jet midair than tell Gretchen we aren't actually together, but I also can't force him to participate in this insanity and risk his job, too.

"Honestly, I'm just taking it all in," he says when he notices me staring at him intensely, awaiting my fate.

"I'd understand completely if you were pissed. I mean, this is *a lot*. God." I proceed to smoosh my forehead into the seat in front of me before looking at him again. "I'm so sorry. I'm very aware of how ridiculous this is."

"Why do you always do that?" he asks, holding my gaze.

The serious inflection in his tone stops me in my tracks. "Do what?"

"Apologize incessantly for things that aren't your fault? Roll over immediately to please people?"

I blink down at my tray, dumbfounded. "Oh. I didn't mean to. I'm sor—" I squeeze my eyes shut, catching myself red-handed in the reflex. I don't have a response, because it never occurred to me that I do this. All the time, apparently. And I certainly never expected him to notice.

Nolan offers me a sympathetic smile before standing. "I've got some things to do before landing."

CHAPTER 14

Andi

Despite my best efforts to claim it's too late to change the room booking, Gretchen wasn't having it. That's how Nolan and I find ourselves in a room with one queen-size bed.

"This is . . . small," he remarks, closing the door behind us, the automatic whirr of the mechanical lock cementing this strange reality. This room can't be more than 300 square feet, despite it being a luxury hotel.

My shoulders dip and I'm unsure where to even sit. The bed feels a little too intimate. "It is very small." Compared to Eric and Gretchen's suite of soaring wooden beams and massive windows, boasting panoramic views of the mountains. A silence falls between us as we quietly unpack our belongings. "Mind if I take the top drawers and this side of the closet?"

"Yeah, take whatever you need," he says, unconcerned as he takes his jacket off, revealing a white dress shirt.

I stop folding my clothes to work down the lump lodged in my throat. Is it just me, or did he get even broader in the past three years? The sleeves of that shirt are doing some serious overtime over his biceps. "Hey, I just wanted to say, I really tried to avoid this whole sharing-a-room thing."

"I know you did. It's really fine. It's only two nights. I'll sleep on the couch—" He pauses to survey the space, only now realizing there is no pull-out couch, just a single desk chair, which is not conducive to sleeping unless you're the approximate length of an infant. Great. "The floor."

"No! I'll take the floor," I insist, cringing at the thought of him not getting a good night's rest. For the PM's bodyguard, being well rested is a necessity on the job. Besides, my conscience can't handle some tragic incident occurring because he wasn't on his game due to floor-induced back pain.

He swings me a look as he tucks his suitcase in the closet. "I'm not letting you sleep on the floor, Andi. It's fine. I've slept in worse conditions."

"It just feels wrong, since I got you into this whole mess," I add as a condolence.

"And like I said, I really don't mind."

I don't have the energy to put up much of a fight, because what's the alternative? As a romance writer, I'm familiar with scenarios involving shared rooms with Only One Bed. In fact, I've written many of them myself. They usually go as follows: One or both parties decide they won't allow the other person to sleep on the floor. They invite the other to share out of the goodness of their heart (not because they're horny or anything). Inevitably, they wake up the next morning locked in a full embrace.

There's usually an involuntary boner or two, and maybe a sexy dream thrown in the mix. In reality, there will be no boners and definitely no cuddling. I'm making sure of that.

"I hate to ditch you right away, but I'm due upstairs to brief the team about emergency procedures," he informs, peering at his phone.

I straighten my spine, trying to hide my disappointment. I'd hoped we could talk it all out ASAP. But duty calls. "Right, of course. I actually have some stuff I need to work on for Gretchen, too."

He lingers by the door as he puts his jacket back on. "We need to talk about this, though. I'll be free later tonight. Probably around nine thirty. Late dinner?"

I watch him for a beat. His expression is sincere, earnest. "Sure. I'll make a reservation. Again, I'm sorry about all of this. If you have a girlfriend or wife or something, this is really inappropriate—"

"Andi?"

"Mm-hm?"

"Stop apologizing. Right now," he says, halfway out the door.

I squeeze my eyes shut. "Right. Force of habit."

"One last thing," he adds, poking his head back in. "I don't have a girlfriend. Or a wife. I'm still very single. By choice."

CHAPTER 15

Andi

Not to sound ridiculous, but after the shitstorm of media today, I selected a restaurant that listed "private" in its description. I just didn't realize it would be located on top of a mountain.

I thought I'd be grateful to be out of that tiny hotel room, especially after Nolan confirmed his "very single, by choice" status. But as the ground below us shrinks away while the gondola ascends into the sky, I'm having regrets.

"You scared of heights?" he asks, noting my death grip on the bench beside my thighs.

"I didn't think I was. But this is . . . ridiculously high," I say as the wind rocks the gondola with a startling creak. I peek down at the river snaking through the expanse of lush evergreens below. We're only a quarter of the way up, and we're already approaching clouds. Technically, it's excellent inspiration for the romantic scene I was writing at the hotel earlier, if I weren't so petrified of an imminent demise. "You?"

He leans back on the opposite bench, lips curving into a cocky smirk that makes my thighs clench involuntarily. "If I had a fear of heights, there's no way I could have gotten into JTF2."

"You were in special forces?"

"Yup. For a couple years." He says it so casually, as though he were a run-of-the-mill, low-level public servant, wasting away (physically and spiritually) in a windowless cubicle at the Department of Finance.

To be fair, I'm not surprised. It's pretty common for the private CPOs to have a special forces background. Besides, Nolan just seems the type. He has that quiet confidence, punctuated by an I-could-kill-you-in-two-seconds-flat intensity.

I lean forward with interest, resting my chin on my hands, determined to keep my eyes on him and not the 2,900-foot distance between this glass hexagon and the ground below. "Isn't there a huge screening process to join? Crazy fitness tests?" One of Gretchen's main CPOs used to be JTF2, and he'd mentioned how strict they are about who's even invited to try out.

"The physical tests are honestly the least of your worries. It's mostly mental, psychological," he explains, one muscly arm draped over the back of the bench. "They try to break you, exploit your fears, your weaknesses. They want to know that under immense pressure, in the worst circumstances, you can act right, make the safest choices. Most people fail. Ninety percent, at least."

I gulp, mentally scanning my laundry list of fears. Heights, unfinished basements, public speaking, mole rats, being tagged in negative book reviews, readers taking the time out of their lives to email me about typos or grammatical errors in my books, disappointing Gretchen and my mother into oblivion, among many others. Any would suffice. "What fear of yours did they exploit?"

He gazes out the foggy window, contemplating. We're on what looks to be the last stretch of incline. "This sounds ridiculous, but things like small spaces and heights don't bother me."

"What about death? Isn't everyone afraid of death?" I ask, white-knuckling the bench as the gondola sways to the side from a gust of wind. Yup. I'm definitely not special forces material.

"Probably. But I'm not scared about it happening in those ways, I guess."

"So what are you afraid of, then?" I ask, growing even more curious.

"I've been trying to figure it out, which is why I spent so much of my twenties pushing myself. Doing reckless shit. Trying to find out why things that should be scary as fuck don't faze me. I haven't come up with the answer," he says honestly.

"You don't even have weird, irrational phobias?" I prod, growing increasingly convinced that this man is some sort of lab-grown Captain America type (the bearded, maple-syrup-infused Canadian edition, obviously) with zero weaknesses.

"Aren't most phobias irrational?"

"No! A phobia of snakes is perfectly rational. Some types can kill you. Same with grizzly bears, like the ones probably roaming the forest below us," I note, avoiding looking down. "But I mean weird ones . . . like on that old TLC show? Remember the person who was afraid of tinfoil? Or grapes?"

He barks out a laugh as we reach the top. The A-frame restaurant looks irresistibly cozy from here. "Grapes?"

"Yes, grapes," I insist, trying to keep a straight face as the gondola lurches to a sudden stop. "You could choke on them. They could roll off the counter and you could slip on them."

He grabs my arm, steadying me before guiding me onto the platform. "Okay, fair point. But tinfoil? What's so terrifying about a thin sheet of metal?"

"Tinfoil is sharp. Paper cuts," I argue, grateful to be back on solid ground.

"That's true. I'll be more sensitive," he promises, stepping aside to let me walk ahead.

The restaurant is rustic-fancy, which suits my choice to wear a simple chiffon floral print dress (a decision I angsted over for the better part of my evening instead of hitting my word count goal, not that I needed to, since it's not like this is a real date). It's also fairly empty. Large windows line the far wall, offering near-panoramic views of the mountains. A large fireplace stands in the middle, the flames casting a warm glow around the dining room.

We select a wooden booth tucked into the far corner of the bar, sitting for only a couple seconds before a young waiter with a gloriously curly man-bun approaches with menus. He introduces himself as Ralph over the distant strains of folk music playing through the sound system. The moment the name leaves his lips, Nolan shoots me a wide-eyed look over the top of his menu.

I tilt my head knowingly when the waiter leaves. "Why the look? What's wrong with poor Ralph?"

A shrug. "Nothing. He just doesn't look like a Ralph. He gives me Randy energy."

"How so?"

Nolan subtly eyes Ralph, who's innocently chatting with the

bartender across the room. "Ralph strikes me as a banker who collects stamps as a side gig. This waiter looks like he lives in a vintage van and knows all the best surfing spots. He probably owns a Hawaiian shirt or two. Or five."

A bubble of laughter comes out, muffled by the menu in front of my face. It reminds me of how he critiqued my main character's name the night we met. "You're really big on names, aren't you?"

"Names set the tone for a person's entire life," he explains, doodling a swirl on the wooden tabletop with his index finger. "A name can affect someone's entire first impression of you. Make you think certain things."

"Good point. I never really thought about it like that. When I name characters in my books, I look at a list of common names from the year they were born, close my eyes, and choose one in under ten seconds."

Amusement flirts at the corner of his lips. "Like Bryce?"

"Exactly. For the record, I changed his name to Brady at your suggestion."

He scrunches his face, pained. Before he can express verbal disapproval for Brady, he's interrupted when Ralph returns with a pad of paper and pen in hand. "Random question. Do you own a Hawaiian shirt?"

"Yeah, man! I lived in Hawaii for a couple months," Ralph says before taking our orders. Nolan gets the bison short ribs and potatoes, while I opt for a pesto pasta with a side of fries. I regret it immediately, because pesto tends to get stuck in your teeth. But by the time I come to my senses, Ralph is already speed-walking away, man-bun bouncing happily on the top of his head with each step.

Nolan flashes me a knowing look. "Told you. Shoulda been a Randy."

I rest my elbows on the table and lean forward. It's one of those booths that's a few too many inches from the table. "What about me?"

"Well, you surprised me. I wouldn't think an Andi would be a beer girl," he says, rolling up the crisp white sleeves of his dress shirt.

I shrug, fiddling with the salt and pepper shakers. They're hand-carved brown bears with massive bellies. "No?"

"I would have pegged you for a red wine girl. Classy, sophisticated."

A snort escapes me. "You think I'm sophisticated?"

"You rub elbows with the prime minister, his wife, and members of Parliament on the daily. That makes you one of the most sophisticated people I know."

"So do you," I point out.

Nolan takes a long sip of his beer. "I'm security. That's different. I don't talk shop."

"Neither do I. If people bother to talk to me, they talk at me. Not with me. And I wouldn't know the difference between a cabernet from a French villa and the bottles they serve at East Side Mario's. I don't actually drink a lot in general. I mean, besides that night we met," I add.

"Ah, that night," he says wistfully, his grin tilting.

"Thanks, by the way," I say, mindlessly spinning the bear shakers, my cheeks growing hotter by the second.

"For what?"

"For being so nice. Not taking advantage of me. I was not in the best state of mind." That's putting it mildly.

He levels me with a look, only partially distracted by the arrival of our drinks and food. "Please don't thank me for not taking advantage of you," he says once Ralph walks out of earshot.

I pull my bowl of pasta and my emotional support side of fries closer. "Okay, fair. But I will thank you for putting my desk together. I wrote a lot of words at that desk." It makes me smile, thinking about how much of a role he played in my writing without even knowing it. Not only did he encourage me to do it, but he literally set up my physical space to do so.

His lips curve in the tiniest grin before he unrolls his cutlery. "It wasn't any trouble. Took me like five minutes on my way out."

"God, the whole night is so embarrassing to even think about," I say, plucking a piping hot fry out of the basket. It burns my mouth, but I deal with it, because I refuse to spit it out in front of him.

"I don't think it was embarrassing. I had a lot of fun, actually. Honestly, I felt—I feel supercomfortable with you, just talking. Hanging out. I got some nice hugs from your dog, too," he adds with a wry grin, taking a bite of his food.

"Ted's dog," I correct.

"How is Lars? And Ted?"

"They're both great. Ted got a job and has his own place now." While I let my pasta cool down, I dig my phone from my bag pocket and pull up a photo of Lars curled up in his bed with his favorite stuffed hamburger chew toy.

Nolan's face lights up. "Aw. You must miss him."

"I do. I never thought I'd miss his hundred-pound self sitting on my lap, or taking over my chair by the window. But I know how happy he is with Ted. The day they moved into their place,

Lars got so excited, he ran around the living room fifty times, peed himself, and then lay belly up under the ceiling fan panting."

He snickers, piercing a roast potato with his fork with startling accuracy. "I can picture that. Does he still like cheese?"

"Apparently. But he's developed a taste for Gouda. The expensive stuff. I drop a wheel off at Ted's place every so often."

A smile plays across his lips, and I can't help but think about how they felt against mine. How his beard scratched against my skin. The pressure of his teeth against my neck. His eyes drop to my lips, too, and an electric charge passes between us.

"Well, we should probably discuss the matter at hand," I suggest, letting my traitorous gaze rest somewhere around the top of his head.

"You mean the fact that we're canoodling in closets at work?" he says with a straight face.

I break a sweat at the mere thought. "Ha ha."

"Can you just tell me . . . is this a PR distraction or something?" he asks through a bite of his ribs.

"Basically," I say, grateful he put two and two together. "I mean, Gretchen legitimately thinks we're a couple. But she's using it to her advantage. She thinks if people know I'm dating you, they'll be less likely to think something is going on with Eric."

"Why does she care? Based on the anniversary dinner the other night, it seemed like she was done with Eric."

I blow on my pasta to cool it down. "Maybe, but an affair would be humiliating, especially one that isn't even true."

"I guess that makes sense. Not that it should be anyone's business."

"It shouldn't be, but you know how politics works," I say, trying to figure out the most polite, delicate way to twirl the noodles onto my fork without looking like a total slob. One of the noodles flops in the opposite direction, flicking a glob of pesto dangerously close to his wrist on the opposite side of the table. He doesn't notice. Or at least he doesn't acknowledge it.

"So, what do you need from me?" he asks simply as I brave a bite.

"Well, first," I start, swallowing hard, "I should reiterate that you don't have to do anything you're uncomfortable with. But if you did feel inclined to go along with this, it would be pretty chill. We'd live our normal lives, with the exception of select public appearances, like the football game, random all-staff events like the staff appreciation event at the River House. There's also Gretchen's breast cancer gala at the end of summer, if this is even still a thing by then. Basically, Gretchen wants everyone on the Hill to know we're together."

He dips his chin in a nod. "And we do this until the rumors blow over?"

I push my near-empty beer to the side, brushing a finger over the condensation on the outside of the glass. "I don't expect it to last past a month, really." When it's said out loud, a month does seem like forever. I don't know if it's adequate time for everyone to forget about the whole scandal entirely, but I'm trying to be optimistic for Nolan's sake. Surely something new will crop up by then. Or at least, all the election season headlines will ramp up, completely drowning out all of this nonsense.

"We'd pretend to break up after that?" he confirms.

"Exactly. Simple as that," I say, really trying to sell it. It's not like my entire reputation, career, and sense of self-respect are on the line or anything.

He nods again, surprisingly casual, like we're agreeing to trade library books, carpool to work, or water the other's plants while they're away. "All right. We're doing this."

"Wait, really? You're fully okay with this?" I ask, forcing down a mouthful of pasta.

"Why are you so surprised? It seems like a good cause. Helping you, Gretchen, and Eric save your reputations. And your job."

"I mean, it's a commitment. And you said earlier you were very single by choice. I can only assume you like your freedom."

"I guess you could say that. My job isn't exactly conducive to a long-term relationship. Ask my last girlfriend." There's a glint of sadness and regret in his eyes.

"How long ago did you break up?"

"Three months ago," he replies, clearing his throat as he pushes his empty plate away.

"I'm sorry." I shift in the booth, feeling guilty for asking so brazenly, and also for barely having made a dent in my own meal.

"It's fine. The long-distance wasn't working, which is for the better. I don't even know where I'll end up next. Hoping to get a new posting in the fall, but who knows. Postings can be unpredictable."

Most CPOs stay for a couple years. It surprises me that it's so short-term, given all the complexities of the job. A strange sensation coils in my stomach that I can't identify. Disappointment, maybe? Shock? I go with the latter. "Any places you're hoping to go?"

"Nope. I'm open to anywhere, as long as it's not here," he says with conviction. It all makes more sense, actually, why he's not afraid of risking his job or reputation to "date" me. He's not sticking around.

"Not a fan of Ottawa?" I ask, half joking but genuinely curious.

A shrug. "It's just . . . I grew up here. I know it well enough to know it's not where I want to stay long-term."

"That's fair. We do have shit transit. And terrible weather."

"Horrific weather. Snowiest capital city in the world," he chimes. "I spent my whole childhood shoveling driveways. Not looking to continue that into adulthood."

"So since we're doing this, we probably need to work on our story in case people ask. Maybe also establish some ground rules," I note, the tips of my fingers tingling with something that feels a little too much like excitement. Not that this should be classified as that. Anxiety-inducing, maybe. But not exciting.

His eyes meet mine with interest. "What are you thinking?"

"Well, we will need to have at least one photo together on social media," I say, trailing off at the sound of cheering coming from the other side of the dining area. About five waiters have emerged from the back to sing "Happy Birthday" to a man at a table near the fireplace. According to the balloons decorating the table, he's celebrating his "25th," despite his snow-white hair and walking cane.

Nolan temporarily spins around to watch the spectacle. "Gotcha. I'm not on social media, so that's all you."

I clear my throat. "Okay. We should also discuss PDA. Are we going to stick to holding hands? Hugging? We probably don't *need* to kiss, do we?"

He shrugs, one arm slung across the back of the booth like it's no big deal. "I mean, we already kissed. Most real couples kiss, I'd assume."

My face burns at the mere memory. "If you remember, things were kind of a disaster between us physically."

"Physically?" His jaw twitches. "Was it really that bad?"

I blink. Is he serious? Has he magically forgotten? Have I lain in bed for hours and hours, replaying the whole thing in my head and withering to dust from embarrassment every time, all for nothing? "I mean . . . we had *no* chemistry," I say bluntly, though I really mean I, Andi Zeigler, have zero chemistry in this body.

He sits back in the booth, evidently offended. *"No chemistry? That's a pretty big statement based on one drunken instance three years ago."*

I sit back to let Ralph clear our plates. "I busted your lip. And smashed my head against the dresser. All within a span of less than thirty seconds. Do you actually not remember?"

He lets out a hearty chuckle, sure of himself. "I remember, Andi. But it was a long time ago. Maybe we've improved."

"If anything, I've probably gotten worse. I'm extremely out of practice," I tell him honestly, playing with the hem of my sleeve.

He appraises me, his eyes twinkling with interest. "You haven't dated since?"

"Nope. And I don't plan to. Similar to yours, my job doesn't leave much time for dating. Or writing, for that matter."

"Right. Well, maybe we'll just need some practice," he suggests, far too casually.

"Practice," I repeat, staunchly ignoring the prickles of heat spiking down my back. "Practice kissing?"

"By practice, I mean a very regimented, highly professional practice session." When he senses some hesitation from me, he adds, "No one is going to believe we're together if we don't kiss."

"Some couples aren't that touchy. Especially in a professional setting, which we'd be in," I point out, a little too harshly.

He appears to disagree. "It wouldn't be natural to me. If I'm with someone, I'm going to want to kiss them. Touch them. Regardless of where we are."

My elbow jerks involuntary at the words "kiss" and "touch," knocking the spare spoon off the end of the table with a clatter. "All right. Sure. We'll practice," I say, leaning down to pick it up.

"Deal."

I lean forward. "Can I ask, what do you get out of all of this? Or are you just doing this out of the goodness of your heart?"

His eyes sparkle in the glow of the fireplace. "You don't think I'm generous like that?"

"I just . . . assumed there was something you get out of it." After working in politics for so long, it's difficult to imagine people being motivated by the goodness of their hearts, with nothing to gain for themselves.

He tilts his head in consideration. "Well, I would take payment in the form of cheesecake."

A giggle rises out of me. Maybe Nolan is the exception. "Ah, right. The cheesecake. That's a very noble and understandable motive. I think I can appease you. Though it has to be store-bought. I can't bake for shit."

"Deal." He pauses, assessing me for a beat. "In all seriousness, it would be cool to hang out. You know, as friends."

Friends. I like the sound of that.

CHAPTER 16

Nolan

Mom has been texting me nonstop since I left. Mostly, she has questions about where I left certain things, like her slippers. Otherwise, it's pictures of flowers in the garden, her tea, her and Theresa on a walk, a squirrel in the yard. She also uses excessive emojis, which drives me nuts.

As a kid, I would have died for her attention. Any measly scrap of attention. Emma and I lived for those rare five-minute phone conversations. When all you know are weeks, sometimes months, of silence for most of your life, the sudden bombardment of messages feels like overkill.

It sounds terrible, but every time Mom's name appears on my phone, I'm overcome with anxiety. I never know if it's bad news or not, just like I never knew whether she was calling to tell Emma and me she'd be back in a few days, or she didn't know how long she'd be gone. Usually it was the latter.

I still remember her cheerful voice telling us, "Absence makes the heart grow fonder," like that could ever resonate with a ten-year-old.

Mom likes to refer to those years as her "struggling musician" days, not bothering to acknowledge the months, even years, at a time when she'd leave Emma and me to be shuffled from family member to family member or family friend. She was always off with random boyfriends who she thought would help her "make it" in the music industry so she wouldn't have to keep singing shitty '80s covers in grimy bars. And every time she'd turn back up (out of the blue), we'd be living somewhere new. I can't actually remember more than six consecutive months that she'd stuck around after I was five years old.

I react to her photos with a casual thumbs-up, admittedly grateful she's getting exercise and spending time in nature. It was the number one recommendation from the doctors to keep her physically and mentally active. Then, I toss my phone onto the desk chair and stare up at the popcorn ceiling, trying to cleanse my mind.

"Are you okay in there?" I call toward the bathroom door. Andi has been in there for nearly half an hour since we got back from the restaurant. And while I know from growing up with Em that a skin care routine can take time, this seems a little excessive.

"Uh, yeah. All good," she croaks from behind the door. She doesn't sound great. Maybe she's a little lightheaded from the elevation. Or worse, uncomfortable with me.

"You sure? Look, if you don't want to share a room, I can head down to the lobby right now and book a separate room on my own card. Gretchen won't have to know."

A pause. "No. It's not that. I promise."

"Okay. Then what is it?"

"I didn't realize we'd be sharing a room, obviously. So I only packed one pair of pajamas."

"Well, at least you packed some. All I have is boxers," I offer as a consolation.

Another pause. "Okay, but the pajamas I brought are hideous."

"Andi, I'm not going to judge you on your pajamas. And I bet you they aren't even ugly."

"They are."

"Well, I don't care if they are. It's not like you need to impress me," I remind her. It feels weird to say that, but it's true. The woman would look good in a brown paper bag. I consider saying that, but it feels like an overstep for our very, very new friendship.

Her sigh is audible from behind the door. "Can you turn the lights out and close your eyes?"

"Fine." I sit up and turn the lamp off. "Lights are off. Eyes are closed. It's safe to come out."

A couple seconds pass before she opens the door. I can hear her footsteps shuffling to the bed, and I crack my eyes open, just a little, catching a blur of red before she dive-bombs under the covers. Her pajamas aren't nearly as bad as she claims. They're an old, oversized T-shirt with a logo I couldn't make out, with an old pair of sweatshorts. She looks like the Michelin Man, wrapped in that puffy white duvet. It's pretty adorable, actually. "They aren't ugly, by the way."

She gasps and tosses a pillow down at me. "You were supposed to close your eyes!"

"I know. I'm sorry. You made such a big deal about them being hideous, I had to see for myself."

"What if I'd been entirely naked?"

"I've basically already seen you naked, so . . ." I say honestly. The words hang between us in a thick, lingering silence. Shit. She isn't responding. Not that I blame her. I promised I wouldn't bring up that night. Why am I the way I am? The panic sets in and I scramble to fix it.

"Not that it really counts. I don't remember it—you. Your body. Naked." I press my pillow to my face to stop more words from coming out of my mouth. It's a total lie, of course. I've thought about her so much over the years, the image of her in front of me, topless on the dresser, is permanently tattooed onto my brain, stored with my oldest formative memories. I've never wanted to punch myself in the face more.

"Right," she says, tone laced with what sounds like relief. "It was a long time ago."

It's quiet again for a few beats, and I lie there, staring into the dark, debating whether to just flop onto my other side and go to sleep. We both have a packed day ahead of us. But after so many years of wishing for one more moment with this woman, just to talk, it feels ridiculous not to take advantage of any time I get with her. There's so much more I want to know.

"Hey, so I was thinking, if we're going to be a believable couple, we should know some basics about each other. In case people ask questions," I add pathetically.

"Good thinking."

"Ask me anything. Question for question?"

We go back and forth, getting the basics out of the way, like our ages (she's twenty-eight, I'm thirty-one), coffee orders (black for me, vanilla latte for her). She's from Toronto (though her mom now lives in Oakville), while I'm from all over the general Ottawa area. She loves it here, whereas I've been desperate to leave since I was a kid.

"Favorite music?" she asks.

"I'll listen to anything, except country," I note.

"Do you like Nickelback?"

"It disturbs me that the lead singer is named *Chad*, but yes, I'm a fan," I reply without hesitation.

Her eyes cut to me. "Shut up."

I shoot upward from my makeshift bed. "Do not tell me you're a hater."

"They're just not my thing."

"I bet you know all their songs," I wager.

"I do know that one . . . *Never made it as a wise man*," she sings, entirely off-key, before snickering to herself.

I smack the edge of the mattress, vindicated. "See? Admit it. 'How You Remind Me' is a banger."

"Okay. Fine. It's a banger. But don't tell anyone I said that." The mattress shakes above with her giggle and it's fucking adorable.

"Wouldn't dream of damaging that hard street cred of yours," I assure. "Favorite candy?"

"Oh, definitely licorice allsorts," she says with far too much enthusiasm.

I let out a rather violent cough. "Wait, what? Those old people candies?"

"Excuse you! They're amazing, colorful, and cute. You never know what you're getting with each handful."

"Either death, depression, or decay, but with sprinkles. Do you wash them down with a glass of prune juice?"

Her gaze rivets down to me as she tosses her hair to one side, exposing her bare neck. "Wow, Nolan Crosby. You are a savage."

"Sorry, this has me questioning who you are, what you stand for, and what I got myself into."

That teases a snort out of her. "Well, now is your opportunity to find out more. Ask me anything."

"What do you do for fun?" I ask.

"Work," she says, which sounds familiar. "When I'm not at work, I'm at home recovering with snacks and a blanket."

"No hobbies?"

"Well, I used to write as my hobby. And after Ted took Lars back, I did some volunteering at a farm outside the city that takes in rescue dogs that are at risk of being euthanized at the shelter—dogs like Lars. They've got a bunch of other animals, too, like goats and pigs. But I haven't been back in a month or so. Things have gotten really busy."

Picturing her swarmed by a cluster of needy rescue animals tugs at my heart more than it should. Maybe even more so than my memory of her feeding Lars cheese slices in her living room. "Rescue dogs? That sounds like a lot of fun. What did you do there?"

"Mostly just walk them, pet them, play with them. It was pretty relaxed."

The thought of going there makes me smile. I could use some time with dogs. "Maybe we can go sometime."

"Sure. I'd like that."

I turn to face Andi on her bed. "Why do you work so much? Passion?"

"Passion originally. That's why I got into politics. I studied political science in school. When I was in my master's program, Eric came to speak at my school when he was first elected as the leader of the DPP. He talked about the importance of voting and all that stuff people roll their eyes about. The world had kind of gone to shit; at least that's how it felt. And the way he spoke about unity and fighting for what's right for the average person, I don't know what it was, but he wasn't like all the other politicians talking out of their ass just to get some votes. He was genuine. Someone who really believed in helping people, especially marginalized people. I wanted to be part of that. Part of change, all that idealistic stuff you think you can do when you're twenty years old," she explains, her hopeful tone transitioning to jaded toward the end.

"I don't think it's idealistic. Eric has made a massive impact. You can see it by how popular he is."

"True. Anyway, my goal was to be on the communications team doing things like messaging, drafting talking points, writing speeches and press releases. But when that didn't work out, I took the job with Gretchen. When you met me, I'd just started a week or so before. Things hadn't gotten crazy yet, so I was still really into writing."

"You're not writing anymore?" I ask.

"Unless the odd chapter or idea here and there counts, no. I don't have much time anymore."

The thought of her no longer writing makes me sad. "You're really talented, by the way. I never got a chance to tell you that."

"You read my book?" She peeks down at me, brows raised in pure surprise.

"I'm not done yet. But I had to read it for the internal investigation. Though seeing as we're *dating* now, another guy on the team will take over the investigation." It feels good to admit that. The last thing I wanted was for her to find out I was reading the book behind her back. "I provided all my notes, all of which come up with nothing compromising, security-wise. So hopefully all this speculation will be over soon."

She's quiet for a moment before speaking again. "I never got the chance to thank you, by the way."

"For what?"

"You were the first person to believe in me. In my writing."

"I'm sure that's not true—"

"It is. You encouraged me to publish without even reading a word. Up until then, I was too terrified of what people would think to even consider it. It meant everything to me. If it weren't for you, I never would have taken the leap."

"You would have," I assure her, though the thought of me being the only person to encourage her makes me really sad.

"Even now, you're still the only person who knows. I never told my family, especially not my mom."

"Why not?"

Her face hardens, and she flops onto her back. "My mom clutches her pearls when people kiss on TV. If she found out her daughter wrote face-sitting smut, she'd have a heart attack."

"If my kid was a bestselling author, I'd be proud," I tell her.

"Thanks, Nolan."

I want to ask if she has any other book ideas, but she beats me to it with her own question.

"So how did you end up in JTF2? Was it a dream of yours?"

I wish I could say I enlisted at eighteen to serve my country. That's the answer I give to people I don't know, because that's what people want to hear. But something about Andi brings out my honesty. "Honestly, I originally enlisted in the military because school wasn't for me. I didn't have the grades to go to university, I didn't care for trades. I needed financial freedom, fast. And I was desperate to get the hell out of Ottawa and see the world, so I joined the infantry."

"And did you see the world? Once you joined?"

"Oh yeah. Did my first stint in Kabul a year and a half in. Then found myself in JTF2 after a stupid bet with a buddy of mine to see who could hit the requirements to go on selection, which sounds pretty fucking reckless now that I look back on it, given what the job is. I've been to every continent, I think."

"Sounds like you like the lifestyle."

"Yup. Can't stay put for long. Can't picture doing anything else, really. I mean, where else would I get to learn how to jump out of a plane? Or rappel down a mountain? Or run sources? But I do miss the adventure. Being on the go. It also has some strange stipulations, pretending to date the PM's wife's assistant, you know."

She lets out a quiet chuckle. "It must be really cool. To be able to walk around anywhere, knowing you could take anyone down at any time, if you really wanted to."

"You could, too, with the right training," I argue.

Her raised brow says, *Fat chance*. "I think you underestimate how weak I am. Sometimes, I have trouble opening the caps on water bottles."

"It's not about strength or size. It's actually about timing and physics. Stand up," I order, pushing my makeshift bed a couple feet toward the TV stand. There's not a lot of room.

She slinks out of bed reluctantly and flicks the lamp on, arms folded across her chest to hide her PJs. I now see her thread-worn T-shirt reads CARLETON UNIVERSITY. "This is gonna end badly."

"It won't. Watch closely," I instruct, trying not to notice how good she looks with her dark hair loose, cascading down her back. I step forward, motioning to her arm. "Can I?"

She nods, and I gently guide her arm upward and to the side in a swift arc, demonstrating how to shift my weight onto my back foot, using the momentum to unbalance the other person. She tentatively copies.

"Step back with your left foot," I say, "and as you do, pull your wrist toward your opposite shoulder. It's all about the angles and timing, not about overpowering physically."

We practice the sequence a couple times: the wrist escape, the pivot, the takedown. With each repetition, she gains more and more confidence.

"Now, I'm going to pretend to come at you and you're going to wait until I've exerted all my force, and then you'll step back with your left foot. If you pull your wrist toward your opposite shoulder, you should theoretically be able to get me on the ground."

"'Theoretically' being the key word." She follows my orders and is able to twist out of my grasp to gain the momentum she needs. To be fair, I'm going pretty easy on her, but she seems so unsure of herself, I want her to have the win.

As I "lose my balance," she places her palm on my chest and pushes me down.

Only, she comes down with me, her knee pinned into my chest, wholly satisfied with herself.

"See? Told you," I manage, struggling to get air from where she's got her knee shoved into my collarbone. "Um, could you—"

"Oh shit. I'm sorry." She shifts her knee over to the other side of my torso, so both of her bare legs are on either side of my chest. I don't think she fully meant to move into that position, because her breath hitches and quickens when she realizes it.

I expect her to get up immediately, but she doesn't. Heat rises in my chest, flowing everywhere, as if I've just dunked myself chest-deep in a hot tub. In the glow of the lamp, her eyes look almost golden as they snap to mine. Hungry. And maybe even a little curious as she circles her thumbs over my chest, studying me, feeling every little pulse and pull, leaving sparks scattering in their wake. She likes this as much as I do.

Fuck me.

The warmth of her body on top of me, the way her nipples are hard underneath the thin fabric of her shirt, the way those soft lips are parted ever so slightly, the velvety softness of her thighs clenching over me. My whole body stiffens and I struggle to swallow what little saliva I have left in my mouth. I never want to move. Ever.

She sucks in a long breath, her chest rising and falling, as though she's just come to that same realization. And that's when she breaks eye contact, her incendiary gaze flicking to my lips. The silence pulses between us and it's almost unbearable.

This is where I'd normally take control, pull her in, grab her ass, and roll her hips over me, over and over again, until we both come apart, until she's screaming my name. But then my stupid conscience steps in. I think about our conversation earlier tonight. Our agreement. She seemed dead set on this idea that we had no chemistry, which was exactly why our "situation" was going to work so well. As friends.

And then there's the fact that I'm not in any position to entertain a relationship, including something casual.

So even though she's currently looking at me like she wants to fuck me right here on this floor, I don't want either of us to have any regrets. I don't want to complicate an already complicated decision.

I do exactly the opposite of what I want. I give her a light tap on the thigh and whisper, "We should probably get some sleep now."

That snaps her out of it. "Yes, yes, we should." She rolls off me instantly and practically dives back into her bed and turns off the light.

We lie there in silence for what feels like hours. I try just about everything to purify my thoughts (including picturing every family member, including my grandma, in a muumuu). Nothing works.

I contemplate addressing what just happened. But what the hell would I say? Technically, nothing happened, which is for the best. Making something of it would just heighten the awkwardness.

So I pathetically settle on, "Good job, by the way. You're a natural. Remind me never to get on your bad side."

Her easy laugh is the last thing I hear before I fall asleep.

CHAPTER 17

Andi

The two days in Squamish go about as well as they could, considering the circumstances (the circumstances: when I mounted him without notice on the floor of our hotel room).

To be fair, we were practicing self-defense. He was meant to be on the ground. But I wasn't meant to straddle him like a horse. I don't know what the hell came over me. Maybe it's the fact that I haven't had sex in three years and am basically a born-again virgin. Maybe I'm ovulating. Maybe I felt like I had something to prove after he admitted my boobs weren't memorable. Or maybe it's the fact that he's offensively attractive, shirtless, and sleeping mere feet away from me. I'm only human.

I also hadn't expected to love the feeling of his body underneath me, the friction, the way I could feel every beat of his heart like the softest vibration. If he hadn't ordered me off him (in the nicest way possible), I probably would have kissed him or worse. If history is any indication, it would have gone south, because that's just my life. A series of failed social interactions. And I need him for the summer, possibly until Gretchen's gala.

Fake dating aside, we mutually agreed on our friendship status. It would be nice to have a friend I can talk to about (mostly) anything. I can't let my overactive hormones screw it up.

So I spend the next day solidifying my permanent residency in the friend zone. I barely spare him a passing glance when he's shirtless after a shower, water droplets clinging to each ridge and groove of his hard-earned abs (okay, maybe I snuck a peek or two, or twelve).

Thankfully, work is busy for both of us. Eric has a meeting with the premier of BC (the head of the provincial government), followed by a press conference and a couple community appearances. Gretchen has a visit to the local soup kitchen, as well as an elementary school. When I'm not following at her heels and doing gala prep on the side, I'm on the hunt for fresh flowers for her hotel room and a very specific face serum she once found at a farmer's market six years ago but can't remember the vendor's name (really narrows it down). If that weren't enough, her publisher has also requested her proposal for her next book, a vegan cookbook. Naturally, she's asked me to write the whole thing based on exactly two handwritten bullet points.

By the time Nolan returns to the room around nine, I'm almost too exhausted to talk. But one can't be too careful. As an added precaution, I've tucked myself into a cocoon of blankets in my ugly pajamas and turned the lights off. No talking of any variety, including small talk. He seems fine with that, settling into his makeshift bed on the floor without a fuss.

The morning we're set to leave is our first test. At the strong suggestion of Bethany from PR, I help Gretchen and Eric snap some "casual yet romantic" photos on the hotel balcony for social media. I'll hand it to them, they really do look like they're in love. You'd never know there's turmoil by the way Eric wraps his hand possessively around her waist, or by the way Gretchen beams back at him.

Once Bethany is satisfied with the photos, Gretchen turns her attention to me. "You two should get a shot," she suggests, wagging her finger in my direction. I glance over my shoulder at Nolan standing a couple feet behind me, his hands in the pockets of his slacks.

"Us?" I clarify, still not used to being referred to as "you two."

"Who else?" she says with an eye roll, gesturing for him to come closer. He inches forward reluctantly, so reluctantly, she has to urge him to pose closer to me.

Realistically, it is an opportunity to get a good picture for social media.

Nolan shoots me a funny smile before wrapping an arm around my shoulders. I lean in, resting my head on his chest, allowing myself one liberal sniff. He smells like a mixture of minty toothpaste and fresh laundry, just like he did the night we met.

"Okay, act like you really like each other. Give us a quick kiss," Gretchen prods, unimpressed by our lack of PDA.

"She wants us to kiss," I whisper to Nolan.

I expect him to scrunch his face at the prospect and give me horror movie eyes that scream, *You really want to try this again?* Instead, he just watches me for a moment, a look of curiosity fleeting across his features. "Do *you* want me to kiss you?" he whispers.

I study his face for a moment, really study it. I take in the perfect slope of his nose. The fullness of his lips. The tinge of pink in the crests of his cheeks. Damn right, I want him to kiss me. But I settle for, "It would be weirder if we refused."

This is the part where he could run away entirely, or laugh in my face—either would be an appropriate reaction. But shockingly, he nods and leans in.

A millisecond after he dips his lips toward mine, I spring forward on my toes like a jack-in-the-box, entirely misjudging the distance.

Your Honor, it's a disaster. Let the record show, I'm an abysmal kisser. Gretchen clicks away as his perfect nose clumsily grazes the side of mine. Thankfully, this time it's our cheekbones that collide first, not our lips. The pain makes me lose my footing, and I stumble into his chest, stomping on his polished shoe in the process.

He pulls back abruptly and his brows lift. *You nearly took me out*, they say.

Before I can curl into a ball and roll down the mountainside, he closes the distance between us again, steadying his hands on the small of my waist. I surrender, letting him take full control of this one. And he really does. He comes in slow, his thumb brushing against my cheek in a sweet, adoring way I've only written about in my books, never experienced. His lips follow, brushing against mine in the softest whisper. It's so light, I have to open my eyes for a fraction of a second to confirm contact.

A confetti cannon goes off in my chest, exploding all the way to my toes. I shiver from the sensation, exhaling disappointment when he pulls back.

He inhales, his eyes fluttering to a close before his mouth catches mine. Fast. And this time, I'm ready. And when he slips his tongue against my lips, I part them immediately, my knees nearly buckling at its searing warmth.

He tastes pure, like water and nothing in particular except maybe a hint of mint. His tongue slides against mine and I can't help but whimper into his mouth. At the sound, he tightens his grip on my waist, letting his hand creep up my spine, vertebra by vertebra. I press myself forward, my breath shallow, frantic to have him closer. He gives me a quick squeeze, giving my bottom lip one last suck, which nearly unravels me entirely. I don't know how much time passes. It could be an hour, or two seconds. But when he finally pulls away, my lips are swollen and my chest is heaving.

Holy shit.

That wasn't like the first time. Not at all. I am officially short-circuiting, unlike Nolan, who looks cool as ever, smirking at me like he's expecting me to say something.

"I got some cute ones. I'll text them to you," Gretchen says. "Oh, when we get in the car, I need you to go through my phone and delete everything I don't need. My phone is running out of storage."

I nod, so utterly dizzy and flustered by what just happened, I barely compute a word.

"Was it as bad as last time?" Nolan whispers as we follow Gretchen and Eric to the cars.

I swallow and my throat is like sandpaper. It's an unfair question, really. If I say yes, it could hurt his feelings. If I say no, I'm opening things up into dangerous territory. So I settle on, "It was similar."

"Similar? As in bad?"

I level him with a look. "I mean, do you think it was good? I hit your face with mine."

He scratches the side of his head, like he needs to really think about it. "It wasn't the best, but it wasn't *horrible*," he assures. "But if you're worried about it, we have all summer to work on it."

Great. Just great.

CHAPTER 18

- - - - ◆ · ◆ - - - -

Nolan

No chemistry.

Those words have haunted me since we got back to Ottawa. I've never thought of myself as having a fragile ego, but damn. That stung.

Sure, our first kiss years ago wasn't the smoothest. But that second one in Squamish was light-years better, on my end at least. I don't know if it was her swollen lips, or the little breathy noise she made when I pulled her flush to me, or the way she tasted, sweet like the lemon tea she was drinking earlier. In any case, it's a good thing our bosses were there, because I'd have been tempted to keep it going as long as she'd let me.

Regardless, whatever I think about our chemistry (or alleged lack thereof) means nothing, because Andi thought it was shit and I just have to fucking deal.

It reminds me of when I was in fifth grade. I had an embarrassingly pathetic crush on this girl at school, Jolene Smith. Like every grade school boy does when they like someone, I chased her around the playground, teased her, did anything I could to get her attention without actually being nice, to no avail. At the encouragement of Em on Valentine's Day, I gave her a handwritten card asking her to be my valentine. She handed it back immediately.

"I already have a valentine," she told me in an ultraserious tone. "Joe Jonas." Joe fucking Jonas from the Jonas Brothers. Her celebrity crush. It was traumatizing, to say the least. I spent the whole weekend sulking on my grandma's couch, playing video games and speaking to no one. And I've hated Joe and his thick, sweeping bangs ever since.

This feels ten times worse. I've been moping around over Andi and our *no chemistry* since I got home last night, which is just sad. Being around Andi is effortless. I don't feel like I have to put on a show, or worry she'll take my dry humor the wrong way. Sure, she's shy, a little reserved, but I appreciate it, because she doesn't talk for the sake of talking. She speaks with intention, not just to fill the dead air. Contrary to my first impression of her, she doesn't take herself too seriously, at least not with me. In Squamish, she let her hair down, let her goofy side come out. And fuck. That smile. Not the fake, tight-lipped one when she's trying to appease someone. The genuine one that unfurls slowly when something amuses her, or when she's talking about her writing. It's the way it spills across her whole face. The way her eyes crinkle a little in the corners. The way it reaches her eyes, illuminating them like little goblets of sunshine in a way that makes my resting pulse go haywire.

God. I really need to get a grip. I already have my hands full with Mom, making sure she has everything she needs until

September. I don't need more complications in my life. And the last thing I want to do is start something I can't finish.

Speaking of Mom, the distinct smell of grease wafts through the crack under my bedroom door. It smells like . . . bacon? I toss on a T-shirt and jeans and pad into the kitchen to make sure everything is okay.

Sure enough, Mom is at the stove flipping sizzling bacon strips in a skillet, while stirring eggs in another and singing a Madonna song. Alarm is my first instinct. Mom shouldn't be making food over a hot stove, especially not food with boiling grease. Theresa and Em hid most of the unsafe cooking ingredients and tools out of reach in the upper cabinets, all of which are open. I make a mental note to add childproof locks.

I go to clear my throat and ask how she got up there, but the moment my toe passes over the ceramic tile, she turns and offers a coy smile, like she senses my presence. "I knew you couldn't pass up bacon."

She's right. Emma and I always begged for bacon like we saw families eat on TV. One night for dinner, when Mom was feeling particularly good, she fried up some bacon and potatoes. We talked about it for months, hoping she'd surprise us with them again. She never did.

This is my time to say something, to remind her how dangerous it is to cook something like this, but one look at her face and I can't bring myself to do it. Instead, I park myself at the table, entirely dumbfounded.

She's practically vibrating with excitement when she serves me my plate. I can't help but wonder whether she remembers that one dinner or if whether she just made bacon because it's a normal breakfast food. Either way, she seems to be having a good morning. She's even dressed in a pair of pleather leggings and a faded leopard print T-shirt, a relic of the past.

"Wow. Thanks, Mom," I say, a little taken aback. Last night when I got back from Squamish, she was confused, thinking I was back from tour. In fact, she was mad at me for coming home "without prior notice." "How'd you get into the cupboards up there anyways?" I ask.

"The chair. Not sure why you keep insisting on rearranging my stuff. But it was driving me crazy, having all my things out of place."

"Remember, if you want anything, all you have to do is ask me or Theresa."

I expect this to start an argument, but she just nods like a child, purses her lips, and watches me with interest as I clear my plate. "So I've been wondering."

Oh no. Do I even want to know? Probably not.

She catches the alarm in my expression, but presses on. "Whether you'd thought about settling down before you go off gallivanting around the world again."

"No," I say through a mouthful.

She remains unconvinced. "You don't want to give yourself some time to find a nice hometown girl? There's a woman in my book club. I think her name is Sari, or Sarah. Anyway, the important thing is she has a daughter." She takes a couple moments to debate whether Sari or Sarah's daughter is thirty-five or forty-five, but I gather she's single and works as a preschool teacher, which Mom points out means she's good with children. "I told her about you and how you're newly single and lonely—"

Despite all she's going through, obsessing over my dating life is something that's remained pretty constant in her mind.

"Mom, I appreciate your concern for my relationship status, but I'm good. And I'm not lonely, for the record."

She brushes my words away with her fork, the sunlight from the kitchen window drenching half her face. "You are lonely. All alone in the world." Jesus. She needs to work on her delivery.

"Ouch, Mom. That's harsh."

"Life is harsh, honey. You know, the doctor told me Alzheimer's is genetic. Do you really want to die alone with no one around? No wife or children?"

What's the point in having a wife and children if I'm barely going to be in their lives like she was? I'm tempted to ask that, but I refrain. "Well, no—"

"You must miss the intimacy."

"Mom!" A violent shudder snakes down my spine, taking me out emotionally and physically. Dearly beloved, we are gathered here today to witness the death of Nolan Crosby.

She doesn't register the abject horror on my face. Either that, or she doesn't care. It's probably the latter. "I know you don't feel comfortable bringing women back here, but our bedrooms are on opposite ends of the house—"

"Can we please stop talking about this?" I beg, pushing my plate forward to shield my head in my hands.

She leans forward and peels one of my hands away to maintain direct eye contact. "Sweetheart, there's no shame in getting help to find the right person. Someone you want to settle down with." The very thought of "settling down" makes me itchy. I've never been settled anywhere in my entire life. I don't even know what that would feel like.

"Well, actually, I met someone." It seemed like a good idea to say it, for a fraction of a second. Just a white lie to get her off my back. But when she shifts forward, her eyes round and big like saucers, the regret crashes through me like a car accident.

"You met someone?" she practically yells. I'm not sure I've ever seen her so excited on my account. There were plenty of times she'd get riled up when she'd get a date, or when she'd get a lead to perform at some random bar. But never did she express that sort of excitement when it came to me and Em. Until now, I didn't know she was truly capable of caring about anyone but herself.

I shift uncomfortably, grateful she's moved on from talking about *intimacy.* "Yup."

"Who is she? When do I get to meet her?"

I back away a little. "Soon. It's, um, new." Why do words keep coming out of my mouth?

"New? How new?"

"Like . . . a week ago? But if it gets serious, I will absolutely introduce you."

"What's her name?" she asks, not missing a beat.

"Um, Andi," I say through a glug of tea, wishing I could swallow my lie down with it.

"Andi," she repeats with emphasis on both syllables. "Interesting. Short for Andrea?"

I have no idea, but I assume so. So I just nod.

"Classic and timeless," she says in a singsong voice. "Sounds like a girl with a good head on her shoulders." And it occurs to me now that when I was a kid, she used to comment on names, give her honest first impression. That's where I must have picked up the habit.

The next few minutes are filled mostly with her firing off questions. *Where is she from? What's she like?* Pretty much everything short of *What's her blood type and medical history?*, though I wouldn't put it past her if I sat here long enough.

"You know, my birthday is next week. January twentieth," she says.

"Uh—" I'm about to remind her that her birthday is in August, not January, but then I remember what all the Alzheimer's experts say. When someone mistakes facts, it's best not to confuse them more, especially if it's inconsequential. "I'll have to see. She's really busy with work and—"

"I want this birthday to be special. You'll bring Andi," she insists, standing to take my plate.

My first instinct is to be annoyed by it all, but I also see how giddy and energetic she is over the prospect. Despite myself, it feels good to see her in good spirits, even if it'll be short-lived. And even better that I've had a part in it.

CHAPTER 19

Andi

The Prime Minister & Me is now in the top 10 in the "Contemporary Romance" category, where it's hovered for two days. Sales for my other books have followed suit. My author DMs and social media following have exploded.

Before now, I always assumed highly successful writers unlike myself lived glamorous lives, typing away at their computers oceanside, watching the waves crash against the rocky shore while cradling a hot beverage, getting inspiration from the call of the gulls over the coastal breeze.

Despite the new zeros in my bank account, here's the cold, hard reality. I'm braless, slumped over in my chair in dim lighting, ruining both my posture and eyesight in one fell swoop; double-fisting a Diet Coke and a tea that's long gone cold to jump-start the creative juices; eating Ritz Bits with reckless abandon; typing furiously. I'm working on a new, half-baked romance idea involving a reclusive former musician, a beach, and mysterious messages in the sand.

It's my first proper stretch of time to write in ages. I have two full days off, a rare luxury. I haven't had this much time to myself since . . . two Christmases ago. And even then, Gretchen texted me at 11:30 p.m. Christmas Day to confirm that everything was set for her charity Santa event at the children's hospital.

In just a day, I manage to write the entire first act of the book. Each word typed melts away the anxiety that's accumulated from years of staring into the void, waiting to be struck by inspiration.

It also proves an excellent mental break from the fear of being doxed, fired, and blacklisted from politics forever. When I'm writing, I also can't hyper-fixate on that hotel room in Squamish. I don't have to suffer, replaying our conversation in my mind, or angst about how good it felt to talk to someone freely. Or lament over not having someone to laugh and make jokes with. I haven't had that in a long time, not since Laine and Hunter, really. And then there was that moment in the hotel room when we were on the floor. And the kiss, which was for show but certainly didn't feel like it.

I don't let myself think about it too hard, because he's leaving in a couple months. What's even the point?

Once I'm satisfied with my word count, I make the mistake of texting Gretchen, asking if she needs anything. She wastes no time replying that the kids' closets are a "straight-up mess."

Only, when I arrive at the house, the closets are still immaculately organized from when I did them a couple months ago. I refold some things anyway to keep Gretchen content while Jason runs rabid in circles around me, undoing all my progress.

Gretchen comes in and sits cross-legged on the floor as soon as she finds out I'm here.

"Everything okay?" I ask over the shouting. Jason is belting the lyrics to a Miley Cyrus song, which seems a little inappropriate for his age.

She shakes her head, but not before asking Jason five times to go play with the Legos in the corner. Thankfully, he obeys. "No. This whole rumor situation is out of control."

Since Squamish, the media hasn't let up on the affair rumors. Even a popular gossip blog published NSFW excerpts of the book, which were dissected and mocked all over the internet (hence my spike in sales). Apparently healthy depictions of consensual sex focusing on a woman's pleasure are gross, especially if written by a woman. If it's sad, tragic, and written by a white man, it's high literature.

"I'm really sorry, Gretchen," I say, grateful for the laundry folding so I can avoid her eyes. I feel beyond guilty.

She stretches her legs out and exhales a long-suffering sigh. "It's not just these ridiculous affair rumors. It's tiring in general, constantly living in this push and pull of scandals and strategizing. Imagine every day, someone is questioning, hey, did you see she wore that purple coat? Clearly that means she's getting divorced. The symbolism of purple." She's never admitted that before.

"I bet. It's not exactly something the average person has to deal with," I point out.

She lifts a shoulder. "People on the internet say I deserve it. That we signed up for this the moment Eric ran for office."

"First, the internet was a mistake. Who cares what those keyboard warriors think? They don't even know you. Besides, *you* didn't sign up for it, Eric did."

Looking at her right now, with her head slumped down, she's a shell of who she was when Eric was first elected. She was so vivacious, with a personality that could only be described as sparkly enough to match Eric's charm. They were a force. They couldn't even enter a room together without winking at each other and smiling with their own little jokes. You wouldn't know it now.

"But I supported him. I pushed him to go into politics. It wasn't even on his radar, you know. He would have been perfectly happy as a public defender his entire life. But I thought . . . a man like him needs something more. And, well, we got more. I never thought he'd actually win, you know? That sounds awful, because of course I believed in him. Still do. I know he's the best thing for our country; I believe that with my whole heart. But Eric was so young and a man of color. All the odds were against us. So when he actually won, I thought, okay, I can give up four years of my career for the greater good. But now . . . with the reelection coming up . . ." She bites her lip. "That's four more years, after I already took so much time off work having the kids."

I nod in solidarity. It feels unfair that the woman always seems to have to make the sacrifice. It's why there are so few women at the highest levels of politics.

Gretchen runs her finger over one of Jason's tiny knit sweaters. "I know it sounds awful, but I miss my life. Don't get me wrong, I care about the charity work, but I miss getting my hands dirty, going through case law, poring over files, being up late into the night. Going to court the next morning and eviscerating the other side. I feel resentful that I've lost that part of me."

This is one of the reasons I've always had a soft spot for Gretchen, even if she's not the easiest person to work for. She's basically a prisoner in her life. She can't just go for lunch with a friend on a whim. She can't go anywhere unless it's cleared and approved by security. And when she does, there's no hope of privacy with security and the public watching her every move. I can't even imagine what that must be like, especially for someone who was always so independent. "I don't blame you. It probably doesn't help that you're alone most of the time."

"Eric always worked long hours. We both did. But this is on a whole different level. He's somewhere else all the time. Even when he's physically here, he's got his nose buried in files, he's memorizing speeches, he's on his phone answering texts and emails. And he's . . . stressed-out." She's not wrong. Since he took office, he's gotten much grayer than he was before. The lines on his forehead and around his mouth have become deeper, more pronounced.

I hate seeing her like this. She doesn't seem happy, and I can't imagine what another four years of this would do to her soul. I've never wished for Eric not to win. I want him to win, he deserves to win, and I think Canadians deserve for him to win. But at what cost to his personal life? "Have you talked to Eric about this?"

She nods. "He knows how I feel. But I can't expect him to walk away from what he was born to do." She doesn't say it outright, but I think she's seriously considering leaving him. "Not that I have a choice," she adds.

"Technically, you do," I remind her, though she isn't far from the truth. Separating right before the election wouldn't be ideal. It would be used as fodder by the opposition to prove Eric isn't fit to run. I can hear the sound bites now. *"How is Eric fit to run a country when he can't even keep his family together?"*

"What would you do in my position?" she asks.

My jaw hinges open. Is she actually asking for my advice, like we're friends or something? I honestly have no idea what I would do. "I'd do what makes me happiest, deep down."

She nods, teary. I can't tell if it's the answer she wants to hear or not. "Thanks, Andi."

A soft knock at the door interrupts the moment. I expect it to be one of the housekeepers, but it's Nolan. My stomach twinges and patters when I see him. I haven't seen him since we came from Squamish.

"Hey, I hope I'm not interrupting," Nolan says from the doorway, his eyes widening when he spots Gretchen. "Oh, I'm so sorry. I didn't realize you were in the middle of something."

Gretchen waves his words away with an exaggerated smile. "Nolan! It's so nice to see you. And no, you're not interrupting." She gives me a swift elbow. "What can we help you with?"

"I just came by to see if you wanted to sit on the back patio and have lunch." He holds up a brown paper bag, flashing me a sheepish grin. "But it looks like you're busy, so we can re—"

"No! Not busy," Gretchen corrects abruptly. "Andi was just finishing briefing me on some gala logistics." She stands and brushes off her outfit, giving me a knowing look.

"Uh, are you sure?"

"Of course! God. I remember when Eric used to give me little surprises like this. You two are in the best stage, when it's still fun and exciting. I wish I could be your age again, with all that freedom to be young and in love." It occurs to me that, in a way, she's living vicariously through me, which makes me sad for her.

"And I'm heading out to meet with Leslie," she informs, referring to one of the gala donors.

"Don't forget to bring her gift!" I say, passing her the small gift bag of prosecco I picked up this morning.

Gretchen takes it and gives us both a wink before she exits the room, leaving Nolan and me alone.

He flashes me a boyish smile and swallows. "Do you have lunch plans?"

"Lunch?"

"If you're too busy, no worries. I just thought, you know, since we're supposed to be dating, eating lunch together is something couples do if they work together. At least I assume so?" He scratches the back of his neck, unsure. I don't blame him. The last time we were pretending to be a couple in public, we kissed.

A warmth overtakes me before I can stop it. Maybe it's the memory of the kiss, or the fact that I've never actually taken a real lunch break since I started working for Gretchen. That, and no guy has ever brought me lunch before.

"Yeah, I think couples definitely have lunch together."

CHAPTER 20

Nolan

I t's the mozza sticks from Roger's Diner! These are my favorite." Andi's eyes are so wide, you'd think she was staring at a pot of glittering gold, not a greasy container of deep-fried cheese sticks.

We're outside at a picnic table on the stone patio area, off the staff's entrance. According to Andi, this is the perfect place to go to be "seen." She's not wrong. It's sunny out, so some of the other staff are soaking up the weather, loitering in the back chatting, eating their lunch, and doing a terrible job of pretending to mind their own business. The whispers are more distracting than I'd like to admit.

"I know. You said they were your writing fuel . . . that night." I whisper the "writing" part, pushing the box across the table, trying to hide my nerves. This all feels a little grimy, like I'm trying to bribe her with food or something.

She pops a cheese stick in her mouth nearly whole, only to

regret it instantly, cover her mouth, and blow the piping hot air from her cheeks. If she were a cartoon, lines of steam would be floating around her. I hand her a bottle of water, which she gratefully takes. "We need a code word. For writing," she whispers back, eyeing the rest of the staff, who are hovering a little too close for comfort.

"What about . . . karate?"

This makes her crack a smile and nod. She watches in amazement as I pull out two burgers, one plain with multiple toppings in individual containers to the side. "I didn't know what toppings you liked, so I got them all just in case."

"Oh, I like them all," she assures me, piling them on top of her patty and bun. "Sorry. I didn't get a chance to eat breakfast this morning."

"No judgment here," I assure her. "So you mentioned you were going to do some *karate* on your days off?"

She nods, her eyes lighting up at the mere mention. "Sure did. Made a lot of progress. My moves are still pretty rusty, though."

"I'd guess karate is something you have to practice, or you'll lose the muscle memory."

"Totally. And the last time I did karate, I was doing it for me and my small number of . . . students," she says, using "students" as a stand-in for "readers." "Suddenly, I'm a black belt. I have thousands and thousands of students. My classes are sold out everywhere."

I'm tempted to stand and hug her, but her enthusiasm doesn't match. She looks entirely guilt ridden. "That's fucking amazing, Andi."

"I always dreamed of this happening. But now that it has, it feels a bit . . . wrong. Like a fluke I didn't deserve. People aren't taking my classes because they like them and think I'm talented. They're there for the gossip."

"Most people aren't going to dedicate almost six hours of their life doing karate if they aren't enjoying it. It doesn't matter how they found your class. It's that they like it and keep coming back for more, even if they don't want to admit it."

"Even if my classes are good, what if my next class doesn't live up to expectations? What if people think I'm a one-hit wonder?"

"They won't," I say confidently. "You have a lot of . . . enthusiastic students in my mom's . . . karate club. And they think it's badass. They're even taking more of your classes." It's true. The other day, Mom mentioned how excited the ladies were about the book and how some of them had ordered the other two A. A. Zed books.

"Really? They like them?" she asks, hopeful.

"Yes, really. They'd be devastated if you didn't keep doing karate. And so would I."

She considers this. "Hopefully I'll be able to finish this one in the next few months. My goal is by end of fall, though it'll have to be piecemeal. I don't get a lot of time off."

"You don't get time off, or you don't ask for it?"

"Both," she admits, finishing her burger. "I've only asked for a few days off here and there. I think that's why Gretchen likes me. Because I basically dedicate myself to her. I know that probably sounds sad, but I don't know any different. I've worked since I was fourteen. Between juggling school and a part-time job, I've never really had a lot of free time."

I relate to that. Sacrificing your life for work. "What was your first job?"

"Unofficially, I babysat and stocked shelves at a corner store down the street. When I was legally old enough for a job, I worked at Tim Hortons pretty much every night and weekend after school," she recounts.

I lift a hand in a high five. "Hey, Tim Hortons was my first job, too, aside from cutting lawns and shoveling driveways. Hated it. I had this boss who insisted on being called Rage."

She snorts. "Rage?"

"His real name was Kevin, but he'd get pissed if you called him that. He'd spend the whole shift double-fisting Timbits and throwing them at us if we weren't working hard enough. Eventually he got fired for refusing to wear a hairnet. And his hair was shoulder-length."

"Ew. Good to know we both paid our dues."

"Why did you work so much as a kid?" I ask.

"We went through some hard times, and I never wanted to end up in a similar situation. It was important to me to make my own money."

My brow flicks up. "Hard times?"

Her expression clouds. "My dad lost his job when I was around eight after hurting his back. One thing led to another and we ended up getting evicted from our house. We actually lived in our car for a couple weeks before my parents could get into social housing."

I work down a swallow, imagining how hard that must have been. "Shit, Andi. I'm so sorry. That's really rough."

"Honestly, at the time, Amanda and I had no idea what was

really going on. We were so young. My mom told us we were going on a camping adventure, and we thought it was fun, living in our car. We had school during the day and my parents would take us to the rec center to shower in the evenings. Amanda and I were just excited we could swim in the huge pool."

I think back to the night we met, how she bought food for Ted and took care of his dog like it was nothing. I knew that kind of generosity stemmed from somewhere meaningful. "When did you finally realize the truth?"

"A few years later, I overheard my mom bring it up to my dad. They were fighting all the time pre-divorce, and my mom had a lot of resentment toward him over our finances and his health issues. She actually comes from a really rich family, who disowned her when she married my dad. He didn't have money or a stable job. He was a bit of a free spirit, kind of like my sister. Stability wasn't exactly his main priority," she explains.

"Damn. Must have put a lot of strain on the relationship."

"Yup. She got sick of it all and left him and went back to her family, who introduced her to my stepdad, Dave. When we were in high school, she married him. He's . . . the complete opposite of my dad. Stable, works in finance, has his shit together. The man even does his own taxes. Eats pizza with a knife and fork."

"Whoa, whoa, whoa. Is he okay?"

"That's exactly what Amanda said. But he's good for her, even if they don't see each other often," she says with a resigned shrug.

"They don't?"

"He works a lot, travels. He's barely home, based on what she tells me. Sounds romantic, doesn't it?"

I tilt my head. "Depends on who you ask."

Half our lunch hour passes by in a blink by the time we update each other on the past few days since we got back to Ottawa. We keep it casual, seeing as we're still under the watchful eyes of the lingering staff members near the door. With every minute that ticks by, I'm growing more and more aware that I'm deliberately wasting time—not that time feels wasted with her.

"Finally," she groans, stretching her arms, eyeing the handful of staff as they head inside. We're finally alone back here.

"Pretending to be my girlfriend is exhausting, huh?" I smile, piling the take-out containers.

"You're not the problem. It's being watched that weirds me out. It's awkward."

"Are people still being weird with you?" She mentioned in Squamish that the staff were either ignoring her entirely or being a little too friendly, trying to extract information.

"A little. There's a lot of whispering going on. Though I suspect it'll die down within a week," she notes. "Anyway, thank you for bringing me lunch. I'm beyond full," she says, stretching her arms over her head. "I think you might have to carry me back inside."

"That's too bad. We still have to eat this," I say, taking a plastic container of cheesecake out of the brown bag.

Her eyes widen at the sight. "Hey! I thought I was the one who's supposed to repay you with cheesecake."

I fidget with the napkin in my lap, terrified to come out with it. "Well, speaking of. Before we head back inside, I actually did have one small—well, not really small—thing to ask. And please don't laugh at me."

She leans in, curious. "And you're bribing me with cheesecake? And mozza sticks?"

"Yes."

"Smart. I would do unspeakable things for cheese in any form." She pops open the container, fork at the ready. When she moans, closing her eyes at the first bite, I smash my knee reflexively against the picnic table. Why am I so nervous?

"My mom," I say, quickly rubbing my now sore knee. "She's been on my ass about having a girlfriend."

She raises a brow. "Really? Why?"

"Partially because she wants me out of her house. And mostly because she thinks I'm lonely. Apparently, I work too much and don't prioritize my personal life," I say honestly. "Which is ridiculous, because this gig is really tame compared to my last one."

"Is that why you took this job? To be home more?" she asks gently through a bite.

In a manner of speaking, yes. But now feels like a bad time to get into the whole thing. Instead, I settle for, "Sort of. Until I get a new posting."

"Right. A new posting." I might be imagining it, but I think there's a tinge of disappointment there. But before I can determine either way, she flourishes a hand in my direction. "Anyway, sorry, back to you. Your mom wants you to have a girlfriend."

"Yeah. She's been talking about setting me up with random women and I got frustrated and . . . well, I told her I had a girlfriend to get her off my back," I say, horrified by hearing myself say it.

She lets out a low whistle, sitting back on the bench. "Wow, that's quite the lie."

"It just kind of came out," I explain. "One minute, she was interrogating me. The next, I was telling her your name."

"Let me guess, you need me to make an appearance or two

so she knows I'm not a figment of your imagination?" she clarifies, pointing at me with her fork.

"She wants me to bring you to her birthday dinner next week—" I stall out, tempted to explain it isn't actually her birthday without having to explain the whole diagnosis. I'll have to tell her before the dinner, but now doesn't feel like the right time. "I know it's a lot to ask, but do you think you could come?"

"Of course," she says easily, as though I've merely asked her to go for coffee. "Tell me about your mom. I want to be prepared."

This should be an easy question, but it's not. "Uh, my mom. She's . . ." I stammer, unsure where to start. Because talking about her in any accurate light requires me to tell Andi everything. According to my watch, we have five minutes left of lunch, not all day.

She must sense my unease, because she follows it up with, "Are you close with her? You talk about her a lot, so I figured."

Here's where it gets dicey. Women like it when men are close to their moms (up until a certain point). Penny straight up told me it was a "red flag" that my mom and I didn't have much of a relationship. And while I agree in theory that people should be close to their parents, usually that kind of sentiment is expressed only by people who were raised by good parents. People who don't know what it's like to have their mom put herself, her boyfriends, and alcohol first, at the expense of them and their siblings.

"No," I finally admit shamefully. I brace myself for a similar sentiment along the lines of *family is everything*, the usual BS I've heard over and over from girlfriends past. But Andi just dips her chin in solidarity.

"I'm sorry. I'm not close with my mom anymore, either. After my parents split, she kind of reshifted her focus to my stepdad and his family." She chews at her bottom lip, avoiding eye contact as she says it. It feels like a heavy admission, something she hasn't shared with many people.

I fight the temptation to reach out and touch her, comfort her. I remember that feeling, of wondering whether it's your fault, if you were just not interesting enough, not good enough for them to want to be in your life. I fucking hate that anyone could make her feel like that.

"She's missing out," I tell her. And I mean that.

We both sit with that for a few moments, something flickering wordlessly between us.

"Either way, I'd be happy to come to your mom's birthday dinner. Just tell me when and where," she says after a while, flashing me a soft, reassuring smile, which lights me up from the inside out.

"Really?"

"Of course. What are fake girlfriends for?"

CHAPTER 21

Nolan

can't believe you still do that," I say.

"Do what?" Emma stuffs the last piece of blueberry muffin (top) into her mouth like a hyena.

"Eat only the tops off the muffins and leave the bottoms, like an absolute monster." She'd always give me the bottoms. I'd always eat them, even if I wasn't hungry, because I hate wasting food.

"I am who I am." She shoots me an unapologetic, crumb-filled smile, and I'm reminded of how much she looks like Mom. It's not just their same hooded blue eyes and sharp features; it's the mannerisms, the way they scrunch their eyes closed when something amuses them. The soft arch of their brows and the quirk of their lips.

"Does Trav know this about you?"

She taps a rogue blade of grass sticking to her Converse. "He does and he's willing to accept it, so long as I don't say anything when he guzzles milk straight from the carton."

"Ah, breakfast crime on breakfast crime."

"The secret to a healthy marriage," she says through a yawn, unable to hide her fatigue. She stopped by this morning to "visit Mom" before heading to the salon for the day, even though I know she came over to check in. Last night was rough. Mom tried to leave the house at nine in the evening to go to "an appointment," and became irate when I wouldn't give her the car keys. She accused me on the front lawn of keeping her prisoner in the house, which drew the attention of the neighbors. It took at least an hour before she calmed down with the help of medication.

"So Mom mentioned how excited she is about your new girlfriend and your football date tonight. Why haven't I heard about her?"

I immediately look away. The last person I want to lie to after Mom is Em. So I settle on half-truth. "It's not as serious as Mom makes it out to be. We're just friends from work."

"Just friends? Going to a football game alone, just the two of them?"

"We're spending time together, enjoying each other's company."

She ignores that and makes a grabby hands motion for my phone. "I need a picture."

I pull up the only photos we have together, the staged ones from Squamish, and toss her my phone.

She grins wildly and kicks her feet. "She is adorable. You two are adorable. Look at the way you look at each other! When is the wedding?" She toggles back and forth between a photo of me looking at Andi, and another one of her smiling up at me.

I snort, plucking my phone from her grasp. "Okay. Next topic."

She raises a brow, unimpressed. "Defensive much? It's a legitimate question."

I swipe the photo away with exaggerated annoyance, making sure she sees how much this conversation is ruining my life. "Because we're not talking about that right now, okay? Next."

She leans in, squinting at me with mock seriousness. "Has anyone ever told you you're a buzzkill?"

"Has anyone ever told you you're nosy as hell?"

She rolls her eyes, unfazed. "How are things with Mom?"

"Honestly, I'm not certain this woman is our actual mother," I say, motioning toward her. She's at the far end of the yard, singing and plucking weeds from her bed of geraniums. She's even wearing one of those floppy straw hats.

"See? I told you. She changed a lot while you were away. Did the work in treatment and therapy. In more ways than one." She has told me that, about a thousand times, though I've always taken Emma's Mom-related opinions with a grain of salt. She was always the first to forgive her. The first to run into her arms when she'd come back for us, no matter how long she'd been gone.

Being two years younger, Emma wasn't fully aware of how bad things got. I always made sure she was safe in her room, either asleep or with the television on loud enough to drown out the yelling and commotion when Mom and one of her boyfriends would fight. Or the nights Mom would come home stumbling and belligerent. Emma never saw me carry Mom to bed wasted. She never saw me pushing Mom on her side so she wouldn't choke on her own vomit.

When Mom would inevitably take off, some family members would lie to us, claiming she left "to work." Emma believed it more often than not, whereas I knew the truth. I was old enough to understand the whispers between adults, the complaining about how she always did this. I knew how frustrated they were with her for leaving them with two extra mouths to feed and no timeline for when she'd return, if ever.

Sometimes it's frustrating that Emma has such a rosy perception of who Mom was, but I wouldn't have it any other way. Not only do I want to protect Emma, but the two of them formed a close bond over the years that I'd never want to tamper with.

"But, Em, she's been . . . making me breakfast. Actually asking me about my life, meddling, when she's not pissed at me for existing," I say, pacing up and down the driveway. I have the day off before the football game with Andi tonight, and I've been antsy about it since I woke up at the crack of dawn.

She slants me a *Where have you been?* look. "Yup. That's what us moms tend to do. It was hard for me, too, you know. I had a lot of resentment toward her. But when I had kids, it changed."

"How so?"

"On one hand, I knew I'd never repeat her mistakes. I couldn't and still can't understand how someone could leave their kids like she did. But I also look at them and think about how I'd feel if they turned their backs on me. If they looked at me like a massive disappointment after I'd turned my life around. I'd be brokenhearted." Emma is highly empathetic and has been ever since she was a kid. "I know it's weird for you, but you have to realize Mom isn't the person she used to be. She got help, she got better. For us. It would be nice if you could see that . . . before it's too late." I know what she means by that. She wants me to forgive Mom before her mind is gone entirely. As great as forgiveness sounds in theory, actually doing it is a whole different story.

I sigh. "Trust me, I want to be in a good place with her, too. But I'm scared it's too late. She's having way more bad days than good now."

"I noticed," she adds, her mouth curling into a small frown. "Mom and I argue more than we ever have, too, even before she went to rehab. Like whenever I visit and start cleaning or doing anything for her, she gets annoyed if it's not done how she likes it. She was also upset for a while because I came over too much, and then when I didn't come over enough. I think she's still mad at me for starting up the salon."

"She's not," I insist, if only for her sake. "She's proud of you. She told me the other day."

"I still feel guilty, though, leaving you with Mom, especially since things are getting . . . worse."

"Em, don't even think that. I was gone for ten years. Coming back for a couple months was the least I could do. Besides, it's not as bad as I thought it would be, especially if it means you finally get to do what you love. How are things going at the salon anyway?" I ask.

"I didn't realize how much goes into it. Hiring, marketing, product inventory, payroll. I've been getting there at, like, five in the morning and staying until way past dinner."

"Shit. A lot more complicated than cutting people's hair."

She tips her chin in a nod. "Sure is. The other day, I had to bring the kids because day care was closed. In the span of an hour, Maisey almost drank bleach and Carter waxed one of his eyebrows off."

I snort. "Jesus. They are feral."

"But honestly, I didn't realize how much I missed working, though. Not that being a stay-at-home and taking care of Mom wasn't work. It's just . . . having something tangible of my own. Being an entrepreneur, it's something I never thought I could do. And I'm doing it."

"You are."

"If you hadn't come home and been here to help, none of this would have been possible. I'm really grateful. Actually, speaking of, I have some good news."

I brace myself. "Good news?"

"I got the call yesterday. Lakeside officially has a spot for Mom at the beginning of September."

I can barely comprehend what she's saying. "But wait, what about the other place? The Marshes?"

"It's less ideal. She'd be on a dementia floor with mostly men. And there's less one-on-one care and activities. It is cheaper, though, so I understand if that's something you're concerned about."

I stare down at my feet, taking it all in. "Holy shit."

"It's good news, Nolan," she says.

"Does Mom know?"

"Yeah. I talked to her this morning. She really preferred this place, so it's a done deal."

"Wow," I say. "That escalated quickly."

"We'll need to put the house up for sale, go through everything and figure out what to keep, what to get rid of." As much as none of us want to sell, we need the house money to pay for the facility.

Em goes on about how she has a friend who's a Realtor who

can get us on the market quick. Frankly, I'm still overwhelmed by the prospect of clearing out the house, let alone listing it.

We chat a bit about the kids and work before she's due to get to the salon. When Em leaves, Mom suggests we take a walk.

"You look like you could use the distraction," she says, wiping the sweat from her forehead with the back of her gloved hand. I think about what Emma said about forgiveness. Mom is definitely trying; there's no doubt about that. Me giving her attitude like I'm an angsty sixteen-year-old isn't helping matters. Besides, I could definitely use a distraction, so I take her hand.

"Theresa will be coming over tonight to keep you company while I'm at the football game with Andi," I remind her as we make our way down the street, which is shaded by mature oaks lining the sidewalks. It's an old street, filled with old homes on large lots that are in high demand with upper-middle-class professionals due to its proximity to downtown. We moved into this house when I was in high school. Back then, the neighborhood was sketchy. Undesirable. But it was a big deal, because it was the first place we ever lived in that wasn't an apartment. Emma used to call it a mansion, despite it being a small two-bedroom bungalow. Back then, it was by far the most run-down one on the block. But Mom's done a lot of work on it since then, because it looks as well-kept as the rest.

Mom nods, seemingly remembering our conversation this morning at breakfast. I always spell things out now, because as the day wears on, her memory worsens. "Are you two football fans?"

"Not really." When she swings me a curious look, I add, "But her boss gave us the tickets for free."

"Is this your first formal date?"

I shrug. "Technically. We had lunch together the other day at work, if that counts."

"Do you want some advice?" she asks. Her question shocks me, because she's never been the kind of mom who doles out advice. Before I get the chance to say yes or no, she leans in. "When you go out to eat, sit on the same side of the table."

I flash her a puzzled look. "On the same side? Why?"

"Sitting across the table is so . . . formal. Like a business meeting. Whereas sitting on the same side is romantic," she tells me, a glint in her eye. "You can cuddle, touch, read the menu together, share each other's food, whisper sweet nothings in each other's ears."

I can't help but smile. "I never knew you were such a romantic."

"Me serial dating your entire childhood wasn't your first clue?" she replies, a wry grin spreading across her face. It occurs to me that she's poking fun at herself.

A laugh bursts out of me. "You did have a lot of boyfriends. I wouldn't consider any of them romantic, from what I remember." And that's putting it nicely.

She nods in hearty agreement. "Remember Vic?"

"The one with the tribal tattoos?" I confirm. Vic wasn't terrible, compared to the rest. And by that, I mean he never yelled or hit her (that I know of). He was a quiet guy, uninterested in Emma and me. But he seemed to hold down a job at a mechanic shop down the street, which was a plus.

"That's the one. I don't think I ever told you, but he proposed. With a ring from Walmart."

I snort. "Did he tell you it was from Walmart?"

"He didn't have to. He got down on one knee right there in the Walmart jewelry aisle before he even paid for it." She starts full-on belly-laughing in the middle of the sidewalk. It's contagious, to the point where I'm laughing with her. I've noticed she enjoys talking about the past, even if it's not entirely rosy. Maybe because those older, core memories are the clearest, compared to recent memories.

"And what did you say?"

"I said yes, of course. We broke up the next week. Anyway, all that to say, Vic was the one who taught me about sitting on the same side of the table. I've done it with every boyfriend since."

I consider that, swinging her a curious glance. "You haven't dated in a while, have you?"

She shakes her head. "No. I've only had one relationship since I got sober."

"Why is that?"

"In my treatment program, my therapist talked to me about how I was using men as a way to fill the void."

"Void?"

"The one your grandfather left. I was looking for love to replace my father's love, and my mother's." I don't know much about my grandparents, aside from the fact that he left early on in her childhood. I've always known that as a fact, but for the first time, it occurs to me that she didn't have things easy growing up, either. How could she be expected to be a good parent when she didn't have that herself? "In treatment, I realized the only way to fill that void is by finally loving myself. By taking care of myself and being pickier about who I date."

"Wow. That's really great, Mom," I say, though it sounds a

little weak coming out of my mouth. I hadn't realized the extent of her therapy or that she'd worked that deeply on herself. "You deserve to be pickier."

"Turns out, when you're sober, men are terrible."

I laugh, despite the pang of sadness at the fact that she never found anyone to settle down with. "You deserve someone good," I tell her, and I mean that.

She smiles. "You think? By the time you get to my age, all these men want are wives to cook and clean for them while they're out playing golf all day."

"Maybe you'll meet someone at Lakeside," I say, finally broaching the topic.

"That would be nice. Though I hear dating can get competitive in these places. Honestly, I'm just happy to be going there instead of that other place. There's a beautiful waterfront trail I can take my morning walks on. They have so many activities, too. I think I'll be just fine on my own."

"Then why are you so adamant about me settling down?"

She stops walking and appraises me. "You and I are very different. I spent my whole life chasing after love, after terrible men, desperate for their approval, trying to be what they wanted. But you've spent your whole life running from love."

Her words strike me hard in the chest. My first instinct is to deny it, because that's what I do when it comes to anything she says about me. I've always deduced that she doesn't know me. But maybe she knows me more than I thought.

We walk the rest of the block in a comfortable silence. As we pass by a field of wildflowers, I spot a group of daisies and stop to gather some, handing a bunch to Mom. Her eyes light up.

"You used to pick me daisies when you were a little boy," she says, a massive smile splitting her face. "Remember that day we spent at Dow's Lake?"

I nod, vaguely remembering it. I think I was about seven. I'd faked sick that day because Mom was home and I wanted to spend extra time together, just me and her. She took me to the park and we lay out in the grass on a giant picnic blanket. She'd brought snacks, and we looked at shapes in the clouds.

It was a good day. A really good day.

Maybe not all days with her were as bad as I thought.

CHAPTER 22

Andi

The stadium is overflowing with patrons double-fisting foamy beers, their voices mixing together with the music in thunderous chatter. It's a sea of red and black, people dressed in jerseys, faces painted. It's a fuller stadium than I expected, not that I've ever been to a game before to compare.

Eric and Gretchen's box is center field, boasting a long buffet table filled with food and desserts, as well as its own bar. Even the seats are premium leather. By the time I arrive, it's filled with people milling about and socializing. They're mostly senior staffers or Cabinet members, but there are some younger staffers in the mix, who were likely given tickets by their bosses.

The moment I set foot in the box, everyone seems to stop mid-conversation, solely to stare. At me. And while it's just the box, it might as well be the entire stadium.

Until these rumors, I've always been a background character in my own life. Not a side character, or even a tertiary character.

And certainly not the main character. Just a faceless, nameless blur of a person blending into the background.

Standing out was something I actively avoided, because that offered a new opportunity for critique. If Dad, Amanda, or I did anything wrong, Mom called it out immediately. That's her personality trait, to find a flaw in literally anything. Our clothes, hair, grades, the way we spoke or acted in public.

So naturally, I'm a millisecond away from bolting when someone shouts my name. "Andi!"

It's Nolan. I know his voice instantly. It cuts straight through my nerves, putting me at ease, if only a little. He's waving at me from a pair of plush seats in the front and center.

My eyes latch on to his like a life raft as I make my way through the crowd. I feel like I'm tiptoeing through an active minefield, putting one foot in front of the other until I make it to the end. To him.

He's in dark-wash jeans and an off-white waffle crewneck, sleeves pushed up a little to the elbows. Even his dark hair is a little more mussed up than usual. The casual look suits him. I'd like this look spread on a cracker and served to me on a platter, thanks.

As I approach, he gives me a smile that illuminates his whole face, the corners of his eyes crinkling adorably. And then he does something near fatal. It's not the fact that he stands, moving swiftly to meet me at the end of the aisle. Or that he pulls me into a warm embrace, his fingers drawing little circles into the small of my back. It's the press of a kiss on my forehead.

Everything numbs and fades around me. The crowd, the stadium. It's only silence. His fresh-showered, minty scent enveloping me. His lips, pillowy smooth against my skin, sending little sparks cascading down my spine, unhitching my insides. No one has ever kissed me on the forehead like that—like they were claiming me.

If you were to play it back in real time, it's probably just a quick dusting. A terse kiss for the duration of a blink in front of everyone for show. An act, like we agreed upon. So why did it just tilt my whole world?

We kissed back in Squamish and acted couply at lunch the other day. But I've never entirely lost myself. I've never lost sight of what it really was, even if it felt like something more.

Just be cool. He's doing this as a favor, as a friend, I remind myself as he ushers me to our seats.

You wouldn't know it. Not when he smiles at me like this, so big it practically splits his face. His gaze roams over my T-shirt and denim shorts. It's probably the most casual I've ever dressed in front of him, aside from my PJs. "You look beautiful." His voice is so low, I'm not certain anyone could have heard it, aside from maybe the people in the row behind us.

"Thank you. You look great. I was starting to forget what you looked like out of a suit. What's with the bag?" I ask, nodding toward the comically large IKEA shopping bag at our feet. "Security barely let me bring my purse in."

"You said your favorite thing was to hang out at home with snacks and a blanket." He proceeds to pull a soft, fluffy blanket out of the bag, followed by what appears to be the entire contents of the snack aisle at a gas station. All varieties of chips, chocolate bars, and candy, including licorice allsorts. "I may or may not have bribed the security guard with candy to let me bring it in."

Holy shit. "You brought licorice allsorts? I thought you said they taste like depression, but with sprinkles."

"I stand by it. But you said they were your favorite, so who am I to deprive you?"

I am officially a Popsicle melting in the sun. "You really didn't have to do all this. Honestly, I don't expect anything but for you to show up—"

He spares a glance at each person milling about behind us, some of whom are most definitely looking at us, probably wondering why the hell we're here instead of Eric and Gretchen, before leaning in. "Andi, if there's one thing you should know about me, it's that I don't do things half-assed."

"No?"

"Nope. If I'm going to be your boyfriend for the summer, I'm going to do it right," he declares.

Warmth flares in my chest, lighting me up in long-forgotten, dusty corners of my mind that haven't been activated . . . ever. "You're definitely doing a good job. Is everyone still staring at us?" I whisper, the awareness of our surroundings creeping back.

He angles himself to the crowd of senior staffers behind us. "Yup. Still staring, which is a good thing. The more they talk about us, the less they'll talk about you and Eric."

His reminder is the only thing that keeps me from sinking low in my seat. He's right, after all. And I use it as the perfect excuse to take his hand, shift my knees toward him, and let myself imagine this is all real. Like I'm one of those women in my books with a doting partner, someone thoughtful and kind.

"Did you play sports? As a kid?" I ask as we watch the players warm up on the field.

"Yup. Not football, though. Played pretty much everything else. Mostly hockey. Not that I could afford to play in a regular league. I played a lot of road hockey and for school teams," he explains.

"I'm guessing you're a Sens fan?" I ask.

"Like every Ottawa native should be. You?"

I laugh. "I don't really follow hockey. But if I did, I'd probably cheer for the Leafs, I guess, being from Toronto."

He gives a low headshake. "And there it is."

"What?"

"The flaw in our relationship."

I slap his knee. "Hey! If anything, it shows I'm loyal during times of adversity."

"Perpetually optimistic, too," he adds.

"This year could be their year. You never know."

He snorts. "Leafs fans have been saying that for a century now. I'll believe it when I see it."

"I knew you had hockey vibes the night we met."

"What gave it away?"

"I dunno. I think the hair," I say, imagining running my hand through it, tugging it a little. God, I need to rein myself in.

He smirks, pushing it back from his face. "My mom keeps telling me to cut it. She says it makes me look like a *lout*."

I snort. Before I can tell him not to cut it, someone wraps their arms around my shoulders. "Hi, stranger." It's Laine. Voice aside, I know it without even seeing her based on the cinnamon-and-apple scent of her perfume.

I whip around to her sitting in the seat directly behind me, barely concealing my shock. "Laine, hi! I didn't expect to see you—here—"

She explains how sometimes Hunter's boss gives them her box seats, though I barely listen through the shock. We haven't seen each other since a coffee and donut date back in early January, a few days after New Year's. Admittedly, the whole thing was rushed. We'd barely gotten past the "What's new with you?" small talk when Laine received an email about an urgent briefing and took off immediately, full latte and donut in hand.

She flicks her curls over her shoulder, revealing new highlights that make her hair appear almost copper. "Since when are you a fan of football?" The moment she asks, her eyes dart to Nolan, and her brow quirks in recognition.

"Oh, um, this is my friend. Boy. Boyfriend. Nolan." God. Lying is hard. Especially to Laine. We may not be close anymore, but she's still the closest thing I have to a best friend. "He's Eric's new CPO," I add.

She recognizes him from that night at the bar, based on her knowing expression. Her mouth quite literally forms an O as she leans forward to shake his hand over the back of the seat. "Nolan. We've . . . met before."

Apparently he recognizes her, too. "We have. Nice to see you again."

Her eyes flick back to me. "Clearly, we have a lot to catch up on. Hunter was telling me things are a little wild at work, after those headlines. I totally meant to reach out and see how you were doing."

"Oh, no worries. I'm great. I mean, obviously there's no truth to the rumors, so . . ."

She waves away my words like she already came to that conclusion on her own. "Obviously. Everyone knows the opposition is feeding the media all these BS stories. I'm honestly offended that people think you'd write filth like that." Grateful as I am for her defense, the word "filth" sticks. Nolan gives my hand a firm squeeze, stopping the pit in my stomach from expanding.

There's an awkward pause as Hunter inches into the seat beside her, two frothy beers in each hand. Of course, he's wearing a sweater-vest.

"Andi?" Like Laine, he looks shocked by my presence, and even more shocked by Nolan's.

"Hunter, remember all the slogans Andi used to come up with for the campaign?" she asks pointedly, forcing a weak nod out of him. "Wild that they think it's the same person who wrote that porny book."

"Uh, yeah," he says passively, handing her a beer.

"Anyway, I was just being reintroduced to Andi's new boyfriend, Nolan. Eric's CPO. Remember him from that night at the pub all those years ago? The guy she went home with?" she adds in a not-so-discreet whisper.

Hunter's eyes go wide in faux recognition, grateful for the topic switch. "Right! I've seen you with Eric but I thought you looked familiar. Nice to meet you, man. I'm Hunter."

Nolan tightens his lips, his gaze flicking to me for a millisecond before he extends his other hand in a greeting.

A beat goes by where we all just sit there, nodding, waiting for someone to break the painful silence.

Laine is the one who breaks it. "By the way, did you get our invitation?"

Shit. I consider lying and feigning surprise, but it seems like a fruitless endeavor. "I did. The cardstock was so . . . thick," I say, immediately regretting it. Who cares about the damn cardstock?

"That was Hunter's mom's choice. Like most things," she informs with a knowing brow raise, like I, too, know the struggle. I met Hunter's entire family once at a holiday party. They were nice and welcoming (aside from his bigoted uncle Frank), a family I could picture myself getting to know over time.

"Hey, it's taken all the work off your plate," Hunter reminds her.

"True. You know me. If I had it my way, we wouldn't even be having a wedding. I've been making sure it stays really low-key. I don't want any of it to feel like a traditional wedding, you know?"

"Right." A destination wedding in Mexico? Real low-key.

She goes on and on for at least fifteen minutes, listing all the ways their wedding is "not like a normal wedding," despite going on a long-winded rant about napkin colors. She's wearing a black dress, for one thing. The ceremony will only be two minutes, max. And there will be a buffet, no multicourse dinner. "Basically, I want it to be like a big party."

"Totally," I say, flashing a syrupy-sweet smile over my shoulder, desperate for the game to start so I can turn back around.

"Anyway, the deadline to RSVP is this week. I'll make sure to add a plus-one for you," she says with a wink. "We need to coordinate with the resort to make sure we have enough rooms blocked off—" A woman I recognize from Privy Council sinks into the seat next to Laine, capturing her attention, leaving Nolan and me with Hunter.

I'm about to come up with a bogus excuse to leave the conversation, but Hunter keeps talking. "Honestly, we won't be offended if you aren't able to make it," he says out of nowhere, which I interpret as, "Please don't come."

"I'll have to see. I need to confirm my vacation time—" I start.

"We'll let you know," Nolan declares.

"Great. Glad you're considering it. Laine was really worried you'd feel awkward." Hunter gifts me a sympathetic look, which makes me want to bash my forehead into the railing around our box.

"Why would I feel awkward? Because of our history?" I ask innocently. Maybe it's the fact that Nolan is at my side, but I'm overcome with the urge to make Hunter sweat a little.

"Exactly! I mean, you and I dated for, what—a couple months? I keep telling Laine how it wasn't anything serious, but you know her. She just cares so much."

Something twists through my chest. Hurt? Annoyance? Frustration? Probably a mix of all. I open my mouth to reply, but my mind is stuck on "a couple months" and "wasn't anything serious." Is he for real right now? *So the entire year we dated, lived together, and talked at length about our future wasn't anything serious?* I want to ask. I want to slap him. But of course, I'm me. I freeze.

Sensing my discomfort, Nolan swiftly tugs at my arm, gaze narrowed. "Let's grab a drink. The game is about to start."

"Yes!" I pop up, a little too enthusiastic.

We shuffle out of our seats and slip into the crowd, tucking ourselves into an empty spot near the bar to order our drinks.

Nolan absorbs me for a couple beats before speaking. "I know you said he wouldn't be the type to put his lips on the fountain nozzle, but I'd bet you a hundred bucks he did."

A deep laugh finds its way out, so much so, I nearly cough up my drink. "Thank you. I needed that. The conversation about cream or blush napkins almost did me in."

He snorts. "I must have blacked out before then. Probably

somewhere after she brought up the pros and cons of chair covers."

"I mean, I'm all for big, extra weddings if that's what people want. The part that gets me is that she keeps following everything up with *but it's going to be so chill*," I admit, feeling both relieved and also a little guilty for complaining about her.

"*Not like a regular wedding*," Nolan adds, doing his best Laine impression.

"Right? It's kind of annoying."

"Are you actually thinking of going?" he asks.

The million-dollar question I've been avoiding for weeks now. "Even if I wanted to go, I don't know if I'd be able to take three days off from work. Unless I get a bunch of my to-do list completed before."

"You know, you don't *have* to go," he reminds me, sensing my turmoil.

"I know. But how do I say no?"

"Easy. You check decline on the RSVP card and never think about it again."

Just the thought of it makes me shiver. "I don't know if I can do it."

"That tracks," he says, gently pulling me into his side.

I tip my chin up to meet his gaze. "What tracks?"

"You and your need to please people."

I set my drink down on the bar. "It just feels too harsh to decline. I owe it to my and Laine's friendship. If I didn't go, it would be a clear message that I don't want to be friends anymore."

"Are you still really friends?" he asks gently.

"Technically speaking, we're still friends. But we don't really hang out anymore, aside from maybe once or twice a year." It's only when I say it out loud that I realize how sad that sounds. It might be acceptable if we actually had meaningful conversations during those hangouts, but we don't. We don't have much in common anymore at all, really.

"She also called romance novels filth," he points out.

"I know. She can be a bit of a snob. And then there's the whole Hunter thing."

"Can I ask . . . is it hard being friends with someone who's dating your ex?"

I shrug reflexively, my go-to when anyone asks me that. Only, I'm with Nolan, probably the only person I can be honest with. "It threw me for a loop at first. It was so soon after our breakup that it made me kind of paranoid, wondering whether they had feelings for each other while we were together. But I felt like I couldn't say anything because it's not like I wanted to be with Hunter. At the end of the day, she deserves happiness."

"You're a better person than I am."

"What would you do? Go and object at their wedding?"

He laughs, considering this for a couple seconds as a voice over the loudspeaker announces the start of the game. "I'd probably go enjoy the vacation out of spite and get completely wrecked at their open bar."

"That sounds . . . ridiculously fun."

"Right? You know what? You should do it."

"Object at their wedding or get wasted at the reception?"

"The latter."

I bite my lip, tempted. "What if I do or say something stupid?"

"You won't. I'll be right there to stop you from making bad choices."

I balance myself against the bar, blinking until his mischievous smile comes into sharp focus. "Wait, you want to go with me? To Mexico? What happened to not people-pleasing?"

"It wouldn't be people-pleasing. We'd be going for a vacation. The wedding would merely be a one-night obligation and excuse to drink for free." He grins sideways at me as I ponder. "Why not? I have the vacation time, and so do you on paper, even if you don't feel like you can take it."

The thought of going alone was terrifying. But going with Nolan? That changes everything. So I hold out my hand to lead him back to our seats, raising my head a little higher than before. "You know what? Let's go."

CHAPTER 23

Nolan

The crowd buzzes with excitement, animatedly recounting the notable plays, the wild touchdown that tied the game. Admittedly, I didn't see any of it. In fact, I didn't pay much attention to the game at all.

Even when Andi and I weren't talking, my mind was racing. First, there's all the questions I want to ask her, all the things I want to know about her. Then, there's the fact that we were holding hands. We've held hands before, but sitting there today with her made me feel like a ten-year-old again, pathetically losing it over the weight of her fingers intertwined in mine. The barely there thrum of her pulse, making me startlingly aware of every movement, every flex and squeeze. The way the warmth of her spread into my entire body, lighting it up.

By the time we funnel out of the stadium and onto the sidewalk, I'm not ready to end the night. So I suggest we take a walk along the canal. It's a warm night. It feels peaceful, especially with the city lights shimmering over the still surface of the water.

"Tonight was . . . fun." She says it contemplatively.

"You say that like you're surprised."

"I was pretty nervous to come here tonight," she admits, her eyes fixed on the pathway ahead. "I know we're not actually dating, but in social situations, I always overthink it and blank, especially with guys. Then I end up rambling and talking about embarrassingly niche topics, like emissions reduction targets. That actually happened, by the way. I almost put a guy to sleep on a date in grad school talking about climate change policy."

God, this woman is smart. I love it.

I resist the urge to tell her I could listen to her talk about climate change until the ice caps melt. Any policy. But I settle on, "Anyone who thinks saving the planet is boring strikes me as a massive asshole."

"He was a dick, come to think of it. He told me that he didn't recycle because it was *too complicated*. Anyway, that guy aside, I'm terrible at dating in general. That's why I don't do it."

My chest pinches when she says that. "I think you're probably better at it than you give yourself credit for. But how will you ever get good at it if you don't try?"

She shrugs. "I—I don't know. I don't enjoy trying things I'm not good at. It's one of my worst traits."

"One of?"

"I have a couple," she says wryly, the moonlight catching her profile. She looks obscenely gorgeous tonight. "I'm really selling myself here as a great fake girlfriend, huh?"

A snort rises out of me. "You know what? I like the honesty. I feel like this is how people should date. I feel like people aren't really themselves on first dates."

"That's very true," she says, her gaze following a couple strolling hand in hand, chatting softly. "That's the problem, actually. People are too busy putting their best foot forward, and then inevitably the flaws start coming out after you're already dating, little by little, which is probably why most relationships don't work out."

"Possibly," I say, considering it. "It would be ideal, knowing someone's bad traits before getting in too deep. A flaws section should be up front on every dating profile."

"Exactly. Then you can decide if you're willing to live with it."

She swings me an adorable, squinty smile. "Did we just revolutionize love and dating?"

"Sure did. We deserve a Nobel Prize. It would save a lot of broken hearts."

I turn, absorbing her like a sponge. "So what's yours? Your actual worst trait?"

Her gaze cuts to my eyes as she considers. "People-pleasing, probably. As you already pointed out earlier."

"Have you always been a people-pleaser?"

"Oh yeah. I was a rule follower. Never stepped out of line. Always did what I was told. I've spent my entire life being agreeable to make my parents happy, because they were miserable together. Mostly my mom. I felt like I had to keep the peace and make things happy for Amanda."

"Is your sister like that, too?"

"Nah. Amanda doesn't care what people think, which is my favorite thing about her. She's a free-spirited artist. She takes after my dad, which drives my mom nuts," she says with abundant sarcasm. "My mom has tried really hard to forget about the past and move on with Dave and his family, who are all . . . rich and uptight. Like her family."

"They sound amazing. When am I meeting them?" I tease.

"For your sake, hopefully never," she replies, dodging a cyclist coming in hot behind us. "Luckily, my mom rarely visits. I haven't seen her in, like, six months. Most of the time when I call, she gives me three minutes tops before she urgently has to go. She always says she'll call back, but she never does."

"Do you want to see her more?"

"I don't know. I always get excited at the prospect, but then actually being with her is really stressful. She's always critiquing, nit-picking. I can never do anything right. My job is never enough. My clothes never fit right. It takes a long time for me to recover."

My heart pinches at the sight of her, eyes cast downward at the ground. "Jeez. Sounds stressful. I can see why you never told her about your books."

"Precisely. I get enough critique from my readers. I don't need it from my own mother."

Frankly, this woman sounds fucking awful. I hate that she's made Andi feel so small, so self-conscious over the years. I'm struck with the overwhelming urge to stop walking and hug her. But instead, I settle for, "For the record, I don't think people-pleasing is a completely bad trait. I assume it's one of the things that makes you really good at your job."

She considers that over a burst of laughter from a group of teens taking selfies on the grass. We've walked so far, we've nearly reached Elgin Street. "Maybe. My sister says I'm desperate for Gretchen's approval in lieu of my mom's."

"Are you?"

"Probably. It sounds weird, but it feels nice to be needed, especially since my mom doesn't need me anymore," she admits plainly.

"That makes perfect sense, actually. I mean, that's part of what motivates people to do well. Everyone wants to feel valued and appreciated."

"That's true. Maybe it's stupid of me, but I really like Gretchen as a person. Despite what people probably think, she's a good person. She genuinely cares about all the causes she promotes, which is why she's so neurotic about all the details. And she's going through a really hard time, especially with the scandal, which is my fault. I guess I feel like I owe her."

It strikes me that Andi's dedication to her work is beyond "career." She has a huge heart. She truly cares about Gretchen, Eric, and their family. I don't think they realize how lucky they are to have her. "Between you and me, do you think she and Eric are happy? I mean, in Squamish, they didn't really talk much, did they?"

She shrugs. "They used to be the happiest couple. Lately, no. I mean, he's almost always gone. And even if he's home, he's in his office reading through briefings—not that he has a choice. It's the job. But they don't get a lot of quality time together."

I nod, taking a moment to rest on an empty bench. "I get that. It's kind of like long-distance. After so much time apart, you stop really knowing the person."

"It's a doomed way to live unless it were short-term," she agrees, parking herself next to me. My body buzzes at her proximity, at her thighs in those shorts. "How do you really get to understand what it's like to be partners when the other person is never there? You'd get used to being alone, and when they're finally back, it would be like getting to know them all over again. I guess you'd know. You mentioned in Squamish that your last relationship was long-distance."

I nod, explaining what happened with Penny, about her meeting someone else while I was away.

Andi cringes, stretching her legs in front of her, the muscles in her thighs flexing. "I'm sorry. That's really shitty of her."

I shrug. "Relationships rarely last in my line of work. There's always resentment because of the crazy schedule, sometimes cheating. Not worth the trouble, in my opinion."

"And you picture doing your job for a long time?"

"As long as my body will let me, yeah."

"You're okay to be single for the foreseeable future?" she asks, meeting my eyes.

"I don't know. Guess I planned to work so much, I wouldn't have time to think about it."

"Sounds familiar," she says with a chuckle. "Okay, it's your turn. What's your worst trait, aside from being a workaholic?"

"Okay, I don't know if this counts because I don't think I do it anymore, but when I was a kid, I had a sleepwalking problem."

"Sleepwalking problem?"

"Oh yeah. I moved around a lot as a kid, so I'd get confused about where I was. I'd go all around wherever we were living at the time, trying to make food, and make a huge mess. One time at my grandma's, I heated up water to make mac and cheese and I guess I decided to go back to bed and left the pot boiling on the stove. Another time, I literally left my aunt's house in the middle of the night in the dead of winter and went into the backyard to make snow angels."

She barks a laugh. "Sorry. I don't mean to laugh. That's actually terrifying and potentially dangerous."

"It's okay. You can laugh. It was so bad, I had to wear mittens to bed and sleep in a sleeping bag for a while."

She tries to bite back a grin, but fails and snorts instead. "Sorry. I'm picturing you all bundled like a gigantic burrito."

"I basically was."

"I can see why you don't do relationships," she teases. "The sleeping bag and mittens might be a deal-breaker."

"You don't think mittens in the bedroom are sexy?" I ask, in a mock serious tone.

She grins, but her expression quickly morphs into something heavier. "Can I ask you something?"

I nod.

"You mentioned a couple times living in a lot of places. Staying with your grandma or your aunt. You don't have to answer, but I was just curious—"

"No. It's okay. Um, my mom was in and out of our lives, pretty much from the time I was around four or five."

I explain how my dad wasn't in the picture and how Mom's life revolved around her boyfriends. How one of them convinced her she could become a singer and how she'd use it as an excuse to leave every few months, on this quest to be discovered. It feels easy, telling her this. It makes me wonder why I held off for so long like it's this big secret.

"So what happened to you guys when she'd leave?"

"Usually it was without notice. I remember a lot of times sitting with Emma on the curb, waiting to be picked up from school, but no one would be there. And then the office having to call all our relatives, asking them to pick us up." I tell her how we bounced between family members, none of whom wanted the burden.

She wraps her arms around herself and lowers her head, as though she's taken on the weight of my story. I feel immediately guilty for dumping all of that on her at once. "Shit . . . That's . . ."

"Heavy? Yup. That's why things are a bit complicated with my mom. Anyway, I really dampened the mood," I say as she shakes her head to deny it. "Now you're obligated to cheer me up with another bad trait."

She kicks her feet against the ground. "You did not ruin the mood at all. But okay, let me think . . . I'm too sensitive. Like . . . I'll cry at just about anything. If I'm stressed, I'll probably cry. If I'm mad, I'll cry."

"Ah, so you cry easily. How is that a terrible trait?"

"I don't know. It gets annoying for some people. Like, for example, orangutans are my favorite animal of all time. If I see a video or picture of them, I'll cry and it'll ruin the mood."

"Okay, I need to test this theory." I whip out my phone and search for orangutans on Google Images. "Does this make you cry?" I show her a photo of a large orangutan with flanges, eating a juicy-looking orange.

The photo draws out an instant beam. "No. Just baby orangutans."

I show her another. This time, it's a bunch of babies in a wheelbarrow. She immediately starts to tear up. I lean in to look closer. "Oh my god. You're actually emotional about it."

She wipes her watery eyes. God, she's fucking cute. "See?"

"Shit. I'm sorry for purposely making you cry. That makes me a horrible boyfriend," I say, forgetting to add the "fake" descriptor in there.

She doesn't appear to notice. "No. It's not your fault. I'm ridiculous."

"Not ridiculous. Adorable," I say. "Actually, I wish I cried more. I don't think I even remember the last time I cried."

"Really?"

"Nope. Haven't cried since I was a kid." I was on the phone with my mom, telling her I'd been a good boy, that I'd behaved at school, basically begging her to come get Emma and me from my aunt's. I'll never forget what she told me: "Nolan, you're ten years old," she said, even though I was nine. "You're a big boy. No more crying."

"Do you . . . want to cry?" she asks, eyes narrowing to slits.

"I mean, there's been a lot of times I probably should have cried, like at some of the shit I've seen overseas. But I don't know, my body won't let me."

"I'm going to give you a list of my top five saddest movies of all time. You're going to watch them and report back," she decides. She texts me a list of movies with *The Land Before Time* at the top. "If you don't cry at the part where the mom dies, you're officially a robot," she warns, standing with a stretch. When she lifts her arms, the hem of her shirt lifts a little, revealing a small patch of soft skin around her stomach. And don't even get me started on the way her shorts hug the curve of her ass.

I smirk, questioning my ability to stand at this point. "Okay, challenge accepted."

While we wait for her Uber, we go back and forth for a little while, telling each other about our terrible habits. I'm a horrible loser when it comes to games. She likes to fall asleep with the TV on. I tend to let my dirty clothes pile up for a couple days too long before doing laundry. She takes showers long enough to drain the hot-water tank.

She turns around before getting into the Uber. "Nolan?"

"Yeah?" I manage, taking her in. Shit. She's gorgeous.

"This was the best date I've ever been on. Even if it was fake." She fiddles with the sleeve of her sweater, her clear, twinkling eyes reflecting the golden light of the streetlamp above when they find mine again.

I don't stop smiling the whole way home.

CHAPTER 24

Andi

I didn't think the sales for *The Prime Minister & Me* could get any better, but I've finally cracked #1 on Amazon in multiple categories. Never in a million years did I think that could happen to me. In a twisted way, it's all thanks to the opposition. Bethany confirmed during a meeting with Gretchen that they've been aggressive in peddling the affair stories.

I know that what's happened has nothing to do with raw talent. It's pure dumb luck. It's about striking gold, writing what people want to read at the right time, and being privileged enough to get the visibility.

After years of struggling to hit readership in the four figures, despite endless hours on social media, trying to connect with readers, making elaborate promo graphics, always being behind the eight ball on marketing trends, I'd always assumed it was me. Maybe people didn't connect with my writing. Maybe I simply didn't have the talent. Because of the self-doubt, I used my day job as a scapegoat. An excuse not to write anymore. What was the point in breaking my back, finding time to write books hardly anyone read? But I'm starting to wonder if I was wrong.

My DMs and emails are out of control to the point where I can't even keep up, let alone respond. Most are positive: people begging for a sequel, saying they binge-read it in one sitting. So I'm taking Nolan's advice and embracing the only positive to come out of this shitstorm.

It's encouraging, at the very least. Ever since I met Nolan, my creativity has sparked to a level that I can't ignore or neglect any longer. But now that so many new readers are finding my books, it's like a fire hose, ideas coming at me before I can make an excuse not to do anything with them. I'm even coming up with lines and dialogue in my head while at work, all of which I furiously record in my notes app for when I can spin them into magic late at night.

Of course, life finds ways to keep me humble. The AC in my apartment stopped working for unknown reasons and I had to sleep two nights nude, with a fan on full blast, until my landlord finally decided to send an HVAC guy to fix it.

"I'm going to Laine and Hunter's wedding in Mexico, by the way," I tell Amanda casually.

"Shut up! You are not!" she yells, to the horror of the woman in downward dog next to us. Hot yoga isn't exactly my first choice of activity on a Saturday morning, especially when my apartment has been a sauna the past few days. But I'm willing to suck it up for my sister.

"Yup. It's the third week of August."

"Why are you flying to Mexico for them?" she asks, annoyed on my behalf.

"Because I'm happy for Laine and I want to support her," I say truthfully. "And because Mexico might be fun."

"Um, only if you have someone to hang out with. I volunteer as tribute!"

"Well, about that. I actually have a date." My face involuntarily softens into a giddy smile when I say it.

She springs up, catching my smile before I can force it back to neutrality. "A date? I thought you were 'too busy to date'?" She makes air quotes.

"I am. He's just a friend from work," I inform with a casual wave of my hand, even though it's starting to feel anything but casual. The Redblacks game confirmed the worst. Something I've been scared to admit since Squamish, or even the first night we met: that I have a crush. A *crush*. On a man who'd rather eat glass than stay in this city much longer.

Not that it matters, because he doesn't see me that way. In fact, he specifically said he appreciates our "friendship" because we can talk about anything, which is true. I've opened up to him more than I've ever opened up to anyone. And maybe that's a normal thing friends do. Maybe I've been so starved for friendship all these years since Laine and Hunter, I can no longer tell the difference between a reciprocal friendship based on a solid foundation of trust, and a romantic relationship. That must be it. Either way, I need to get my feelings in check, quick.

Amanda slow-blinks and gives me her *Are you for real?* head tilt. "Ands, you don't have friends, last I checked. And Laine doesn't count, even if she did pity-invite you to her wedding."

I give her a swift kick in the thigh with the ball of my foot. Damn her for being entirely correct. "You think it's a pity invite?"

She nods. "A hundred percent. She still has lingering guilt over breaking girl code, which is why she's kept you strung along all these years."

"Well, that's harsh," I note, scratching my head in thought. Is that really what Laine has been doing? Maintaining a thread of friendship because she feels bad for me? Not because she still enjoys my company from time to time? Not because she still cares about me as a person? "I don't think she's been stringing me along. We've each been taking turns reaching out to catch up."

Amanda doesn't look so sure. "All I'm saying is, it's okay to admit that your friendship has . . . expired. You don't need to have some epic argument for a friendship to end. Some really amazing friendships just fade away with time, without any rhyme or reason. And that's not a bad thing. It means you're evolving, changing."

Evolving. Changing. "I'm not so sure. I've felt stagnant the past three years," I point out. The only time I don't feel stagnant is when I'm writing.

"You have been," Amanda agrees. "But I mean you and Laine specifically. You two are in entirely different places than you were when you first met, and I don't just mean Hunter." She's right. I've gone through a whole relationship and gotten my job with Gretchen, which has taken over my life. Laine is equally busy working her way up the ranks at PCO . . . and now getting married.

"Yeah. Maybe," I say, mostly to appease her. Truthfully, what she's saying rings true. Laine and I have little to nothing in common anymore, aside from Hunter. At the same time, she was my best friend. All those days working side by side, laughing over our cubicle walls. The late-night takeout at the office when we were slammed with data entry and cold-calling. She was the first true best friend I really had. It's hard to come to terms with leaving her in the rearview entirely. I care about her and I still want her in my life, even peripherally, even if it means I have to put up with Hunter from time to time. And fly to Mexico.

"And she's asking a lot of you with this wedding," Amanda says, reading my mind. "Going to Mexico for three days isn't exactly cheap. Not to mention, that's three days of awkwardness, pretending to be happy for them."

"I am happy for them," I point out. "Laine deserves happiness. And Hunter . . . he isn't my favorite person. Do I wish for someone better for Laine? Of course. But he makes her happy and that's the most important thing. Besides, it won't be as awkward with Nolan."

I make the grave mistake of inadvertently smiling when I say his name, which causes Amanda's jaw to drop. "Are you two fucking?" she asks straight up. That's the thing about Amanda—she doesn't have a filter, even around Mom and Dave's crusty family.

"No! Just hanging out. Platonically." I consider explaining our *arrangement* and why we've been spending so much time together, but telling her we sometimes pretend to be in love in front of colleagues would only add fuel to the nonexistent fire.

"And he wants to go all the way to Mexico with you, for a wedding of total strangers, to hang out with you *platonically*?"

"Neither of us wants a relationship. He's not planning on staying for long."

"It's not a relationship I think he's after," she says knowingly, stretching her leg back so far, my body hurts just looking at her.

"He wanted to support me because he knew it was going to be a weird situation. Trust me, he's a really good guy."

Her eyes flatten into slits. "I'm sure he is. Doesn't mean he isn't hoping to hook up with you after a few too many glasses of champagne at the reception."

"He's leaps and bounds out of my league," I assure, second-guessing myself as it comes out. Is it possible he does want to hook up? We did have that moment in our hotel room in Squamish where it felt like he did—until he put a stop to it. I pull up the photos Gretchen took of me and him in Squamish and scroll to my favorite one before handing my phone to Amanda, who's now transitioned to cobra pose. I'm smiling into the camera while Nolan is looking at me with an open-mouthed smile, like he's amused by something I've done or said. I like it because it doesn't look too posed, even though the whole thing was heavily orchestrated.

At a single glance, she throws my phone back onto the yoga mat like it's coated with infectious bacteria. "Holy shit. Why didn't you tell me he looked like that? I deserved some fair warning!" she screams, chin hitting the mat.

"I basically just did!" I holler back, matching her volume, to the horror of our fellow yogis.

"Why are we screaming?!"

"You started it," I note, reverting back to my indoor voice before whispering, "Sorry, I'm, um, new to yoga."

She sits up on her knees. "I didn't expect him to look like Jack Ryan."

"My point exactly. He could probably sleep with anyone he

wants. Why would he want to hook up with me? I look like a librarian."

"Librarians are hot, Ands. Shushing people with authority? Punishments for overdue books? Some people are into that. Besides, it's always the serious ones who have a wild side."

I work through a violent cough. I am not having this conversation with my little sister. "Anyway, Nolan is coming with me as moral support."

"If you say so," she says knowingly, clapping her hands together. "I can't wait to know what Hunter is gonna wear for the ceremony. How much do you want to bet he'll be in a vest?"

"What's wrong with a vest?" I ask innocently to rile her up.

"Oh, nothing if you're a fifty-year-old man on the brink of collecting that sweet pension." She was never a fan of Hunter, even while I was dating him. She thought he was a smarmy, power-hungry social climber. "Mark my words. He's gonna look like that guy from *Peaky Blinders*, but the cheap knockoff version from Shein."

I let out a loud snort, earning a warning look from the instructor at the front of the room.

By the end of class, I find out about the new guy she's hanging out with, Geo. They met on Hinge and she has a theory he's lying to her about his career.

"He says he's a pilot," she tells me. "But his friend told me he actually works at the Booster Juice in the airport."

"That's . . . a really odd thing to lie about. Like . . . you could find out really easily."

She shrugs, like it doesn't matter to her. And it probably doesn't. "I figure he'll tell me when he's ready to. Hey, by the way, did I tell you I'm probably heading to BC with Hannah in the fall?"

"The girl who used to live in a storage space?" I confirm. Amanda has so many friends of all varieties, it's hard to keep track. Whenever I talk to her, I'm reminded how remarkably boring my life is in comparison. We get together around once a month, and every time, she has new friends, probably a new gig, and a new place to live. She's always in motion. Meanwhile, I've had the same apartment, job, and general routine for over three years.

She nods. "Yup. She has a really nice studio off Rideau I was going to move into, but it might have roaches and a poltergeist, so we decided to break the lease and go to BC for a couple months."

"BC, interesting," I say.

"I've actually been talking to Dad about it," she says nonchalantly.

"You have?" I haven't talked to him in a while, though he does text me every so often with funny anecdotes and dad jokes he thinks I'll like.

"Yeah. He's living in the Interior right now. I was thinking of seeing if I could stay with him for a few days. We haven't seen him in, what, almost two years?"

"At least," I say. It makes me sad that it's been that long.

Her posture stiffens. "You won't tell Mom, right?"

"Why would I tell Mom, of all people?" In fact, I've been dodging her uncharacteristically frequent calls the last few weeks. She leaves long-winded voicemails every time someone new (of societal importance) asks whether I'm a mistress or whether I wrote *The Prime Minister & Me.* The latter of which is somehow worse in her mind.

"I don't know. You talk to her more than I do. She came to visit you at Thanksgiving."

I snort. We used to be closer before she remarried, before I moved to Ottawa, back when I was desperate for her approval. "Yeah, she came for, like, an hour. She complained the entire time about the homeless people outside my apartment. Went on a tirade about how one person was wearing a Columbia coat that looked expensive. Because apparently you must wear rags as a poor person. She basically threatened not to visit until I move."

Amanda frowns. "God. She really is delusional, isn't she? I told you. She completely forgot that used to be us. Erased it from her memory entirely."

"I think it's the opposite. She remembers it so much, she's desperate to put herself as far away from it as possible."

"It's kind of sad, really," she decides. "Imagine being so insecure that all you care about is what people think."

I work down a swallow. "Really sad," I agree, even though I understand it a little more than I'd like.

CHAPTER 25

Nolan

Who knew an animated movie for children could be so depressing?

Andi texted me her list of top five saddest movies while we were at the game the other night. I started with *The Land Before Time*. I don't normally watch a lot of movies. I tend to fidget, unable to let my mind rest and escape. It's a symptom of the job, being on guard, assessing, watching for danger. It's my default state. But this one held my attention, maybe because it's designed for kids with an equivalent attention span, or maybe I'm just desperate for something to talk to Andi about. Either way.

Based on the cover and description, I didn't think much of it. I was wrong.

NOLAN: Watched land before time.

I stare at the screen, waiting for a reply. She takes forever to text back. And by forever, I mean half an hour. It might as well be an eternity.

ANDI: And?

NOLAN: Still not crying, but pretty damn close.

ANDI: Haha. You should move on to #4. I have a feeling that one might spark something.

Fourth on her list is a '90s movie called *Stepmom*. I consider asking her to watch it together. Then again, I don't know if I can handle another sad movie. Not after what happened yesterday.

When I came home from work, Mom had pulled all the files from the cabinet. She was on hands and knees on the floor among the mountain of scattered papers, frazzled, convinced she had a tax return she needed to fill out by the end of the day. I made the mistake of telling her there was no form, which frustrated her to the point where she hurled the cabinet padlock at me.

I've never in my life seen her that angry, let alone violent. Not even when one of her boyfriends stole hundreds of dollars' worth of savings from under her mattress. After getting her to bed, I panicked and called Emma. The doctor had warned us about the possibility that her disease could manifest in unpredictable, violent outbursts. But it's one thing to hear it in theory, and another thing when a piece of steel is being hurled at your head.

When she woke up this morning, she was back to her normal self, '80s music blaring, asking if I wanted to join her for breakfast.

"What are you doing alone on a Saturday?" Mom asks, eyeing me suspiciously from her chair. After our walk, she napped while I did a quick workout. Her nap went a little longer than expected, which was how I found myself on the couch watching a sad children's movie. After it was over, Mom came out and put on her favorite show, *Coronation Street*.

"I'm not alone. I'm with my mom." It actually feels good saying that.

"Watching British cable dramas," she reminds me. "What's Andi doing today? Is she busy or something?"

"We don't have to hang out all the time. And I'm texting her right now."

"But you'd rather be with her, in person," she counters, smirking. Am I really that obvious?

"We've both been busy with work. I didn't want to bother her on the weekend. And I'm spending the day with you—"

"I don't need to be babysat," Mom says firmly, entirely forgetting yesterday's events. "Besides, Katrina is coming over to watch a movie with me in an hour," she adds, referring to our longtime neighbor. Katrina has been wonderful, always offering to fill in if I need to go out or want a break. I've never taken her up on it, mostly because I feel too guilty asking.

I shoot Katrina a text to confirm the plan. She responds immediately, saying that she's happy to stay until midnight and that I should go out with my "lady friend." Clearly she and my mom have been talking.

Still, I'm hesitant. "I don't know, Mom. It's last-minute. What if Andi already has plans?"

"You won't know if you don't ask."

"You think I should call her?"

It feels a little weird to call Andi out of the blue to hang out on a random weekend, seeing as it's outside the confines of our arrangement. After the football game, our only obligations are work lunches, the all-staff summer social, Mom's "birthday" dinner in a few days, and the gala.

I'm also not looking to cry in front of Andi, which I feel closer to doing after that movie than I ever fucking have. Something tells me spending time together is asking for trouble. Besides, asking her to hang out would involve growing a pair, which I'm apparently incapable of doing where she's involved. I've literally jumped out of planes, engaged in close-quarter battle, been involved in hostage rescue, been shot at. Yet talking to this woman is scarier. That probably says more than I'd like.

"Why not? You want to hang out with her. I bet she wants to hang out with you, too. You're wasting way too much time worrying about what she thinks. Take it from me, days like this might feel slow, like you have all the time in the world. But you'd be surprised how fast months and years go by. Don't miss an opportunity to make memories with people you care about. They're all you have at the end of the day, unless you're me," she says with a snort.

"Did you just make an Alzheimer's joke?"

She nods, satisfied. "I did."

"That was dark, Mom. But actually, though, if you lose those memories, does it matter if you made them to begin with?"

"I may not remember everything, let alone what I did this morning, but what I do remember is how things made me feel. Happy, sad, it all sticks with you. That's worth its weight in gold."

I'm still thinking about Mom's words by the time *Coronation*

Street ends, and by the time I distract myself by tidying up the kitchen. Sure, Andi and I may not be dating. But I care about her as a friend. It's within the normal confines of friendship to ask her to hang out, isn't it? When I can't think of any more excuses to delay, I head to the back deck and take Mom's advice. I call.

She answers after two rings. "Hello?" Usually, Andi's voice is calming and sweet, like she's leaning in to share a secret. But right now, she sounds alarmed.

"You sound seriously disturbed. Everything okay?"

"Oh, uh, everything is fine. I'm just not used to people calling out of the blue, except for work."

I carefully lower myself into Mom's rickety folding chair, uncertain it can hold my weight. "Not a fan of phone calls?"

"People don't tend to call me in my personal life unless they have terrible or urgent news. Even Gretchen tends to text, asking me to call her for urgent matters."

"Well, I apologize. I thought since you're my fake girlfriend, I'd graduated to calling privileges. But I won't call anymore."

"No!" she assures. "I don't mind."

"Are you people-pleasing and you actually do mind?"

A pause. "Okay, maybe I'd prefer you to at least text me first and say you're going to call. Unless it really is an emergency."

"I can definitely do that."

"So what's up?" she asks, tone back to soft and casual.

"I was wondering if you had any plans today." The moment the words leave my lips, I squeeze my eyes shut, regretting my entire life.

"I was planning to write, but turns out, I have to work." I don't want to make assumptions, but she sounds a bit stressed.

"Gretchen's got you working on a Saturday?"

A sigh. "She's writing a vegan cookbook and asked me to batch-test eight different cookie recipes. A dozen each. I'm at home at least, but it's a little overwhelming."

I cough. "Eight types of vegan cookies? Holy shit."

"Yup. Vegan oatmeal raisin, vegan matcha, vegan lemon crinkle, to name a few."

A snicker escapes me. "Oatmeal raisin, huh?"

"Hey, those are actually my favorite."

"That tracks. With the allsorts."

She laughs. "In my defense, they're amazing and soft and chewy. Though I'm not overly optimistic about gluten-free, egg-less cookies. Anyway, sorry if I sound a little off. She sprang it on me this afternoon and I don't bake and—"

"I'll help," I cut in. "Not that I'm any good at baking, either. But I can follow instructions. Measure ingredients."

Another pause. "Nolan, are you actually offering to help me bake vegan cookies on a Saturday?"

"Yes." A resounding yes.

"You don't have other plans?" she asks skeptically.

"Well, I was watching *Coronation Street* with my mom. But she got annoyed with my questions and said I should be hanging out with my girlfriend. I basically got kicked out."

"So you're saying even your mom didn't want to hang out with you?"

"She did not. Pretty dismal, actually."

"A little bit. But if you're serious about helping, I'm heading to Peevey's in half an hour to get ingredients. Hopefully they have them. Do you think they'll have tapioca starch?"

"I have no idea what that is," I admit. "But if you need that amount of ingredients, I'd say our best bet is to start at Costco."

"Costco," she repeats. "Don't you need a membership to shop there?"

"It's your lucky day. I have one—well, my sister has a family membership." I never used to be a Costco shopper, but there's one just down the road, which is convenient. "I'll pick you up in exactly half an hour."

CHAPTER 26

Andi

Nolan stays true to his word and picks me up half an hour later, on the dot, which is sexier than it has any right to be. Why am I getting so hot and bothered by a man who abides by a strict schedule? My standards are devastatingly low.

When he rolls up in a champagne-colored PT Cruiser, he has to honk the horn and wave me down through the crack in the window before I recognize him.

"Sorry! I didn't realize it was you." I inhale a potent cloud of floral perfume as I slide into the passenger seat. An Alanis Morissette song is playing faintly on the radio.

"Didn't expect me to show up with these wheels?" He pats the dashboard affectionately, as though it's his trusty golden retriever, and flashes me a blindingly adorable smirk. I promptly shift my gaze for my safety. Maybe hanging out with him today was a bad idea. Maybe I'd said yes a little too hastily, without fully thinking it through.

"When you rolled the window down, I thought you were some creep offering me a ride or some loose candies," I inform.

"I don't have loose candies to offer you, unfortunately," he says, digging around in the console between us. He extracts a worn, wrinkled ziplock bag of what looks like birdseed crushed into a fine dust. "But I do have this bag of my mom's trail mix. Can't confirm how long it's been here."

I snort, reaching for my seat belt. "That's very generous of you, but I'm good."

Once he confirms I'm securely fastened, he rests his ropy forearm lazily on the wheel as he pulls onto the street. "Sorry for the subpar snacks and music. This is my mom's car, which she inherited from my grandma when she died, if you were wondering. The radio is permanently stuck on Easy Rock 103.4."

"Honestly, I kind of love this for you. I would have guessed you'd drive a truck, or something hardcore."

His mouth parts ever so slightly as he shoulder-checks me. "Ha, good guess. I used to drive an old Jeep, actually. But it crapped out when I first came home. It sat around all winter while I was overseas. My mom doesn't drive anymore so I've been commuting in this one."

"Well, it very much suits you. Thanks for coming and offering to help, by the way. I was really stressed-out." That's putting it lightly. When he called, I was close to a breakdown over almond flour, of all things. Just hearing his deep, reassuring voice was enough to put me at ease. Temporarily, at least. Because now, the nerves are bubbling to the surface in my chest like a shaken carbonated drink.

"We'll try not to burn your apartment down." He shoots me a quiver-inducing smile as we pull onto the highway.

The conversation is easy, like it always is. We mostly talk about work. I tell him how the gala prep is going. He tells me about his upcoming travel with Eric to Montreal and how he needs to pick up some groceries for his mom for while he's gone anyway. It strikes me how sweet he is to his mom, despite what he told me about their relationship and his childhood. I shift into the passenger-side door until my shoulder is squished against it, trying to resist the overwhelming, unsettling urge to hug him.

Thankfully, all it takes is one glance at the Costco parking lot to evaporate all those warm, fuzzy feelings. It's an absolute madhouse, with lines of cars zipping up and down rows in search of someone leaving. "Does this place always require police to direct traffic?" I ask genuinely, eyeing the stone-faced police officer in the intersection.

"Oh yeah. It can get pretty wild," he replies, nodding toward the fray. "I once witnessed a fistfight over a parking spot. A guy threw his fully loaded hot dog at the car's windshield."

"What a waste of a hot dog."

"That's what I said." He turns left, only to get honked at as we attempt to go down a lane, and then another, getting stuck behind at least five other cars vying for spots. Another loud honk pierces the air.

"Did that person honk at us? How are you so calm?"

He shrugs, entirely unfazed. "When you've driven in some of the places I've driven, a Costco parking lot in Ottawa is nothing. I take it you don't come here often?"

"Nope. As a single person living alone, I've never needed to shop in bulk— Oh!" I yell, pointing a couple rows over. "There's a spot!"

"Is your seat belt on?"

I nod and we rip over, only to be beaten out by a granny in a van. It happens at least three times before we finally manage to get a spot at the farthest edge of the lot.

"Wait, did you say you're a Costco virgin? You've never been, ever?" he confirms.

"My parents couldn't afford bulk shopping. And I tend to avoid crowds," I say, following him through the parking lot toward the entrance.

"Ahh, that's why you shop in the middle of the night."

"Precisely."

He lowers his shoulders and angles his head to the door. "Shit. Well, in that case, I feel bad dragging you here. Let's go to Peevey's."

"No, it's cool. I'll be fine," I say, gazing at the entryway filled with massive carts. I've always had anxiety about crowds, but I also know it's good for me to get out of my comfort zone. Besides, the drive to Costco wasn't exactly short. I don't want to waste Nolan's time, so I grab a humungous cart and push it through the entrance.

He saddles up beside me and inches me out of the way with his body, taking control of the cart. "I've got the cart, you'll read the list of ingredients."

I nod, scanning the vast expanse of aisles filled with everything from jumbo packs of toilet paper to fifty-gallon drums of olive oil.

"But first, we get ice cream," he says. When I swing him a questioning side-eye, he adds, "It's just a rule."

We stop at an area that serves an impressive array of food, including pizza and massive hot dogs. Nolan gets us two towering, perfectly crooked soft serve cones, which he insists on paying for. "Soft serve. To dull the ache of getting your toe rammed by a gigantic cart," he says, passing me my cone.

I thank him for the ice cream, ignoring the flutter at the base of my stomach when our fingers brush together for a millisecond. "No one rammed my toe, by the way."

"By the end of this, someone will have. Trust me."

Weirdly enough, navigating the crowd isn't as terrible as I'd imagined. Maybe it's the ice cream. Or maybe it's just a symptom of shopping with Nolan. The crowd tends to part for him in a way they never do for me, maybe because he's a tall man with a commanding presence.

"Is that a sample station?" I ask, nodding toward a spiky-haired lady behind a table serving little muffin holders of fresh banana bread.

He immediately swivels the cart toward it. "It is. Let's go."

"I thought Costco samples were the stuff of legend."

"Nope. You could come here for a whole meal's worth of food if you wanted to."

The lady looks like she'd rather be literally anywhere else, but he manages to charm a smile out of her. "Can I get one for my girlfriend as well?" he asks, so naturally, I almost believe him.

"Anything for such a beautiful couple," the lady says, revealing her dimples. She happily hands him a second sample, which he passes to me, his lips turning up in a grin. Not just any grin, but that boyish, infectious grin that makes my heart do a back handspring. For a couple aisles, I let myself imagine we're a real couple here on a Saturday afternoon. It's good practice for when we're at work, I justify to myself.

We make a game of it, grabbing ingredients and beelining to every sample station. I'm basically a kid in a candy store, indulging in everything from teriyaki chicken to smoked Gouda to chocolate-covered almonds.

We weave through the crowd, zeroing in on the quiche samples. Nolan checks in every so often to make sure I'm okay, which I am. By the time we reach the checkout, the cart is full, and Nolan is carrying a tray of mini cheesecakes he insisted we buy (to keep up the tradition). "So how was your very first Costco experience?"

"It's my new favorite place," I say, leaving out the fact that it's only because I was with him.

* * *

"How does it taste?" Nolan asks hours later, leaning his weight against my kitchen counter.

I stare up at him, letting the spicy cinnamon flavor melt over my tongue, attempting to mask my expression as I pass him the other half. We're so close, there's got to be less than an inch between our chests. And it's not by choice. That's how small my kitchen is.

Baking Gretchen's cookies was a tricky affair, between trying to keep all the ingredients organized and navigating such a narrow space between the two of us. There were multiple moments where we brushed against each other. Like when he reached around me to grab the sugar from the cabinet behind me, his beard grazed my cheek, our chests pressed together, and I lost a couple years off my lifespan. Maybe it was the shock, or the fatigue, or the cookies (though I don't think anyone in history has ever been turned on by a vegan cookie), but there was a beat where we both lingered there, frozen, until he pulled away abruptly and spun around to measure out a cup of sugar.

"Um, it tastes like . . . vegan," I say honestly, pulling at the fabric of my dress, which is basically glued to my chest with sweat. It's ridiculously hot in here, even with my AC fixed. That's the downside of living on the top floor of an old building. And then there's the fact that the oven has been on for four straight hours.

His lips twist as he finds out for himself. After one bite, he hits his own chest to force it down with a vicious cough. "That's . . . grainy. Do you think we messed up the recipe? Added too much cinnamon?"

"Nope. We read it over like, five times. I think it's supposed to taste like this . . ."

"Like potting soil?" he clarifies. He's not wrong. It does have a rather . . . earthy aftertaste.

I gobble it down like a hyena anyway, because eating myself into intestinal distress is my go-to coping mechanism when I'm tense (or in this case, an unbearably horny mess). "Good thing it's Gretchen's opinion that matters."

"At least we can say we tried," he says with a shrug, helping me pop the rest of the cookies into an old Christmas cookie container before I can do any more damage.

I pull myself onto the one free space on the counter, relishing the feeling of the cool laminate against my thighs. "Thanks for all your help. I feel bad that you spent your whole Saturday baking cookies with me." It took four hours, but we've made and labeled them all, except for the last batch of devil's chocolate chip, which is still in the oven.

"Nah. If anything, you helped me. I was having a crappy couple days. It was just nice to get out of the house and do something."

I consider asking him to elaborate on his bad days, but I don't want to pry. It doesn't feel like my place. "Seriously, though, I have no idea what I would have done baking these all by myself."

"You would have pulled it off. You're self-sufficient," he teases, leaning back against the counter next to me, hands planted on either side of him. It's not lost on me that his pinky is grazing my thigh, ever so slightly.

I force down a swallow at the contact. "When you've been single as long as I have, you don't really have a choice."

"Do you ever feel lonely?" he asks, immediately regretting it. "Sorry. That was rude. I've been spending too much time with my mom lately."

"No, it's okay. I do. Sometimes. When Hunter and I broke up, it was the small things I missed, more so than him. Like doing mundane things together. Errands, chores, even getting up in the morning, drinking coffee, all those small things that suck when you're by yourself." I still remember shuffling around the grocery store with my cart with that thickness in my throat, the deep ache I felt in my bones in those first few weeks after Hunter. "It's nice to have someone to do those things with. Someone to make the boring things tolerable, maybe even fun." *Like shopping with you at Costco*, I want to say. "What about you? Do you feel lonely?" I ask instead.

He tilts his head in thought. "I guess I probably am lonely, but usually too busy to notice until I'm in between assignments. I don't know if being lonely is enough of a reason to get into a relationship with someone."

"Right? Is it worth the stress? The potential heartbreak? All the emotional demands of being in a relationship? The independence is nice, too, once you're used to it. My mom was always so reliant on my dad or stepdad to do things for her. I like knowing I can figure things out for myself. Except building my IKEA desk," I add wryly.

He swings me a knowing look. "Or getting your patio door lock fixed."

"It's not that big a deal, though. I mean, I'm on the top floor." Truthfully, it's one of those pesky tasks I've always had on my to-do list but never gotten around to dealing with because other things always end up taking priority.

I try not to stare too long as he strides over to the living room to assess. "You don't think someone could climb the fire escape to the balcony? It's only six floors."

"The average person definitely can't," I say, following him.

He looks out the window and peers down. "They could. I'd bet my life on it."

"Maybe you could. If you really tried," I wager, trying to avoid the mental image. Too late.

"I wouldn't really have to try." He gifts me with a confident smirk over his shoulder. "Seriously, though, what if a crazed fan of yours finds out where you live?"

I snort. "Crazed fan?"

"You're a bestselling author, Andi," he points out. I wait a beat for him to laugh or crack a smile, but it doesn't come. He's dead serious.

"Under a pen name."

"Who's been doxed," he adds.

"Fair. But I still don't think I'm at the point where fans are going to come to my house and hold me hostage and demand I write, *Misery* style," I say, laughing at the mere thought that anyone could ever be so invested in my work that they'd bother to find out my personal information.

"I wouldn't be so sure. You're seriously talented. Have you ever thought of quitting your job? Writing full-time?"

I head to the kitchen to fetch the tin of leftover burned cookies again (because I'm weak and I never claimed to have an iota of self-control). "Oh, hell no. That was always a pipe dream of mine, to write full-time. I barely made enough money to cover the expenses of self-publishing. Before, at least."

"And now?" he asks as I pass over the tin. Realistically, I've made more money in the last month than a year's worth of salary. But it's hard to say how long it'll last.

"Technically I could quit and be okay for the next year. Though it would be a leap of faith. And I worry that if writing was my only source of income, it would feel more like an obligation. Something I have to do rather than something I love. That could change everything," I say, biting into a particularly burned oatmeal raisin. "Do you ever feel like a fraud in your job?" I ask, immediately regretting the overshare.

He shrugs, braving a bite of burned cookie. It's so incinerated, it crumbles immediately in his hands. "Maybe in the beginning. But the nature of my job makes it easy to measure my skills. I always knew I deserved my place, if that makes sense. Why? Do you feel like a fraud?"

"Not as a PA. As a romance writer."

His eyes rivet to me as he forces down a bite. "Why is that?"

I swallow a clump of raisin, finally coming out with it. "I haven't done any of the things my characters do in my books."

"What things are you referring to?"

I meet his gaze for a hot millisecond before I say it, eyes to the ceiling. "Sex."

"You haven't had sex?" His brows shoot up to his hairline; he's apparently startled by my admission.

"I have. Just not . . . good sex. Not that my books are only about sex. I know it's a small part of them, but still."

His hands tense at his sides, and he shifts slightly on the couch. I feel guilty that I've made him uncomfortable with my overshare. He pauses for a couple beats, collecting his thoughts. "For the record, it's not the sex that drew me into *Prime Minister*. It's the story, the tension between the characters. You do an amazing job writing people to root for. To care about. And also, murder mystery writers don't go around killing people to make the murder in their books more authentic. Doesn't make them frauds. You'd never know you were inexperienced to read your work."

"Really? I always feel like people can read right through it. Like they know I'm just some weird, nerdy girl who's barely done anything aside from . . ."

His jaw ticks. "Aside from . . . ?"

"Missionary."

"Just missionary?" His jaw goes slack. He looks alarmed. Offended. Aghast. Not that I blame him.

I cover my face with my fingers. "I can't believe I'm telling you this. You must think I'm a weirdo pervert."

"The only thing that's weird is that you only did missionary with your exes. I mean, did you even get off?"

"No," I admit. It was always so quick, there was never even a chance I could get there. "But that's common. Seventy percent of women don't come from penetration."

He sits forward, mouth shaped into a grimace. "That doesn't mean you should never come. There are many other ways."

"It's okay, honestly—"

"You don't know how amazing you are. Any guy lucky enough to have a chance with you would be an absolute tool not to learn what you like and get you off. Bare minimum. If I were your boyfriend, I'd . . ." He trails off without finishing that statement. His hand flexes at his side.

"You'd what?" I dare to ask, leaning forward to meet his fiery gaze in a challenge, his knees just barely pressing into mine. It's the smallest brush of skin, but it's enough to set me ablaze.

He's so close, I can make out the little rings of gold around his irises, the soft mossy hue that blends seamlessly into brilliant blue. I can smell the cinnamon on his breath as it feathers over my jaw, exploding in little shock waves over my skin.

I shift, crossing and uncrossing my legs, all too aware of the heaviness growing between them. Maybe it's all the sex talk, but my brain has left the station. It's long gone to a traitorous place. A place where all I can think about is what his lips would feel like. How the rough pads of his fingers would feel digging into my hips, skating up my thighs. How it would feel to be touched like no one has ever touched me.

Something has shifted between us, like it did that night in the Squamish hotel room. It's something in the added millisecond of a glance. I wonder if he notices, or if it's all in my head.

That's when he clears his throat and pulls his knees back, ending the contact. "Oh shit. I didn't realize how late it was. I'm supposed to get back to my mom by midnight. I should probably get going."

"Right. Of course," I say, blinking from the whiplash of the conversation. My entire body is on fire as he stands and heads to the door.

"See you at work tomorrow? Lunch?" he asks over his shoulder.

"Yeah. Lunch."

CHAPTER 27

Nolan

I t's been a full day and I still haven't recovered from that conversation about sex. Maybe it's the unfair, mind-blowing fact that Andi hasn't been treated the way she deserves in bed. Or maybe I'm just an asshat baby who can't handle a simple conversation about sex with a platonic friend—who happens to be obscenely attractive.

I was a half second away from kissing her, and I'm fairly certain she wanted to kiss me, too. The only problem is, I would have wanted to do a lot more. Things could have gone from zero to a hundred quick if I hadn't left so abruptly. It's for the better, I keep telling myself, especially since I'm leaving. In fact, Jones texted yesterday to let me know he might have some good news about a posting soon, though there were no details. He doesn't like to say too much until it's a sure thing.

I don't want to make things more complicated than they have

to be. Besides, I like hanging out with Andi. Really like it. If we got physical beyond our arrangement, it could get awkward, which is why I've decided that intimate hangouts at her place are probably a bad idea.

The next time we see each other at lunch, I act like nothing happened. Like I didn't have a hard-on the entire rest of the night just thinking about the way the thin fabric of her dress clung to her skin. We keep our conversation casual and light, neither of us bringing up what happened (or didn't).

It's better this way, because after work, we take the forty-five-minute drive to a farm to spend some time with the rescue dogs. I've been stoked about the idea ever since she brought it up in Squamish.

The place itself is a little hobby farm southwest of the city. It's a nice setup, with a massive gated area divided up into various pens and enclosures, all connected by a dirt pathway. There are also communal covered areas for the dogs to come and go for water and shelter. We're immediately met with wagging tails and yips from particularly excitable ones running up and down the fence, seemingly rejoicing in our arrival.

A sturdy woman in overalls and muddy rain boots trudges over to meet us. Three large dogs follow close at her heels, nipping playfully at her pockets, presumably for treats. Her weathered face breaks into a smile when she spots Andi. "Andi! Great to see you. It's been too long."

"I know. I've been so busy this summer. But I see you remodeled the enclosures." Andi gestures toward the pens.

"We did! Finally got Hank to build 'em. Took a while for the dogs to get used to, but now they love 'em," she explains, her gaze shifting to me.

"This is Nolan," Andi says, stepping aside so I can shake Deidra's calloused hand.

"Nice to meet you. Welcome to the farm." Deidra glances at the dogs, now sitting obediently at her feet. "These three here are some of our permanent residents," she explains, her voice softening with affection. "Bernie is the golden retriever. He's one of the first ones I ever took in, five years ago. He was found with mange in a parking lot dumpster. The collie is Brenda, a puppy mill rescue and the boss lady. She's a herder so she likes to keep everyone in line. The big guy is King. We think he might have some wolf in him, but we don't know for sure."

Andi bends down to stroke King's head. "Deidra takes in the dogs that are surrendered from death row at the main shelters," she explains. "She's able to adopt out most."

Deidra gives a modest shrug. "Usually, they just need some basic obedience training and a lot of belly rubs. Nine times out of ten, they make amazing pets. And the ones that don't, we keep here."

"Wow, running a place like this sounds like a lot of work," I say, impressed.

Deidra nods, chuckling as Max nudges her hand for attention. She obliges, ruffling his fur. "It is, but it's worth it. Every one of these dogs deserves a second chance at a happy life.

"We have about ten rescues right now," she explains, taking us to the pens for a mini tour. They lead into a larger, grassy area, where the dogs without behavioral issues can socialize with one another. A couple bigger dogs follow us in, all vying for attention. "We try not to take more than that, given the space. But the shelter is always calling us. They're overrun, especially after spring litters."

My heart clenches seeing Andi kneeling in the muddy grass, giving each dog much-needed love. A mix of dogs surround her: a couple of Lab mixes, a fluffy husky, a doodle mix. Off to the side, a midsize dog catches my eye. It's standing alone at the edge of the group, sniffing the perimeter of the fence. Its fur is sparse, with patches of sad-looking white fuzz clinging to raw, red skin. Its legs are thin and shaky, like they could give out any second.

"What happened to that one?" I ask Deidra.

"That's Cody. He's been here a couple months. He's an Airedale terrier, not that you can tell. He was surrendered by his owner because he kept chewing off all his hair. The vet thinks he has food and environmental allergies that led to a severe skin infection. We're trying to work out a proper diet for him. He also needs daily medicated baths."

"Poor guy," Andi says, holding her hand out to coax him over. He eyes her but doesn't approach.

"He doesn't have a lot of confidence. I think it's because of his fur," Deidra whispers, as though he can understand us.

I extend a hand toward him. He eyes me warily before backing away into his corner. He looks like he needs a bit of space, so I back off and join Andi to run around with the more outgoing dogs. Over the next hour, I notice Cody's sad brown eyes longingly following our movements from his corner. While Andi helps Deidra dole out some special snacks, I decide to try again. I approach slowly, stopping when he cowers again in the corner.

Instead of going closer, I sit in the grass nearby with a treat on my knee. I avoid eye contact, waiting for him to come on his own terms. After a couple minutes, he eventually does. He takes a tentative step forward, barely close enough to sniff my hand and take the treat before darting back again, his little nub of a tail tucked tightly between his legs. I wait a little longer for him to gather the courage to return. This time, he sits a couple feet away. His skin looks raw and a little shiny, probably too raw to pet, so I give him a soft pat on the head where some thicker tufts of fur remain. He flinches at first but relaxes slightly. He seems to like it, because his breathing grows heavier.

For the next fifteen minutes, we sit together quietly, him inching closer and closer until he finally plunks next to me, his back resting against my hip. He watches Andi frolicking around the pen with the others. Finally gaining his trust feels rewarding. More so than any job, any mission.

When I go to stand, he follows me. In fact, he follows me around the pen for the rest of our time.

"Wow, Cody took a liking to you," Deidra remarks, genuinely surprised when she returns. "He's been so timid since he got here. I've been worried he wouldn't get adopted if he couldn't build trust with someone."

"He's got so much potential," I say, stroking Cody's greasy head. "A little TLC and he'll be an amazing dog."

Deidra swings me a hopeful look. "We just need to find the right owner for him. Are you in the market for a dog?"

"I wish," I reply honestly. "I travel a lot for work and I'm not staying in Ottawa long-term."

As Andi and I prepare to leave, the thought of saying goodbye to Cody makes me feel like shit. He follows me as far as he can, his small frame lingering at the gate as Deidra gently closes it. Through the narrow crack, he watches us pull away, his eyes filled with a desperate longing that just about kills me.

Andi glances at me from the passenger seat. "We'll come back," she says, voice soft.

I swallow hard. "Tomorrow?"

CHAPTER 28

Andi

For the rest of July, we settle into as much of a routine as we can with our schedules. We do lunch together so we can keep up appearances. We attend a coworker's going-away party. Our relationship is so believable, even Ann, the head chef for the Nichols family, corners me in the staff kitchen one day to ask whether I can introduce her to Nolan's CPO coworkers.

In our off-time, we'll take walks, grab takeout, watch TV together. Nolan is also keen on going to the rescue farm to see Cody, so we make sure to go at least once a week.

It's wildly adorable, seeing Nolan with Cody, with his peach fuzz and scrawny little body. But the two of them have developed a close bond. In fact, Nolan even bought him a soft blanket to sleep with at night, a sweater (in case he gets cold), and some chew toys.

Nolan also keeps offering to let me come to Costco with him. I never thought I'd ever look forward to grocery shopping.

Maybe because it was a stark reminder I was alone, shopping for one. Sure, Nolan and I aren't actually together, but it's nice to have someone to share your cart with, someone to help you find random ingredients, someone to convince you to get the extra tub of ice cream you've been eyeing.

Today is Eric and Gretchen's staff appreciation barbecue, which is being held at the NCC River House, a heritage building with a public dock for swimming on the Ottawa River. It's a gorgeous wooded location, though neither of us actually swims or fully enjoys the day, because he's doing security while I'm caught up with logistics—coordinating food, overseeing entertainment, and making sure everything runs smoothly.

It's become a more arduous task than normal, because today, Eric and Gretchen aren't speaking. Gretchen didn't tell me much, aside from calling him "that man." They spend most of the afternoon on opposite sides of the docks, asking me and Eric's assistant to play telephone all day over trivial things, like condiments for the barbecue food.

I'm exhausted by the time everyone filters out at the end of the day, so I'm extra grateful when Nolan offers to stay and help with the cleanup.

"Want to take a dip before we go?" he asks, tilting his head back to the water with a playful grin. The sun has just set and the lake is still, almost glass-like.

It's tempting, though there's one huge problem. "I don't have my bathing suit."

He arrows me an impish look. "You don't need a bathing suit to swim. Come on."

I count the seconds, saying a silent prayer as he drops his tie, jacket, dress shirt, trousers, socks, and shoes on the dock. I gape at his perfectly honed pectorals, layered with dense muscle over muscle. A lump forms in my throat when he gets to his briefs.

Only, I barely catch a glimpse before he's in the water with a massive splash that breaks the stillness.

A bra and underwear are the same thing as a bikini, I remind myself, unzipping my dress.

His searing gaze burns a trail from my eyes, down my breasts, over the valley of my stomach, and down before he seemingly snaps out of it. "The water's great. Really warm!" he calls out.

I take his word for it. With a running leap, I plunge in. Holy shit. It's ice-cold. "You liar," I say, splashing him. "It's freezing."

He tosses his head back in a carefree laugh, which echoes across the lake. "I forgot to mention that I did underwater diving training in Antarctica. My idea of warm is probably skewed."

I snort, my body adjusting as the water gradually becomes more bearable, enveloping me like a sheet of chilled silk. "See any penguins?"

"Of course. And walruses. They're pretty friendly, actually."

I chuckle, floating on my back next to him. "How many oceans have you swum in, Mr. Antarctic Diver?"

He pauses, doing the mental math. "All of them, except for the Indian Ocean, I think."

I let out a whistle, both impressed and also entirely unable to imagine living that kind of life. I can only imagine how stifling a boring government city must feel for him. How much he must miss traveling to far-off, far more exciting places than here.

"Do you think you ever want a home? A permanent one?" I dare to ask, regret clawing its way up my throat instantly. It's probably too personal a question, even though I already know the answer. Nolan wants thrilling new experiences, adventure, unpredictability, not the same old routine every day, in bed by ten. He wants more than I could ever offer.

"I don't know. It's hard to imagine." He wades a little closer, shaking the beads of water from his face. The droplets cling to his beard, sparkling in the moonlight.

"Understandable," I say, swallowing as the distance between us closes. "Especially if you haven't stayed in one place in so many years."

"I used to, though. When I was a kid. There was actually a house at the end of my grandma's street that I loved," he tells me, his tone tinged with nostalgia.

"What was it like?"

"Em and I called it the yellow house, because it was the only house on the street with colored siding. All the other houses were brick. It had this white front porch that was always over-flowing with flowers in the spring and summer, and covered with leaves in the fall. Every night, the lights would be on and they'd have the fireplace going in the living room. I think a couple lived there, though I never met them."

I close my eyes and imagine the warm, inviting glow on a snowy winter night. "That sounds magical." I don't miss the way the moonlight catches his lips.

"It was magical," he continues. "There was this little trail next to the house that led to a forest with a ravine. My sister and I used to spend hours in that forest, running wild, playing hide-and-seek, fishing, and catching frogs. In the winter all the neighborhood kids would skate on the frozen water. Whenever I was back there, I didn't have to think about anything else. I didn't worry about my mom, or where Em and I would end up next."

"Have you been back since?" I ask gently.

"No, not since long before my grandma died. I actually forgot about the house until just now when you asked." He pauses, expression growing forlorn at the bittersweet memory. "How about you? What's your dream home?"

"I've never thought that far ahead," I admit. "It's funny. When I was writing all the time, I'd think about my characters' futures, mapping out their lives in vivid detail. But I never did the same for myself. I guess I've always lived to get through the day, the week, the next project."

"Live to get through," he repeats, as though tasting the words.

"I'm fully aware of how sad that sounds."

He shakes his head, his eyes latching on to mine. "No. I get it. The future is scary."

"It is. I don't even know what I want anymore." Being with someone, sharing my life with someone, is overwhelming. But being completely alone suddenly doesn't sound as appealing as it used to.

"Maybe," he says, voice calm and steady, "you could start with slowing down. Living in the moment. It might help you figure out what you really want." He gestures around us, as though asking me to take it all in. Even in the moonlight, it's hard to see anything except the blackness of our immediate surroundings.

I do absorb it all. The glow of our skin, contrasting the cool darkness of the water lapping against us. The chirp of a distant bullfrog. For the briefest of moments, everything fades around us, aglow.

"Is it working?" he whispers.

I nod, a small smile tugging at my lips as the tension melts away into the water. "Kind of." Truthfully, I'm not sure I'm able to see past what's directly in front of me. Him. I don't say that part out loud. A soft breeze blows over us, and my teeth begin to chatter.

"You're freezing, aren't you?"

"No," I say, because under his gaze, I feel the opposite. I wade a little closer and so does he.

"Come here," he says gently, his eyes like beacons, as though we weren't already floating toward each other.

It's probably a bad idea, touching him. I have half a mind to backstroke away before it's too late, but when my leg accidentally brushes against his side, any remaining reservation splinters away.

I hook my arms around his broad shoulders, letting my body dangle below until he brings me in close, my chest pressed to his. The soft waves crash against us, knocking my hips against his at a steady, rhythmic pace, until the friction becomes unbearable.

When he pulls back to study my face, I know he feels it, too. The charge between us, a spark away from igniting. "Fuck," he whispers, eyes on fire. "You have no idea how badly I want to kiss you right now."

"I want you to," I whisper back.

He holds my gaze for a beat longer than normal. His eyes flick to my lips, confirming he wants to kiss me. We both move closer, the distance between us closing until our breaths mingle.

A swell of heat pools in between my legs, and for once, I'm not thinking. I'm doing.

I hinge forward and we practically collide. His hand drifts to the small of my back, tilting me closer and closer until our lips catch. It's soft, delicate, testing.

"Is this okay?" he rasps, feathering a couple slow kisses along my jaw and down my neck. Holy shit.

I mumble something that sounds like a cross between "fuck" and "yes," not that it fully captures the way I'm feeling.

He pauses against my lips. "Are you sure? I didn't hear you."

"Don't stop," I order authoritatively, pressing a soft nibble into the bottom of his lip, kissing away the pearl-like water droplet hanging there.

In response, he makes a low, guttural sound at the back of his throat that lights a match within me, within both of us. He wraps his arms under my ass and hoists my legs tight around his waist. His tongue slides hungrily against mine, dropping down to my neck, skimming my shoulders. He tilts his waist toward me, and I arch against something heavy pressing into my lower stomach.

The kiss deepens until there's absolutely no space, no water between us. It's lip biting, tongues colliding, him pulling me so flush against him, I could combust. It's commanding yet desperate all at once, the way we're hungry for each other, as though we've both wanted this for longer than we'd like to admit. Or at least I have.

A pulse drops from my stomach to between my legs. I smooth my palms over the hard ridges of his shoulders to stabilize myself. The water makes it easy to roll my hips against him in a ravenous frenzy. I feel like I'm in some sort of Nolan-induced trance, and I never want to snap out of it. No one has ever kissed me like this.

His hands work their way from the small of my back up under my bra. He runs the pads of his fingertips up and down my thighs, touching me the way I've only ever fantasized about in my books.

My breath hitches when his hands reach my ass, cupping it hard, using it to set the pace.

"That's it, sweetheart. Just like that, nice and slow." He arches himself back to me, planting kisses all the way down my throat, stopping at the base of my ear before slamming his mouth back to mine. His fingers play with the lacy hem of my panties, and I'm seriously regretting not wearing a thong—not that he seems to care or notice.

"That feels so good," I whisper. Even in the water, the friction is about to set me ablaze, so much so, an embarrassingly loud moan rockets out of me, reverberating across the lake. I've never been particularly vocal or boisterous while being intimate with other men, but there's something about Nolan that makes me feel like another person entirely. It feels like an otherworldly experience, getting out of my head, letting my body take the lead. Because I've never, ever let myself let go like this, with anyone.

"Fuck. The way you sound." His thumb presses deeper under the hem, followed by another finger, just barely grazing me, almost teasing as he works his fingers closer and closer to my clit.

I rake my fingers over his chest, up to his neck, holding him close, letting myself feel every single sensation, letting myself moan into his ear as loud as I need to.

Apparently, he loves it, because he kisses me even harder. It's wet. It's needy. It's electric. And then he nearly loses it, bucking in a frantic pace against me. This is officially the hottest moment of my life.

I'm utterly throbbing, desperate for him to touch me, ready to beg for release.

A low buzzing sound on the dock yanks us out of the moment. His phone.

His gaze snaps up. He shifts me off him, his breath coming in ragged bursts as he scrambles to hoist himself onto the dock to check the screen. "I'm so sorry," he murmurs, voice strained. "Shit. It's my neighbor. Hold on."

Dripping wet, he takes quick, unsteady steps up the dock, his usually smooth movements now sharp with urgency. I follow him, climbing the ladder as fast as I can.

Shit. Is she okay? I'll be home in half an hour. Leaving now.

He rushes back to me, his shoulders rigid, his eyes wide with a mixture of guilt and unmistakable worry. "Andi, I'm really sorry. I have to go. Now."

"What's wrong?" I ask, wringing water from my hair, which is plastered to my face in a complete sopping mess.

"It's my mom."

CHAPTER 29

Nolan

I hadn't intended for Andi to find out about Mom this way, but after I get off the phone, she immediately says, "I'm coming with you," no questions asked.

Even though she's not fully aware of the situation, she seems to understand that I need the support. I appreciate it, more than I can ever express.

Whatever spell came over us minutes ago vanishes entirely. We both switch into emergency mode, drying off, getting our clothes back on, and jumping into the car as fast as possible, like we weren't making out like teenagers in the lake.

It's strange, having her with me the entire drive home, not just because of what happened between us. Ever since I moved back, I'm used to having things under control. But with Mom's condition worsening, it's starting to feel like the opposite. Andi's mere presence is a comfort I never anticipated. There's something inherently reliable and reassuring about her presence that makes it feel like everything is going to be okay, even if it's not.

Once we're about five minutes away from Mom's house, I finally speak. "You should probably know, my mom is sick."

"Sick?" She eyes me curiously, though she doesn't look surprised.

"Alzheimer's," I reply, the weight of the words settling like a sandbag between us.

Her face falls with gentle empathy, though she doesn't say anything, which I appreciate. Whenever I tell people, they usually start asking a million questions, like *When did it start? What were her first symptoms?* A bunch of facts I have to rattle off for their own knowledge, which actually makes me feel worse in the moment. And that's not even scratching the surface of our history, before the diagnosis.

I've been that way my entire life. If something is wrong, I've always been the type of person to close off and bottle it all up. Talking about my feelings never did me any good.

But there's something about Andi that makes me talk. "She was diagnosed three years ago." I explain how she started having issues with her memory even before that, while I was overseas. According to my sister, it was small things, like misplacing keys or forgetting people's names. Emma was the first one who noticed, though Mom also hid a lot from us, because she was embarrassed and in denial.

"She was doing relatively well up until the last few months. She's become really short-tempered, easily agitated. She also gets . . . confused sometimes and will go out and wander around the neighborhood, trying to see old friends. Tonight, our neighbor caught her walking down the street in her pajamas looking for my sister," I explain. It's not until I'm finished talking that I let out a long breath, all the tension releasing from my body. Maybe it's the fact that talking kept me distracted from whatever the hell I'm about to walk into, but regardless, it felt fucking good to get all of that out.

Andi softly places her hand on my forearm and gives me a reassuring squeeze. "God. I'm sorry, Nolan. That must be really hard on you, especially given your childhood."

I stay quiet, focusing on the road ahead. But something about her words hits me square in the chest. No one's ever said that to me before. Even Emma and I, who both know what it's like to be Mom's caregiver, have never really acknowledged that fact. It's always been about duty, about action, what to do next for Mom.

We pull into the driveway. Andi and I agree it's best she go to my place while I fetch my mom next door. The fewer people, the better.

"Hey, thank you so much. I'm so sorry about this," I say when Katrina opens the door.

"It's fine, Nolan. She came in and asked to have some tea. She wanted to watch Bon Jovi concert clips on YouTube," she tells me, adjusting her pink bathrobe over her round middle. I'm beyond grateful for her. She's been really helpful and under-standing about Mom, unlike some of the other neighbors, who see her as a nuisance when she shows up at their door.

Mom is in her nightgown, casually sitting on the couch with a cup of tea, bobbing her head to "Livin' on a Prayer." When I walk in, she looks up and smiles, her eyes wide. "Hon! You're finally back from tour?"

Strangely, this greeting gives me relief. She may not know

what day it is, but at least she knows who I am. I keep waiting for the day she won't recognize me at all. I've been trying to prepare myself mentally, trying to tell myself it won't affect me as much as it does other people. But I'm starting to doubt that.

"Yeah. Just got back," I say. "Hey, let's get you home and to bed."

She frowns. "But I'm not tired. I'm still in the middle of the show."

"We can watch it at our house," I insist.

It takes a solid ten minutes to convince her, but eventually she gets up and lets me lead her home. She quickly spots Andi waiting in our kitchen and eyes her with curiosity. "Who are you?"

Andi briefly glances at me before holding her hand out. "I'm Andi. It's really nice to meet you, Mrs. Crosby."

"Are you Nolan's girlfriend?" she asks, which surprises me. I didn't expect her to remember about Andi, given she's still at least three years behind in her head.

Andi nods. "I am."

Mom claps her hands together in delight. "Oh, I'm so happy to finally meet you." She turns to me. "She's way more beautiful than you let on."

I smile involuntarily. She's not wrong.

Mom is quick to offer her some wrinkly grapes from the fridge, which Andi happily accepts. Before I have any say, they're both sitting at the kitchen table, which is filled with random boxes and spilled ingredients. I feel a surge of embarrassment, given how clean her place is in comparison.

Andi doesn't seem to mind. She's good with my mom, sticking to neutral subjects, like the weather and '80s bands.

Mom leans in and whispers, "My music skills aren't what

they used to be. But I used to be quite the performer. I'll make sure to dig out the videotapes next time you visit. There better be a next time," she says, winking at me.

"Mom, Andi will be back to visit really soon. We should get you to bed," I say.

Thankfully, she doesn't protest and heads to bed without much of a fuss.

When I come out of the bedroom, Andi is elbow deep in the sink, cleaning. "You really don't have to do that," I say, startling her slightly when I walk up behind her.

She waves my words away like flies. "You helped me bake eight dozen cookies the other day and helped me clean up a whole party today. The least I can do is wash a couple pans. And by the way, I already ordered an Uber home."

"What? No. I'll drive you."

She shakes her head. "No. You shouldn't leave your mom."

Fuck. She's right. I duck my head, feeling both guilty and overwhelmingly grateful for her understanding. "Thank you, Andi. For everything tonight. I'm sorry I didn't tell you about her earlier. It's just—"

"It's okay, really. I understand it's probably not an easy thing to talk about. Especially with someone you don't really know."

I nod. "The whole situation is hard to explain to people."

"You're a good person, Nolan. For taking care of her so willingly."

I wince at the compliment, sweet as it is. "Actually, when my mom was first diagnosed, I left." She eyes me curiously. "About a week before that first night we met, she was officially diagnosed. I was home at the time and was supposed to be for a couple months. I thought about quitting and staying to help Em, but I didn't. I fucked off—the day after we met, actually. Took the first opportunity I could to leave. Avoided coming home, actually, because I was bitter about the whole thing. About her needing our help when she'd never been there a day in our lives."

She considers that for a beat. "Honestly, that's really understandable."

"Is it? Because I don't think most people would take off when their mom is given between four and eight years to live."

"I think your reaction was human. Of course you'd be scared. Avoidance just happened to be your first reaction. It doesn't mean you didn't care or love her any less." I may not fully believe that, but damn, it feels nice to hear. Until now, I'm not sure I knew how much I needed to hear it.

"You really think so?"

"Maybe it's not that you resent her, but that you don't want to lose her all over again?"

Her words pummel me in the face. Sure, Mom can't physically leave me anymore. But she can leave me mentally. She's going to, in fact. It's only a matter of time. And I don't know what's worse. "I feel like shit. Putting her in a facility."

She reaches to give my forearm a squeeze. "My grandpa on my dad's side was diagnosed with Parkinson's when I was a kid, and my grandma was the same way. She didn't want to put him in a home, because who does? But Alzheimer's is a serious disease. Sometimes, there comes a point where it's detrimental not just to the caregiver's health, but to the patient's. And unfortunately, that means the best place for them is somewhere they can get specialized care."

I nod. "I know. Thank you for the reminder. And I'm sorry about your grandpa, by the way."

"Thanks," she whispers. "And seriously, I know it's impossible not to feel guilt. But you're an amazing son. She's lucky to have you."

"It was the least I could do. I'll be leaving soon." Something rattles in my gut when I say it. For the first time, saying I'm leaving doesn't feel like relief. It doesn't feel exciting. It feels sad. I'm actually going to miss Ottawa. Because Andi is here. My family is here. And of course, Cody, the little bald gremlin of a dog I can't stop thinking about.

"Right." She stiffens a bit, nodding, but avoiding eye contact.

Andi's never been one for prolonged eye contact. But after the past few weeks of spending so much time together, I can feel her opening up to me, becoming more comfortable with me, especially tonight.

Now, her body language is telling me she's taken a step back, and it doesn't take a scientist to figure out why.

Still, I don't push it. I'm not normally one to beat around the bush if there's an awkward conversation to be had. But honestly, I have no idea what the hell to say. I've kissed my fair share of women, but that kiss was . . . something. Maybe it's because I've been imagining how her skin would feel against mine ever since that first night we met. The way she would feel against me. The way she tastes.

I'd be lying if I said I didn't want to do it again, and more. But I don't say that, or anything remotely close, because I'm a straight-up chicken.

So instead, we sit on the porch and make stilted conversation about literally anything else—the cookies, Lars, Cody, how she wants to go back to Costco. Anything but what happened between us tonight before Katrina called, until her ride shows up.

I don't think it's my imagination that she practically runs for the car.

"You still good for dinner tomorrow? So long as my mom is up for it?" I confirm.

"Yup. Totally!" she squeaks, already sliding into the back seat.

"Okay. Well, uh, enjoy the ride?" I call before closing the door.

"Enjoy the ride"? That's all I have to say after what happened at the lake? After she came with me to help with Mom?

I am an absolute asshat.

An hour later, I'm lying in bed, trying to get any semblance of sleep, when she texts me.

ANDI: How's your mom doing?

NOLAN: Good. Still sleeping!

ANDI: So about tonight . . .

I nearly die in anticipation, watching the little dots appear and disappear for what feels like forever.

NOLAN: Yeah?

ANDI: I think it's best we don't do that again.

Well, fuck. I don't know what I expected her to say, but it wasn't that. Before I can respond, another message comes through.

ANDI: With everything going on with the media and our situation, I just don't think it would be a good idea. Besides, I don't want anything to happen that could risk our friendship.

Reading those words feels like a gut punch. At the same time, she's entirely right. Hooking up would complicate things, especially since I'm leaving, at some point, in the near future. And even though I've been second-guessing that lately, leaving Ottawa is the smart thing. Temporary. Just as I like it.

NOLAN: You're right. Just friends.

ANDI: Perfect ☺

CHAPTER 30

Andi

Friends.

That's what Nolan and I are. The last thing I need is to get emotionally attached to someone who's leaving?

Maybe because I have a deeper understanding of him now, knowing what I know about his mom. I never understood why he took the posting here in the first place if he intended to leave within a few months. It all makes sense, the mixture of sad puppy and frustration on his face whenever he brings up his mom, the guilt in his eyes when he talks about leaving.

It's easy to see how much he loves and cares about her, despite the past. The look of utter terror on his face when he got the call from his neighbor was proof of that.

All I wanted to do last night was hug him. Absorb all of his sadness. If anything, it's even more of a reason things need to stay simple between us. He's here for his mom. Nothing more. End of story.

Still, I can't stop thinking about what happened at the River House and how badly I want to do it again, particularly when I'm alone and in bed, just me and my fingers. And it's more than just that. It's his smile, his relaxed, self-assured laugh, all these little things about him that I shouldn't care about. I've been strangely jittery and distracted all day at work. So much so, I even messed up Gretchen's morning coffee order, which has been the same every day for the past three years.

I thought I'd be able to make out with Nolan in the lake and move on with my life as normal. But I haven't been able to stop thinking about it all day, the way he felt against me, being on the verge of coming from the pressure alone.

It takes me a solid hour to pick out what to wear for his mom's (sort of) birthday tonight. In my defense, dressing to have dinner with someone's mom is not easy. Most of my work clothes give off a "devout Sunday school teacher" vibe.

I don't know why it's weighing so heavily on me, or why I'm so desperate to impress Nolan's mom. Eventually, I settle on a thick-strapped, square-neck, fitted black midi dress I bought years ago for one of Gretchen's galas. I pair it with black strappy heels I rarely get the chance to wear, because work demands more comfortable, supportive footwear.

Simple and platonic, I murmur to myself, my heart lurching into double time as I enter the restaurant.

Nolan stands immediately when he sees me, and my stomach does a barrel roll. I've seen him in slacks and a dress shirt countless times, but it hits different tonight. Maybe it's the way his eyes wander over me, electrifying my spine, or the way he wraps his arms around me in a greeting, pulling me snugly into his chest. There's something softer, gentler about the way he presses us flush together, his palm steady on my back, our breathing syncing. "You look insane in that dress," he whispers. His breath ghosts my neck, and I sigh into the warmth.

And then he does the unthinkable: He plants a soft kiss on my cheek. My knees nearly buckle. I know it's bad, but I let myself sink into him. Because if I can't actually do anything with him, I can at least take advantage of the times we're pretending to be together.

Friends, I repeat, my attention turning to his mom.

She doesn't seem to remember meeting me last night, evidenced by the way she springs from the table as I approach. "You have no idea how happy I am to finally meet you."

I'm a little taken aback at first by how alive she is tonight compared to last. She's in full color, vibrant and sharp-eyed. "Likewise. Nolan doesn't stop talking about you, Mrs. Crosby," I say, hugging her back, relishing how warm she is. It occurs to me that I don't think my own mother ever hugged me like this.

I don't know what I expected, based on everything Nolan told me about her, but it certainly wasn't this. A surge of guilt rockets through me as I struggle to reconcile the mother she was to Nolan with the woman in front of me, who so clearly loves her son.

"Call me Lorna," she insists, adjusting the leopard print shawl around her bony shoulders.

Nolan pulls a seat out for me across from his, but Lorna shoots him a look. "Remember what I said? Same side."

"I don't mind—"

"I insist. It's good for couples to sit on the same side at restaurants," Lorna informs us.

Nolan swallows and nods, ushering me to the seat next to his. It's a cute little wood-fire pizza shop with seating in a courtyard with vines snaking up the side of the brick building. Lorna's favorite, according to Nolan.

The conversation flows easily. As we eat, she asks me a lot of the same questions she did last night about where I grew up, what I do for work, my hobbies, though I don't mind, because she genuinely seems to want to get to know me.

When she tells me she loves reading and recently joined a book club, I'm tempted to tell her about my writing. I've never had an impulse to share that secret with anyone else, aside from Nolan. But I manage to keep my mouth shut, instead asking about her favorite books and authors. She also spends half the meal telling me all about Nolan when he was a kid. I give him a reassuring smile when he begins to look uncomfortable.

"As a baby, he was such a little cuddle bug. From day one, he only wanted to contact nap. If I tried to get him to nap in his bassinet, he would just howl until I held him. He also absolutely hated wearing a diaper. Much preferred being totally naked."

Nolan's face turns a deep shade of crimson. "Mom," he groans.

She flashes me a funny look. "He'd throw a tantrum whenever I made him wear clothes. One time, when he was around two, we were at the mall and he marched right into the middle of the food court and stripped, proudly showing everyone his belly button, among other things."

I throw my head back in a laugh, imagining it.

Nolan buries his face in his hands. "We are not having this conversation."

"He ran circles around and over the tables until I could finally catch him and toss a blanket over him. You should have seen the looks some of those old ladies gave me. They thought he was absolutely feral. I guess he kind of was."

"Is this something I should be on guard for? You randomly stripping in public if the mood strikes?" I ask, pushing my empty carbonara plate away.

Nolan cracks a smile. "Yup. This is your fair warning now."

Lorna bursts out laughing. "Nolan was always a little daredevil. Never wanted to be still or do anything that didn't involve a thrill. It got him into trouble around town. That's why his grandma and I were so happy he went into the military after high school. It really gave him the discipline he needed."

"Okay, Mom. No more stories." The more she talks, the more agitated Nolan is getting. I can't tell if it's because he's embarrassed.

By the end of the night, Lorna is getting tired and is starting to forget some of her words. She also becomes agitated when Nolan reminds her to finish her food. Soon after, he decides it's time to get her home.

I wait in their living room while he gets her into bed and arranges for Katrina to come over while he drives me home. We make a quick pit stop for gas on the way. And when he smiles at me through the window as he fills the tank, my soul leaves my body.

"Sorry for the pit stop," he says, sliding back into the driver's seat.

My brow quirks. "No worries. I'm not in a rush to go back home."

"Why not?"

Because I'm alone. Because I want to stay with you. "I don't know. The silence. It stresses me out. Makes me think about all the things I need to do."

He drums the steering wheel, his eyes narrow, deep in thought. "Want to go somewhere?"

"Where? It's a Tuesday night."

"I know a place."

• • •

We drive up an old street in a neighborhood on the south side of the city near Carleton University. It's a mature, quiet area lined with little brick bungalows backing onto woods. As we approach the end of the street, I spot a charming little house that stands out among the rest. It's set back from the road, its siding butter yellow, with little white shutters and trim, and a gray porch that looks like it used to be white. It's the perfect size for a little swing, or a pair of Adirondack chairs. Someone is home, because the lights are on inside, casting a warm orange glow over the lawn. I imagine the inside of the house smells like caramelized sugar, vanilla, and a touch of nutmeg.

"This is the yellow house," I say, in awe of it. No wonder he was so drawn to it as a kid. It looks straight out of a storybook, surrounded by lush greenery, including a large willow tree in the front yard.

He nods. "It is. It's a little more run-down than I remember."

"It's twenty years older," I remind him, opening the car door.

"Where are you going?"

"You said there was a magical forest back there," I say, hopping out of the car.

I've never seen him unbuckle his seat belt so quickly. In a heartbeat, he's out of the car, and taking my hand to lead me down the worn trail only wide enough for one person at a time. I don't miss the childlike giddiness, the hop in his step.

Despite the pink-and-orange sky, it's already dark back here, with the tall ancient trees canopying the trail, blocking out the remaining August daylight almost entirely. Back here, the world fades away and disappears.

It's quiet. No more sounds of city traffic or barking dogs in the neighborhood. Just us and the satisfying sounds of our shoes crunching the leaves, pine needles, and fallen acorns. The hum of crickets and the burble of a stream ahead. The air is also cooler, filled with the earthy scent of damp leaves and moss. I can picture young Nolan with messy brown curls, getting lost in his own little realm.

As we continue down the trail, the tree line starts to thin as the sound of water gets louder. The trail slopes down to water, trickling over smooth rocks and fallen branches. There's a little grassy bank along the edge speckled with wildflowers, where I imagine Nolan and his sister used to fish. Across the ravine, fireflies flicker in the brush like little beacons of light.

The opposite way stands the yellow house, with all of this magic in the backyard.

Nolan still hasn't let go of my hand as he guides me to a flat patch of grass near the edge of the ravine. Something flutters in my chest as we lower ourselves onto the cool grass, the length of our hips and thighs touching ever so slightly. Neither of us moves to adjust.

"I used to love it back here," he says, his gaze following the mist rising from the water, swirling lazily into the night.

"I can see why. It's like a whole different world back here."

"Honestly, it's probably one of the only places I was ever really happy. By the way, I'm sorry about tonight. About my mood," he says regretfully.

"It's okay," I say. "I'll admit, just talking to her tonight, I wouldn't have known she basically abandoned you guys."

A bitter laugh escapes his throat. "She puts on a show on her good days. It sounds bad, but sometimes her good days are harder for me than her bad days. At least when she's mad at me, I know how to deal with it."

I bow my head.

"A lot of the stuff she says about me isn't accurate. For example, that story she told you about me jumping off the counter as a kid? That never happened."

"Is it because of her memory?" I ask.

Frustration flickers over his expression. "I don't know. Maybe a little, which is why I never say anything. But she did this even when we were kids. She'd make up random things, trying to act like she has some authority or knowledge about Em and me."

"Maybe she did it out of guilt. Because she knew she wasn't there for you like she should have been," I suggest.

He looks at me. "I never thought about it that way. You might be right."

"I understand how it can be frustrating, though," I continue. "It's hard, her living in this alternate reality that she was there more than she was."

"Exactly. It's like she's falsely assuming credit. She never knew or cared what my favorite cereal was, or when I lost my first tooth. And sometimes I get so fucking mad. All I want to do is call her out on it, tell her how I feel about how we were raised. But I can't."

"Why not?" I ask.

"Because by the time I thought I'd found the courage, she was diagnosed. And I just . . . can't do that to her now," he says, his voice cracking a little.

At the pain in his eyes, my heart aches for him. I'm desperate to hug him. To go back in time and hug his child self and protect him. "It sucks for you, though, to never be able to tell her how you feel."

He nods. "Yeah. It really does. I feel really resentful about it. All the time. Even though she's been so great. Ever since I moved back, she always wants to talk, always wants to go for walks—when she's not mad at me. It's so weird."

"Maybe this is her way of trying to make up for what she did. Maybe she really does know how much she failed you and Em."

"Maybe," he says quietly. "I just wish I could be more like Em. She forgave Mom instantly. Well, actually, I'm not sure Em was ever angry at her."

"No?"

"She didn't even hesitate when it came to taking care of her. If she was bitter or had any kind of resentment over it, she never told me. She's never said it outright, but I'm sure her having to take care of our mom took a huge toll on her personal life. She didn't have a lot of friends eventually, aside from ones that stuck around town. So when she met Travis, they got married immediately and had four kids. She leaned into the mom lifestyle and put everything into them to give them the stability we didn't have. I chose a completely opposite life. I mean, I guess I just continued living the way I'd always lived. With no roots. Nothing to ever hold me back."

"It makes sense. Why would you long for stability when you've never had it?"

He looks at me, really looks at me, and there's something vulnerable in his gaze. "That means a lot. In all seriousness, though, I'm sorry for all of this."

I furrow my brow. "Sorry for what?"

He's quiet for a moment, though I sense his thoughts are still racing. "I don't know. Bringing you into all this stuff with my mom. I know it's a lot. It's not fair that I didn't tell you when we originally agreed on all of this."

I shake my head, my lids growing heavy. "It's not. I mean . . . it is. But it doesn't scare me or make me think any less of you. Thank you for telling me. And for trusting me with this."

Everything grows fuzzy around us as he wraps his arm around my shoulders, curling me into him. As the blues, greens, and brown hues of the coming night and the trees blur around us, I let myself relax into his embrace.

Being with him here, in the one place he felt safe as a child, feels heaps more intimate than when we were at the lake. And god, it's been nice, having him to spend time with, having someone to talk to, someone to share my whole self with. I don't want it to end. I don't want him to leave. The pit in my stomach expands at the mere thought.

Shit.

I'm already dreading it and he's not even gone yet. So I let my lids flutter to a close, committing it all to memory. The damp, earthy smell of the forest. The trickle of the ravine. The way my heart cartwheels as my body molds to his. The way he glances down at me, his pensive gaze sweeping over my face. And I hold on tight a little longer.

• • •

"Can you believe the latest story?" Gretchen tosses her phone at me. The headline reads, INSIDE THE NICHOLS' TROUBLED MARRIAGE. Below is a rather unflattering photo of her and Eric from two years ago at a state dinner in Washington. Gretchen is squinting from the sun, but from that angle, it looks like she's death-glaring at Eric. "Apparently, an insider claims everyone on staff knows about Eric's alleged affairs. Plural."

"They're saying there's more mistresses in the mix?" When the rumors first began, I assumed they'd only last a month, tops. But they've been going strong all summer.

She rolls her eyes. "Well, this is Spotlight. They also claim Princess Diana was abducted by aliens. It's laughable, honestly. Anyone who knows Eric would know that the man barely has time to poop unless it's scheduled into his calendar. Let alone service multiple women."

I snort. "Truth."

"You're distracted again today," Gretchen points out, her freshly waxed brows raised knowingly. "The email you just sent used 'there' instead of 'they're' and you spelled 'meeting' like 'meating.' Sounds a hell of a lot more interesting, but frankly illegal."

I rub my temples, embarrassed. "Sorry. I'm tired today."

"Is the CPO keeping you up until the late hours?" she asks with no shortage of gleeful curiosity.

I nearly choke on my coffee. "No. We're slowing things down a little, actually," I inform, trying to keep my tone casual. Seeing as we're "breaking up" in a few weeks, I've been looking for small ways to plant some seeds of doubt about the relationship so the news doesn't come out of nowhere. I've also been avoiding him entirely. I've come up with a valid excuse, that I'm busy with writing and gala prep.

Gretchen gasps and I immediately recoil, assuming I've made another glaring typo in the email. "What? Why?"

I shrug. "He's leaving in a few weeks. Location TBD."

"He's still wanting to leave, huh? And you're not going to try long-distance? I feel like it's easier than ever nowadays, with video calls."

"I don't know if there's even a point, because he doesn't ever plan on coming back," I note, as if that's the final nail in the coffin.

"Fair point," she concedes, but then her eyes narrow, and I can practically see the wheels turning in her head. "But I don't know if you should throw in the towel just yet. What if he changes his mind? Or—hear me out—he leaves after a tearful goodbye, only to realize wherever he is isn't for him. And then, after a dramatic forty-eight-hour montage, he turns up at your doorstep, possibly holding a boom box over his head."

I snort. "Gretchen, you've been watching too many romance movies."

She waves a dismissive hand in my general direction. "Maybe. I don't know what's gotten into me. Anyway, it's a possibility, is all I'm saying."

"Not a likely one." After all my conversations with Nolan, he has zero intent on staying. Regardless of what happens, he's leaving, and I'll still be here, as I've always been. It would be smart of me to detach now to avoid the inevitable: emotional ruin.

She sighs dramatically, like I'm an annoying main character who won't get out of their own way. "Doesn't mean you need to end things. Might as well make the most of the time you have. You're still going to your friend's wedding in Mexico, right?"

I nod. We have a week until we go to Mexico, where we'll be sharing a room. A room. I need to get my feelings in check.

"Go for a grand finale, if you know what I mean," she says with a wink.

I think about that for the better part of a day. I think about the night we first met and how liberating it felt being with him, even if we didn't actually hook up. I've been telling myself getting physical with him will make things worse. But maybe it's the opposite.

Saying goodbye is going to hurt like hell either way. If I'm never going to see him again regardless, why not do something for myself? Why not let go, even just for a little while, and enjoy the ride before it ends?

CHAPTER 31

Nolan

I haven't seen Andi in days, since Mom's "birthday" dinner. Not that I haven't tried.

I've texted, asking her to go to lunch, asking if she's up for a movie. But she says she's swamped with work and writing in her small bits of spare time. Understandable, yet frustrating.

Sure, it crossed my mind that maybe the whole thing with Mom scared her off, though I didn't get that impression. I think the real issue is that she's been avoiding me since we hooked up at the River House. Part of me thought kissing her would feel like relief. That I'd be satisfied after that and move the fuck on with my life. But it's only made things worse. The time away just makes me miss her more.

Luckily, life is busy enough to keep me at least semi-distracted from staring at my phone, waiting for her to text me. Even without Andi, I've been going back to the rescue farm a couple days a week to spend time with Cody.

Each time I show up, he comes bounding toward the fence, his little nub of a tail going wild, rejoicing at my mere presence. It feels amazing, knowing he's as elated to see me as I am to see him, even if I don't know what I did to deserve the affection. When I tell Deidra that, she laughs.

"That's the thing about dogs. Their love is unconditional. It doesn't matter how much money you have, what you look like, what you've done, a dog will love you all the same," she says with a smile. "And that little guy loves you."

"I love him, too," I say, without even thinking. Honestly, leaving him here every time kills me. Knowing he doesn't have a warm person to sleep against every night. No one to cuddle his shivery body and give him his medicated baths.

"You sure you wouldn't consider taking him?" she asks again.

I sigh. The past few weeks, I've researched all the intricacies of bringing a dog to different countries. Turns out, you can't—easily, at least. Every country has a shit ton of regulations and standards when it comes to transporting animals, which really fucking sucks. Not that it really matters. Wherever I go, I wouldn't have the time or the capacity to properly care for a dog like Cody anyway. He's better off with Deidra, or another family with an actual permanent home.

Cody isn't the only thing I'll miss. Things are still tough, but I think Mom has finally gotten used to me being around. We've established more of a routine, and I've learned how to counter some of her anger and frustration. Mom has insisted on making a ritual out of breakfast at the sun-drenched kitchen table. Those slow, golden mornings are when she tends to be at her sharpest. Whenever I'm home in the evening, we take a walk around the neighborhood as the sun sets. Most of the time, we have the same conversation about old music. It's a safe topic. She gets frustrated if we talk about anything recent, like TV shows she watched that morning, because she doesn't remember most of it. She asks me a lot of the same questions over and over about my time in the military. Of course, there's lots I can't tell her, but she seems fascinated by what I can reveal. We also talk a lot about Emma and the kids. It's become such an embedded routine, I'm probably going to miss it the most come fall.

And then there's work, which takes up most of my time. One of the pros of the job is that Eric loves physical training. He loves staying active, like I do. So whenever he works out, I work out with him. On my first day, I stayed in my suit and he looked at me like I had five eyes. "You're not working out with me?" he asked.

"Uh, am I supposed to?"

"I'd rather not have a man in black staring at me while I work out. Besides, if I'm going for a run, it would be weird for you to run after me in that suit."

I wanted to tell him I've run with a rucksack and gear that weighs nearly his body weight, but I refrained and borrowed his gym clothes. Since then, he's treated me more like an old friend than an employee, which I appreciate, especially after missing the camaraderie in the military.

He likes to do a bunch of types of workouts: lifting in his home gym, runs on the property, swimming, and even some mixed martial arts.

Shockingly, Eric doesn't have much of an ego and is always asking me for fitness advice, wanting to try new things like ju-jitsu. I keep joking with him that he needs to start paying me double, for being both his CPO and his personal trainer.

Today we're doing some boxing. It's his first workout in a couple days since his schedule has been packed with back-to-back meetings.

"All right, don't go easy on me," he says.

"Right. Can't mess your television face up for your Montreal trip. You'd scare the nation with a shiner." Tomorrow, we're heading to Montreal for two days. Eric has a couple meetings and an announcement about new steel factories.

"Oh, come on. I'm tougher than I look. I survived my last diplomatic meeting without punching anyone, didn't I?" A smirk plays at the corner of his lips.

"Just barely."

Eric shrugs, adjusting his boxing gloves with a nonchalant grin. "Hey, a black eye might actually boost my approval ratings. People love a leader who can take a punch, right?"

I step into the ring. "Yeah, well, let's see if you still feel that way after I land one on you."

Eric raises an eyebrow, a mischievous glint in his eye. "I don't plan on making it easy for you."

We spar for about half an hour before taking a break.

"So you and Andi, eh?" he smirks.

"I was waiting for you to bring this one up." Damn, I hate lying to him. "Actually, I meant to thank you and Gretchen for being so cool about it. I know it's not ideal to date someone you work with, but we're both committed to keeping things professional."

"Glad to hear it. And treat her well. She's the best PA Gretchen has ever had," he says.

"She loves working for her," I say. Andi talks about all the latest bills, things Eric is working on. She knows everything and is so smart, which is really sexy. I almost feel too dumb to be in her presence.

"Your face just went bright red when I said her name. You must really like her." Somehow, even that statement doesn't do how I feel justice.

"I do." I work down a hard swallow, finally admitting the words out loud. The truth I've been avoiding for weeks. I have feelings for her. Feelings that scare the shit out of me. Feelings I'm not sure I can ignore any longer, or outrun, no matter where I go in the world.

"If you don't mind me asking, how are you planning to make it work when you leave? I know you don't plan on extending your contract for much longer."

"Long-distance, I guess," I say, avoiding his stare. Just saying that phrase out loud evokes dread, even though Andi and I aren't actually together and won't be doing long-distance—or anything, for that matter.

He raises an eyebrow, his expression a mixture of curiosity and concern. "What's stopping you from staying?"

"A lot of things," I admit, searching for the right way to put it without having to lie. "But mostly, what if I give up my whole life plan, put roots down here, and it doesn't work out?"

"That's a possibility, sure. But if that happens, wouldn't you be in the same position you're in right now? You could always get a new contract and leave."

"True." He's not wrong. I'd be begging Jones for a new posting anywhere but here. At the same time, I don't know if Andi would even want me to stay. In the entire time I've known her, she's never expressed wanting anything more than a temporary friendship, which is a far cry from a real, serious relationship. "I wish I knew how she felt."

"You haven't talked about it?"

"Not in so many words," I say. That's putting it mildly.

Eric flashes a knowing smile. "Gretchen isn't the best with expressing how she feels, either. I've learned a couple things. When she tells me she doesn't want to talk, nine times out of ten, she *wants* to talk. It's not always what she says, but what she does. How long or how tight she holds my hand. The way she used to lean in and brush her arm against mine during meetings or events." He pauses, lost in thought. "Anyway, sorry for the ramble. I'm sure you don't want to take relationship advice from me, of all people," he says knowingly.

Andi has never been one for grand displays of affection. She's generally subtle, a little shy. But I think about the way she kissed me with reckless abandon in the lake. The way she folded herself into me and clung for dear life in the forest behind the yellow house. The way she listens when I talk and effortlessly understands me like no one else does.

There's no fucking way we're *just friends*.

"No, actually, I think that was exactly what I needed to hear."

CHAPTER 32

Andi

I'm on my way to grab lunch from the kitchen when I spot Nolan power walking toward me from the end of the hallway.

"Hey!" he calls out, waving me down. If I'd seen him an hour ago, I'd have ducked into the kitchen and pretended not to hear him. Admittedly, I've been avoiding him the past few days, making excuses not to see him because I'm a weak individual. But since talking with Gretchen, I'm feeling bold.

Besides, my guilt triples at the mere sight of him, so earnest and adorable in his suit, which is uncharacteristically wrinkled. His hair is also mussed up and unstyled. He looks a little . . . disheveled. I stop, waiting for him to catch up. "Do you have a second to talk? Somewhere private?" he asks.

"Sure," I say, nodding toward the door to the supply closet.

He follows me in. It's just as small and crammed full of junk as it was the first time we talked in here. Only right now, it somehow feels smaller.

"What did you want to talk about?" I ask, trying to sound casual, definitely not on pins and needles, waiting with bated breath for what he has to say.

"I like you." He blurts it out so fast, it comes out more like *Ilikeyou*. "I like you," he repeats, slower, more deliberate this time.

My jaw goes slack and I stumble backward, leaning my entire body weight on the shelf behind me in order to stay upright. I think about the way he touched me at the lake, the way he's opened his life up to me.

I try to say something, but everything in me is crackling and short-circuiting, like I've dumped a bucket of water on an electrical control panel. "Are you saying you have feelings for me? Real feelings?" I finally manage. I need the clarification.

He rests his hand near my head and exhales, like he's trying to calm himself down. "I do. And I have no idea what I'm accomplishing by telling you this. I don't know if it changes anything for you. Or if you'd at all be interested in being more than just platonic friends—not that I don't love being friends. I do. I guess I was wondering if you, at all, feel the same way?"

I've never heard him ramble like this. He's generally well-spoken and articulate, able to keep his cool in pretty much any scenario. But seeing him like this—unraveled, unfiltered, barriers down—gives me the courage to do the same for him.

So I come out with it. "I do." It comes out in a whisper, like confessing it too loudly might burst the bubble we're in. "I've wanted to be more. I just . . . didn't know you felt the same way."

"Seriously? I thought you said we didn't have chemistry?"

"I lied. Of course we have chemistry. Now, at least. Not so much that first night—"

"Wait, wait, wait. I need you to repeat that. I didn't quite hear." He makes a show of leaning in, his hand forming a shell around his ear.

I roll my eyes, repeating, "We have chemistry."

He flashes me a self-satisfied smirk. "Thank you."

"You enjoyed that way too much."

"I did," he happily admits.

We stand there in the closet, smiling wordlessly in the darkness like complete nerds until he clears his throat. "Look, I know I'm supposed to leave, and I know that makes things complicated. But the fact is, I have no idea when that's even happening, or if it will—"

I place my finger over his lips before he can continue. "Stop. Let's not talk about that."

"You don't want to talk about it?"

I don't know what's come over me, but I can't stop thinking about his words at the lake. About living in the present. Maybe I need to do a bit more of that and less planning. "Not right now, at least. We don't have a lot of summer left. Why don't we make the most of the time we have and go from there?"

He smiles. "I like that. A lot, actually. Though that sounds very unlike you."

"You were right the other night. About me not taking the time to really let myself feel. Enjoy. Listen to myself and trust myself to know what I want without overthinking."

We both just stare at each other for a solid beat as I think about what this means, my mind in overdrive at the very thought of him touching me beyond the confines of our fake-couple agreement. "Are you overthinking right now?"

"No. I'm only thinking about one thing," I admit, biting my lip under his searing gaze.

His brows draw together. "What's that?"

"That I want you to kiss me. Need you to kiss me." *And sit me on the shelf and make me scream.*

His eyes simmer and his mouth curves into a wicked smile, drinking me in. Then he bends down, brushing his lips against mine. It's almost exploratory, how slow and teasing it is.

His breath is warm against my neck, sending sparks scattering down my back. I nearly lose it until my tongue grazes his bottom lip, until he catches my mouth entirely in a full brush of my lips. I need more, desperately. And for the first time in my life, I'm more than willing to ask for it. I press my mouth into his and we meld together, pulling apart in tiny gasps, until my hands are clawing the dense hardness of his muscled back, dipping underneath his jacket.

Our kiss grows more urgent when I press down on his bottom lip, moving over his neck, making little marks that are sure to last for days, marks that claim him. He seems to love it, if the low groan he makes is any indication.

He reaches to tilt me closer, pressing himself into me until my skirt is bunched at my hips, and my legs are wrapped around his waist, my heels digging into his backside. Until he's backing me against the shelf, feathering kisses down my jawline, past my neck, claiming me in return. Until I'm running my hand over his thrashing heart, simultaneously arching myself against his thigh.

"Does that feel good?" he whispers.

"Too good," I manage through a moan as he traces circles on my inner thigh, going higher and higher until they graze my center, stirring something wild inside me. Even the tiniest movement feels tenfold.

"I can't believe you're this wet for me already." He runs a finger over the smooth satin fabric of my panties where they're embarrassingly soaked in the middle.

"I've been thinking about you fucking me in here," I admit, my cheeks blooming with heat, my legs trembling.

He cups my jaw, and my blood sizzles at the eye contact. "I'm not fucking you for the first time in a closet. But I will make you come," he promises, his voice so low and ragged, it makes me clench.

He swirls his finger over the fabric until I'm tensing and shifting, grinding down on his hand. "Good girl. Keep going."

My body reacts instantly when his index finger dips under the wet fabric, brushing and thrumming in slow, deliberate strokes exactly where I need it, winding me so tight, I forget where I am or who I am. Instead, I focus on Nolan. I toss my head back to meet his eyes, begging, saying all kinds of filthy things I'd never imagined I would say out loud.

He's barely slipped the tip of his finger in before my whole body clenches around it, contracting, shaking, thrusting into his hand in the most intense climax I've ever felt. It splinters and fractures everywhere, hot liquid rolling through me long past the point I thought possible. He holds me as I unravel beneath him, his nose tucked into my neck.

I take a couple seconds to catch my breath before placing my palms on his chest, lowering myself back down, my chest still heaving as the aftershocks keep coming. "That was . . . holy shit."

All I can think about is how badly I want to make him come. How I want to see his face when he loses all control. I want him so badly, it physically hurts. I bite my cheek guiltily, knowing full well I needed to get to a meeting. Five minutes ago. "I'd love to stay and take care of you, but I have to go," I explain, pulling my skirt down.

"Don't even worry about it," he says. "You have no idea how badly I needed that. Just that."

I bite my lip, my stomach dipping. Gone are the courage and unabashed confidence I had all of two minutes ago. "Do you, um, want to hang out tonight? We could, um, continue this?"

His breathing is still heavy, labored as he tries to collect himself. "Fuck. I do. More than anything. But Em's youngest is sick and my mom's nurse is on vacation. I have to stay at home."

"No worries at all. Totally understandable."

"Unless . . ." He eyes me for a moment. "You could come to my place?"

"I can definitely do that!" I say, far too eager for my liking.

"Fair warning, my mom's house is going on the market, so things have been a little crazy the last few days. There are boxes and piles of junk everywhere."

He'd mentioned that a couple times, that they were selling his mom's place. "Oh, that's right. Did the listing go up yet?"

"Not yet. We've been trying to get the house sorted for photos. Em put a hard deadline on next week, though they don't think it'll be on the market for long. Apparently, the Realtor already has clients who are interested based on the lot alone." His mom's house is older and small, but the lot is huge and private, with tall hedges in the backyard. It's also in a prime location just west of downtown. I have no doubt people will flock to it.

"Don't even worry about it. I'm not coming over for the aes-
thetics."

His entire face lights up at my response. "Great. Around
eight?"

"Sounds good. Well . . . See you tonight?" Before I back out
of the closet, I give him an awkward thumbs-up. God no. Not
the thumbs-up. Why am I suddenly feeling so shy again?

Another blinding smile. "See you tonight, Andi."

Despite embarrassing myself into oblivion, I can't stop smiling the rest of the day.

CHAPTER 33

Nolan

EM: I just got an opportunity to go to a beauty convention in Toronto this week. Huge opportunity for networking. Thoughts? I know I'm supposed to stay with Mom overnight when you're in Montreal, but I was curious if Theresa could fill in?

NOLAN: Go! It shouldn't be a problem. I'll text her and ask.

I'm counting down the hours, minutes—who am I kidding?—seconds until Andi comes over. It took me longer than expected to recover from our "talk" in the storage closet today. And even hours later, I'm still not a fully functional human being.

Not to be too dramatic, but seeing her lose it like that in my arms was otherworldly. Utterly addictive. I would have lost it right there with her if it had gone on much longer. I already can't wait to do it again, but better.

Before heading home, I make a pit stop at the farm to spend some time with Cody. I can't stay long today, though it's better than nothing. I need to get home and prep for Andi.

My first order of business when I get home is to do a deep clean of my room, as well as the living room. Not that I'm expecting anything. I want to go at Andi's pace, whatever she's comfortable with. Mostly, I really want to hang out with her, breathe the same air, even if it just involves us watching sad movies together with cheesecake.

Either way, a cleanup is overdue. Emma texted the other day to ask whether her Realtor friend could come take photos of the house for the listing, and as it stands, things are still in a state of chaos with half-packed boxes stacked in the hallway and piles of random items, which I'm still unclear as to whether they're to keep or toss.

I'm in the kitchen wrestling with the overflowing garbage when a piercing scream cuts the air. *Mom.* I drop the bag immediately and sprint down the hallway.

It takes a few frantic seconds to figure out where the sound came from. The bathroom. When I find her, she's lying on her side against the cold, hard tiles. Her clothes are drenched, clinging to her frail frame, and her entire right arm is an alarming shade of crimson.

"Mom! What happened?" I shout, rushing to her side.

"Water. Too hot," she manages weakly, her voice shaky through the tears.

The bathtub is still running, steam billowing out, and the water is scalding, as hot as it'll go. I turn the water off, my mind racing. She must have tried to take a bath and scalded herself.

I help her to her feet, though she's unsteady. Before I wrap a towel around her, I get a closer look. Her skin is angry and red, blistering. Fuck. She's seriously hurt.

I've seen people in the field wounded ten times worse than this—I've carried men out of the line of fire, patched up injuries that would haunt most people's nightmares—but this is different. This is Mom. And seeing her like this, so vulnerable, so hurt, it hits different.

My hands tremble as I dry her off as best I can, then dress her, my mind a blur of panic and guilt. Why didn't she ask for help? And worse, why wasn't I there to help her? How long was she lying there?

"Mom, we need to get you to the hospital," I say, trying to keep my voice calm, though inside, I'm anything but.

I help her to the car, every second feeling like it's dragging on forever until we get to the hospital.

Thankfully, the ER nurses push Mom through to see a doctor fairly quickly. While we wait, a nurse treats the burns with a saline solution. I'm texting Andi to let her know I have to cancel due to an emergency while Dr. Rathbone, a calm woman with a reassuring presence, examines the burns closely, her expression serious but not alarmed.

"These are second-degree burns," the doctor explains, her tone steady. It's a slight relief to hear that. It means the burns are deep, but they haven't damaged the muscle or bone. Still, they're far from minor. "Good news is, they should heal within two to three weeks, depending on how her skin responds to the treatment and so long as the burns are kept clean and dry. We'll need to monitor for infection and she'll require a change of dressings a few times a day."

While the nurse treats the burns and wraps Mom's arm in a bandage and gauze, Dr. Rathbone asks to chat with me privately in the hallway.

"I see from her medical file that she's an Alzheimer's patient," she says, eyeing me over her iPad with thick-framed glasses. "Are you her primary caregiver?"

"Um, kind of. I'm her son. I live with her. She has a nurse who comes by during the day and sometimes at night when I'm working."

"Private or through the Alzheimer's Society?"

"The Alzheimer's Society. We can't afford private nursing."

Dr. Rathbone lowers her chin in sympathy. "It's a great temporary resource, but they aren't always reliable, especially for Alzheimer's patients who require constant care, as well as familiarity and routine."

I nod, knowing she's right. Emma and I have done the best we can with what we have, but based on recent incidents, it's clear Mom now requires more and more intensive supervision.

"I'm curious if you've considered full-time care for her? In a facility? With someone in her state of decline, living at home without trained professionals is eventually going to become a hazard. It's not to say her care at home isn't adequate, it's just, with these types of conditions—"

"Actually, she has a spot at Lakeside in the fall." Saying that out loud makes it all the more real. Soon, Mom will be in the facility and I'll be gone. We won't have our morning chats anymore, or our walks. My stomach dips at the thought, and it reminds me of how I used to feel as a kid whenever I missed her.

She dips her head, noticing my expression. "I know it's difficult, but I think it's the best place for her. At least you'll know she's safe and potentially catastrophic accidents like this won't happen." I know she means well, but I leave the hospital with Mom feeling like complete shit.

"I'm sorry about this," Mom murmurs on the drive home. She feels guilty. It's hard to imagine feeling worse, but somehow, her apologizing for an accident makes me feel like complete garbage.

"Mom, it's not your fault," I say, trying to mask my anger with reassurance. The truth is, I'm pissed at myself. How could I have let this happen? She shouldn't have been trying to bathe without her nurses in the first place.

The what-ifs start an aggressive invasion of my stream of consciousness, each one more terrifying than the last. What if I hadn't been home when it happened? What if I hadn't heard her scream? The thought of her suffering alone, in pain, makes me want to throw up.

I glance at Mom, who's resting her head against the window, eyes closed, looking more fragile than I've ever seen her. I swallow hard, forcing myself to focus on the road. This can't ever happen again.

I called Emma earlier while we were in the waiting room, which I felt terrible about. She was busy packing and getting things ready for her convention. The last thing I want is her thinking I'm a total fucking disaster taking care of Mom without her. But she made me promise to keep her posted on everything.

Things get even worse by the time I get Mom to bed. A text comes in from Theresa, confirming they still don't have anyone to cover the two night shifts while Emma and I are away. I think about what Dr. Rathbone said about the lack of consistent, reliable care.

What the hell am I going to do? I can't bail on Montreal without jeopardizing my job. I refuse to ask Emma to sacrifice more than she already has, but there's no way I can leave Mom alone. I contemplate asking Katrina, but decide against it because she's already done so much for us lately. I lie back in bed, running through all the options until it feels like I'm drowning.

I'm not sure what prompts it, but I naturally find myself calling Andi. I don't expect her to solve my problems. I just need to hear her voice. Something steady and comforting.

"I'm so sorry about tonight," I croak. When I texted her earlier, she'd told me to call when I was free. "My mom had an incident."

"What happened? Are you guys okay?" she asks, her voice clouded with concern. Still, the warmth in her tone envelops me like a cozy blanket.

I explain how Mom tried to take a bath but put the hot water on full blast instead of mixing it with the cold, scalding herself and falling out of the tub trying to escape.

"You have no idea how much I wanted to see you tonight," I confess, my voice dropping to a whisper. And I mean it—I needed that escape, that comfort, more than I can put into words.

"Don't even think about that right now. All that matters is that your mom is okay. And you. Are you okay? You don't sound good."

My breath hitches in a sharp intake of air. Without notice, my vision blurs. It's moisture, pooling in the corners of my eyes, threatening to burst over my lash line. Shit. Am I actually crying?

My chest tightens and I press the heels of my hands to my eyes, refusing to blink, trying to hold them at bay. Trying to hold it together. "Sorry. It's just been a shit night. And I'm supposed to go to Montreal with Eric tomorrow for two days, and then we have Mexico a couple days after. But Emma was invited to this beauty convention in Toronto and can't stay with Mom overnight. At least not for the next two nights. If I can't get any of the support workers or anyone to fill in, I might have to cancel both trips, and I feel like a total asshole because I told you I'd go and—"

"Nolan, don't even worry about Mexico. Seriously," she says firmly.

I clench my jaw, unable to respond, my throat aching from holding back these stupid tears. The guilt is suffocating.

"Your mom is a billion times more important than a not-like-the-others wedding of some couple you don't even know. And when it comes to Montreal, how about I go over at night when I'm off work? I can sleep on the couch, make sure everything is okay while you're gone, even help a little with some packing for her move. I know it's not a great alternative compared to you or Em, or even her nurses, but it's better than her being alone."

I finally allow a blink, as though that will improve my hearing. Did she really just say that? Sure, we've established we have feelings for each other that can't be ignored. But shit. This is beyond that. Beyond anything that feels reasonable to ask of someone, even someone you're in a kind-of-relationship with. "No, I can't let you do that. It's too much. You're way too busy with work and the gala—"

"I really don't mind," she insists, cutting me off with a no-nonsense tone that leaves little room for argument. "So long as it's okay with your mom and Em." I already know Mom will be okay with it. She loved Andi. Wouldn't stop talking about her after the dinner.

"I don't even know what to say." And I mean that. I can already feel my anxiety slipping away, little by little, just at the sound of her voice.

"Say yes."

It's an easy *yes*. She may not be a professional trained to deal with Alzheimer's patients, but I trust her implicitly for two nights. I trust her to make Mom feel comfortable, to watch her, to make sound decisions. "Only on the condition that you don't sleep on the couch. You'll stay in my bed. Things in the living room are a mess right now, with the packing."

"Okay. Deal. One question: Do you sleep on an extra-firm pillow? I need to know if I should bring my own pillow."

A deep laugh bursts out of me, which I thought I was incapable of five minutes ago.

"You totally do, don't you?"

"What makes you think that?"

"Just a hunch. You strike me as an ultra-firm guy. Mattress, too," she adds.

"You'll have to find out," I say mysteriously. "Seriously, I owe you. I know how busy you are and—"

"Nolan, stop. I'm doing this because I want to, end of story."

"Fine," I say, laying my head back. "But for the record, I'm really annoyed I won't get to see you till after Montreal." After Montreal, we only have Mexico, and then a week and a half left before the gala, before I'm set to leave. It's not nearly enough time.

"It'll go by fast," she assures. "You're going to be too busy to even miss me."

I wouldn't be too sure about that.

CHAPTER 34

Andi

N olan is happier than I've ever seen him, you know," Lorna tells me softly as we meander down the cracked sidewalk outside her house for a quick walk before I head to work. Droplets of morning dew cling to each blade of grass, shimmering under the early sun.

"You think?"

She's in a chipper, energetic mood compared to last night. She was understandably thrown off by my presence and confused me for Emma. Not that I minded. My biggest worry was that she'd eventually realize I wasn't Emma and become upset or confused. Luckily, she didn't. And by the time she woke up this morning, she knew who I was.

Still, the experience made me gain even more appreciation for Nolan and the emotional toll this must have on him day to day.

I watch as she runs a finger over the bandage extending up

her thin forearm from her burn. "Oh yes. He always has a sunny smile on his face, especially when he's talking to you. He's constantly talking about how wonderful you are, how smart. I've never seen him like this with anyone."

"He makes me really happy," I say, trying to ignore the lingering question in my gut. Where can this lead, in reality? I've done a great job at compartmentalizing those worries and focusing on the now. But with Nolan gone, it's become harder not to think about.

"He's a good boy. Good to a fault. I know how much he worries about me. He always has, ever since he was a little boy," she says. Before Nolan went to Montreal, he left me detailed notes about Lorna, everything from when to serve her pre-prepared meals to how to administer her medication and how to dress her burns, and he included a list of numbers for her nurses and doctors. He also insists on calling me every couple hours to make sure things are okay, which is really sweet. "It feels like yesterday he was taking care of Em, making sure she did her homework, got to school. Gosh, he grew up fast."

I nod.

Her eyes well appreciatively. "You'd be amazed by how fast the decades pile up and pass you by. How little time we have, even the luckiest of us. That's why I'm so grateful he found someone like you. Someone who lights him up from the inside out. He needs that."

I think about how quickly the past few years have flown by since I've worked for Gretchen. I'd be lying if I said I took advantage of all that life has to offer. If anything, I've been going through the motions, just getting through the day, trying to stay as busy as possible so I don't have to think too hard about my life.

I think about that as we finish the block before Lorna starts to get tired. I can tell by the way she's losing her train of thought mid-sentence.

Theresa is at the house by the time we return so I can get to work. It's a busy day, as Gretchen has an appearance at the children's hospital. It gives me a couple free hours to get things done in advance before Mexico.

Normally, I'd work past dinner, but tonight, I make sure to head back by four to relieve Theresa. Lorna still remembers me by the time I arrive, thankfully, and we spend the night chatting on the deck, followed by some TV before she turns in early.

It's only eight, which is more time than I usually have to myself before sleeping, so I use the extra time for writing. It's not my desk at home, but it's near perfect. Nolan's bed is comfier than I expected for a firm mattress and pillow. Though I noticed Nolan purchased two brand-new soft pillows, which he left on the end of the bed in their original packaging.

I slide under the crisp sheets and pull the comforter to my chin, inhaling his scent, cocooning myself in it as I write (more accurately: type and delete, repeat). About an hour in, my phone dings.

NOLAN: Hey, let me know when it's a good time to call.

ANDI: Feel free!

He calls a couple minutes later. "Sorry I haven't checked in since this afternoon. Things were busy with Eric tonight. He had a town hall that ran later than expected. You know how he is, always wanting to stay and chat. His stalker was also here, so I had to fill out a report."

"Oh no! Don't apologize, though. It was a good night."

"Did my mom think you were Em again?"

"No, actually." I tell him about our night and how she seemed to be in good spirits today. He seemed pretty down last night when I told him about her confusion, so it's nice to give him some good news. "Are you back at the hotel?"

"Mm-hm. What are you doing?" His voice is a little gruffer, slower. He sounds tired.

"Your mom went to bed half an hour ago so now I'm lying here, in your bed, struggling to write," I add, sinking back deeper into the pillow.

He mutters something pained that sounds a lot like *shit*. "What are you struggling with? Maybe I can help."

"No. Not with this particular scene."

"Why?"

"Because. It's, um, X-rated." My cheeks heat at the admission.

He lets out a low hum. "It's a sex scene?"

"Yup. Now you see why I can't ask you to help brainstorm ideas."

He chuckles that low, grumbly laugh, and my heart rate doubles at the mere sound. "It's not weird at all. Set the scene for me."

I blow the air from my cheeks. I've never confided in anyone about my writing, aside from the odd beta reader online, let alone solicited help for the steamy scenes. But he sounds eager for distraction, and I could use some input, even if it's awkward. "Well, it takes place on the beach. The couple had a fight and the heroine stomped off on a long walk. The hero follows her to a rocky area and things get . . . heated. I can't figure out a way to make it feel fresh since there are already two intimate scenes before this one. It's an emotional one, so I want it to reflect that."

"What about oral? Sixty-nine?"

"I've never understood sixty-nining. Wouldn't that get complicated, especially with the sand?"

"It's really not as hard as it looks." Jesus. His voice.

"What if there's a height difference? He's really tall. She's really short. I mean, would that work, logistically—" I'm rambling now and my skin prickles with sweat. I throw the comforter off me for some air.

"It can still work," he assures me, his tone serious, as though he's running me through the logistics of Eric's motorcade. "Basically, she has to straddle his face backward."

"While doing oral," I say, scandalized by saying it out loud. I would never say something like that in public, but on the phone I feel freer, probably because he's not in front of me.

"Exactly."

"That sounds hard. No pun intended." My laugh is a little strangled, and I notice my fists are clenched at my sides.

His rumbly amusement vibrates through my phone. "Again, it's not."

"You seem very pro sixty-nining. Is it your favorite position?" I dare to ask, my mind circling back to the storage closet. The roughness of his beard against my temple. The spread of his fingers pressing into my ass, leaving imprints long after.

"One of," he tells me. "It's really hot, the angle, the view—everything."

My body is on fire, pulsing everywhere. "You actually like

eating women out?" In romance novels, heroes love it. But I always thought it was a known fact that men in real life don't enjoy it.

"Fuck yeah."

At his enthusiasm, a raspy breath escapes my throat as all the tension pools between my legs. "You must be one of the few. Most guys don't."

"Has anyone ever eaten you out before?" he asks unapologetically.

"No. Not that I've ever really asked. I've always been paranoid. I don't know—"

"Would you like someone to?"

"You. Only you," I say reflexively. "And only if you want to," I add, burrowing lower under the covers, tracing circles around my inner thigh, imagining it's his hands and not mine.

"Are you kidding me? God, Andi. The way you would taste." The way he says it, so longingly, so confident, my stomach tightens and coils to the point of discomfort. No one has ever talked to me like this before. "There's nothing I'd rather do right now." His voice rumbles through my phone, and it feels like he's right here next to me, parting my legs. "Fuck," he breathes over what sounds like the rustling of the covers. "I'm sorry I can't be there to do it. To make you come in my bed. Do you want to come, Andi?"

Goose bumps erupt down my legs, over my arms, and my pulse goes into triple time. "Yes," I whisper as my fingers circle back up to my breasts.

"Are you wearing those lacy panties again?"

"No. I'm in pajama shorts and a tank top," I say, blinking hard to ground myself. This is real. This is happening.

He huffs a breath. "Fuck. Can you feel my hands, pulling those shorts down?"

"Yes." I nod, sliding my hands down in unison to kick off my shorts. I swallow as the cool air hits me, a stark contrast to the warmth of the rest of my body.

"What are you thinking about? Be honest," he rasps.

"How badly I want you. How I want to touch you," I admit in a pained effort to keep my voice steady as I picture him and his ropy arms, hovering over me.

"Where would you touch me?" he asks.

I slow my breath. "I'd swirl my tongue up and down your cock, sucking harder at the tip." I can't believe those words just came out of my mouth. And most of all, I can't believe how much I liked saying them.

He lets out a hard breath. "Fuck. Are you touching yourself?"

"I am," I manage, a shiver cascading down my back. My eyes flutter to a close as I let my fingers dip dangerously close to where I want them. Where I want him. "I've touched myself a lot thinking of you."

He lets out a strained groan that makes my pulse race. "Me too. Ever since that first night, I've thought about you more than I'd like to admit."

"Even though I embarrassed myself?"

"Listen to me. I literally didn't stop thinking about you for three fucking years. Do you know how hard I came just from thinking about you? Every time?"

I don't know how to respond other than to let out a whimper.

"What do you imagine when you think about me, Andi?" he asks, his voice commanding, grumbly, and warm against my neck.

"You on top of me, your hands touching me everywhere," I admit, dropping my hand from my stomach, lower, to where I'm strung tight.

"Where are your hands right now?" he asks, like he can sense my every move.

"Um, my thigh."

"Close your eyes, okay? And imagine it's me touching you. Dragging my finger up and down your inner thigh. Are you doing it?"

I do as I'm told. I imagine the warm length of his body pressed next to me. The scruff of his beard scratching against my jaw. The rough pads of his fingertips digging into my skin. All the blood whooshes down, lower and lower, until I'm squirming under the sheets. "Yes," I manage through a whimper.

"Good girl. Where would you want me to touch you now?"

"You know where," I rasp, desperate to touch myself even lower to soothe the ache between my legs.

"Not yet," he orders. "Drag your fingers up to those gorgeous tits."

I do as I'm told, circling my fingers around my nipples, driving myself wild with need, chasing what I imagine is his touch.

"You have the nicest tits, you know that? Do you know how much I've wanted to touch them? Suck on them?"

I let out a low, grumbly sound from the back of my throat. I've never wanted anyone more.

"Okay, now drag your hand down, over your stomach, and down. You're wet for me already, aren't you, baby?" he asks without hesitation, because he already knows the answer.

"Soaked," I admit, a thrill rocketing down to my toes.

"Swirl your fingers around that swollen little clit, just a bit, okay? I want to hear it. Don't put your fingers in yet. Just imagine it's me down there, working you until your pussy is dripping wet and ready for me." There's a huskiness in his voice, an edge to match the intensity pulsating through me.

"Fuck," I moan, swirling my fingers over myself, quickening the pace as the tension pulls tighter in my belly at his voice alone.

"Faster, Andi. I want to hear you beg for me."

"Okay." I hold back a desperate noise, letting the feeling simmer and swell there for an unbearable stretch of time.

"Now slowly slide your index finger in."

"Fuck," I moan, clenching around myself, imagining panting against his bare skin as he holds me, guiding me through it.

"You're doing so good. Now put another one in. Is that pretty pussy as tight as I'm imagining it is?"

The moment my second finger slips in, everything feels heightened. The buzz of the ceiling fan, blowing cool air over my naked body. The sound of my own heart hammering against my chest. "So tight. Oh god, it feels so good. You feel so good."

"I wish I could see your face. I wish I could fuck you myself. Press those legs down, spread you open, and—"

"I want you to fuck me. I need it so badly." Being here in his bed, enveloped in his scent without him next to me, feels brutally unfair. So I close my eyes, picturing him burying himself in me, losing himself in me entirely.

"Faster, okay? God, I can hear it, the wet sound of your fingers in your pussy. You're drenched," he says with a pained grunt, like he knows it. Like he can see me.

"Nolan. I'm close," I rasp, my other hand swirling over my nipples, pinching, deepening the sensation.

"Open those legs. Wider for me," he commands.

I do it. I'd do just about anything he wants me to, at this point.

"That's it, fall apart with me." Just the sound of his voice alone drives me senseless with need. I think he could order me to do just about anything right now, and I'd do it. No questions asked.

That's when the tension breaks. He sucks in a breath and then there's only silence, as though the entire world has frozen over. I let out a wild sound I can barely even hear over the ringing in my ears, suppressing it with my other hand as the shock waves erupt. As I spiral into another galaxy, imagining him next to me, entirely spent, gaze heavy and satisfied. Me tracing my fingers over his chest, over each groove and freckle, like a treasure map.

"Feel better?" he asks, breathless after a stretch of blissful silence.

"Yes," I whisper, my body still feeling warm and fizzy, like it's hovering.

"Good night, Andi."

"Good night."

CHAPTER 35

Nolan

You'd think traveling with Eric would be exciting, but I find myself itching to get home the entire time.

Maybe it's because I've been a CPO for so long. I've gotten used to these types of trips with former clients. It's always somewhere nice, like Paris or Madrid. Private jet, Michelin restaurants, expensive-ass hotels with nightly rates equivalent to a month's salary. But there's never any off time to actually enjoy yourself. Not when you spend the lead-up scanning the bowels of the internet for regional threats, planning driving routes, casing out hotel and event venue floor plans, and generally being on high alert for any potential risks.

It's been two days, but I'm anxious the entire drive home, feeling like I can breathe again only when I pull into the driveway. I've never missed home. Until now.

Mom is sitting on the couch reading *The Very Hungry Caterpillar* with Maisey, Em's youngest, tucked into her lap.

"Uncle Nono!" Maisey screams in that sweet, high-pitched little voice of hers. She flings herself off Mom's lap and rushes to hug my legs. I take a couple minutes to play with her on the floor. I try peekaboo, though she specifically tells me she's "too old" for peekaboo at three years old.

"This is what happens when you spend so much time away," Emma calls from the kitchen.

"Oh, don't listen to her. I barely remembered you were gone," Mom quips playfully, coming to my defense.

She stands slowly, stabilizing herself on the side of the couch before pulling me in for a hug. I really fucking missed her.

"How are you feeling, Mom?" I mumble into her shoulder.

"A little tired today," she admits. I ask what she did this morning, but she doesn't remember. Instead, she pulls Maisey in for a tickle, and the two of them resume their book on the couch.

I head into the kitchen to find Emma on hands and knees, buried under a mountain of random sauces and spices scattered around the kitchen floor. "Did you know Mom's been trying to poison us?" she asks, holding up a dusty jar of god-knows-what like evidence from a grisly crime scene before tossing it into the garbage.

I plunk into the chair closest to the stove. "Huh?"

She tosses a small canister of green powder at my chest. "Look at the expiration date of this oregano. It's from 2012!" Indeed, the expiration date is May 2012. A relic.

"Slander! Spices don't expire!" Mom calls from the living room.

"Oh really?" Emma plucks a bottle of balsamic vinegar from the floor, holding it up like she's about to unveil a deep, dark family secret. "This balsamic expired six years ago. And you said Mom wasn't a pack rat."

"Hey, I never said she wasn't a pack rat—just that she's selective about what she hoards," I argue.

Mom, still within earshot, fires back, "It's called being prepared! You never know when you'll need a dash of aged balsamic. It tastes better that way, in my opinion."

"Sorry for the mess," Emma whispers to me as she continues her archaeological dig through the pantry. "I want the place to be in sparkling condition for showings. Hard to make a house shine when the pantry looks like a scene from *Hoarders*."

I laugh, catching another outdated spice jar she tosses my way. "Yeah, nothing says 'buy this house' like decade-old oregano."

"In better news, did Mom tell you what Andi did?" Emma asks, gesturing to the fridge.

"No?" I poke my head in to find fresh produce and containers stacked and labeled. Holy shit. I know how much she hates grocery shopping, and I also know how little free time she has. I'd never even asked her to do that, or alluded to it, even though it was a task that was going to stress me out in the lead-up to Mexico. It's like she anticipated exactly what I'd need without me even voicing it. I've never had that before. My heart swells with a mixture of gratitude and something I can't quite put my finger on.

"Andi did this?"

"Sure did," Mom says, entering the kitchen behind Maisey, who Emma has to coax not to touch the dusty pantry items. "Andi was absolutely wonderful company, by the way. Invite her back more often."

Em's eyes widen. "Speaking of Andi, I meant to tell you, I hired new staff. Met a couple girls from Ottawa at the convention who were looking for work."

"That's great news," I say. I know how badly she needs reliable staff to help her out at the salon. "But what does that have to do with Andi?"

Em swings Mom a look. "It means I'll be good to stay with Mom a couple days while you're away. In Mexico!"

My stomach does some sort of nervous twist. "Em, you really don't have to."

"I insist. It's no big deal."

I shake my head, eyeing Mom. "I don't know. I don't want to leave again." As badly as I wanted to go to Mexico with Andi, the thought of leaving Mom so soon feels daunting. It occurs to me now that, despite myself, I've actually been enjoying Mom's company on her good days. I enjoy our conversation, even if she can get on my nerves at times. I'm not sure what changed with her over the years, or whether she's always been this person deep down, but something about her energy is infectious.

"Nonsense. I'm not letting you. Consider yourself kicked out," she says.

"Evicted," Emma emphasizes, tossing me a yellow tube with a cartoon banana on it. "By the way, here's some suntan lotion for Mexico. It only expired in 2009."

* * *

Seeing Andi again adds years to my life.

When I pick her up for the airport, I have to smother the temptation to run to her and jump up and down like a maniac. I hug her tighter than I intended, taking in the fruity smell of her shampoo, the way she pops onto her toes with a little squeak, how she lets her lips graze my skin as she presses her nose into the nape of my neck.

That phone call was the only thing that kept me going. And I've had far too many long showers replaying it in my mind.

I can barely believe she's finally here, within reach. Right in front of me.

I cup her face, strumming her jawline with my thumb for a heartbeat before tilting her chin upward. "I missed—"

Before I can finish that sentence, she presses her lips to mine. It's hard, desperate, the way her hands clasp each side of my face and beard, tugging me down toward her. It's like she's needed this, needed me. I let her take whatever she wants as she slides her tongue against mine, coaxing a longing groan from deep within my throat.

When we pull back, she smiles up at me, her nose still grazing mine. She's so fucking cute, I'm never letting her go.

Travelers dodge us and race past with their luggage around us in fast motion. But we stay rooted in place, frozen, my forehead resting against hers like we're in our own sparkly snow globe. We stay like that for longer than it's convenient, seeing as we're late.

Apparently, it doesn't matter. The flight to Mexico is a clusterfuck.

By the time we get through security and to the gate, we learn the flight is delayed due to a freak windstorm, forcing us to wait at the airport for an extra six hours before boarding. It means we'll be missing the first night and won't arrive until early morning the day of the "non-wedding." Then, we're in middle seats sandwiched between two families with screaming children in front of and behind us. Because of the delay, it's a two-hour wait for another shuttle to the resort.

Regardless, it's still enjoyable. We pass a lot of time working through plot holes and brainstorming for the book Andi's working on. There's a lot of time I just sit there and watch her type on her iPad. It's magical, seeing her at work, witnessing the creative gears turning. Sometimes, she'll read me a passage she's unsure about, her voice shaky and hesitant at first, but once she hits her stride, she loses herself in the flow of the words. There's nothing better than seeing her eyes light up when she slots a challenging puzzle piece of her story into place. It's contagious, the spark in her when she comes up with the perfect line of dialogue. She'll sit up straighter, her eyes narrowed, entirely in her element.

"You good?" I ask her as we pull into a narrow, palm-tree-lined lane leading onto the resort grounds. It isn't lost on me that we've arrived at her ex-boyfriend's wedding weekend.

She squeezes my hand. "Yeah. I'm actually excited. And on the bright side, we got to miss the awkward welcome mixer where everyone tries to act like it's totally normal that I'm there," she adds in consolation.

I tilt her an encouraging smile. "Remember, if you need me to fake food poisoning, or a grave injury, I'm game."

She laughs and our eyes snag.

I think about what she said that one night, about how having a partner for all the good stuff isn't even the best part. It's about the mundane times when all your plans go to crap. Doing that flight alone would have been a fucking nightmare. But it's hard to stay annoyed or stressed for too long when I'm with her.

CHAPTER 36

Andi

'm Hunter's aunt, Janine. I recognize you but I can't recall your name, dear," says a sunspotted woman in a wide-brimmed hat. She's the first to greet us at the beach for breakfast, where we came directly after checking in.

I vaguely recall meeting her briefly at Hunter's parents' holiday party. She was wearing one of those ugly Christmas sweaters with battery-powered string lights. I swallow. "Nice to see you again. I'm Andi."

Apparently, she recognizes the name, because her eyes go wide like saucers. She lifts her gaze to meet mine suspiciously over her plate of shrimp, like I'm here for nefarious purposes. "Andi. Right! You were Hunter's . . ."

"Ex-girlfriend," I take the liberty to say. Might as well bite the bullet. "Don't worry, I was invited. I'm not here to object or anything," I joke. It doesn't land; she recoils.

"Babe, do you want any French toast?" Nolan asks, sidling up to me, saving me. Thank god. He leads me away from Aunt Janine, who's still eyeing me warily as she returns to her seat.

"She's a hundred percent convinced I've crashed this wedding," I say with a snort as we head to the end of the table. The sun's already warm, the scent of salt water and sunscreen filling the coastal air.

Without thinking, I slide my hand into Nolan's, not for appearances, but because it feels right. Just like it had felt natural to rest my head on his shoulder during the flight.

Under the pavilion, we have the perfect view of the beach. It's massive, the white sand stretching at least a mile or two on either side. It's dotted with little straw huts, chaise lounges, and the odd palm tree swaying in the breeze. The water is glittering in the sun, boasting a wild shade of blue that reminds me of Nolan's eyes.

Just as we go to sit down, Laine finds us. She's in a black bikini, a fruity drink in hand. "I'm so glad you guys made it! I heard about the storm. A bunch of people got delayed."

"I wouldn't miss it," I say. "The resort is absolutely stunning, by the way," I add as Laine greets Nolan with a sandy hug.

She ushers us to sit with our plates and pulls up an empty chair next to me, where she launches into a story about how Hunter's mom had a lot of trouble communicating with the resort coordinator, and how frustrating it was that no one understood it wasn't a "wedding" but a "celebration of love."

"Hunter and I spent last night together," she makes sure to tell us. "No rules, no tradition."

We chat for at least fifteen minutes, and it feels like old times. Maybe it's the coastal breeze, the tan, but she's absolutely glowing. Even Hunter comes by for a quick greeting. He's seemingly in a good mood—I can tell by the animated way he's talking, telling us all about the excursions available. You'd have to be a monster not to feel happy for them right now.

It doesn't take long before Hunter's parents spot me at the end of the table and come by to greet me. It's a bit of an awkward exchange.

"Andi, it's so nice to see you again. You look absolutely lovely," Hunter's mom says warmly, mid-bite of a piece of pineapple before adding, "How have you been?" I don't miss the sympathetic look in her eyes.

"I've been good. Busy with work." Is that really all that's new to report?

"I'm sure. I hear you're quite the talk of the town," she says with a raised brow.

I fight to swallow my bite of toast. "Yup. Luckily everyone knows none of the rumors are true."

A woman in a yellow beach dress I don't recognize angles herself toward us with interest. "So it really wasn't you that wrote the book?"

I shake my head instinctively. "No."

She frowns. "Shame. It was one of the best books I've read in a long time."

"Don't listen to Gloria," Hunter's mom says, leaning in like she's telling a secret. "She's a pervert who only reads Fabio smut."

Gloria shamelessly throws her head back in a throaty laugh. "If it doesn't have a shirtless man on the cover and at least three questionable uses of the word 'throbbing,' it's not worth my time."

I can't help but snort, trying to hide my amusement.

Hunter's mom looks both amused and horrified. "You know, Gloria, there are books out there with actual plots. Substance."

She waves a dismissive hand, taking a liberal sip of her mimosa. "Please. Romance has more substance than your left toe. Give me all the heaving bosoms and throbbing members." She says "throbbing" so loud, like she doesn't give a single flying fuck. I officially love Gloria. I'd die for Gloria. She's my favorite kind of romance reader—proud and unashamed of what she loves to read, despite people making fun of her to her face. I respect that immensely and I tell her so.

"I used to hide the covers of my books behind other books," she says with a snort. "When I was young, I even glued the cover of my dad's legal drama on a Harlequin to bring to school. But now, at my big age? I can't be bothered."

"What changed?" I ask.

"This world is too dark, too negative, as it is. You have to find joy where you can. Joy, by the way, isn't frivolous. It's foundational."

"Joy is foundational," I echo.

Gloria watches me for a beat before she leans in and whispers, "The shame fades quick when you stop giving it a seat at the table."

Her words light something inside of me. Before I can respond, Hunter's mom shakes her head. "Well, I better move along. I'm proud of you for having the gumption to come and support them. It's very nice of you."

"Thanks," I say, forcing a grin.

After a long chat with Gloria about recent romances she's read and how she gets all her recommendations from a bookstagrammer called TaraRomanceQueen (who apparently raved about *The Prime Minister & Me*), Nolan and I head to the beach to play bocce ball, the waves lapping against the shore. It's more fun than I expected. I'm absolutely terrible at it, launching it like a fastball. When Nolan realizes the first terrible throw wasn't an anomaly, he stands behind me to adjust my stance, my shoulders, and my hips, and helps me guide the ball. His breath skirts over the back of my neck as he places his hand on my wrist to guide the ball to the left. It still manages to veer off course. I start laughing so hard, I nearly topple back into him.

By the end of the game, I'm tipsy after too many fruity beachside drinks, too loud for someone who planned to fly under the radar all weekend. And somehow my flip-flop met an untimely death during bocce ball. The sand and asphalt are so hot, you could make a perfect fried egg on them.

"Hop on," Nolan says immediately, bending down. In one swift, practiced motion, he swoops me onto his back. I barely have time to react before he starts down the sandy path.

I rest my chin on his shoulder as we make our way toward the villa. "Was I really that bad at bocce ball?" I ask.

Nolan chuckles, adjusting his grip as he navigates the uneven ground. "Yes."

"Ugh. It's petty, but I really wanted to beat Hunter and Laine," I admit.

"You're allowed some pettiness. You've been handling this whole thing like a champ."

"Honestly, it's easier than I thought it would be," I admit. "For a long time, it bothered me. I don't like the way it happened, but I know they really tried to spare my feelings. It wasn't perfect, but they tried." I pause, my gaze drifting to the sky. "I always say love stories don't have to end perfectly to be beautiful or worth telling. I've always liked books without those perfect epilogues. But something I've realized lately is that love doesn't have to start perfectly, either. It doesn't always come wrapped in a pretty package with a perfect bow."

"That's true."

"Sometimes it's messy, uneven, jagged. Something we can't quite tamp down. It's scary when it sneaks up on you when you least expect it, because it's not something we can fully understand or control. It's scary." I pause. "Shit. Sorry. I'm rambling. I do that when I drink. I probably make zero sense right now."

He chuckles softly beneath me. "No, you're making perfect sense. It's scary, sure. But still worth it, I think."

"It is. It's raw and real. And beautiful in its own messed-up way."

CHAPTER 37

Nolan

After the beach, we finally get a chance to unwind and unpack for a couple hours before the non-wedding. We've been in our room for a total of twenty minutes and I'm officially nervous. I haven't been this anxious around a woman in ages. I'm second-guessing, checking in the mirror.

As soon as we crossed the threshold into our room, the air shifted. Maybe it's the afternoon humidity, but there's always been an energy between us, and now it's quadrupled. It's like something has been unleashed. The anticipation of knowing things aren't off-limits anymore.

As Andi unpacks and organizes her things ritualistically, I can barely take my eyes off her. When she disappears into the bathroom, I head onto the balcony for some air.

It's private, on the corner of the building, with two cush-ioned chaises. To my left, the coastline stretches out like a giant, rocky puzzle waiting to be explored. Above me, the sky is a brilliant blue dotted with fluffy clouds.

When I turn on the resort Wi-Fi, my phone pings with a message from Emma.

> EM: Huge news. Mom's house sold!!

> EM: Well, kind of.

I knew it was officially going on the market today. But I never would have guessed things would move that quickly.

> NOLAN: What?

> EM: It was on the market for half a day and it got three offers OVER ASKING PRICE. Hallie has given them 24 hours to put in their best offer. It's a bidding war!! So exciting!

> NOLAN: Whoa. That's amazing. Keep me posted.

I'm still reeling from the news when Andi comes onto the balcony.

"What's up?" she asks from behind me. I spin around to find her glowing, her skin tinted peach from the sun. She's put on a bikini. A small one, with very little fabric, to be precise—not that I'm complaining.

"There's a bidding war on my mom's house," I tell her, barely able to look away from her. The way the strings of the bikini bottoms hug the small of her waist.

Her eyes widen. "Holy crap. Already?"

I nod, explaining how we got three offers on the first day.

She doesn't jump for joy, or react. Her soft gaze just roams my face, like she's trying to read me. "How do you feel about it?"

"I feel . . . bittersweet, I guess. Em and I have lost hours of sleep worrying about how we'd pay for Mom's care at such an expensive facility. But it's sad in a lot of ways, making this transition. It feels like admitting defeat, realizing that Emma and I don't have the ability to take care of Mom. Knowing her health is declining too rapidly for us to manage."

She runs a hand over the underside of my forearm. "I know it's hard. But you guys are a hundred percent doing the right thing. Your mom knows it, too. When you were in Montreal, she was telling me about all the field trips and activities they do at Lakeside. She's such a social butterfly, I think she'll love it there."

I squeeze her hand, grateful for the reminder. Grateful to be here with her.

"Can you do my backside?" Andi asks. When she turns to get set up on the chaise, the small width of fabric barely covers her perfectly round ass.

Jesus Christ. If I die right now, at least I'll die happy.

Before I succumb to death, a couple things happen. First, I fling my hand back to stabilize myself on the balcony railing. Then, I mumble something in the affirmative, trying to ignore the slight jiggle of her backside as she flips around on the chaise. Who am I kidding? This image is now permanently imprinted on my brain. I will never be the same.

Like a complete Neanderthal, I forget my name, where we are, what I'm supposed to be doing, until she gives me a look over her shoulder, her eyes darting to the oil.

I set myself on the side of the chair and pour the oil on her back. I start with small circles at the nape of her neck, slowly skating down her shoulders. The tips of my fingers tingle; I'm desperate to explore every surface of her body.

I make my way down, over the backs of her thighs and up. The only place I haven't done is her ass, but I don't want to presume anything. Her breath quickens as my fingers dance dangerously close.

As if she can sense my hesitancy, she says, "Make sure you get everywhere."

CHAPTER 38

Andi

Nolan is trying to kill me. There's no other explanation for the way he's teasing me. I've given him outright permission to touch my ass. I want him all over me. I want him to brand me. But he's taking his sweet time. By the way his breath is ragged against my back with each touch, I can tell he wants this as much as I do.

I didn't know how much I needed this until now. My whole body ignites in tiny explosions, lighting up every nerve in my body as his fingers move down my back, his thumbs skimming over the sides of my breasts.

As he runs his fingers south, I arch my back and he seems to get the hint. His fingers move down, molding over my bottom. He spends an obscene amount of time there, like he's giving each cheek special attention. Every so often, he slips his thumb under the small strip of material, applying the softest amount of pressure where I never knew I wanted it.

"Is this okay?" he whispers, moving down, gliding the tips of his fingers over my center under the fabric.

"Yes," I manage, parting my legs slightly to give him access.

He shifts the material over completely, and his thumb fully slides over my seam. I let out an embarrassingly loud moan, which disappears into the hot, open air.

"Goddamnit," he hisses, running his thumb back up over my slit, stroking me through the oil, still managing to dodge my clit. I'm absolutely throbbing now, pushing back for more pressure.

"Does that feel good?"

"Yes. Please keep going," I grit out, melting into him.

The wet noises should be illegal as he slides his index finger and thumb up and down my slit. My vision turns spotty when he finally grazes me where I need it.

"You are going to be the end of me." His voice alone threatens to detonate me. Just as the pressure begins to mount, a voice from the pathway reaches us. It's another couple, walking hand in hand toward a pair of chaises below on the beach.

Panicked, I push up, until Nolan shushes me and pushes me back down. He tosses a towel over my lower half. I stay silent for a few breaths as he continues touching me under the towel, completely discreet.

There's something about the risk of getting caught that riles me even tighter.

He gently presses his finger to my entrance, teasing me. "You want me inside you? Ask for it."

"Please," I whisper.

One finger slides in, hooking inside me in a way that makes me jolt, makes me desperate for more fullness, more friction.

He follows it up with a second finger, filling me completely in a perfect rhythm. It's like a spark catching fire, lighting me up from the inside out. "Holy shit. You're so tight. I can feel every pulse."

His touch renders me completely mindless, to the point where my body has completely taken over. I naturally arch for him, propping myself on all fours, utterly begging for more as the pressure builds.

He eases his fingers in and out, teasing, torturing me, burying them in me in a way I'm positive only he knows how. I squeeze and push back against his fingers until the flames dance and twist their way through all the forgotten parts of me. Until I can't keep still. Until I'm gripping the sides of the chaise so hard, my knuckles are white. Until I'm cursing and mumbling incoherent nonsense under my breath. "Oh fuck, Nolan."

"Keep fucking my hand, baby. That's it, just like that."

The pressure dilates to a point of no return. The pleasure tumbles down my spine in a spasm so intense, it nearly takes me out. I grasp for the towel slung over the top of the chaise to muffle my cry as it pounds through me, over and over again. It's never felt this way before. Ever.

Eager to return the favor, I motion for him to sit on the edge of the chaise, and I drop to my knees, running my fingers over the hem of his shorts.

He swallows, helping me take them off. I do a double take when I pull him out of his briefs, entirely mesmerized. Let's just say, size is not a concern of his.

I plant a map dot of kisses all along his inner thigh, teasing him until he can't take it anymore. He grips my jaw and looks me in the eye. "I'm gonna need you to stop teasing me," he commands.

I reach to grip his wide base with my hand. I give it a couple strokes before licking around the tip, barely taking him in before he nearly falls back on the chair, glossy-eyed, his jaw clenched. He's been mouthy this whole time, but he looks so completely and utterly wrecked, I think he's lost all ability to speak.

"Fuck," he finally manages, his legs trembling. Heat blooms through me, just seeing him out of control like this.

I've never done this before. And while I've written about it, it's a whole different story actually doing it. Encouraged, I lean forward, taking as much as I can, which isn't even half. I use my hand on the base, setting the pace, slowly lowering myself deeper and deeper until he can't take it anymore, until he grips my hair and pulls me back.

"Do you want me to stop?" I whisper.

"No. Yes. I just . . . We need to slow down. That mouth of yours is going to make me lose my mind."

I flash him a smirk, settling back on my knees, waiting for instructions.

"Let's go inside," he grits out.

CHAPTER 39

———————◆•◆———————

Nolan

Apparently, I lose my mind anyway.

The moment my lips touch hers at the foot of the bed, I'm a goner. Of all the things I've imagined doing, this is what I've craved the most. The feeling of those soft, plump lips against mine. She tastes so fucking sweet, like the pineapple juice we drank in the front lobby on the way to the villa.

She sighs into me and steps back, just enough for my eyes to rake over her. "Let me see you."

She swallows, reaching back to unclip the straps behind her neck. My knees go limp when her breasts fall out. They're the perfect teardrop shape, full at the bottom, nipples begging for me. I immediately drop to my knees, worshipping them. They're so full, each hand can barely contain them. I take each one in my mouth, running my tongue over her until she's gasping, until she pushes back.

"You want me to stop?" I ask.

"No. I want you to fuck me," she says. For a moment, I think she's slightly embarrassed, but she can tell by the way I feel against her stomach how much that turns me on.

"I'll fuck you on one condition," I say, sitting back on the bed, her in between my legs. "You're going to tell me what you want. Every step of the way."

She blinks up at me as I run my hands down her backside, over her ass. "I wouldn't even know where to start."

"What haven't you done that you've always wanted to do?"

"Literally anything."

"No," I say sternly, giving her a soft tap on the ass. "No more people pleasing. I want you to tell me what you want me to do to you."

She swallows and it occurs to me she's never been asked what she wants. "I don't know if I can," she whispers.

"Sweetheart, look at me." I wait until she makes eye contact with me. "Listen, anything you want me to do to you, I guarantee I've already thought about it a million times. You have no idea how much I've wanted you like this, how many times I've come in my own hand thinking about you."

She tilts her head, taking it all in. For a second, I'm terrified I've freaked her out. But she nods, straightening her shoulders slightly. "Okay."

"That's my girl. Now what do you want me to do?"

"I—I want to sit on your face."

"Fuck," I hiss. "You want to sit on my face while I eat your pussy?"

"Mm-hm."

I back up on the bed and motion for her to come with me. She straddles my chest, a little unsure what to do with herself. I pull her arm upward, bringing her over me, taking a second to stop and admire her. "Stunning" doesn't even start to describe her.

"Hold on to the headboard," I instruct.

She does as she's told, and I can tell by her face that she's a little anxious. I start slow and soft, running the flat side of my tongue over her, and it's game over. For both of us. She gasps, nearly collapsing over me. "Fuck, Nolan."

"You okay?"

She nods, her legs still tense on either side of my head.

"Do you know how long I've imagined this? How long I've imagined how good you taste?" I ask, which makes her ease up a little. "So fucking sweet."

When I sweep from the front to the back, she nearly loses it, tensing her stomach. "Fuck," she manages.

"If you like it, I want to hear that you like it. You're holding back. If you want me to stay on your clit, tell me."

"Keep going, right there. Please."

"Keep going until you come?" I clarify, ready to absolutely devour her.

"You're going to—" she starts, finally letting herself relax into me, grinding herself into my face. Her thighs clench as I lap her up. It's not long before she's riding my face, taking what she wants, angling me exactly how she likes it.

"Scream. Show me how much you like this," I say, my lips vibrating against her. And she does. Loud. It's music to my ears as she grips the headboard, her body trembling over me as she rides my face with abandon. I want to burn this image of her losing it, of her tits bouncing over me, into my memory for all of eternity, if possible.

"I'm sorry if I was a little much."

"Are you kidding me? Andi, do you know how hot it is that I can get you off like that?"

"You're lying."

"I swear on everything, it was. I almost came just from the sound and taste of you coming alone."

"That was . . . I've just never done that before. And not just sitting on someone's face. Actually being vocal, you know? It was different."

"Good different?"

"I think so."

"Well, good. Because I like a woman who knows what she wants in bed."

Her eyes blaze. "Oh yeah? So if I beg you to fuck me right now, that would turn you on?"

"Sweetheart, you don't ever have to beg. How do you want it?"

"I want you to fuck me from behind."

"Get on your hands and knees," I order, grabbing a condom from the drawer. When she does, I inch myself forward into position right behind her, rolling it on. "Spread your knees."

I run myself along her seam and nearly detonate right then and there. I've imagined what it would feel like to be inside of her, and fuck, I don't know if I can handle it.

Finally, she pushes back against me, absorbing my tip. I suck in a breath, feeling her close in around me. It's the best fucking feeling in the world.

"We have to go slow," I manage. "You're so tight."

She nods, rolling her hips back to take a little more. "More," she whispers. We go glacially slow, not just for her, but for me. As she sinks lower and lower, she pulses and grips around me, and I swear to god, I feel every single thing. It's disorienting, how every single nerve ending is pulsing and tensing. I am officially ruined.

"Oh fuck, yes," she hisses, taking me fully. It takes a couple moments, but she finally adjusts around me, just barely.

"Don't fucking move," I order, holding her hips to keep her still.

"Why?" she whispers, her tone laced with a need that drives me wild.

"Because I'm going to come and I'd prefer not to embarrass myself entirely."

She smirks, leaning forward into the pillow, moving in a way that nearly ends me. "Please fuck me," she begs.

Even teetering on the edge of a near-death situation, I don't know if I'd be able to say no to this woman. I rear back and enter her again, my vision going fuzzy at the sound of her soft whimpers. I lean forward, kissing her neck, desperate to be as close to her as possible.

We find a rhythm, going slow at first. And then she starts bucking her ass against me and I lose it. I start to thrust hard into her once I know she can take it, relishing each moan, each cry, each "Fuck."

And when she tells me she's going to come again, I hold her tighter, reaching around her front to touch her the way I know she likes it. It doesn't take long until she starts shaking and collapses onto the mattress, contracting under me.

As it rips through her, she closes her eyes and tosses her head back, her plump lips parted, the flush of her pleasure warming her cheeks and her chest. I've never seen anything more beautiful.

I don't know how I manage to hold back as long as I do, but I come with her. It's so intense, my ears ring and my vision goes entirely. I lose all ability to do anything but ride out the explosions of pleasure, which last for a scary amount of time, eventually settling in small pulses.

I kiss her neck, tracing my finger over every curve and slope, treasuring her the way she deserves. I roll her into my side, chest to chest, relishing her warmth, every point of contact, our fingers intertwined. She blinks up at me, resting her forehead against mine, holding it there, our breath syncing.

I don't know that I've ever been more connected to someone else than I am right now. I think about how right it feels having her here with me. How right I feel at home with her.

It's official: I have never felt something so fucking good in my entire life. And it's not just the orgasm. It's *her*.

CHAPTER 40

Andi

The thought of leaving this bed to go to the non-ceremony feels like pure torture. In fact, I'm convinced my legs have transformed into noodles, incapable of carrying me any farther than the edge of the mattress. I might as well resign myself to living here forever, like the grandparents in *Willy Wonka and the Chocolate Factory*. Only instead of lying in bed and making snarky comments about the outside world, I'd be with Nolan.

Nolan is in the shower, whistling what sounds like the "Wedding March." So I avoid reality a little longer and check my author email account. I haven't looked at it in days, and the thought of doing so is almost as daunting as attempting to move from this bed.

I start scanning the A. A. Zed emails on my phone. It's the usual, a bunch of spam mail, author newsletters, and promotional offers. As I scroll, one email stands out. Its subject line practically jumps off the screen.

Subject: Representation Offer for Your Bestselling Book

Dear A. A. Zed,

My name is Cher Reynolds and I'm a literary agent with Reynolds and Holburg Literary Agency. I recently had the pleasure of reading THE PRIME MINISTER & ME and I was absolutely captivated by your writing. Based on its tremendous success over the last few weeks, I believe there's potential for your work to reach an even wider audience.

I'm reaching out to you today because I would love the opportunity to represent you and your book. Between you and me, many large publishing houses have expressed interest in purchasing the rights. I'm genuinely so excited about the possibility of working together and helping you achieve even greater success in your writing career.

Please let me know if you would be interested in exploring this opportunity further, and we can schedule a time to chat at your convenience.

Warmest regards,
Cher

Holy shit. Cher Reynolds is a powerhouse, representing some of the biggest romance authors in the business. I came across her name over and over back when I was researching the traditional publishing route years ago. And the weirdest part? There are two emails from other well-known agents asking for calls to discuss potential representation, just casually sitting in my inbox.

How is this real? When I published my books, I immediately opted to self-publish. I knew going the traditional route (getting my books published by a large publishing house to be sold in actual bookstores) would be difficult. It would require not only a literary agent to believe in my work, but an editor and an entire publishing team to love it enough to pay me for it. I never imagined anyone would like my work enough, nor did I want to give up creative control, so I never bothered to try.

I try to tamp down my excitement, my urge to finally spring from the bed and dance around the room as I toggle through the emails. When Nolan finally emerges from the bathroom, his hair still flecked with water droplets, he eyes me curiously, clueing in to the mix of emotions playing across my face.

"Everything okay?" he asks, eyes searching mine.

"Yeah. Um, I . . . I got some emails from literary agents who want to represent me and sell my books to publishers," I say, lightning fast.

His jaw unhinges and his eyes go wide, studying me, like he's puzzled by my reaction. "Are you kidding me? That's fucking amazing! How are you not freaking out right now?"

I shift uneasily, still holding my phone. "I don't know. What if no publisher buys it? What if they completely botch the marketing?" Realistically, the book is doing amazingly well as it is. Do I really need an agent and a publisher, who will take an even larger cut of the profits?

While I launch into a speech about all the downsides and risks of publishing through a large house, Nolan's expression morphs into one of genuine confusion mixed with frustration.

He shakes his head, as if trying to clear his thoughts. "Okay, that's a lot of cons. What are the pros?"

"It would reach a much wider audience. If it did well, it could lead to mainstream recognition. Potentially international recognition. And mostly, my book would be sold in brick-and-mortar stores." My heart thrums with longing at the mere thought of casually seeing my book on a shelf at a bookstore. Discreetly watching a customer pick it up and read the back. Maybe even purchase it. The more I visualize it, the more I realize how badly I've secretly wished for that to become a reality, as silly as that sounds.

Nolan senses the longing. "Are you seriously doubting this? You've got agents reaching out to you! This is what every writer dreams of. It's like being scouted for the major leagues."

I sigh, letting my head fall back against the headboard. "I know, it's just—what if it fails, despite an agent and a publisher investing in me? What if this whole thing exposes the truth? That I wrote the books to begin with?"

He takes it all in, really considers it. "That's a completely valid fear. All of it. But you have to know, what happened to you says nothing about your worth or your talent. I think you'd be doing yourself a disservice if you didn't at least take one call. Just one. And if you don't like what they have to say, we don't ever have to talk about this again. Regardless, I'll still be here, supporting you."

One look at him and I'm overcome with instant relief. "You really think it's worth taking the leap?"

"Your books are already bestsellers. They're already successful beyond what you thought possible. Even if an agent or publisher royally fucks things up, no one can take away your success."

"One book is a bestseller," I correct him.

He gives me an eye roll. "Andi, deflect all you want. But having people read your work has always been your dream, ever since I met you. And I'm not talking about making everyone else happy, or pleasing your mom. I'm talking about doing what truly makes you light up. Every time you write, you get this giddy look on your face. You literally glow when you talk about it."

"That's the sweat and angst, but go on," I tease.

"I think you should do this for yourself. Not because you have anything to prove, because you don't. But because you, of all people, deserve to live out your dreams in full."

The breadth of his words hits me in the chest to the point that tears sprout, pouring over my lash line. Not because I'm upset, or scared. But because no one has truly seen me like him. No one has understood what I've gone through or what I need before I even understand it myself.

He wraps his arms around me, pulling me in so tight, I feel entirely sheltered. In his arms, no one can hurt me. No agent, editor, reader. No one.

I finally pull back and nod. "Okay. I'll do it."

● ● ●

Cher calls within five minutes of me confirming I'd like to talk. Nolan goes onto the balcony while I take the call, giving me privacy.

It lasts almost an hour, though it doesn't feel like it. Cher has an immediate warmth, like I'm talking to a dear friend. It feels like it's all over before it even begins, even though she walks through everything extremely thoroughly, graciously stopping to answer any questions I have.

I'm still absorbing it all by the time I head onto the balcony, back to Nolan, who's pacing back and forth.

"How did it go?" he asks.

My lips curve into a small, tentative smile. "Amazing, actually. I mean, I should probably take the other calls, but Cher was so lovely. First, she talked about how much she loved the book and my writing. She thinks it could be really huge in the market and talked about how she thinks it should be positioned and which houses would be best placed for that."

Nolan's entire face lights up, and he steps forward to wrap me into a massive hug. "Holy shit."

When we pull back, my face falls a little. "But what I liked most was that she was honest and realistic. She didn't make any wild promises. And she also cautioned me about the risk of being doxed again when I told her I want to remain anonymous under my pen name, no photos, no interviews."

"But people write under pen names all the time, don't they? I mean, they can't make you go on camera or anything."

"She had no problem with me staying anonymous. But she couldn't promise that people wouldn't be able to find out my identity, especially if the book were as successful as she thinks it'll be."

He nods. "That's fair. But hear me out—if it's as big as we think it will be, will you really need to keep your job?"

I bite the inside of my lip in consideration. "I don't know."

"Even for your dream job?"

I shrug. "It's never been something that seemed possible." It's not that working for Gretchen is something I absolutely love. But I'm good at it. It's a known quantity. And after all this time, working for Gretchen has become my identity. I've never had the confidence to even consider writing full-time, until now. If I did, I'd have no choice but to tell my family the truth.

"But what if it were? I know the job gives you a purpose. And I know how important it is for you. But does it really serve your soul? Or is it just serving your need to please people?" His words drive their way directly to my chest. He's not wrong. I've never felt passionate about working for Gretchen, especially this past year. But the thought of quitting something I know I'm good at for the unknown is terrifying.

"I don't know."

He bows his head. "I get it. And I'm sorry if it sounds like I'm pushing you. You don't have to make any decision now. Sit on it for as long as you need to. And if you ultimately decide that you don't want to go down that route, I'll completely support you."

"Thank you."

"But you have to do one thing for me," he says, stepping forward.

"What?"

He wraps his hands around my waist and pulls me into his chest. "I want you to celebrate this. Regardless of what you decide, this is a massive accomplishment. You are officially the coolest person I know. Everyone wants to write a book, but hardly anyone sits down and does it, let alone does it well and creates something that becomes such a success on such a huge scale, all with a full-time, demanding job no less. And you're such a workhorse, with all these goals. I don't think you celebrate yourself enough or take the time to really sit and think about how fucking amazing you are. You've worked so hard and you deserve every good thing that's going to come your way. So you're going to put a beautiful dress on tonight and we're going to celebrate."

"Celebrate," I repeat.

"Exactly. We're celebrating the fuck out of this win, no matter what happens."

CHAPTER 41

————— ◆•◆ —————

Andi

The ceremony, despite its "non-wedding" label, is absolutely and completely normal—short, sweet, and surprisingly touching. Laine's and Hunter's vows are so heartfelt, so genuinely adorable, that I actually shed a few tears.

The reception is magical, set on the same beachfront pavilion we ate breakfast on. The sounds of waves crashing and the string lights twinkling above us are like a scene straight out of a movie.

Nolan and I spend most of the night on the dance floor, alternating between dancing and making frequent trips to the bar. But what really gets to me isn't just the dancing or the margaritas; it's how Nolan treats me. We haven't made anything official, or talked about the future, but he treats me like his girlfriend, touching me in these small, sweet ways, kissing my neck, wrapping his arms around me and pulling me into his side as we move through the crowd.

By the end of the night, we're stumbling back to the villa,

laughing at everything. At one point, I attempt to kick off my shoes mid-stride, convinced I can walk better barefoot, and I nearly land in a bush. By the time we get to the villa, we're still dying over the random guy at the bar who thought Nolan and Hunter were brothers and spent a solid five minutes trying to convince us of his theory.

"I don't look anything like him, by the way," he argues vehemently. They don't look anything alike, but it's fun to tease him about it.

"I mean, you *do* have similar hair," I tease, resting my chin on Nolan's shoulder as we fumble with the villa door.

"Clearly you have a type," Nolan counters.

I laugh, leaning into him as the villa door swings open, the sounds of the ocean still faintly in the background. It hits me then—somewhere between the bad dancing, the hand-holding, and the ridiculous bar conversations—how much I love being with Nolan. How much I want to do this forever.

"Can you believe Hunter's dad's name is William Williams?" Nolan says, shaking his head in disbelief as he collapses onto the bed, still in his suit. "You can't tell me his parents weren't sociopaths."

I laugh. "Yeah, it is pretty unfortunate."

He continues, his voice full of mock outrage, "It's like they just gave up. 'What should we name the kid? Too much effort. Let's just double up.'"

"Or they *really* liked the name. I actually think it's a nice name," I point out.

He flashes me a smirk, pulling himself into a seated position on the edge of the bed. "You like most names."

"I do! I think they can work for the right person. Will is one of my backup names if I have kids."

Nolan's eyes narrow, his expression somewhere between teasing and scandalized. "Wait, wait, wait. You have baby names?"

"Well, not an official list," I admit, shrugging. "But I've got some favorites in mind."

He leans in, his eyes twinkling. "What are they?"

"I'm not telling you!" I say, crossing my arms. "You'll just make fun of them."

He raises a hand to his chest, feigning shock. "I would *never*. In fact, I'm a huge supporter of well-thought-out names."

I shoot him a skeptical look. "You have opinions—strong ones."

Nolan grins mischievously, motioning for me to come closer. "Okay, fine. I might have *some* thoughts. But come on, before you name your future child Turbo or something, let me help out."

I swat his leg playfully, standing between them. "Turbo? That's what you think I'd name a child?"

"I'm just saying, it could happen. I've seen weirder." He wraps his arms around my waist, hands settling at the small of my back. "All right, hit me with your other picks."

I sigh, knowing this is a terrible idea. "Okay, I like Olivia."

He nods, thoughtfully rubbing his chin. "Olivia, hmm . . . Olivia seems like someone who's super kind but will absolutely school you on trivia night."

I laugh.

"But," he continues, "Liv is the one you have to watch out for. She's the wild card. Probably owns, like, three motorcycles."

I roll my eyes. "Okay, since you're clearly the expert, what names *do* you like?"

I'm half expecting him to dodge the question, but instead, he answers without hesitation. "Pippa for a girl, Jack for a boy."

I blink, surprised. "Wait, seriously? You have baby names, too?"

Nolan shrugs, completely casual. "Not that I'm planning anything, but yeah. Always liked those names."

I smirk. "I like Jack."

"Jack's a classic," Nolan says. "Jack's the guy who'd change your tires and then offer to repaint your house and build your fence because he's nice like that. He's probably mayor of the town, too."

I laugh, shaking my head. "What about Jack Turbo?"

He belts out a laugh. "Interesting combo. Sounds like an accountant by day, vigilante slash street racer by night."

"Destined for greatness."

He snorts, pulling me down onto his lap.

"I'm glad we came. Not just to celebrate Laine and Hunter, but it's been nice, being here . . ." I squeeze my eyes shut, my arms wrapped around his neck. "Sorry. I don't know what I'm saying."

"No, it's been amazing. I don't want to leave tomorrow."

"Though that means you'll get to see Cody again," I remind him.

His whole face lights up. "True. I miss the little guy. I actually texted Deidra asking her how he's doing, but she hasn't responded yet."

I smile into his neck. "I don't know if I'm ready for real life."

"You don't have to be. At least, not yet," he says, a mischievous glint in his eye before he shackles my hands above my head on the mattress. He plants a map of kisses all the way down my body, down my neck, chest, over each breast, over the valley of my stomach, and down to where I'm desperate for him.

And then he does it. He runs the flat part of his tongue from the top, down my center, sweeping my entire length. He takes turns sucking my clit and licking me top to bottom in long, languished strokes, like he's a man starved.

I shift on top of him and he cups my tits, rolling his thumbs over my nipples before grinding my ass to him. He leans over and grabs a condom from the bedside table, slipping it on.

We fall into bed together, me on top of him. The past few times have been slow. Nolan likes to stretch things out, wind me up until I'm begging for release. But tonight, the energy is rushed, needy, desperate, as though we both sense how much we need the connection.

I sink onto him with ease, utterly desperate to settle the ache in my core that blooms whenever he's around. It feels so deep, like he's intrinsically a part of me.

"Andi," he grunts, hands on my hips to set the pace. "You feel so good. So. Good."

He props himself up against the headboard so we're face-to-face. A flicker of sadness passes over his expression before he captures my lips in a kiss so urgent, so deep, I practically dissolve into him. And it feels different, us looking each other in the eye as we move in sync, our bodies trembling, melding into one. It's intimate, like it has been every time since the first day we got here, even if neither of us wants to admit it.

The climb is so fast, I press my hands into the mattress to slow us down. I want to remember everything, how he sounds, how he tastes, what he feels like.

A smile spreads over his face, and it almost takes me out before he brings one palm flush over my heart. "I can feel you, right here. You're already close, aren't you?"

I bite my lip through a sharp gasp, nodding as the heat inside me nearly unfurls. "So close."

I expect him to torture me a little, make me wait. But he starts bucking up into me faster and faster.

I study the way his jaw tenses as he works me, the way he tips his head back, groaning with abandon, the way he looks at me like I'm something to be cherished, even loved. From that alone, the pressure inside me mounts to nearly a point of no return.

"I need . . ." He hesitates, swallowing.

"Need what?"

Our eyes lock and he doesn't waver. "You," he whispers.

At his words, I fall apart entirely as he absorbs every tremble. Every shock wave rippling through my body. It's bigger, more intense than any other time because it's not just about pleasure, or the technique he used to get me off. It's about him. And me.

He thrusts hard into me, finishing violently in a ragged, fractured groan that turns everything upright. I come all over again, in soft, subdued waves. We stay like that, watching each other lose all control in a way we've never been able to do with anyone else.

Our vision tunneled, we go limp in each other's arms, still moving slowly, not ready to end the connection. I don't think I'm physically capable of letting go.

As he holds me, I think about what he said. How I need him, too. How safe I feel with him. Not just because he could probably kill somebody with his bare hands. I've never felt safe like this with anyone, physically or emotionally. I've never felt like I had to put on a persona, like I had to perform for him. I've never felt like he was grading me or that he had any expectations for me. I can just be.

I think about the night we met. How he carried my groceries and filled my world with color all within the span of a few hours. How I pursued my dream, all because he encouraged me to do it. I think about the fog I was in for months after he left and how it never really lifted.

Since he's been back, every second with him feels like standing in the sunlight. How my heart leaps, twirls, and sizzles when his name flashes on my phone screen. I think about how quickly I trusted him and how he never wanted anything in return for keeping my secret. I think about how much he cares about his mom, his family. I've never met someone like him, ever. And more than that, how he sees me. How he believes in me like no one else.

It's all-consuming, how desperately I need him. It scares me. I've never needed anyone before.

CHAPTER 42

Nolan

It's at the luggage carousel that it hits me, all at once. I'm in love with Andi.

Of all the moments for my brain to choose, it picks this one—us sweaty, skin crisp and sunburnt, her head resting lazily on my shoulder as we watch suitcases circle endlessly on the belt. It feels like a confetti bomb detonated in my chest.

I love this woman.

It doesn't feel as foreign as it should, considering I've never been in love—not like this. It blankets me in a steady, affectionate warmth, spreading through me until it fills every corner of my being. Maybe because the feeling has been there longer than I realized, quietly brimming under the surface, waiting for me to figure it the hell out. And now that I have, it feels obvious. As simple as the sky being blue. The earth being round.

She tilts a goofy grin at me, giddy when her bag tumbles

down the chute, entirely oblivious to the fact that she has me wrapped around her finger.

I want to rewrite everything she knows about love—tear down whatever walls she's built—and show her it's not just some fleeting thing. That it can be good, real, and that it can last. We'll surely mess up along the way, we'll have hard times, but we'll make it. Fuck, I want to lie in bed, debating baby names, planning a future. A home.

I'm still reeling from the weight of it when my phone vibrates in my pocket. I glance at the screen and see two missed calls from Jones. Weird. Lately, I'm the one calling him.

As we head to the parking garage, I dial him back.

Jones picks up on the first ring. "Good news, man," he says, his tone oddly chipper.

"Good news?" I echo, half listening. I'm distracted by Andi's ass as she walks in front of me down the narrow space between the parked cars.

"You're going to Denmark."

I stop walking, convinced I've misheard. "Denmark? As in, Scandinavia, Denmark?"

"Is there any other Denmark? Yeah, royal protection. The second-born Danish princess. She's starting university and they need extra security. Two-year contract. And get this—they specifically requested *you*. Apparently, your stubborn ass came highly recommended by a certain sexy PM with luscious locks."

I blink and blink again, trying to take it all in. "When does it start?"

"As soon as you can get out there. Better brush up on your Viking skills," he replies casually, like he didn't just casually toss a grenade my way.

"Holy shit."

"You fucking owe me for this one, Crosby. I'll send you the paperwork ASAP when it comes in. Talk soon."

He hangs up, and I'm left standing there, the phone still pressed to my ear, staring blankly at the dented Honda in front of me.

Denmark? Two years?

I glance over at Andi, waiting for me to unlock my mom's car, effortlessly gorgeous and completely unaware.

"Can we stop for food on the way home?" she asks hopefully.

"Uh, yeah. Sure," I say, making quick work of distracting myself loading the luggage.

She eyes me suspiciously when I slide into the driver's seat. "Everything okay?" she asks, a noticeable edge to her voice.

I swallow as we drive out of the lot, suddenly aware of every second ticking by, the weight of it all. I've just realized I'm madly in love with Andi, and not ten seconds later, the opportunity of a lifetime drops into my lap.

I wanted this for months, begged for it. Royal assignments are sought-after because they come with a lot of perks, despite the archaic protocol. They're prestigious, the operations are complex, there's extensive travel, and they're long-term. An assignment in a nice Scandinavian country to boot? That's something I never would have dreamed of. That said, they require long hours. Everyone knows you give up your personal life for royal assignments, which, until recently, wouldn't have been a problem.

"Jones—my boss. He called to tell me I got a posting. Two years. In Denmark," I tell her, keeping my tone neutral. I have no idea how she's going to react. Even I've barely processed it all.

Her eyes widen, though the rest of her body stays stationary. "Denmark? Wow. When?"

"Starting as soon as I can get out there."

She blinks, like she's trying to make sense of it. A beat goes by before she speaks. "Congratulations, Nolan. That's amazing news, isn't it?"

It should be amazing news. It should feel like freedom, like the break I've been waiting for. But it doesn't. Because I'm not certain I want that life anymore.

I run my hand through my hair. "It is—at least, I thought so. Before you."

She winces. Winces. "Nolan, you've been desperate to leave since the start of summer. This seems like your chance . . . to get your life back."

Your life back. Her words hang in the air between us, echoing in my head. "But what if I don't want it back? What if I wanted to stay?"

Her expression falters. "Nolan, think about this. Do you really want to change your whole life plan for . . . this fantasy?"

"Fantasy?" I repeat, the word feeling bitter on my tongue. Is that what this is to her?

"I mean, that's kind of what this is, isn't it? Pretend?" She hesitates, searching for the right words. "Sure, we may have caught feelings along the way. Lost ourselves a little—"

"Lost ourselves?" I ask, the blood rushing to my ears.

She nods. "Yeah. I don't think we were thinking clearly."

"Andi, this summer with you was the clearest I've felt . . . ever. I know I was supposed to leave, but I can't do that if you feel even the slightest bit the same as me."

"I just don't know" is all she says. Her silence is deafening as she sits there, looking out the window at the parking lot.

I wait for her to turn and look me in the eye. "Andi, don't. You might be able to fool yourself, but you're not fooling me. I haven't felt like this, ever. You're the first person I've ever pictured a life with. A home with. I've never done that with anyone until you. The only pretending I've done is acting like I don't love you. Do you not feel the same way?"

"Nolan, I—I'm not saying I don't feel the same way," she stammers, looking down at her lap, her hands wringing together. "It's the exact opposite. The way I feel about you . . . it scares me. And if you changed your mind and stayed for me and it didn't work out . . ."

"I would be staying mostly for you. But I'd also be staying for my mom, for Em, Cody . . . I don't need to travel and live out of my suitcase anymore. I want my life here. With you." When I say it out loud, it all plays out in front of me, a life of family, not of work for the sake of work. Embracing all of Ottawa's seasons. Barbecues on hot, lazy summer days with Andi, Mom, Emma, and the kids. Fresh autumn afternoons frolicking down crunchy, leafy trails in the woods with Cody. Long, snowcapped winters that call for lazy days inside, curled up under a mountain of covers with Andi, cups of marshmallow-topped hot chocolate warming our hands.

Her eyes well with tears. "I want that, too," she says softly. "But I'm scared. I don't know if I would be okay if it didn't work out, regardless of all the reasons you want to stay. That's why I need you to really think about this. I can't let you make such a huge decision on a whim."

My heart twinges when her voice cracks a little, and it hits me hard. She's scared. Scared to believe in what we have. Scared of what happens if it all falls apart. And to be honest, so am I—only, instead of turning inward to me, she's turning away.

"A whim," I repeat, because it feels like anything but. I understand what she's saying. She needs to know I'm all in. That it isn't just an impulsive decision I'll regret. My word isn't enough.

"You've been through a lot the past few months. Everything with your mom and her move to the facility. I think you need some time. Please, take it," she pleads.

And maybe she has a point. Maybe I do need to think it through.

CHAPTER 43

Nolan

fter Mexico, I can't sleep without Andi curled up next to me, the pads of her fingers tracing little squiggles and hearts on my chest. Her small body managing to hog 70 percent of the bed and covers. There were so many times I wanted to call her just to hear her voice.

Unfortunately, I don't have plans to see her until the gala at the end of the week. I've taken four days off work to handle the move. While we were in Mexico, the house officially sold to the highest bidder, who offered $75K over the asking price. Emma and I have been busy packing and sorting out all the legal paperwork associated with the sale.

Unfortunately, packing is proving difficult. Mom keeps forgetting about the move and is becoming increasingly agitated about all her belongings being moved. This afternoon, she got upset with me when she came into the living room to find her furniture gone. She'd forgotten she gave us permission to donate it. When I reminded her about the move, she became irate. Honestly, it was really hard to watch. Emma had to come and try to smooth things over.

"We're doing the right thing, aren't we?" I ask Em. We're in the backyard, watching Mom putter away weeding the garden while singing. One of the only activities she wants to do.

"Sometimes it doesn't feel like it, but I know it is. For her and for us." She swings me a questioning glance.

"What if she hates it? What if she thinks we abandoned her?" It's my biggest fear, along with her forgetting who we are.

Em is quiet for a moment. "You're really worried about her," she finally says.

"I always worry, Em. She's our mom," I reply, probably more defensively than I intended.

"No. I know you've always cared on some level—"

"I . . . didn't expect to care this much," I admit. "I've been so angry with her for so long, ever since I was a kid. All I felt was this deep-seated resentment whenever I thought about her, whenever I saw her. I never thought there would be a time I could look at her and not feel that way. Because feeling the opposite, feeling hope, always meant disappointment. And I hate that it feels like she's leaving us all over again."

Em sniffs, rubbing her nose with her sleeve. "I know. It's fucking cruel, is what it is. But it always helps me to remember that, this time, it's not her choice."

"I know. I don't know why that makes it worse."

"In some ways, it is. But for me, it's nice to finally know it's not us, you know? I spent so much of my childhood wondering if there was something wrong with me, wondering why we kept getting passed around." We sit with that for a few beats.

I squeeze her hand, the way I used to when we were kids. Whenever we'd be shoved into someone's car, on the way to the next house. "I'm sorry, Em."

"For what?"

"For leaving you right after high school as soon as I could. I was a selfish asshole," I admit, still unable to wrap my mind around how I could leave so easily. How I could compartmentalize, throwing everything into my training, my job. Barely even thinking about my family, because thinking about them hurt too much.

"Starting your career and making money was not an asshole move," she argues.

"Okay, but it was an asshole move to leave again when Mom was diagnosed. You never should have had to step up in the first place. You had a whole family and a husband . . . and I just fucked off."

Her lip twitches. "You did. But you came back. You stepped up this summer. I'm really proud of you for that. And mostly, for giving Mom some grace. For spending more time with her, giving her a chance to show you who she really is before it's too late."

It feels wrong to be thanked for that. For enjoying Mom's company on her good days, laughing at her ridiculous stories, even if she can get on my nerves at times. I'm not sure what changed with her over the years, or whether she's always been this person deep down, but something about her energy is infectious. If anything, finally getting to know Mom over these past few weeks was the privilege of a lifetime.

● ● ●

I get a call from Deidra at the rescue farm the next day.

"Someone put in an application to adopt Cody," she informs.

Her tone is casual enough, but the words hit me like a sledge-hammer to the face.

"Nolan? You there?" Deidra asks after too long a silence.

"Yeah. Sorry. I'm just surprised." I shouldn't be. The little guy is fucking amazing. Of course someone else would want him.

"Yup. It's an older couple whose dog passed a couple months ago. It also had skin allergies, so they know all about his medications and special diet."

"Whoa. That actually sounds perfect," I say, even though it doesn't feel like it. When I tell you my heart drops out of my ass, I mean it plummets through the floor.

"Doesn't it? They want to come meet him tomorrow, and if all goes well with their background checks, I think it'll be a go." She sounds optimistic, and I should be, too. I know it's selfish. I should be elated at the prospect of him finding a forever home. A family that loves him and has the time to give him all the attention he needs.

"Anyway," she continues. "I just wanted to call and let you know because you two had developed a bond. I know you said you weren't in the market for a dog, but I wanted to confirm that was still the case and give you the chance to throw your name in the hat."

I clear my throat. Fuck. Of course I want to adopt Cody. But would I be making an impulsive decision, like Andi said? Is all the stuff with the house going up for sale, Mom's health, and her moving into the facility messing with my head? The last thing I want to do is adopt Cody and then come to the realization that I should take the Denmark contract. It wouldn't be fair.

"Believe me, Deidra, I want to take him, but I don't know where I'll be next week and—"

"No worries!" she says quickly, like she anticipated that answer. "I'm going to proceed with the adoption, then. Feel free to come by today or tomorrow if you want to say goodbye."

I drive to the farm first thing the next morning, my stomach coiled into tight knots. *This is a happy day. This is a good thing,* I tell myself.

When I come through the gate, Cody bounds over, his tongue out to greet me with a million licks. Then, he flops over, giving me access to scratch his oily belly, completely oblivious to the fact that today is the biggest day of his life. He's getting adopted. I run my hand over his peach fuzz and force a smile, but inside, I'm absolutely gutted. It should be me adopting him.

And then something happens. The moment his big, dark, trusting eyes meet mine, something breaks. For the first time in two decades, I cry. And it's not just a few tears I can hold back. It's a full-on, shoulder-shaking, loud sob. A long-overdue one at that.

Cody tilts his head at me, confused, and then, as if sensing it, he starts whimpering, too.

I manage to collect myself (barely) in time for the arrival of his new family. Like Deidra said on the phone, they're an older, salt-and-pepper-haired couple. They're kind and gentle with him, giving him space when he cowers away from them, pressing his whole body between my legs.

They reassure Deidra and me, promising to send pictures and updates. And I nod, trying to stay strong as I hand his shaky little body over to them. He whimpers and cries when they take him. And when they drive off down the dirt road, I let go again.

Deidra awkwardly pats my shoulder, unsure what to do. Not

that I blame her. I'm a six-foot-four man crying in her yard like a child.

I full-body sob the entire drive home. It's the kind that makes your gut ache. The kind that empties you until there's nothing left.

CHAPTER 44

Andi

"He told me he loved me," I confess to Amanda. I called her on my way home from work and bribed her with Chinese food to come save me from fermenting on my couch alone for another night since returning from Mexico three days ago.

Amanda nearly dumps the entire container of General Tso's chicken as she flails on my couch like an eel. She even punches the cushion for dramatic effect. "Shut up. I told you he has feelings for you! Do you feel the same way?" She leans forward, studying my reaction with the intensity of an FBI detective.

The moment I hesitate, Amanda pounces. "I'm taking your silence as a yes," she giddily decides, popping a piece of chicken in her mouth.

"I do love him," I admit from my spot on the floor in front of the couch. I sigh into my lo mein, swirling the noodles around with my chopsticks. I've known it for a while, probably since that night at the ravine. But I think I only let myself truly feel the weight of it when he carried me on his back to the villa in Mexico. My mind drifts back to that moment, the warmth of his arms, and the way I never wanted to let go of him. "But it's more complicated than that."

She blows the air out of her cheeks like a deflated balloon. "How? If he loves you and you love him, what's complicated about that?" she asks simply. I've always appreciated this about her. She's all about emotions. Feelings. No logic.

"Well, he said it directly after finding out he got a job in Denmark. A two-year posting he's been waiting to hear about all summer. And now he's second-guessing. Said he wants to stay in Ottawa, even though he told me when we first met that he never intended on settling anywhere."

"If he wants to settle here—in Frostawa, of all places—for you, why not let him? People are allowed to change their minds," she notes.

I explain that this whole decision is also on the heels of him dealing with the reality of Lorna's health, all while arranging to move her into a facility for her Alzheimer's. It would be unfair of me to let him make such a massive decision, such a huge divergence from everything he stood for, without thinking it through entirely. What happens when he realizes life with me is boring? The same predictable routine compared to the spontaneity and adventure he's accustomed to?

"Poor guy. That's a lot to deal with," she says thoughtfully. "Though it doesn't mean his feelings for you aren't real. Maybe you're the one thing he's sure about."

"Or maybe I'm his escape from reality." My heart lodges in my throat at the possibility. "Anyone in his shoes might make an emotional, impulsive decision. That's why I'm giving him some space. We're supposed to go to Gretchen's gala together on Friday, but I haven't heard from him. I don't know if it's a good idea to pressure him to go. He might need more time to process."

"Give him an out, if you're worried. Just say no worries about the gala and leave it at that. He has a lot going on, to be fair."

I nod, glancing down at my phone. Still no word from him. In three days. "Yeah, maybe I'll do that."

Amanda leans back, a mischievous glint in her eyes. "Or," she says, drawing out the word, "you could throw caution to the wind and offer to go to Denmark with him. I hear they have the best pastries. Did you know they eat open-face sandwiches and bike everywhere? Maybe that's how they stay so fit."

I've thought about it a lot over the last few days. His career is everything to him, and I know how difficult it's been for him to put it on pause. The last thing I'd want is for him to feel secretly resentful about staying. But that would also mean giving up my career with Gretchen. "I could."

Amanda freezes mid-bite, nearly choking on a piece of fried broccoli. "Wait. What?"

I lift a shoulder, trying to appear nonchalant, though my heart is racing. "It's a possibility."

She sets her food down and straightens her spine. "Are you saying you'd actually leave Gretchen and follow him to Denmark?"

"I would consider it."

"Holy shit," she whispers, dropping her chopsticks in the container. "You must be seriously gone for him. I never thought I'd ever hear you say you'd be willing to quit your job. Like, I would have bet my life savings—which is only in the three digits but let's pretend it's more—that you would be working for her until she dies. Or until you die."

She's probably right. Just a few months ago, leaving Gretchen wasn't even on my mind. But a lot has happened in the last few days with *The Prime Minister & Me.*

I signed with Cher before we left Mexico, and she immediately set up calls with editors at all the large publishing houses. Less than twenty-four hours after we got back to Ottawa, I received offers from nearly every house.

Surprisingly, Cher didn't push me to just take the highest offer. Her main focus is ensuring the publisher does right by the book and that the editor truly loves my writing. A couple editors stood out right away, understanding my creative vision. There's also a laundry list of legalities and contractual things to consider. Cher also connected me with a film agent, who's already gotten a ton of interest from Hollywood. I have calls scheduled with three different producers and studios.

Cher goes hard on negotiations, asking the tough questions, ensuring we get the best deal. And we do eventually accept the terms of one of the offers.

After researching the industry extensively, I know none of this is normal. Most talented authors aren't able to get representation, let alone massive book deals, or film deals. There's also a lot of privilege at play. And while I feel undeserving on most levels, I'm trying to take Nolan's advice and let myself soak it in.

And of course, none of this is a guarantee of long-term success. But it gives me hope that, temporarily, I can sustain myself with my writing. It also gives me some flexibility to write the other books in my head that have been begging to be written.

"But what would you do? I can't imagine it would be easy to find work, especially since you don't speak Danish," Amanda points out.

I bite my lip. I didn't expect to tell Amanda the truth about my writing. But it feels wrong to keep it from her, especially considering everything that's going on. "If I tell you, you need to promise you'll keep it between us. Like, full-on blood oath."

She blinks. "Why? Are you starting an OnlyFans account or something? Oh my god. I've never been so proud. I knew you were a freak—"

I hold my hand up in protest. "I'm not—"

"Let me help you with your username! What about Capitol-Crush? CaucusQueen? VotingVixen?"

I stand and wave my arms—the only way to get her attention. "Amanda, I'm not going on OnlyFans. I'm a romance author."

Her jaw drops. "Wait, what? A romance author?"

"I'm A. A. Zed. The author of *The Prime Minister & Me*," I confess, my voice steady, with more confidence than I thought I had.

"What! I saw that book everywhere on the internet." She quite literally screeches. "I can't believe you're a smut writer!"

"Romance writer," I correct her. "And why does that shock you more than the prospect of me being on OnlyFans?"

"I have no idea. I always thought you were so . . . repressed, with your prim-and-proper librarian vibe."

"Well, thanks," I mutter into my chicken fried rice.

Amanda collapses into laughter. "Meanwhile, you're writing piping hot sex. This is my new favorite thing. When did you start writing? I mean, I knew you read romance novels, but I had no idea you even wanted to write."

She listens with bated breath as I explain the whole story. How I started, how I self-published, how, after the pictures of

Eric and me leaked, the book skyrocketed on Amazon. Then I tell her all about Cher and going on submission to publishing houses.

"I can't believe it was you this whole time," she says, still coming down from the initial shock. I wait for her to chew me out for keeping it from her, but she doesn't. "This is freakin' awesome, Andi. I'm telling everyone. I'm going to the store to buy four thousand copies to give to friends—"

"Amanda!" I hiss, shooting her a stern look. "I just said this has to stay between us. My job is on the line," I remind her.

She slaps a hand over her mouth like a child being scolded by her teacher. "Right. Shit. Right. Sorry. I promise I won't say anything, unless you end up quitting? Then can I tell people?"

"No. It's still a secret. That includes Mom. Especially Mom."

"Are you kidding me?" She snorts. "Mom is the last person I'd tell. Though I'd honestly pay good money to see her reaction. She would go nuclear if she knew her daughter wrote smut."

She would probably pass out.

Amanda squeezes her eyes shut. "This is like the coolest thing that's ever happened to me. When you become famous like Stephen King, can I be your assistant?"

I smile, my heart warmed by her enthusiasm. Amanda's completely serious, and the best part? There's not an ounce of judgment in her voice. She's genuinely excited for me, which makes me feel terrible for keeping it from her for so long. Maybe I should have told her sooner.

After Amanda leaves, Cher emails to tell me the deal announcement is up and that I can post it on my author account. Admittedly, celebrating is a million times less enjoyable when you're all alone, with no one to share it with. Just me and my green tea. Like it always has been.

CHAPTER 45

Nolan

ANDI: Hey, I hope everything is going well with the packing. I know how busy you are so I wanted to let you know that you don't have to come to the gala if things are too busy, or if you're just not up to it.

ANDI: Also, I was hoping we could talk soon. Maybe tomorrow after the gala? Let me know.

I grumble down at my phone. I can't tell if she's simply being nice, or if it's a big fat hint that she doesn't want me there. I'd still planned to go, regardless of my headspace. My mind is still a jumbled mess, but all I want to do at this point is see her. I need to see her, almost as badly as I need air.

At the same time, I don't know if it would be fair. Not while my head is still a complete shitstorm. It's been a crap few days, to put it mildly, especially after Cody. Tomorrow is officially moving day, and nearly everything is packed, aside from the essentials. With everything going on, I'm starting to wonder whether Denmark is the right call after all. At least in Denmark, I wouldn't have to feel this kind of pain.

Thankfully, today Mom seems to be in decent spirits.

"Think you'll miss the house?" I ask her. We're sitting in the grass at the edge of the lawn next to her garden, which is where she's most at peace, away from the chaos of moving boxes inside.

The sun casts a long shadow over the lawn, the rickety deck I hated when I first moved in, the overgrown gardens, which are more weeds than flowers. Two months ago, this was the last place I wanted to be, here with my mom. All I craved were those long, adrenaline-filled days on the road, nights alone, never knowing where I'd be next. And now, the prospect of leaving, of leaving her, fills me with dread.

"Yes. But it's okay," she says, pulling a weed. "I want to go. Well, that's an overstatement. No one wants to live in a facility where you're locked down, forced to eat and do what they want, when they want."

"That's fair," I say, the pit expanding in my stomach.

"But it's the right thing to do. I keep having these accidents and I don't want you giving your life up to take care of me like Em did for so long. I can't stand the thought of being a burden on anyone, not anymore at least."

My heart pinches. "Mom, you are not a burden."

She shrugs, her gaze still focused on the weeds. "I'm not sure you would have said the same a couple months ago."

I bow my head, because she's entirely right. Coming back here felt like a massive burden, like I'd put my career on pause. "I'm sorry. I feel like shit for the way I handled things with you. Not just moving back, but since you were first diagnosed."

Her eyes find mine, and the line between her brows intensifies. "What do you mean, how you handled things?"

"When I found out about your diagnosis, I was angry. Not because of how the disease would affect you, but because it meant I couldn't tell you how I really felt about everything that happened back then. And I knew it meant we needed to take care of you. I hate myself for saying that, for ever thinking it. I didn't want to move home when Em left. I was angry about it because—"

"I was never there for you when you were younger," she finishes. It takes me off guard, because she's never officially acknowledged that before. I always thought she lived in an alternate reality. One where she never abandoned us, where she was never a bad mom. I didn't know she was ever capable of acknowledging the truth. That surprises me. I always thought Emma was too soft on her. That she wiped the slate clean with Mom and just brushed over the past. "You have every right to hate me," she says, her eyes welling with tears.

A brick drops heavily on my chest. "I never hated you, Mom. Especially as a kid. All I wanted was for you to come home. And by the time my anger manifested, I'd already gone into the military."

"It's the biggest regret of my life. I wasted so much time. And when you said you'd come back, I thought maybe it could be an opportunity to rebuild my relationship with you. Not that I deserve it." She lowers her head, her voice thick with emotion.

"You do. Of course you do." I lean forward, catching her gaze. "And for what it's worth, I've loved being here with you. I didn't expect to, but I did. I want to help. And believe it or not, I like hanging out with you. I'd keep doing this forever if we could." I say it with my whole chest, because there's nothing I'd rather do.

She looks up, a faint smile tugging at the corners of her mouth. "Well, I like hanging out with you, too, honey. But living with your mother isn't very conducive to dating, is it?"

"Neither is leaving for months at a time," I admit.

"I'm shocked your bags aren't already packed," she says, her smile turning wry.

I shake my head.

"I take it you haven't made a decision about Denmark yet?" I'd told her and Emma about it briefly, dodging giving a firm answer every time they asked.

"I don't want to leave you. I want to be able to visit whenever I want, go for our walks." I pause, faltering a little. For the first time in my life, Mom and I have a relationship. A proper relationship. And if I go to Denmark, I won't be able to visit her in person. And by the time I'm finally able to come back, I'm terrified she won't even remember me anymore.

She takes my hand and gives it a gentle squeeze. "Please don't second-guess this on my account. I'm going to be fine. Em is here," she says firmly. "Besides, you were so excited about the prospect of going somewhere else. I thought you'd always live that way. Always on the move."

"On the move?"

She nods. "I think you've been desperate to run, to leave before you can get hurt, like I hurt you every time I left when you were a kid."

Her words hit me like a gut punch. I've always wondered why I've had the overwhelming urge to be on the move. To avoid settling anywhere for too long. I always used the excuse that I wanted to travel, see the world. That was probably a small part of it, but if I'm being honest, seeing new, far-off places gets old after a while, especially when I don't get to slow down and enjoy them. That's why I threw myself into work. All I wanted was to keep busy, too busy to fully invest in a relationship. Too busy to care about someone on a deep level. If I was too busy to fall in love, I would never get hurt. I'd never get left behind again.

I look at her, the sadness in her eyes reflecting back at me, and I realize she's right. She's been holding on to her own guilt, just like I've been running from my own fear.

"Look, I may not have all my marbles for much longer. So let me share some wisdom. It's not about where you are, Nolan. It's about who you're sharing your life with. You two get to write all your own rules."

I nod, the heaviness gathering in my throat. "It's scary. The idea of staying in one place long enough to give life a chance. To get hurt. What if she gets bored of me? What if I give up my life and she decides she doesn't want to be with me?"

"Love, that big, passionate love worth having, can't be found living a safe, comfortable life, sweetie."

"Why not?" I manage.

"A safe life might look good on the outside, but it's empty beneath it all. True love, or anything that makes life worth living, is worth the discomfort. It's about how bravely and passionately you put your heart into it. Into the people in your life, instead of hiding away and being small because you're scared."

Maybe she's right.

• • •

The one positive among the shitstorm is all the time Em, Mom, and I have gotten together over the past few days. I can't even remember the last time the three of us were together. For our last night before Mom's official move, we spend it in the empty living room, eating bacon for dinner. Mom's idea.

After a movie and some music, Mom retires to bed early, leaving Emma and me on the floor to do some last-minute packing. We still have the house for a couple days after tomorrow before the closing date, which gives me some buffer time to figure out what the hell I'm doing with my life.

As I clear away the bacon-greased paper plates, I catch Em's screen as she scrolls through listings, amazed by how much we got for this place compared to some of the list prices. In a flash, I spot a yellow house.

"Wait, stop. Go back."

She scrolls back up and there it is. The yellow house. Holy shit.

"Hey, isn't that the house that was on Grandma's street?" she asks, squinting closer.

"It is." Frantic, I tap over her shoulder to enlarge the listing.

It's definitely the house, covered in flowers, some of which are starting to wilt, marking the end of a hot summer. According to the listing, it's only been on the market for a day.

I think back to all those chilly, frosty Ottawa evenings, when the sparkly dusting of snowflakes crunched under my feet as I walked back to my grandma's, my breath forming little puffs of white. I think about how I'd gaze longingly into those warm, glowing windows, wishing I could just stay there. Wishing I didn't have to move or switch schools again. Wishing Mom would come home for good.

My mind rewinds back to the night Andi and I went to see the house. When I took her hand and led her down that tree-lined trail to the ravine. How I imagined us sitting in that gazebo on crisp autumn mornings, watching the leaves fall, and then bundled up with frothy mugs of hot chocolate during winter. Waking up each morning to the dappled sunlight filtering through the trees, the birds chirping. I didn't realize it in the moment, but it was the first time I'd ever pictured my future with someone. The first time I imagined myself happy, in one place.

It's strange, actually seeing what it looks like inside after so many years of wondering and imagining. The house itself is cozy—two bedrooms and a single bathroom. The hardwood floors are weathered and could use some refinishing. Wooden beams that match the floors stretch across the ceilings, adding some character. The stone fireplace stands tall in the living room, its mantel adorned with family photos representing a lifetime of memories, all in that little house. The kitchen, with its farm-house charm, boasts a massive window that frames the view of the forest and gazebo in the backyard.

It's undeniably old and has seen its share of life, which is exactly why it's so charming.

"I can't believe it's for sale. And it's honestly a really good price for this market," Emma says, scrolling through the photos. "Someone will probably scoop it up, quick."

For the next hour as we watch some random murder documentary on Netflix, I barely pay attention. I'm too preoccupied with scrolling through the listing on my phone. A strange sensation thrums through me as I tap through the pictures, read every word, even the fine print. I'm not the kind of person who believes in signs, but I can't ignore this. It's like fate or destiny is tugging me in a clear direction. A direction I've known deep down was the only one that made sense.

"Em?" I nudge her, my tone urgent.

She pulls her gaze from the screen and turns. "Yeah?"

"Can you call the Realtor to set up a showing?"

CHAPTER 46

Andi

I've worked a couple black-tie events for Gretchen, but none as opulent as this gala.

To be fair, the Renaissance-inspired grand ballroom at the Fairmont Château Laurier doesn't need much. It's exquisite on its own, with massive crystal chandeliers, ornate moldings from the floor all the way onto the ceiling.

Tonight, it's bathed in a soft, golden glow. Each table is topped with towering floral arrangements, their vibrant petals and greenery romantically spilling onto the tabletops. A live band is stationed in the corner, playing a mixture of classical and jazz music. Admittedly, the champagne ice sculptures Gretchen insisted on look beautiful, backlit along the perimeter of the room.

The crowd is a mix of society people, foreign dignitaries, and high-ranking politicians. Some are mingling near the canapé stations, while others are dancing.

Eric and Gretchen are definitely not dancing. They're noticeably stiff and standoffish with each other, despite the goal to look like a strong couple. Image and countering negative PR were important to Gretchen for so long, but in the last few weeks, I'm not sure she wants to pretend anymore.

It doesn't help that they had another fight today. While ironing and steaming their outfits, I was an unfortunate witness to another bickering session. This one wasn't explosive. It was just a lot of silence and apathy, which honestly felt worse. Explosive arguments at least showed they cared.

Currently, they're on opposite ends of the room, chatting with other people. But the moment she spots me, she beelines it over.

"Thank you for all your work on this event—I mean it," Gretchen says genuinely. She's been complimenting my work a lot more these days, which I appreciate. "I don't know what I would have done the past few months without you."

"Of course. Actually, I was going to check on the candy bar. I didn't see those special gummies we ordered and—"

"Andi, do me a favor and stop fretting. Go have some fun with your man. Is he here yet?" she asks.

"Not yet," I say, brandishing a fake smile. I don't know when or if he's coming at all. He didn't respond to the text I sent giving him an out, which is uncharacteristic. He's never been one to ignore texts. That said, today was an emotional day with his mom's official move. I wouldn't blame him if going to a black-tie event was the last thing he wanted to do.

So I do what most awkward people do at formal events when they have no one to talk to. Head for the food. I park myself at the fondue station and make awkward small talk with an MP from Newfoundland, who has decided I'm the person to talk to about fiscal tax policy, while I pretend to understand all the intricacies.

"Now, if we could just get bipartisan support on the GST rebate expansion—"

I smile and nod some more, all while my brain screams for an exit strategy. I consider faking a cheese-related emergency, but even that seems like a stretch. That's when I spot Nolan.

Holy shit. The air shifts. Even the overbearing scent of expensive perfume and political ambition fades.

He's in a suit, not that I should be surprised. He's always in a suit, looking like he came straight from a Bond movie set. But there's something different about him I can't place. Maybe it's his relaxed posture, or the softness in his eyes when he looks at me, drawing my gaze straight to him.

"Sorry, am I interrupting?" he asks, his question cutting through like a lifeline.

I shake my head quickly, practically diving toward him. "No, please, interrupt away. You've saved me from hearing about marginal tax rates. I owe you big-time," I whisper when we're out of earshot.

He smirks. "I'm glad I could be of service." He steps back to take me in. "You look . . . beautiful." I bought this dress the other night at the mall. It's black meshy material with off-the-shoulder straps, a pleated bodice, and a slit up the left side. It's simple, but elegant.

"Thank you," I say, offering him a soft smile. "So do you. How have you been?" I ask eagerly.

Nolan lets out a breath, his shoulders relaxing slightly. "Honestly, a lot has happened. Cody got adopted, for one."

I gasp. "He did?"

"By the perfect family," he says, though I can see how pained he is over it from the way his eyes drop.

"I know how much you'll miss him," I say softly, reaching out to touch his arm. He glances at me, and I can tell he's grateful for the support.

"And then, of course, there was move-in day today," he adds, rubbing the back of his neck, his hand lingering there as if trying to ease the tension from the long day.

"How did it go?"

"It went well. Mom handled it as well as she could. She got a little teary when Em and I left, but I think she really liked the staff. Some of the women on her floor came over and introduced themselves and invited her to rock-themed bingo tonight. There was also talk of her joining a singing group."

"Wow. She's already making friends." I smile, my heart lightening at the thought.

"There was also a silver-haired guy named Bill on her floor. I think he has a crush on her already, because he came by and offered to give her a tour about three times. Not sure if it was a memory thing, or if he's just persistent. Either way, before we left, he asked if she had dinner plans," he adds.

"Holy crap. Did she like him?"

He slides me a funny smile. "She kept referring to him as a silver fox, so I assume so."

"Sounds like she's going to have the time of her life," I say.

We sit in silence for a moment, the air between us stretching thin and taut, like an invisible thread threatening to snap. I try to read his expression, but it's hard to tell where he stands after nearly a week of radio silence.

"Thanks for coming. It means a lot, especially after today. I wasn't sure if you—"

"Well, I actually came because I wanted to talk to you about something." He nods toward the French doors leading to the balcony.

We step out onto the balcony overlooking the landscaped lawn of Parliament Hill. It's quieter here, away from the hum of voices inside. I wrap my arms around myself, more for comfort than warmth, and I lean against the railing, waiting for him to speak.

"I'm sorry," he says, his expression pained. "About the past few days. I should have kept you updated—"

"No," I cut in. "Nothing in our arrangement says you're obligated to keep me updated on what you're doing."

His jaw tightens. "That's just it, though. I don't want to be in this arrangement anymore. I've given it a lot of thought over the past few days, like you asked me to. I went back and forth over it. I talked to my mom about it."

I take a deep breath, trying to push down the anxiety that's been gnawing at me since we've been apart. "You did?"

"I never understood why settling down was so scary. I feared staying in one place for longer than a couple months, because of the way I grew up. I never felt like I was enough to make anyone want to keep me. Like I was good enough. My mom was actually the one who pointed out that, because of that fear, I've been running. Desperate to leave places, people, things, before I get hurt," he tells me. "And she's right. I've never felt like I needed to be anywhere until I met you. But staying here, being with you, means I could get hurt. And so could you." He works down a swallow, taking my hands into his with a gentle squeeze before he continues.

"Then I thought about what you said. The night we met. About how love stories aren't only about a happy ending. And how a happy ending doesn't mean everything is perfect. We're going to have our ups and downs. We'll probably fail each other, hurt each other. And I know that sounds scary, but it's real. It's something worth nurturing for as long as you'll let me, because I love you, with so much certainty, with everything I am. Please tell me you feel even the tiniest bit of what I do."

He loves me. He told me before, in the car at the airport. But this time feels different. It doesn't fill me with anxiety or doubt. It makes my eyes watery. My arms and my legs go numb as my chest bursts and fills with affection for this man. The only man, only person who's ever truly seen me.

"Nolan, of course I do," I whisper. "Ever since the first night we met, I've thought about you. I constantly regretted falling asleep and letting you leave without getting your number. You scared me, but you also woke me up. You were the first person who ever made me realize there was another way to live. A version where I wasn't lonely, getting takeout for one because it was marginally less depressing than cooking for one. A life where I didn't work myself to death to avoid being alone.

"And when I saw you again at work, I couldn't believe that life brought you back, even if you weren't supposed to stay. I was kidding myself the entire time we were pretending to be friends, stuck in this weird arrangement, because the truth is, I've never wanted to be your friend. I never wanted to be your pretend girlfriend. I wanted you. The man who carried my groceries for blocks in the dead of winter. The man who put together my desk. Who encouraged me to follow my dreams without even knowing me or whether I had a stitch of talent. The man who did what was right and took care of his mom, even when it was hard. The man who fell in love with the ugliest dog at the rescue. You. Someone I could never dare to dream up for my books, even on my best days."

Those blue eyes roam my face as he places my palm over his chest, the steady thrum of his heart palpable even through his jacket.

"I've never pictured my life with anyone, until you," I conclude.

"Me either," he says, the tenderness in his expression threatening to undo me. "And now that I have, all I can think about is the future. With you."

"A future," I repeat, my heart bursting with such an overload of love, it feels like it was spun with sugar. "But that doesn't mean staying here necessarily. I thought about it and I'd love to go with you, wherever you want to go."

Nolan shifts slightly, his eyes flickering with something unspoken. "Actually, speaking of . . . I put an offer in on a house."

I cough. "What? A house?"

"The yellow house."

"Holy shit." I know how much that house means to him.

"It was one of those moments that made me realize I'm meant to be here," he explains, a spark of nostalgia lighting up his face. "Em just so happened to be looking at the listings, and by chance, I glanced down at her iPad when she scrolled past it. I never look at listings, so I never would have seen it otherwise. It was so weird. The moment I saw it and looked at the pictures, I knew I had to put an offer in."

"Of course," I whisper, in complete awe.

"I called the Realtor, who told me they'd already gotten a lot of interest and that I needed to act fast. So I went for a showing this morning and I ran into the owner in the driveway."

"He was there?"

"Yup. And weirdly enough, he recognized me immediately. As the boy who used to 'cut through my backyard and steal crab apples,'" he recounts, his lips unfurling in a nostalgic smile. "When I told him about how much I loved the house, he invited me inside and gave me a tour himself."

"That's . . . surreal. Like lightning in a bottle," I say, absorbing the gravity of it all.

"Exactly. His wife recently passed, which was why he was selling. They'd lived there since they first got married. It was supposed to be a starter house, but they couldn't have kids of their own, so it became their forever home. Before she died, she told him she wanted it to go to someone who would love it as much as they did. All that to say, he asked what I'd offer for it. I made a reasonable offer, no conditions, and he accepted right away. On the spot."

"Oh my god, Nolan. Congratulations!" I pull him in for a tight hug. "So this means you're officially staying?" I confirm, unable to hide the excitement.

"There's absolutely nowhere else I'd rather be." He leans down for a kiss and everyone around us blurs.

I pull back with a teasing grin. "But wait, you said you hate Ottawa winters with a fiery passion."

"Oh, I do. But I learned something in tactical training in the Arctic."

"What's that?"

"Cuddling is a solid way to stay warm," he replies with a wink.

I lean into him, and in a blink, I can see it all. Us, posing for one of those cheesy photos outside the yellow house next to a "Sold" sign. Him, guiding me down the overgrown path into the forest of his childhood, where fireflies dance by the ravine. I see blazing red autumns transitioning to Christmases. Us stringing lights along the windows, hanging stockings on the fireplace, building ugly gingerbread houses. The snowy winters, me struggling with cross-country skiing on the backyard trails while he laughs and encourages me to get back up and try again. The snow melting into muddy, hopeful Ottawa springs, invigorating us to embrace it all over again, even if a surprise mid-April blizzard tries to dampen our spirits.

"Oh, and there's something else," he says, eyes twinkling.

"What?"

Before he can respond, someone grabs my shoulder.

I turn around to find Gretchen, her face pinched with absolute fury. She looks like a storm ready to destroy. "Andi," she snaps.

"What's wrong?" I ask.

"How could you lie to me?" I don't miss the hurt and anger in her eyes as she lobs her phone at me. It hits me in the chest with a heavy thud.

CHAPTER 47

Andi

It isn't until I read the caption under my deal announcement post that I see it. I signed my name—Andi, instead of my pen name initials, A. A.

My stomach plummets and the nausea hits me. I stare down at my screen, my mouth hanging open in disbelief. There's no denying it now.

And then there's Gretchen, standing in front of me, her face pulled tight in a mixture of anger, hurt, and utter disappointment. "Bethany just called. The media has descended like locusts."

A wave of panic washes over me. I can almost hear the buzz of gossip sites revving up, the frenzy of social media. My mind races with images of headlines, tags, and hashtags. Even the room itself feels quieter than before. People are definitely looking at us, listening, whispering.

It feels like a tidal wave of embarrassment is crashing over me, pulling me under.

"Gretchen," I whisper. "You have no idea how sorry I am."

"Sorry? Sorry for what? For lying to me all this time after I gave you chance after chance to tell the truth?"

"I know," I say, my voice trembling. "I was scared that if you knew I wrote the book, you'd think there was truth to the rumors about me and Eric. And the last thing I wanted was for my author stuff to impact my job here."

She shakes her head, the disappointment in her eyes cutting deeper than any anger. "I trusted you. I confided in you more than anyone, even my closest friends. I trusted you with my children," she hisses.

My heart cracks in two when I see the betrayal in her amber eyes. She's entirely right. I should have come clean. I should have told her it was me who wrote the book, regardless of what would have happened to my career. It was the right thing to do, and I was an absolute coward.

I take one look at Nolan out of the corner of my eye. He steps forward to take my hand, but all I want to do is escape. I can't look at him, or especially Gretchen.

So I run.

•   •   •

I don't recommend running barefoot, my dress billowing behind me like some messed-up superhero cape. But desperate times and all.

By the time I get back to the safety of my apartment, my lungs burning from the cool night air, the bottoms of my feet black, all I want to do is collapse into a ball in bed and hide under the blankets for eternity. All the glittery, fancy book and film deals in the world suddenly seem hollow and worthless compared to the betrayal, the humiliation. And I only have myself to blame. I was naive enough to think I could get away with it.

The time passes in a haze. It could have been ten minutes or two hours; I lose all sense of reality as I huddle in the dark, contemplating how I can ever make it up to Gretchen and Eric. The knock at my door startles me out of my cocoon of self-loathing. I hear Nolan's concerned voice through the door.

"Come here," he says the moment I open the door. His suit, which was sharp and immaculate earlier, is now slightly disheveled. His tie is loosened, hanging askew around his neck. He pulls me into a hug so tight, it's like he's bracing himself against the weight of the world. His arms wrap around me with a firm, reassuring grip, holding me upright as I cling to him. I bury my face in his chest, letting his steady heartbeat ground me. In his arms, it feels like everything will be okay, even for a split second.

"I outed myself. On my deal announcement," I say when I let go, blankets still folded around me like a burrito.

There's a brief, heavy silence before Nolan speaks again. "I know. Everyone was talking about it after you ran out."

"I can't believe I did that. God, Gretchen—everyone must think I'm completely unhinged." I cringe, sinking down to the floor, and he sinks down with me.

"Fuck what everyone else thinks," Nolan says firmly. "Especially people on the Hill. You don't need them anymore."

"I do. I feel horrible for what I did. This is so much bigger than even me," I explain. "It could ruin Eric's campaign."

Nolan shakes his head. "It won't. People love him, Andi. Even when these rumors first came out, his approval ratings barely changed."

"Still. I'm going to go resign tomorrow. I can't show my face on the Hill ever again," I decide, not that I'd be welcome anyway. "Though I'm pretty sure I'm already fired."

"Maybe this is the best thing that could have happened, given the circumstances. Now you can write full-time. Do what you actually love."

I shake my head. The thought of my entire life falling from under me is enough to make me want to dive back under the covers. "No. I'm going to call Cher and tell her to cancel the deal."

"Don't, Andi," he says firmly, taking my hands into his.

"Why not? I don't deserve any of the glory. Not on the back of what I did."

"Look, we may not have handled this the right way. I'm not disputing that. But what I can tell you is punishing yourself won't help. Taking away your only source of income, all your potential . . . it feels like a massive waste. The damage is already done, so why not make the most of it?"

I shrug. I don't have an answer for him.

"I think the bigger issue here is that you're scared," he tells me.

"Scared of what?"

"Of being yourself, of getting out of your comfort zone. You're scared of taking risks. You're scared of letting people in and letting people see you. Really see you." He pauses, his gaze intense. "You've gotten used to fading into the background, being behind the scenes. Hiding. Avoiding the spotlight. You avoid attention at all costs. And I don't understand why, because in a room full of people, you're the only one I want to look at."

I nod. "I've always been scared of judgment, ever since I was a kid. My mom was so critical about everything, what we ate, how we ate, how we dressed. If Amanda or I said or did the wrong thing, especially in front of Dave's family, we'd hear about it for weeks. Even now, whenever I do things, I always hear her voice in my mind. Some judgment or criticism. And I think that's why I've always lived my life so safe."

I think about all the reasons I've kept my writing a secret this whole time. Why I chose a pen name. It wasn't just because I wanted to keep my writing separate from my day job. Deep down, I was ashamed. I was embarrassed.

I thought if people knew I wrote books, let alone romance, they'd use it as a window to judge me. I imagined my mom's raised brow, her whispering with her country club friends about me. They'd think a whole host of things, that I'm talentless, that all I write is fluff, or that I'm some weird sexual deviant who fantasizes about her boss's husband. But now I know judgment comes regardless. I can't avoid it. It's up to me not to care.

"I see you, Andi. And I love the person you are. Not put-together, perfect Andi, Gretchen's personal assistant who can do everything all at once. Or A. A. Zed, the bestselling novelist. Just Andi, the sensitive, sweet woman I walked in on in the bathroom, who's owned my heart ever since."

A tear rolls down my cheek. Not because I'm terrified or scared. But because I've never had someone believe in me like Nolan. And it means everything.

"My mom told me yesterday that one of the biggest mistakes we can make is living life small, letting life pass us by because we're scared."

I sniff. "That sounds wise."

"She also said to live a loud life. A life so big, so full of meaning, that even if one day you forget some of the things you've done, you'll have given people one of the most important things we have in this world."

"What's that?"

"Happiness. Hope. Even if it's temporary."

Maybe he's exactly right. I can't continue letting my life pass me by in a whisper. I deserve to pursue my dreams in vivid color. To live loud and live big. Maybe I don't have to be scared or ashamed anymore to be A. A. Zed, or even Andi Zeigler. And I certainly shouldn't have to choose one or the other.

CHAPTER 48

Andi

The headlines have come out this morning, officially linking my pen name to me.

Inevitably, Mom called. Her reaction was as expected. She was scandalized and surprised, but mostly offended that I kept my writing a secret. To be honest, I think she was just impressed by the whole deal announcement. I told her I'd provide her a redacted copy of the book, minus the steamy bits.

Mom isn't the only one who's surprised. Laine comes over, which is unexpected.

"So you actually wrote the book?" Laine asks the moment she steps into my apartment.

"Yeah. I did," I say, managing to maintain eye contact with an iota of confidence.

"Why didn't you tell me?" she asks, not bothering to take off her shoes or coat.

"I'm sorry, Laine. I didn't tell anyone, especially not people I work with. I couldn't afford to have people not take me seriously."

Her brows draw together tightly as she leans against the wall in the entryway. "Okay, but I'm not just some person you worked with. We're supposed to be best friends. You know everything about me."

I don't really know how to respond to that. "Are we, though? I mean, I barely see you."

"What? We hang out all the time. I invited you to my wedding."

"I know. But we only see each other a couple times a year," I counter, the sting of distance between us palpable. "You hang out with your work friends all the time and never invite me. And it's been that way ever since I started working for Gretchen."

"Because we work together. It's easy to go for drinks after work. I'm sorry. I figured you wouldn't want to be invited. It's not like you really like hanging out with them, and you have nothing in common with them. And then there's the Hunter thing. Most of them are friends with him and I figured it would be awkward for you." Her reasoning makes sense, but it doesn't ease the hurt.

"Honestly, I've felt like we haven't been nearly as close over the past few years," I admit.

"So that's why you've decided to have a whole secret life behind my back?"

I squeeze my eyes closed. She's right. "No. I didn't tell you because if I did, you would have judged me. Hard."

"Why would you say something like that? Is that really what you think of me?" she asks, her eyes wide with disbelief.

"Yes. All you used to talk about was serious literature. You turn your nose up at rom-coms. You called them trash. Remember?"

"Well, yes, but—"

"Exactly," I interject, folding my arms tightly over my chest.

"I wouldn't have said something like that if I'd known," she says regretfully.

"See? If you'd known," I point out. "Anyway, it doesn't matter. I was ashamed and I shouldn't have been. That was on me and my own insecurity." If anything, I'm the one who refused to see my writing for what it is. Not just salacious stories filled with steam, but stories about love and all its intricacies—something people universally long for.

She takes a step closer. "Andi, I'm sorry about all of this. I'm sorry we've gotten distant over the last few years. I've missed you a lot, you know."

"Really?"

"Every time I stay late at work, I think about our intern days. Sending each other code words over internal messenger whenever Raj would bring up his master's degree from Queens."

I snort. "I miss that, too."

"And all the days exploring Ottawa when we were new to the city."

"Remember the time we accidentally took the wrong bus to the Bayshore mall and ended up in Orléans?"

She snorts, finally kicking off her shoes. "Oh my god. Don't remind me." After waiting at the bus stop for forty-five minutes, we gave up and took an Uber back downtown and got gross ramen at some random dive.

We spend a solid hour on the couch reminiscing about old times before Hunter picks her up.

When he arrives, she spins around. For a heartbeat, we watch each other, slightly teary, before she comes in for a hug. It's not just a quick, casual, see-you-later hug. It's heavier. We hold it for a long time, because I think we both know this is it.

I settle into her embrace, our friendship playing out in my mind. At the same time, I'm starting to realize that not all friendships are built to last the long haul. Like romantic love, friendships evolve, too. Sometimes too many things happen. Too many hurts. Sometimes you lose what you had in common to begin with. Or your lives simply aren't in sync anymore, causing you to drift away. And that's okay . . . I'll always treasure her role in my life—making me fall in love with this city. This job. Pushing me out of my comfort zone.

Despite everything that happened, Laine was one of my best friends. I still care about her deeply. That will never change, even if things will never be like they were.

• • •

I save the hardest conversation for last: Gretchen. A couple months ago, I'd have rather defected to another country than have this discussion. But thanks to Nolan, I feel brave.

I wait a week or so until the media frenzy is over. This week, they've moved on to a new scandal.

Despite the slowed media attention, my presence still turns heads. The moment I walk through the staff door, it's clear everyone knows. It's a lion's den of judgmental eyes and whispers, reminiscent of that first day the headlines exploded. But today, I hold my head high and walk with purpose.

Nolan's words echo in my mind, giving me strength. I

shouldn't be ashamed of my writing or my books. I've brought happiness and escape to so many people. There's been a lot of luck and timing in my success, but I've worked hard. I've written those books, and people have connected with them in ways I never expected. They've found joy, hope, and even solace in my words.

When I step into Gretchen's office, she's reclining in her chair, her brow raised like she's been expecting me.

"Eric and I are separating," she blurts out.

"Wait—what? Is this about the book?" My voice cracks with the shock of her words.

She nods, her face a mask of tired resignation. "Yes."

"Gretchen. Wait. I can explain. I am so, so sorry for all of this. Mostly I'm sorry for lying to you and to everyone about being the author. I was . . . embarrassed. I know it sounds ridiculous, but I promise I was never harboring any weird fantasy or crush. It was just something that was easy for me to write. Either way, I understand that this is detrimental to Eric's shot at reelection later this year, so I'm going to resign."

She holds her hand up. "I read it. Your book," she says. The room goes quiet, except the thud of my heart. "I've never read anything like it."

I lower my head, the shame creeping back in.

"I've never read a romance, especially not one with steam," she adds. "And I found myself bingeing it in one sitting. After it was done, I was crying. Not because I thought anything in there was real. The characters were all completely different, which I appreciate. But what got me was that I'd never read about a man who was so considerate, so caring. I'd never read a description of such sex or a man putting a woman first in bed. Those things just aren't in movies and TV. And I realized that Eric and I had that."

"You absolutely did."

She sniffles. "But we haven't in a long time. Over the past four years, we stopped putting each other first. We stopped prioritizing uninterrupted quality time, without one of our phones going off and distracting us. I stopped laughing at his jokes. We stopped touching. And mostly, we stopped dreaming together. And before you ask, we did try. We knew what the issues were, and we couldn't fix them all these years. No matter what we did, we ended up at square one, every damn time. And it's exhausting, you know?"

I sit there in complete silence, taking it all in. Of all the things I expected her to say, this was not it. "You and Eric seemed so in love. I had no idea you felt so alone."

"I thought maybe he wasn't trying hard enough. Or maybe it was me not putting in the effort. But I realized after reading your book that the reason we couldn't fix things was simple: We're not in love like we used to be. At least, not in the way either of us wants to be loved in the long run.

"I want what's in this book to last. And I know it's fiction. I know it's an idealistic portrayal of love. I know the characters will go on to have struggles offstage that we don't see. But I just can't give up hope and settle. I don't want that for myself, or for him. So I decided I'm moving out by the end of the month," she continues, a hint of finality in her voice.

"Really?"

"I want you to come with me," Gretchen says, her gaze steady.

"Wait, I'm not fired?"

"Why would I fire you for writing a romance novel? You're the best PA I've ever had, Andi."

My first instinct is to say, "Yes! Of course." But I think about my conversation with Nolan. For the first time, I have the luxury of choice. The ability to ask myself whether this job is really something I want. And when I think about it, I'm not sure it is. I'm not sure I need the approval anymore.

"Gretchen, I don't know what to say."

"You're going to say yes, aren't you?"

"I—I was actually planning to write full-time," I tell her. It feels oddly liberating to say that out loud, even though I'm fairly certain I'm about to break out into full-body hives.

She watches me with an expression I can't decipher.

"I feel terrible leaving you, Gretchen. Especially now," I add.

"No. It makes sense. You should move on. We both have to move on. And it would be selfish of me to take you when you're capable of so much more."

"Thank you," I say, even though I don't feel like I deserve it, coming from her. As I turn to leave, a mixture of relief and dread drops in my gut. At least now there's some understanding, even if it doesn't erase the complications or the hurt caused.

"You're going to change the world with your words, Andi," she tells me, her tone sincere before I cross the threshold. "You've already changed mine."

I nod, feeling a lump in my throat. As I leave her office, the weight of the decision settles in my gut, but there's something else there. A sense of possibility. Of excitement that I haven't felt since I wrote that first line in my first book.

I already can't wait to write the next chapter.

CHAPTER 49

Nolan

I make a drumroll with my free finger on the table as Andi finally signs her contract with her publisher.

It's been two weeks since she handed in her official resignation to Gretchen. It was a tough decision to leave her, but the right one. But because Andi is Andi, she stayed with her through those first few weeks after the separation to help Gretchen organize her affairs.

It's one of the reasons I love this woman so much. Her heart. The woman who comes with me to visit my mom nearly every single day and reminds me to bring her a bushel of daisies each time. The woman who supports my career, my long hours. The woman who's always making sure I have everything I need before I realize I'm missing it. And I can't believe she's mine.

A small tear rolls down her cheek when she sets the pen down. I catch it with my thumb, wiping it away, along with all the loose strands of hair in front of her face. "You really don't have to film this," she says, sniffling, taking a swipe at the camera.

I pull her into me, tracing the delicate line of her jaw, the full part of her bottom lip, partially tucked in. "Oh, but I do. This is a big fucking deal."

"Thank you," she says, her eyes glossy with emotion. "I don't think I would have had the courage to do this without you."

"You would have," I say. "And I'm going to be here with you every step of the way, cheering you on. I'm proud of you, Andi. You deserve all of it." And I mean that. Seeing her live out her dreams is surreal. Honestly, I just feel lucky to be here for the ride.

"So am I. Thank you for making me realize that—"

Something fuzzy yips at my feet, disgruntled by the lack of attention and belly rubs for the past five minutes.

"Just a minute, Cody," I say, despite the way he's wagging his tail and nudging my leg.

I adopted Cody. About a week after he was taken home by his new family, I got a call from Deidra. The adoptive family had brought him back. Apparently, Cody had been terrorized by their cat, who was on a mission to make his life miserable. Cody was so scared, he wouldn't come out from under the bed. When Deidra told me, I didn't hesitate. I hopped in the car and drove straight to the rescue farm.

Now, Cody is back with me . . . well, Andi and me. I'm crashing at her place temporarily until the yellow house closes next month. Andi started feeding him cheese like she did with Lars, and he's never been happier. He's curled up at my feet, looking up with those big, soulful eyes as if to say, *More cheese, please.*

Cody gives an approving yip and rolls onto his back, exposing his fluffy belly. His hair is starting to grow back, now that we've figured out the proper diet.

"Honestly, I think this is the happiest I've ever been," she tells me once we giddily hit send on the contract.

Her words wash over me like the tiniest rays of sunshine. "It's just the beginning."

"Just the beginning," she repeats.

She smiles, nuzzling her nose into the curve of my neck. I feel the warmth of her wide smile against my skin, and everything in me stabilizes. I've lived my entire life in motion, always coming and going—mostly going. Running. Never letting anyone get too close to me. Living in constant fear of being unworthy, of being left behind, forgotten. Of getting hurt.

For the first time in my life, I have this overwhelming urge to stay put. To let her fill my life with her sweet laughter, her smile. I can't wait to get the keys to the yellow house so I can officially ask her to move in with me. Andi has already made a Pinterest board full of design ideas. There are so many little renovation projects I want to start on.

Mostly, I want to walk Cody along the same, familiar route every day in the trails behind the house. I want to go grocery shopping every Saturday and come home to her every single day, smiling at me from over her laptop, her hair pulled into a wild bun.

I always thought I'd be happy anywhere else, somewhere just out of reach. But there's nowhere else I'd rather be than right here with Andi, my home.

And there's not a chance in hell I'd ever trade this life for anything.

EPILOGUE

Andi

THREE YEARS LATER

xcuse me." A woman swivels around in the Starbucks line and does a double take. Instinctively, I shift back, assuming I'm in her way. "Sorry to bother you, but are you A. A. Zed?"

It takes me aback. It's the first time I've been recognized randomly in public, ever, despite my name and photo being national news.

There's a split second when I instinctively gear up to deny it, before I remember that I no longer need to hide. There's no more embarrassment, shame, or severe urge to sink into oblivion. Instead, I relax my posture, smile, and say, "Yeah. I am," with confidence.

The woman lets out a high-pitched squeal, turning the heads of nearby patrons. "Oh my god. I am obsessed with your books. I actually took the afternoon off work to get here on time."

A joyful warmth swells in my stomach, expanding into my chest. I will never get used to hearing that. "Wow, thank you so much. Where did you travel from?"

"Montreal," she tells me. "I'm a little early, but I wanted a good seat. I saw the event was sold out." She's not wrong. The lineup of people waiting for the event to start is currently snaked around the building, spilling into the parking lot. Just to see me.

Today is my launch event for my sixth book, *Into the Blue*, an angsty summer romance that early readers have called my "best work yet." And even though it's my sixth, I'm still in awe when I see my books on shelves. And even more in awe when the bookstore manager gets me set up at a table in front of a stack of preordered books nearly as tall as me to sign.

It takes me a while to work through the lineup. It's important to me to give each reader time, especially when they've spent hours reading my books. I can't help but think about the hundreds of hours I spent typing away, unsure anyone was ever going to read my words, let alone like them or connect with them.

It means a lot to me when they giddily recount their favorite scenes, their eyes shimmering with the same magic I felt when I wrote them. It's the exact fuel I need to keep creating stories that bring joy to people's hearts. The ones that give them a cozy, safe place to escape to when real life gets tough.

Midway through signing, I crane my neck to catch a glimpse of Nolan, my lifeline. He flashes me that sunlit smile as he works his way through the line, handing out custom bookmarks and stickers, and generally charming all the readers. He's become so well-known at my events that I'm starting to think some people are coming here for him. Everywhere he goes, people quite literally salivate over him. Not that I blame them.

He recently took a new job as a CPO for the governor general. While he loved working for Eric, his new schedule is more relaxed. It gives him more time to visit Lorna in the memory care facility. Unfortunately, her memory is getting worse and worse, which only confirms that it's the best place for her. She smiles every time we bring her daisies and play her favorite '80s music, even if she doesn't always remember who we are.

Whenever we're not visiting Lorna, Nolan becomes a walking billboard for my books.

His support for me has never waned ever since the first night we met, when he convinced me that my words were meant to be read by people other than me. If anything, it's grown exponentially. Everywhere we go, he tells everyone and their grandmother to read my books. He's even lurked around the romance section of the bookstore, pouncing on unsuspecting patrons to pitch my books. He's also threatened to have T-shirts made with my book covers on them and script that says READ MY GIRL-FRIEND'S BOOKS. (I saw them in his online cart.) He's basically a walking romance hero, but better, because he's turned everything I thought I knew about real love sideways.

I used to think love was fleeting, a rush of lust, a chemical reaction that was bound to fizzle after the honeymoon stage. I'd seen it happen one too many times. But three years, two homes, and one bouncy, floppy, ugly puppy later, I see how wrong I was.

Sure, those feverish days where all we wanted to do was rip each other's clothes off have softened. We may not do our best every single day. There are days I get irrationally pissed when he leaves his socks in the living room. And he'll get equally offended when I spend too much time scrolling on my phone engrossed in publishing scandals instead of having an actual conversation with sustained eye contact. We may disappoint each other, even hurt each other during times of stress. But that's okay, because that's real life, beyond the crisp pages of a book. Messy, weathered, mundane, sometimes a little topsy-turvy, but beautiful, raw, and real. And with every new layer, every new experience, we'll love each other more and more. We'll also become more resilient. We'll turn toward each other, instead of apart. Stronger as a pair to face whatever life throws at us.

By the end of the evening, when my wrist is sore and my voice is gone from all the talking and shaking hands, Nolan brings me a fresh tea and an oatmeal raisin cookie while I finish up signing and personalizing a stack of preordered copies.

"You need this."

"I'm fine, really," I assure him.

"You're pregnant. You need it."

I smile gratefully, taking the cookie. He takes better care of me than I do myself. I have a tendency to lose myself in my writing, greasy and unshowered, typing feverishly for hours without drinking a lick of water. He's always there with a fresh glass of water and a nutritious meal, slipping it onto the corner of my desk as quietly as possible so he doesn't break my concentration.

His doting tripled (if that's even possible) when we found out I was pregnant two months ago, and I'm currently in the throes of nausea. Not the best timing for my book launch, but I'm managing and trying to come to terms with the fact that I can't do it all, all at once.

"Any good name inspiration?" he asks, leaning over to catch

a glimpse of the books I'm signing. His arm brushes against mine, making my heart patter.

"There's a lot of Ashleys." For someone who's always had a list of potential names, I've found that coming up with the right one is challenging, especially when he's decided I have to choose because he's scared I'll say yes to anything he suggests. It doesn't help that Nolan has opinions on every name that isn't Pippa or Jack. I secretly love both, but I haven't told him, because it's fun to rile him up.

He shrugs. "I don't mind it. But Ashley sounds like a girl who really likes fall and makes it her whole personality."

"What about Doreen?"

"Sounds like a woman who uses a rotary phone and has a chronic smoker's cough."

"This child is going to be nameless for the first month, aren't they?"

Nolan chuckles and crushes me into his chest. His heartbeat thrums steadily against my cheek, and I let myself melt against him, my favorite place in the world. A place of safety, of bravery, of deep feeling, of all-encompassing, enduring love. The kind I didn't believe lasted.

"Even with our nameless child, I couldn't have written a better ending. A better epilogue." I tilt upward to meet his twinkling gaze, catching the smile tugging at the corners of his lips. It's so pure, so earnest, it makes me want to cry.

"You mean a better beginning."

That's what a real epilogue is, after all: the start of the next book.

ACKNOWLEDGMENTS

I moved to Ottawa, Canada's capital city, in 2013 to pursue a master's in public administration and public policy (a fancy way of saying I was gearing up to be a career public servant). As a political science nerd, I still remember my first walk along Sussex Drive, gazing at the Parliament building (albeit through the construction zone) in absolute awe.

For those who may be unfamiliar, Ottawa has a reputation—it's known for being freezing cold (definitely true), for being devoid of good food (semi-true but not nearly as bad as people say), and for being "boring" (fair). But for all its quirks, Ottawa is an understated, quietly romantic city. With its lush green spaces, scenic parks, and the stunning Rideau Canal, there's no shortage of outdoor activities, no matter the season. I've enjoyed watching the city bloom in both literal and figurative ways, from the vibrant autumn leaves in Gatineau Park to the lively energy of festivals and events. And, of course, there's the poutine. Ottawa has been my home for the past decade, and I'm so happy to honor it by setting *The Bodyguard Affair* here.

First and foremost, I want to extend my heartfelt thanks to my readers, who have stood by me over the years. I know this book took longer than expected to reach you, and I truly appreciate your patience and unwavering support! I'm incredibly grateful to the librarians and booksellers who continue to champion my work and put it into the hands of wonderful readers like you.

As always, I'm deeply thankful to my literary agent, Kim Lionetti, and the amazing team at BookEnds Literary Agency, as well as my film agent, Addison Duffy, at United Talent Agency.

A huge thank-you to my editor, Kristine Swartz, and my team at Berkley (Mary, Yazmine, Jessica, Elisha, and Christine) for your understanding and support during my parental leave. Your patience and encouragement mean the world to me.

I'd like to offer a special thank-you to Stephanie D. for your invaluable political insight on the Hill. While much of it didn't make it into the book, your knowledge was crucial in helping me grasp the intricacies of this world. I'm so grateful for all the phone calls, texts, and your enthusiasm—you're the best!

To Kate and Danielle, my fellow Ottawans, thank you for your encouragement as I wrote a book set in our beautiful city—especially one within the wild world of politics. I hope you love the public service references.

And last but certainly not least, thank you to my husband and my parents for being so amazing with Baby C during her first year and a half of life, giving me the time and space to finish this book. And of course, thank you to Baby C for being such a champion napper!

*Keep reading for
a preview of Amy Lea's*

SET ON YOU

Available now!

The gym is supposed to be my safe place. The place I destress, reenergize, and ponder random wonders and mysteries, like: How was I delusional enough to think I could rock a middle hair part circa 2011?

That's why I'm equal parts horrified and appalled that my Tinder rebound, Joe, has sprung onto the treadmill to my right.

I brace myself for an awkward, clunky greeting, but thankfully, his attention appears fixed on the treadmill's touch pad. As he presses the dial to increase his speed, I catch a whiff of eau de wet dog. He not-so-subtly glances in my direction before averting his eyes.

Sure, Tinder Joe was kind enough to order me an Uber after our lackluster quarter-night stand two weeks ago. But it's highly coincidental we'd end up at the same gym, in all of Boston. I wonder if he's stalked me. Maybe I blew his mind in bed? So much so he went FBI on my ass, located my gym, and staged a casual run-in? Given my social media presence, it isn't out of the realm of possibility.

At every opportunity, Dad warns me of the dangers of posting my whereabouts on Instagram, lest I be kidnapped and sold into sex slavery, *Taken* style. Except Dad is no Liam Neeson. He doesn't have "special skills," aside from his legendary sesame chicken recipe. And so long as the Excalibur Fitness Center continues to sponsor my membership in exchange for promotion on my Instagram, I'm willing to risk it.

Tinder Joe and I lock eyes once again as I catch my breath post–sprint interval. Our shared gaze lasts two seconds longer than comfortable and I can't help but notice how his perfectly coifed boy-band hair remains suspiciously intact with each giraffe-like stride. Whether he stalked me here or not, my first instinct is to flee the scene.

So I do.

I take refuge in the Gym Bro Zone, aka the strength-training area.

As a gym regular, I exchange respectful nods with the other patrons as I enter. A familiar crowd of 'roid-pumping frat boys loiters near the bench presses while simultaneously chugging whey protein shakes like they're on the brink of dehydration. Today, they've donned those cringey neon tank tops that hang too low under their armpits. To their credit, they're nothing if not devoted to their daily routines. And after catching a glimpse of my sweaty, tomato-faced self in the wall-to-wall mirror under harsh fluorescent lighting, I'm not in any position to judge.

A guy man-splaying on the bench press grunts excessively, chucking a set of dumbbells to the floor with a loud *thud*. Normally this would grind my gears, but I'm too busy bounding toward a majestic sight to care. My treasured squat rack is free. Praise be.

The window squat rack is one of exactly two racks in this facility. It boasts a scenic view of a grungy nightclub across the street, a long-rumored front for a murderous motorcycle gang. The natural light is optimal for filming my workouts, especially compared to the alternative—the rack cloaked in shadow next to the men's changing room, which permanently reeks of Axe body spray.

The window rack is close enough to the industrial-size fan to let me savor a stiff breeze mid-sweat, but not close enough that I'll succumb to wind-induced hypothermia. It's also in the prime position for gawking at the television, which, for unknown reasons, is cruelly locked to the Food Network. I worship this squat rack the way Mother Gothel regards Rapunzel's magic hair. It gives me life. Vigor. Four sets of squats and I'll be high on endorphins for at least a day, fantasizing about the strength of my thighs crushing the souls of a thousand men.

Giddy at the very thought, I stake my claim on the rack, setting my phone and headphones on the floor before heading for the water fountain. The man with a goatee, who rocks knee-length cargo shorts and an actual Sony Walkman from the nineties, approaches at the same time. He graciously waves me ahead of him.

I flash him an appreciative smile. "Thanks."

My back is turned for all of three seconds while I take a sip. Freshly hydrated and eager to crush some squats, I spin around to find an exceptionally broad-shouldered figure stretching directly in front of my window rack.

I've never seen this man before and I'm certain I'd remember the shit out of him if I had. He's tall, well over six feet, with a muscular build that liberally fills out his unassuming gray T-shirt and athletic shorts. One look at his enormous biceps and it's clear he knows his way around a gym. A black ball cap with an unrecognizable logo shadows his face. From the side, his nose has a slight bump, as if it's been broken before.

I shimmy in beside him to pick up my phone, purposely lingering for a few extended beats to transmit the message that this rack is OCCUPIED. He doesn't get the memo. Instead, he proceeds to clasp his massive hands around the barbell, brows knit with intense concentration.

Either he's fully ignoring me, or he genuinely hasn't noticed my presence. The faint beat of his music is audible through his earbuds. I can't identify the song, but it sounds hardcore, like a heavy-metal lifting tune.

I clear my throat.

No reaction.

"Excuse me," I call out, inching closer.

When his gaze meets mine, I jolt, instinctively taking half a step back. His eyes are a striking forest green, like an expanse of dense pine trees dusting untouched misty mountain terrain in the wilderness. Not that I'd know from personal experience. My exposure to the rugged wild is limited to the Discovery Channel.

I'm nearly hypnotized by the intensity of his eyes, until he barks a "Yeah?" before reluctantly removing his right earbud. His voice is deep, gruff, and short, like he can't be bothered with me. He momentarily lifts his ball cap, revealing wavy, dirty-blond locks that curl at the nape of his neck. It reminds me of the scraggly hairstyles worn by hockey players, the kind you just want to run your fingers through. And he does just that. My throat dries instantly when he smooths his thick mane with one hand before dropping his ball cap back over the top.

Deliberately ignoring the dip in the base of my stomach, I nod toward my headphones hastily strewn at the base of the rack. "I was here first."

Expression frosty, he arches a strong brow, regarding me with contempt, as gym bros tend to do when women dare to touch what they deem as *their* equipment. "Didn't see your stuff."

Undeterred by his brush-off, I take a confident step forward, laying my rightful claim. When we're nearly chest to chest, he towers over me like a behemoth, which is more intimidating than I anticipated. I expect him to back off, to see the error of his ways, to realize he's being a prick, but he doesn't even flinch.

Swallowing the lump in my throat, I find my voice again. "I'll only be a few minutes, max. We could even switch in and out?"

He sidesteps. For a second, I think he's leaving. I'm about to thank him for his grace and humanity . . . until he dares to load one side of the barbell with a forty-five-pound plate, biceps straining against the fabric of his T-shirt.

"Seriously?" I stare at him, hands on hips, gaze settling on his soft, full lips, which contrast with the harsh line of his stubbled jaw.

"Look, I need to get to work in half an hour. Can't you just use the other rack? It's free." As he ruthlessly balances the rack with another plate, he barely spares me a passing glance, as if I'm nothing more than a pesky housefly.

I pride myself on being an accommodating person. I wave other cars ahead of me at four-way stops, even if I have the right-of-way.

I always insist others exit elevators in front of me, as my parents taught me. If he had just been polite, half-decent, even the slightest bit apologetic, I probably would have let him have it. But he isn't any of the above, and I'm shook.

"No," I say, out of principle.

His jaw tightens as he rests his forearms on the bar. The way he leans into it, stance wide and hulking, is purely a territorial move. He gives me one last, indignant shrug. "Well, I'm not moving."

We're locked in a stare-off with nothing but the faint sound of Katy Perry singing about being "a plastic bag drifting through the wind" over the gym sound system and a man grunting on the leg press a couple feet away to quell the silence. My eyes are dry and itchy from my refusal to blink, and the intensity of his stare offers no sign of fatigue.

When Katy Perry fades out, replaced by an Excalibur Fitness promotional ad, I let out a half sigh, half growl. This guy isn't worth my energy. I retrieve my headphones from the floor and stomp to the less desirable rack, but not before shooting him one last evil eye.

11:05 A.M.—INSTAGRAM POST: "ASSHOLES WHO THINK THEY OWN THE GYM" BY **CURVYFITNESSCRYSTAL**:

Real talk: This morning, an arrogant dickhead with nicer hair than me callously stole my squat rack. Who does this? And if you're guilty of this crime, WHO HURT Y'ALL?

I don't know him personally (and I don't want to), but he struck me as the kind of person who loathes puppies and joy in general. You know the type. Anyway, I ended up channeling all my anger into my workout while blasting my current jam, "Fitness" by Lizzo (trust, this song is fire).

Final thoughts: Most people at the gym aren't assholes. I promise. 99% are super helpful and respectful, even the steroid frat boys! And if you do encounter that unfortunate 1%, just steer clear. Never give them power over you or your fitness journey.

Thanks for listening to my TED Talk,

Crystal

Comment by **xokyla33**: YAS girl! You're sooo right. You do you!!

Comment by **_jillianmcleod_**: I just don't feel comfortable working out at the gym for this reason. Would rather work out at home.

Comment by **APB_rockss**: U promote embracing your curves/size but all u do is work out and live at the gym? Hypocrite much??

Reply by **CurvyFitnessCrystal**: @APB_rockss Actually I spend one hour in the gym working out each day. Devoting time every day for yourself, whether it's at the gym, taking a walk, or in a bubble bath is hugely beneficial for all aspects of your life, including mental health. Also, you can both love your body and go to the gym. They aren't mutually exclusive.

• • •

After yesterday's incoherent Instagram rant, I took a much-needed soul-searching bubble bath. My response to the person who called me a hypocrite unintentionally sparked a fierce debate of epic proportions between my loyal followers and my haters. I try not to pay the trolls an iota of attention, but after Squat Rack Thief and two glasses of merlot, I was feeling a tinge combative. And it's been building for months.

For seven years, I've striven to shatter harmful, fatphobic stereotypes in the fitness industry. I've built an Instagram following of two hundred thousand based on my message of self-love, regardless of size. The drama over me being "too big" to be a personal trainer yet "not big enough" to represent the curvy community is typical in the abyss of the comments section. There's no in-between.

The crass body-shaming and occasional racist slurs have become more commonplace with the growth of my following. For the sake of maintaining a positive message, I've ignored the hateful comments. The fact is, I love my curves. Most of the time. I'm only human. Occasionally, the trolls manage to penetrate my armor. When this happens, I allow myself a short grace period to wallow. And then I treat them to a proverbial middle finger in the form of a thirst trap (a full-length body shot, for good measure).

But last night, sometime before my rainbow glitter bath

bomb dissolved entirely, it occurred to me that my followers are probably equally, if not more, hurt by the comments. If I want to stay authentic and true to my body-positive platform, maybe it's time to start speaking out.

Today's workout is the perfect time to ruminate over my strategy.

But to my displeasure, Squat Rack Thief is back again, for the second day in a row. He's stretching in the Gym Bro Zone. Must he have such magnificent quads?

He narrows his gaze in my direction as I shimmy through the turnstiles. Instantly, his expression goes from neutral to a deep scowl, as if my mere presence has derailed his entire day.

I eye him sideways before shifting my faux attention to the generic motivational quotes plastered on the wall in an aggressively bold font: *If it doesn't challenge you, it won't change you.*

Evading him for the duration of my workout is harder than I expected. Wherever I go, he's looming in my peripherals, taking up precious space with his gloriously muscled body.

When I woke up this morning, it crossed my mind that he could be an Excalibur Fitness newbie who hasn't grasped the concept of gym etiquette. I fully intended to give him the benefit of the doubt. Maybe he was simply having a bad day. Maybe he spent the entire night staring into the vast distance, roiling with regret. Lord knows I've had my fair share of rage-workouts.

All of these possibilities lose legitimacy when he conspires to out-pedal me on the neighboring assault bike. When I catch him eyeing my screen, I channel my inner Charlie's Angel and full-throttle it.

At the twenty-calorie mark, we both stop, panting, hunched

over the handles. My "no-makeup" makeup has probably melted entirely, and I'm seeing spots. But my exertion was worth it—I beat him by a whole 0.02 miles. He practically seethes when he reads my screen. Evidently unable to cope with my victory, he pouts, promptly hightailing it to the machines.

Not half an hour later, it's officially game over when I witness him saunter away from the leg press without bothering to wipe down the seat. The darkest places in hell are reserved for those who don't clean the machines after use.

Compelled to speak up on behalf of all hygiene-policy-abiding gym patrons, I set my dumbbells down and march forth.

He's in the zone as he does a round of effortless pull-ups. I stand, mouth agape, unintentionally mesmerized by the taut, corded muscles in his arms flexing with each movement.

He gives me a Chris Evans vibe, but with slightly longer, luscious locks. I don't know if it's the glint in his hooded eyes or the dimples, but he has a boyish look to him that makes him appear faintly approachable when he isn't scowling at me.

When he catches me gawking at him like a crazed fangirl thirsting for a selfie, he pauses, dangling from the bar. "How's the view from down there?"

I'm about to say *godlike*, both because it's entirely true and because it's my default to compliment people. I do it for a living. But the last thing this guy needs is a confidence boost.

I consciously make a flat line with my mouth, channeling Mom's severe expression when she's supremely disappointed in my life choices. I hold out a paper towel, generously pre-sprayed with disinfectant, for his convenience, of course. "Are you forgetting something?"

He blinks. "Not that I'm aware of."

"You forgot to clean the leg press."

He releases the bar, sticking a smooth landing as he eyes the paper towel pinched between my fingers like it's been dipped in sulfuric acid. "Keeping track of my workout or something?"

"No," I say, a little too defensively. "But you need to wash the machines when you're done with them. It's a rule here. People don't want to touch your dried sweat." I inwardly cringe. I might as well have an I'd-like-to-speak-with-a-manager angled bob. But I can't back down now. In fact, I double down, pointing to the sign on the wall to our right that reads *Please wipe down machines after use.*

He doesn't even glance at the sign. Instead, he appraises me, arms folded over his broad chest. "I'm not done with the machine. Are you unfamiliar with supersets? You know, when you cycle through multiple exercises back-to-back—"

"I know what a superset is!" I snap. Heat rockets from my lower belly to my cheeks when I realize I've unjustly called him out. This is mortifying. I silently will myself to disappear into an obscure, nonexistent sinkhole. Maybe this is cosmic retribution for not minding my own business.

He flashes me a knowing smirk and struts back for another set.

As if this painful interaction never happened, I slink away into obscurity to film my back workout tutorial on the cable machine. It's a prime opportunity to promote my sponsored sweat-resistant activewear.

I'm midway through filming a shot of ten cable rows when Squat Rack Thief materializes out of thin air. He chooses to park his massive body directly in front of the camera, of all places, blocking the shot. In my silent fury, I lose all focus, with zero recollection of whether I'm on the first rep or the tenth.

He leans lazily against the machine, wearing a smug grin that I'm beginning to think is his natural resting face.

"Yes?" I ask through clenched teeth, irritated at the prospect of refilming the entire segment.

He produces a paper towel from behind his back, swishing it in front of my face. "Here. So you don't forget to wipe down the seat."

His sarcastic tone combined with his sneer tells me he isn't doing this out of the goodness of his heart. This is a hostile act of aggression, cementing our rivalry.

Before I can formulate a cutting response, he drops the paper towel into my lap and waltzes toward the changing room.

AMY LEA is the international bestselling author of romantic comedies for adults and teens, including *Set on You*, *Exes and O's*, *The Catch*, and Mindy Kaling's Book Studio selection *Woke Up Like This*. Her acclaimed works have been featured in *USA Today*, *Entertainment Weekly*, *Cosmopolitan*, and more. When Amy is not writing, she can be found fangirling over other romance books on Instagram, eating potato chips with reckless abandon, and snuggling with her husband and two goldendoodles in Ottawa, Canada.

VISIT AMY LEA ONLINE

AmyLeaBooks.com
🅞 AmyLeaBooks

Ready to find
your next great read?

Let us help.

Visit prh.com/nextread